Praise for *Gaudeamus*

"A gonzo piece of metafiction that cleverly blurs the line between reality and fantasy." —*Publishers Weekly*

"Brio, zest, clarity, and excitement . . . *Gaudeamus* translates loosely as 'Let the good times roll,' and that's just what Barnes does." —*SciFi.com*

"Inventive . . . Sprinkled with wry humor and colorful plot twists." —*Booklist*

"Expands the borders of narrative fiction to create a sense of plausibility and familiarity in the midst of a surreal cosmic comedy." —*Library Journal*

Praise for John Barnes

"Thoughtful and absorbing . . . A winner." —*Kirkus Reviews* (starred review) on *The Sky So Big and Black*

"A full, rich vision of the future, compressed expertly into 240 pages." —*Publishers Weekly* (starred review) on *Candle*

"I put this novel down only long enough to wipe the sweat from my brow." —Gregory Benford on *Daybreak Zero*

"Barnes's view of the collapse of financial life . . . is so alarming that the book could draw attention in a way no official report can." —*The Atlantic* on *Daybreak Zero*

GAUDEAMUS

JOHN BARNES

 A TOM DOHERTY ASSOCIATES BOOK

TOR® NEW YORK

GAUDEAMUS

Copyright © 2004 by John Barnes

Edited by Patrick Nielsen Hayden

A Tor Book
Published by Tom Doherty Associates, LLC
175 Fifth Avenue
New York, NY 10010

www.tor-forge.com

Tor® is a registered trademark of Tom Doherty Associates, LLC.

The Library of Congress has cataloged the hardcover edition as follows:

Barnes, John, 1957–
      Gaudeamus / John Barnes.—1st ed.
          p. cm.
      ISBN 978-0-7653-0329-5 (hardcover)
      ISBN 978-1-4299-7062-4 (e-book)
          1. Science fiction—Authorship—Fiction. 2. Human-alien encounters—Fiction.
      3. Time travel—Fiction. 4. Inventions—Fiction. 5. Novelists—Fiction. I. Title.
      PS3552.A677G38 2004
      813'.54—dc22   2004048095

ISBN 978-0-7653-1198-6 (trade paperback)

Tor books may be purchased for educational, business, or promotional use. For information on bulk purchases, please contact Macmillan Corporate and Premium Sales Department at 1-800-221-7945, extension 5442, or write specialmarkets@macmillan.com.

First Edition: November 2004
First Trade Paperback Edition: July 2014

Printed in the United States of America

0 9 8 7 6 5 4 3 2 1

THIS BOOK IS DEDICATED TO
ASHLEY GRAYSON,
AND TO
PATRICK NIELSEN HAYDEN,
WHO WAITED SUCH A LONG TIME

Excerpt from an undated "Page 3" of a letter in Travis Bismarck's handwriting, on a page torn out of a steno pad. I think he was writing to me about some book of mine before 1995. Usually he writes to me every time he reads one of my books. I wish I could find the rest of his letter, but it probably went into some box that got thrown away. I don't really remember. I've asked Travis, and he doesn't remember writing it.

So, John, looks to me like another way that there's two kinds of people. 1. People who read too much to have interesting lives. 2. People who read too little to notice how interesting their lives are. And in real life they're never the same people. That's why people love stories about Zen masters & Einstein & wizards & Old Coyote & poets & saints & beats & hobos. It's also how we know that most of them are fictional. Especially fucking Einstein.

GAUDEAMUS

CHAPTER ONE

In the thirty years I've known Travis Bismarck, since my second day at college, he has never driven himself if he could beg some poor fool into driving him. I've often been the fool. So at five-fifteen one morning not long before the turn of the millennium, he rang my doorbell to talk me into giving him a ride to Denver, and fool that I am, I opened the door and welcomed him in and said yes.

I hadn't seen Travis in five years. When the bell rang, I thought it was going to be my neighbor, Ben, looking for some company to shovel walks with and then grab some coffee after.

Most of that year, I got up really early. I had taken a year off without pay from teaching, trying to finish a scholarly book, expecting a quiet year, and then stuff had happened non-stop. The novel that was supposed to finance the whole year took far too long to finish, and then the British publisher who had commissioned it stiffed me. Kara, to whom I was married at the time, went through some very scary surgery and they put her on a strange cocktail of drugs with odd side effects. An old friend's wife died, he lost his house, and he ended up sleeping on my couch for a couple months before writing a screenplay, becoming wealthy overnight, and moving to Idaho to marry a high school girl. Just one of those years we all have now and then, but I was having it right then, and it sucked.

Anyway, I was in serious need of money, and I have shitty getting-rich instincts but great stay-eating instincts, so all the bells in my head were ringing "get to work, get to work, get to work" and I had books to finish. My eyes would slam open like a garage door coming unstuck at four-thirty every morning.

Well, meanwhile, back at the start of the story: I was down in my office in the basement, at five-fifteen in the morning, with a cup of the thick heavy black coffee I prefer when I'm writing regularly. I had *Jagged Little Pill* on the Walkman, big fuzzy *Where the Wild Things Are* slippers on my feet, and my usual writing outfit of an Anderson's of Maumee (a grain elevator company near my home-town) sweatshirt and gesso-spattered black sweatpants. I had been there since about 4:40, allowing for time to trip off the coffeemaker and take a leak before sitting down. I was just on the point of prom-ising myself that, now that I had written the one page I wrote be-fore doing anything else, checked email, and found all the hidden icons in that day's *Gaudeamus*, I would actually do some work. If I was a good boy and got ten pages by seven A.M., I was going to treat myself to a swim at the college and follow it up with breakfast at the Quarter Circle.

At that point I was working on the redraft of the novel I'd been stiffed on, so my agent could go out and peddle it to American pub-lishers. I was staring at a page of research, trying to make myself want to type the next three sentences, which needed to be about daisite. Daisite is a thermite—nasty evil stuff even for a thermite, invented by the French for use on natives and Germans. It sets fires that are almost impossible to put out and burns human beings in a distinctive, horrible way. I needed to mention that without going into details just yet because the complete gross-out scene wasn't supposed to happen for another fifteen pages or so.

When I heard the doorbell, I thought it was Ben, and I should be ashamed how glad I was, considering how many better things I should have been doing than shoveling snow.

It's a rare fall in Gunnison when you don't see some serious snow in October. I hadn't yet looked out the window that morning but if snow had fallen, then Ben, who looks after that neighborhood like a building super with OCD, would be by, shovel in his hand, big happy grin on his face.

The fall after I bought that house, I had discovered that Ben shoveled everyone's front walk as soon as it snowed; he did mine that first day.

I had said, "Aw, Ben, don't do that."

"It's easier to shovel while it's fresh-fallen, before anybody's walked on it."

"Yeah, I know, but *you* shouldn't have to shovel *my* walk."

"It's not that I have to. It just needs to be done, and I happen to be out here when it's easiest to do it, so it's easier for the whole world, on the average, if I do it."

"Well," I said, Calvinist guilt gripping me like a vise, "uh, hey." Stupidly forgetting that in the rural West, people expect you to keep your word, I had added, "In that case, it'll be easier if you have help. So next time, if you see my office light on—the second window from the back on the north side of my basement—ring my bell, and let me come on out and help."

Three days after that my bell rang at four forty-five and I broke from a gruesome decapitation scene to spend three hours throwing snow with Ben. We got both sides of the whole block and all the walks up to the porches. The sun was just coming up as we walked down Colorado Street to Daylight Donuts for a whacking dose of sugar and caffeine.

It was better exercise than swimming, with more company. I had even admitted that I enjoyed it, so it didn't even feel very virtuous anymore.

So the bell rang. Okay, here I am at the start of the story again. The bell rang. Now, this time, I'm really going on.

I was just thinking about how to explain that all thermites release molten metal, usually iron or copper, and that adding sulfur to a thermite makes it spatter molten metal around, and the molten metal carries the sulfur right through flesh to give deep disfiguring horrible burns, and I was already bored.

I thought I heard the bell through Alanis Morissette wailing in the headphones, and charged up the steps, eager for something to do that wasn't writing.

It wasn't Ben, it was Travis. Who I've known for thirty years and given so many rides to.

The contrast between Ben whom I expected and Travis whom I didn't won't mean anything unless I also explain who Travis Bismarck was. And is. He's still alive, despite the efforts of some people who come into the story later. There's going to be some violence. Sex too. Stick around.

I first met Travis Bismarck in August of 1975 in Rubelmann Dorm at Washington University in St. Louis, where we were both freshmen on the same floor. He was twenty-two, old enough to be a senior, but he'd done four years in the Army first. He was immediately interested in me because I was one of the few freshmen with a car; I'd come to St. Louis in June, and taken a job selling radio ads, and you really need a car for that.

Trav was an anomaly. In 1975 at Wash U, freshman dorm floors were jammed with frustrated long-haired free spirits. They had missed everything: already, Nixon had resigned, Saigon had fallen, and most of the bands had broken up. My fellow students, who were all set for it to be 1968 again, didn't have any way to know how good the times actually were: the drinking age was eighteen, pot was as tolerated as it ever got, you could *dance* to disco as opposed to having a hippie spaz attack, punk and wave were coming in, and it was post-Pill and pre-AIDS.

Trav tried to fit in, letting his hair grow out, wearing those silly loose-fitting three musketeers shirts, and so forth. But he was muscular, his posture reeked of sergeant, and he didn't have the Holden Caulfield upper class there is nothing here I need to give a shit about drawl that most of the other kids had. In the vague and scrawny seventies (when only jocks and gays lifted, Alan Alda was a model of masculinity, and forty-year-old men were trying to teach themselves to begin every sentence with "uh, like") he stood out like a racehorse in a herd of sheep.

Most people called him "GI Joe" and avoided him. He tried to explain that he had spent most of his time at "Fort Nowhere, East Dakota. I cleaned my rifle, shined my boots, and smoked dope most of the time. I did half a year in Cheapundgoodbiersburg in West Germany, too, where I cleaned my rifle, shined my boots, and went out with fat blonde girls that couldn't speak English but had good pot. Yeah, I went in while there was still fighting in Vietnam, but by the time I was out of Basic you had to volunteer to go, and Mama Bismarck didn't raise no idiots, at least not no idiots idiotic enough to volunteer their way into 'Nam."

Somewhere during the following spring I realized that Travis's double negatives, and saying 'Nam, and so forth were acquired camouflage to keep an upper-middle-class suburban boy from getting his skinny pink ass stomped flat. The truth was that Travis was from an affluent Dallas suburb. He'd gone to a prep school in New

England and summer camp in Minnesota; his SAT scores were off the map; he had a trust fund. He said his motives for joining the Army were "forty percent James Jones, thirty percent Sartre, and twenty percent Errol Flynn."

Oh, he wasn't a complete fake. Travis *had* been in the Army and *was* Texan, and he did have some authentic prole tastes. Fat girls, for instance. But who ever heard of a redneck Texan that didn't like to drive?

Freshman year, Travis and I developed a pattern. I'd drive him out to some place way out in the county that had Wild Turkey on special. He'd buy a case and give me a bottle of it. Then he'd use the booze to attract a girl or two to his room, get all of us roaring drunk, and tell preposterous tales of great overseas bars, getting laid in Mexican whorehouses, the awesome marijuana of Costa Rica, and so forth, till we all got too drunk to listen.

His favorite stories were about the bizarre sexual behavior of Texans. Years later, driving from Raton to San Antonio in a single day with a busted car stereo, I amused myself for hours trying to figure out where, in all the miles and miles of miles and miles that you see there, all the pervs from Travis's stories were hiding. Over that hill, perhaps, was a family reunion turning into a drunken orgy. Maybe, as I slowed momentarily on my way through the cluster of ten buildings with a town name sign and a single stop sign, I was passing the Baptist church in which the preacher had concealed a movie camera in the floor in front of the altar, with its lens flush with the floor and pointed upward, to take shots up skirts during altar calls. Perhaps that RANCH ACCESS NO SERVICES sign was the gravel road that led to the home of the wealthy rancher who kept six pigs, all named Barbara, in his house, bathed them daily in the same tub he used himself, and never, ever sold them. The small town of forty-five double-wides, a gas station, four churches, and two block-long facades of shops might harbor, somewhere, "the undertaker you never want to use for your daughter, John, swear to god, everyone for a hundred miles around knew it was true, the one time the head majorette at the high school in that town didn't beat a train to the crossing, and that guy got the body, everybody said he put her back together prettier than she was in real life, but her own daddy checked that coffin after the viewing to make sure that old boy hadn't kept no souvenirs. Honest to god and jesus and that whole crowd, John, I don't make this stuff up."

Anyway, that was Travis, and I had driven Travis many places off and on for years, though not at all during the five years just before he rang my doorbell, at five-fifteen on an October morning not long before the turn of the millennium.

Well, here we are at the start of the story again. I really am trying and stuff does happen in this story. It's just that I promised some people I wouldn't just make things up in this book, and nonfictional things make no sense without the context. So I keep giving context. I'll stop soon.

All right, so it was a very early morning, full of contrasts between the expected and the unexpected. I expected Ben and a snow shovel and I got Travis and a duffel bag. I expected to write a story and instead I got told one. Come to think of it, even *Gaudeamus* was unexpected that morning, and the truth is—I did promise to tell as much of it as I could—I wasn't actually working on the book right at that moment, I was working on making myself get back to working on the book, after looking at *Gaudeamus*. And *Gaudeamus* was even more surprising than usual that morning.

Writers don't dress trendy or dance trendy, but they read trendy and they listen trendy; it has to do with what you can do in a small room in which you are trying to avoid writing. And *Gaudeamus* was trendy—oh, it was trendy. Somebody got me hooked on it, I thought

Kara because she was in constant email touch with her very trendy Minneapolis friends, but she assures me that I got *her* hooked on it; she thought one of my grad school buddies introduced me to it, but it could also have been somebody I knew on GEnie.

Anyway, I do remember for sure that I was hooked on *Gaudeamus* not long after we moved to Gunnison, and from then on it was a mandatory part of every day. By the time we bought our house, in the summer of 1996, it was a genuine phenomenon and it seemed like everybody and all six of his illegitimate brothers was always trying to introduce those of us who already knew about it to *Gaudeamus*.

It's weird how devoted so many of us were to *Gaudeamus* considering how forgotten it is now; one of those in-groupy things that flickers and goes, like Minneapolis in 1988, like Cathy Chamberlain's one album, like *The Rakehells of Heaven* or *Liberty Meadows*. It was the kind of thing that might be discussed at a Renaissance or Heritage Weekend (Al Gore and Newt Gingrich both claimed that they followed it). An alt-weekly columnist might denounce it for its terrible attitude or praise it as the next big thing or complain that it was going downhill, only to get a note back from the editor saying "never heard of it—SIGNIFICANCE?" Somebody might leave a pile of the first year of *Gaudeamus* on CD with accessing instructions on a table outside a rave, and nine-tenths of them would end up like AOL coasters, but some of them would be on the projection screens at a goth gather the next week, and some of the .wavs would find their way into a DJ's mix.

Places that had a "No Downloading *Gaudeamus* at Peak Hours" rule included Sandia, CERN, and Livermore, but also the Centers for Disease Control, Lindesfarne, Industrial Light and Magic, *Mother Jones*, the NSA, Arcosanti-Banff, and Lucent's Deep Black Facility. The poet laureate of the United States admitted that she was a fan but she didn't understand it; the First Lady said it was an "ugly, ugly thing"; a Nobel laureate in economics used incidents from *Gaudeamus* to illustrate his BBC lecture series; one very tense night when it looked like *Politically Incorrect* might go up in an actual brawl, Bill Mahrer cracked an inside joke about that day's *Gaudeamus*, and the whole thing fell into a gigglefest between Martha Stewart, Jack Welch, Anthony Hopkins, and a fat woman from PETA.

And nowadays it's at least as forgotten as Apollo 2000, Pugwash, *My Name is Not Bitch,* or Dyna-Soar.

Gaudeamus was described, by the sort of people who are paid by *Time* or the *Atlantic* to explain trends to nonparticipants, as a "comic-book serial on the web," an "interactive anime soap opera with footnotes," "an online hybrid between a computer game and an editorial cartoon," and "the product of one weird mind." That last came closest.

Each day at exactly 3:26 Mountain Time (the slugline was always in mountain time), it would be available for download from www.gaudeamusonline.com, a black web page with the single red word "Download" at the center in 18 point Courier. Click on that single word and you would download a self-unpacking compressed file—pure executable machine code, smart enough to know what operating system it was talking to. (That, and the fact that the phrase "One True" appeared in several notes in the code, gave me an idea that I'm still pumping money out of.) Once it got onto your PC or Mac, it locked up your system for seven to twelve minutes while it ran like a shrew on crack through a half meg of free space, generating a complex animated cartoon with many clickable objects.

Most comparable self-unpacking stuff would have needed half an hour and three to five megs, or so my computer-jock friends told me, so whoever packed *Gaudeamus* was a genius in something other than satire. Several different things, if I understood what people who cared about stuff like that were telling me. Files like that should take weeks or months—or a large staff and a dedicated Cray—to create, and yet they sometimes referred to events as little as seven hours before posting time. If Richard Reno really was the sole creator, he must have animation, editing, and compression technology far beyond what was commercially available, and work faster than any artist anyone had ever heard of, to put *Gaudeamus* out on a daily schedule.

The decompressed presentation would invite you to click on a start icon.

That would launch a two-minute animated clip, a different one every day, loaded with icons. Clicking an icon might reveal panel comics (with headings like "earlier that day," "what he was really thinking," and "a random silly drawing"), short text essays (tightly edited tirades on everything from the way people treat their dogs to the failures of NASA to why high heels are sexy), photos of all kinds of things (sometimes the relation to the link was clear, but other times it was a complete mystery, just a picture of a fighter plane, or a bottle of ketchup, or a family standing in front of the Grand Canyon), and dead tree links to articles in dozens of publications, everything from *Nature* and *Aviation Week and Space Technology* to *Double-D Hos, The Unspeakable Visions of the Individual,* and *Direct Action!*

The ongoing story itself was set in wildly inconsistent locations—if there were two characters talking, say O. B. Joyful and Harris McParris, in the first shot they might be whispering with heads together in a coffeehouse, in the following middle-distance shot they might be in tuxedos riding a camel across a desert as McParris turned around to address Joyful, Joyful's reaction shot might show him (her, it? The character was as sexless as Tweetie Bird) in a grass skirt in a polar waste, and then the two characters might laugh together about the answer in shorts and t-shirts, obviously in a movie theater, with their feet up on the seats in front of them and a big bucket of popcorn between them.

The characters bore about as much resemblance to any real living beings as the characters in *Pogo, Krazy Kat,* or *Bloom County;* there was no character named Gaudeamus (though O. B. Joyful might be a pun on it) and there was no known reason why the thing was called that, except, perhaps, that it made those of us who liked it unreasonably happy.

The plot was intricate and complex, with a heavy dose of political or social satire. For example, *Gaudeamus* fans heard about the Monica Lewinsky affair about three days before Matt Drudge, if they clicked on the book on one shelf in one scene (the title was *Fat Beaver and the Cigar of Joy*). The week that Travis dropped by, in late October 1997, many of the fans were complaining, in the many dedicated Usenet groups and online bulletin boards, that *Gaudeamus* was getting too morbid and into very bad taste, because it contained many references to the ongoing hunt for the Hardware Store Killer.

The main Usenet *Gaudeamus* group had around two hundred postings per hour, round the clock, from all over the world, so that no one could hope to follow all of that.

As far as anyone could tell, the one and only creator was Richard Reno, who had drawn a panel called *Gaudeamus* from November 1978 through June 1981 at Moloch College in Indiana—in fact I'd read it in its early paper incarnation, because Travis and I had had a fling with two girls that went to Moloch.

Several of the major characters were the same, or had the same names and seemed to be the same idea allowing more than ten years' drift in drawing style and ideas. But it was impossible to prove that Richard Reno had even been on the planet between June 9, 1981, when he was photographed at the Moloch College graduation, and August 6, 1993, when *Gaudeamus* appeared on the web.

When *Gaudeamus* vanished again, it went so suddenly that there was practically no evidence of its passing; within a short time everyone forgot that there had ever been such a thing. Nowadays radio guys refer to it as a trivia question on those 80s-90s mix stations. But this was in 1997, and I had been following *Gaudeamus* for a couple of years already, and there was no sign that it was going to go away; it was eternally there, like Montgomery Ward, the Soviet Union, or Johnny Carson. And in 1997, I think three-quarters of the professional writers in America were following it, with at least as much devotion as *Sluggy Freelance* got a few years later.

It was not only that *Gaudeamus* was funny and dramatic and sad, silly an instant before it was touching, strangely moving and exciting so that many people confessed to having *Gaudeamus* daydreams. Every good comic had always been like that.

Nor was it just that it was so amazingly alive in a way that reminded you of how strange our own world is, or the weirdly consistent physics that somehow reminded me—without being directly like—the odd extra joints in the middle of their insteps that people have in Don Martin drawings. It felt like a world that lived more than our own, like classic cartoons from back when studios could afford armies of in-betweeners to make every petal on every flower wave separately. You could come up with pages of comparisons and not really get what it was like. Surreal as Fleischer's *Betty Boop*, political as *Pogo,* an eternally continued open-ended novel like *Bruno* or *Gasoline Alley,* a glimpse into the eternal present like *Calvin and*

Hobbes or the later Roadrunners, a bitter sneer at an ugly world like *Li'l Abner,* brave and hopeful as *Peanuts* and dark as *The Watchmen:* all that with characters who combined the exuberant silliness of Bugs Bunny, the "Whatever!" acceptance of the Three Stooges, the never-say-die courage of Goofy, and the anarchic defiance of Hekyll and Jekyll. Think of all of that, all at once, seamlessly, and now you are nowhere near what it was like.

You just had to be there.

So anyway, this particular morning, I had been trying to make myself want to sit down and explain daisite, and why it's such thoroughly horrible stuff. And I didn't feel like writing that, but if I could do two pages of that, I could then return to Kit Miles, who was a character I really liked, in a scene with another character I really liked, and then eight pages would just fly out and I'd be all set to go swim a mile and have breakfast at the Quarter Circle with my conscience clear. But I just couldn't stand to even type the word "daisite" again, and something about the phrase "spraying molten metal and burning sulfur into human flesh" wasn't quite singing as it should.

And my escape, as it so often was from everything else that wasn't going well that year, was *Gaudeamus.* This morning seemed to be the bridge between two sequences. Usually I wasn't as fond of the sequences that were Ower Gyro's dreams, but this one was better than average. Ower Gyro was tucked into bed, looking like Ower Gyro—a sour-faced middle-aged squirrel in a baby bonnet— sound asleep. The viewpoint panned the room, and I saw that he had a picture of Merle the Killer Squirrel (whom O. B. Joyful had gunned down in the Christmas episode the year before) on his nightstand next to an ashtray overflowing with cigar butts. I clicked on the ashtray and found a link to the official web page for *E.T.* with a note that said "He was here but he doesn't look like this." I clicked on Merle and discovered that I could download an mp3 of a song called "Gone But Not Too Gone," from a band called Skin2Skin. Nothing interesting so far, or at least nothing I got.

Then the image wavered in the way that denoted the start of a dream. Ower Gyro dreamed of God sitting at the computer, using a mouse—a real one, his tail tied in a shoelace knot to a wire that led into the computer. God was playing a dirty video game called "Who Fux Hu," and on the computer screen Cindy Lou Who was riding astride the Chinese politician. A caption read "Who Gets Past First." There was nothing to click on.

God pulled off a mask to reveal that he was actually O. B. Joyful. The scene cut back to reality as Ower Gyro sat up in bed, tearing off his baby bonnet, and then looking at the alarm clock: 3:00 A.M. Next to the alarm clock, where the ashtray and the photo of Merle had been, there was now a small white box, about the size of a cable box, with three LED readouts; the readouts spelled out GAUDEAMUS across them. That white box was the only clickable artifact on the screen, so I clicked it. My screen went solid blue except for a blinking white message: "GAUDEAMUS. Password?" Beneath that was a blinking entry line.

I tried entering "Gaudeamus" and got back "NO ACCESS. HAVE A NICE DAY. GAUDEAMUS!"

Well, everyone had to admit that there was some large percentage of *Gaudeamus* that they just didn't get. Obviously this was one of those for me. Kara and I were having lunch with Melody Wallace today, and Melody was Western State's other semiotician besides me, and a big *Gaudeamus* fan. Maybe she'd have seen something I didn't.

With a sigh, I clicked on the Word icon, cranked up my Walkman, and typed:

". . . carries the burning sulfur deep
inside the flesh"

and looked to see if I could get by with just that much—daisite was just a digression. All I really needed at that point was to say "French-made incendiary grenades" and let it go, but I have a hard time trusting people to be interested in things without my supplying an enormous load of context.

Oh, hell, supplying context was my *life*, if you came right down to it. I liked teaching humanities classes, and writing novels rather than short stories, and working out the unseen areas offstage of all my sets. My friends are always demanding that I get on with the story and stop telling them who everything and everybody is in it.

I opened a new file and typed in

IDEA:

STORY BEGINNING:

The Last Ride of Context Man

by John Barnes

He never knew how to start a story because
the beginning needed a context, and the
context demanded an earlier beginning, and
in ten minutes he'd be all the way back to
the big bang.

The doorbell rang, and I heard it faintly over Alanis Morissette. At least I thought it rang, and that was good enough. I turned off the Walkman, got up, and hurried all the way upstairs, through the tiny kitchen and into the dark living room.

I thought it was going to be Ben and his snow shovel, which

would mean a much better day than it looked like being, but when I flipped on the porch light and opened the door, Travis Bismarck was standing there, holding a big duffel bag, just as if it hadn't been five years since I'd seen him last, and at that moment I already knew that he'd be asking me to drive him somewhere, and that I would do it.

CHAPTER TWO

I was so ready for the pretty, Christmas-card-y scene that Colorado Street always is after a fresh snow that I was startled to see just a light scattering of crusted gray corn snow on my flowerbeds, left over from an inch that had fallen earlier that week. The walks and street were clean and dry.

Then I realized with a start who this person who was not Ben was. "Travis Bismarck."

"Right," he said, imitating the way I say it. For some reason people have made fun of that, since I was quite young.

At that hour, *every* street in Gunnison is quiet. Not just "the occasional car passing" quiet. Really quiet. No moving cars, no people. You're more likely, even in the middle of town, to see a deer than to meet a neighbor.

Travis stood in the hard-edged yellow downlight of my porch's overhead flood, looking like a sentimentalized painting of himself. That's what light in warm colors with sharp shadowing will do. (I would need to remember this to use as an example in teaching lighting class, when my sabbatical was over.)

Travis is just over six feet tall with no extra fat, long in the legs and arms, narrow all the way down, with muscles that are flat and hard more than bulging and thick. I'd sparred with him in a few different martial arts here and there, and though, if I got him cornered, I could pound his guard down and then manhandle him, first I had to catch him, which was unlikely. I was far too slow ever to foot-sweep him or beat him to a punch.

He has coarse, planar features, but smooth soft skin, as if the sculptor had said well, fuck the detail work, I'll just go right to the sanding. His nose, like mine, is a little frog-button that barely keeps his eyes from scrambling in the middle. But he has a strong, square jaw, his hair is black without the aid of dye, his face doesn't bag and wrinkle and run down the front of his skull the way mine does, and he has marvelous, clear, piercing blue eyes. He always looked handsome standing next to me, and now he looks fifteen years younger than I do. And he's four years older, may God fling his filthy soul onto the hottest coals in hell.

For five years, our communications had been a few Christmas cards and a couple of late-night drunk dials.

"Well, come on in." His boots were clean, so I motioned him to Kara's huge old futon couch and said, "All right, what brings you to my door?"

"Well, a nice old boy driving a load of cows from Saguache on up to some ranch by Crested Butte brought me most of the way. I hitched a ride into Gunnison—still had your address in my electronic palm dingus, and was about to tell that trucker to dump me at the four corners and I'd look around for somewhere to get coffee and directions, when I saw the sign for Colorado Street, and had him let me out.

"So then I just walked on up here, saw you had a light on in the basement, thought maybe you were up early writing—or up late—and rang your bell. I would've called ahead but I wasn't even sure I'd be stopping in Gunnison; it kind of depended on where my ride turned off. And I didn't want to wake you up. But when I saw that your light was on down there, and knowing two writers live here, I figured either you'd let me in or old Kara would."

"And you were right," I admitted. "I have no judgment where old friends are concerned, and she has an irrational desire to populate the house with vagrants. Anyway, try not to look around too much. The place is a fucking sty. Are you up late or up early?"

"Up late. Gonna be up longer, too."

"Coffee, or Wild Turkey?"

"Let's compromise and do both," he said, which had always been our mutual favorite slogan. "Double up the Turkey. *You're* up early to write, not late to finish, right?"

"Right."

"So you got any of that Pure Black Evil you drink while you write?"

"I like to be able to taste *coffee*, not just warm brown water." I went back to the kitchen, poured another big mug of nice fierce coffee for me, then poured one for Trav and added his two shots of Wild Turkey.

I settled back into a big papasan chair that Kara usually sat in, facing Travis, and took a glorious sip of coffee, realizing that I was not going to have to explain daisite, shovel snow, or swim, for several hours at least. The day was starting off great.

"So, John, is the little woman asleep?"

"Kara's asleep," I said, "and that might be the stupidest possible thing you could call her."

"God knows why, John, but your lovely wife forgives me."

"She says you amuse her. She says the same thing about the guy that eats live chickens in the sideshow, by the way." Kara liked

Travis, which was a puzzlement to me. My first wife had hated him, and I certainly understood that. But no matter who liked him, or not, he has stayed in my life longer than both of them, and all the girl-friends between, all put together.

I got married just a couple years after graduating from college, and started my alternation between getting tired of good jobs and getting tired of grad school. By then Travis was just finishing his second stint in the Army and trying to start his business as a private detective. Trav and I stayed in touch but not as much; he had de-cided to set up in Billings, Montana, and we lived in St. Louis and then in New Orleans. Besides, my first wife thought he was a jerk, and definitely not the kind of friend her husband was supposed to have.

But then after a while we moved to Missoula, and even though that's 350 miles from Billings, Westerners don't think of that as much of a distance. (Hell, we used to drive to Spokane and back, about four hundred miles round-trip, for a decent Chinese dinner and a chance to see a movie the first weekend it was out.) So Travis and I saw more of each other—he'd drop by for the Missoula science fic-tion convention, or I'd be over there for some academic conference at Eastern Montana College, or he'd come out to see a Montana Repertory performance if I was road-teching, or we'd go to some ski area in between on a weekend. One way or another we were in touch.

Then I moved to Pittsburgh, and I'd see Travis whenever miss-ing persons cases took him that way, or whenever Kara and I took a trip up to Montana. (We did our honeymoon up there, and went through Billings on our way west; after all these years, Kara and I can still crack each other up by referring to our night in Billings, the second night of our marriage, which involved Travis, the Worst Country Band On The Planet, a pack of very obese coyotes, and "okay, so let the blind guy drive." But that's an entirely different story.)

The last time I'd seen Travis in the flesh had been when he was tracking a deadbeat dad in the northern part of West Virginia, and had stopped in for an evening to visit Kara and me; it was during the ten days or so while we were packing to move out of Pittsburgh, off to my new job in Gunnison.

We'd stopped long enough to clean up and grab a meal with Travis at the Star of India, near the Carnegie, a great little restaurant which was kind of a magnet for events in my life. It was there that I'd started writing *One For the Morning Glory*, successfully hit on a Norwegian grad student in robotics by getting into a conversation about glue, planned a huge all-day-long outdoor theatre cycle with four friends (it was never produced, foundations having no vision and us having no money), told my parents I was going to marry Kara, and broken up with a stripper. Not all on the same night, by the way.

Looking back, that evening at the Star of India might have foreshadowed something, if anything had happened connected with that evening, instead of the utterly different things I'm reporting in this book.

Travis and I were now both five years older, and none of it showed on him; all ten of it showed on me, I'm afraid. Small college theatre professors work a lot of hours. I was glad to see him but he could have had the decency to be a bit less of a contrast to me. "Okay, Travis, why are you here? And don't tell me it's because your old man was too impatient to go to the drugstore."

"Damn. Another corny joke shot to hell with overuse. Well, all right. You've always been willing to give me a ride when I needed one, and I don't forget that." He took a big swallow of his coffee-and-Turkey, about half the cup I would judge, which would have made my eyes sting and my head ring—I keep my coffee at least as hot as McDonald's keeps the stuff they use for giving old ladies third-degree burns in the crotch. Add that much good whiskey and it will open up your sinuses right through the top of your head.

"Travis," I said, "of course you don't forget that I give you rides when you need them. Sometimes you need another ride. And within reason, you're welcome; I have to go to Denver tonight anyway."

"Goddam. Perfect. And I knew I could count on you, John, I knew it." He took another big gulp of that fierce stuff.

Travis is a very sentimental guy, but he hates to admit it, so he normally doesn't say that kind of thing. I looked at him a little closer.

I knew that having him as a friend meant he'd show up irregularly and ask strange favors. I have several friends like that. It's part of their charm, really, even if I do get grumpy and unhappy when I can't do them the particular favor they ask for. It's worth the frustration, though, because often I can, and anyway, having friends like that is kind of like being unexpectedly dumped into a scavenger hunt or improv comedy sketch (or both at once) a few times a year. Anyway, I don't want that side of my life to change.

But drinking Turkey-and-Evil that fast . . . and something about his expression . . . this was more than Travis's usual embarrassment at needing some odd favor. More than his usual pleasure at bringing me a weird story. He looked *scared*.

"Trav, are you in some kind of legal trouble? Or being followed by somebody violent?"

"Maybe both, John. I'm sorry. I know you got a house and a respectable job and you're up for tenure and everything, and your wife's just a little bitty thing, and all. I'm pretty sure I shook off anybody following me but you know that's never certain. I wouldn't be here if I had much choice."

"So you're being followed, or you might be?"

"I *was* being followed. As far as Alamosa. I changed IDs and rental cars in Santa Fe, but they stayed with me, so I ditched that car in Alamosa in long-term parking at the airport, took a cab out to a truck stop, hitched to Saguache, then found a ride with another semi this way. That Alamosa airport only has flights to Denver, and the other side must know I'm going to Denver eventually, so basically I faked for Denver and zagged here. Even if they tracked me to Saguache, where I changed rides, they'd be expecting me to be headed for Denver, either the Fairplay way or the Leadville way."

"Who are they?" I was *not* pleased. Everything he'd said was true—I had plenty to lose by getting involved in the kind of thing that was Travis's bread and butter. Plus, I'm no good at it. I *write* about adventures. Having them is something else. I had stiff joints and a big gut, and very likely was a coward too since nothing had tested my courage in a while and it probably atrophied like a muscle that isn't used.

Travis sometimes had enemies who were not gun-averse and didn't seem to think bystanders were innocent. I don't keep a gun in the house because I wake up disoriented and do strange things till I'm fully awake. I once picked up my cat Anata, held him to my ear, and said "Hello?" when I was awakened by a friend knocking on the door. I'm always finding half-finished cooking projects in the kitchen, later in the day, that I can't remember starting.

So if Travis had brought trouble with him, I was in for a good stomping, followed by god-knew-what happening to Kara. That's the kind of thing that can make you angry, even at an old friend that you normally forgive for everything.

And that awareness just rubbed in how jealous I was about his youth and energy, compared to the way I was wearing out. We'd gone down such different roads. In my college days I'd almost kept up with him. He'd dropped out of Wash U after sophomore year—a little matter of not having attended classes. By then he was working part-time for a detective agency in Brentwood. He went back into the Army again to be an MP.

They stationed him at Fort Leonard Wood, so he came back to St. Louis pretty often. He'd let me know he was coming, and if I didn't have a judo tournament or a tech rehearsal on a Saturday, he'd call me late Friday night from some truck stop out on the edge of town, and I'd drive out to wherever the semi had dropped him. Then we'd spend the weekend wandering around the Delmar Loop or the Central West End, eating, drinking, and annoying women who were way out of our league.

A few times, when he could give me more notice, I managed to find a great big fat girl with long hair for Travis, and someone short and tiny for me, and the four of us drove out to some little river town down towards Cape Girardeau for what Trav called a Redneck Heaven Weekend—even though he was a fake redneck and I wasn't one at all. We'd stay in a cheap hotel, go to someplace where the girls could sunbathe and we could drink during the day, then dance and drink at some roadhouse Saturday night, then back to the room for drunken sex.

When I divorced the first time, and moved to Pittsburgh, Travis came along on the trip to keep me more or less sane. Depending, of course, on what you call sane.

One night in Sheridan, Wyoming, my truck had been broken down for two days, with a day yet to go before it was fixed. It was the height of tourist season, so there was nowhere to stay through the whole time; we had to move on a night-to-night basis. That night all we could find to stay in was a bridal suite with two huge heart-shaped beds and a six-person lipstick-red hot tub. I kept speculating about how many guests the average couple brings for the wedding night these days, but Travis told me that this was the cynicism of the newly divorced.

For old times' sake we went out and located two cases of Pearl beer, which is terrible stuff but Travis likes it, plus one big heavy prostitute and one tiny little blonde one. I guess that was when I started to notice who was aging faster. I had a nice time but I was all done well inside my hour; the girl just hung around because she was waiting for her next call, and besides she and I were watching, in a spirit of complete awe, what was happening on the other side of the room.

After all those years, Travis still had all the single-minded endurance of a priapic sheltie. He also still made those weird noises. The small blonde woman nestled under my arm would periodically whisper, urgently, "Are they okay over there? She's kind of my friend . . ."

I suppose I should have rejoiced that something, at least, was stable in my universe, and just the way it was when I was twenty-one, but mostly it just made me feel old.

And looking at him, right now, on my sofa, clear-eyed and vigorous and looking like he was more up for a brawl than ever, apparently after being awake for many hours and having just breakfasted on bourbon—all right, Travis still looked like he could handle anything. But the contrast only made things more acute for me. I felt even older—and in danger—danger I couldn't hope to cope with.

"Relax, John, your shoulders are up to your ears and you look like you're going to need your blood pressure medicine. I don't think you or Kara is in any danger. I shook my tail hard and doubled back and shook it again. If trouble does show up, I'm here and it's me they're after. As soon as I go, you'll be out of this again, and don't you dare even think about lying or not talking if someone turns up asking questions. Just tell them whatever they ask, so they leave you and Kara alone, and you let me worry about whatever happens, 'kay?"

I took a bigger swallow of the coffee than I intended, enough to make my eyes tear a little, swallowed hard, counted ten, and remembered that without Travis, and certain other friends like him, my life would be entirely vegetative, and I would be even more depressed, even fatter, and feeling even more old. "All right," I said, "suppose you tell me what we're at no risk *of*. I doubt I'm getting any more words today, anyway."

He finished his cup in another gulp that would have melted my head. "'Spose I can get a refill? Just one Turkey this time. I want to try to fool you into thinking I'm coherent."

"I don't know if that's possible at this point, Trav." I went out to the kitchen, topped up my own cup, gave him another shot of Wild Turkey, and topped up his.

When he'd had a sip—he didn't seem to be gulping this one—he curled one leg under the other in a peculiar way he has that looks like a teenage dance student. He rubbed the back of his neck, and began. "Now you're John again. Now you're my favorite old bewildered small-town Midwestern boy."

"The man with the word 'chump' glowing on his forehead."

"The man who always listens when it gets weird. Because it *has* been getting weird. I need to talk it over with somebody who's used to thinking about weird stuff, because it's been wall-to-wall weird for the last few weeks."

"I gather it's been weird."

"You never did do irony well," Travis said. "You smirk too much." Then he leaned way back and appeared to be reading the story to me from a screen that only he could see, on one of the thick log beams of the ceiling. After a few minutes I slipped into Kara's office for a second and borrowed a notepad from her pile of them—we both did that all the time—and began to take notes. Travis didn't stop, or even seem to notice.

CHAPTER THREE

When I got the call from Xegon, all they said was that it was an industrial espionage case. That was no surprise at all. I'd worked for Xegon before; they're a high-tech company in Albuquerque, with an office in an old storefront building along Montgomery Avenue and a lab in the secure area out east of Kirtland AFB. Which ought to be enough to tell you they're on the spooky side of defense.

Companies like that live in a permanent cloud of worry about spies, all the time; their military masters worry about foreign spies, and they worry about their rivals. What they worry about, more than anything else, is the employee with the hidden problem who needs a pile of money to deal with it, because that's the guy who will shoot a pile of documents over to the competition.

So I'm always getting hired to find the man with the golden nose, or the geekamatoid engineer that thinks he's in love with a teenage crack whore, whenever management has noticed that the competition is suddenly right up with them in the proprietary areas and they're wondering who might have sold them the voodoo. It's a nice little sideline because those places always pay promptly and at a premium, and I'm always glad to get the work.

Xegon was good for about a job every other year, all very routine stuff; the most interesting Xegon job I had had up till then was a good Christian girl particle physicist who had paid for some grad school textbooks with a porn shoot some years before. Then she'd found Jesus and married his right-hand man, who wasn't quite as good at forgiving as his homie was. So she was being blackmailed by her old-hippie California mother. Two weeks of banging my head against the wall while nobody would tell me anything that was going on, and then I found myself in a happy little family conference that was like a successful attempt to do ten hours of the Springer show in forty minutes. But that's another story for another time.

Apart from that one, no previous case had taken more than a week, or been difficult at all, but all of them had been way, way lucrative. So when I came back from Anaconda, where I'd been doing insurance work, photographing a guy who was supposed to be crippled up with a bad back while he taught an advanced techniques in rock-climbing class, and found that message from Xegon on my answering machine, I figured, hot puppies, I'm gonna pay my rent for a while. I called them back, they booked me the flights, and I caught the first flight out of Billings to Denver, and then a flight from Denver to Albuquerque.

It started out completely usual. The taxi dropped me off in a parking lot surrounded by little strip malls, most of them fake Southwest mission stuff; that whole part of Albuquerque, just west of the intersection of Montgomery and Tramway, is a mixture of CBS block buildings and places that look like they used to be Taco Bells. I went through the phony-stucco arches into the lower gallery, then up the stairs to the nondescript second floor. Xegon had acquired all the offices on that floor and put in connecting doors, so it was a bigger place than it looked like from the outside.

The only person I recognized from any previous trip was the receptionist, and I didn't know her name. Every time I've ever gone there, the person who gave me the assignment, the person who accepted my report, and the person who had me sign all the in-strictest-confidence documents and handed me the check, had been three different people, with no overlaps between any trips.

The guy whose office they sent me in to was a Mr. Hale, who they said was head of security.

Hale was a familiar type, but not familiar for where he was, which was maybe my first hint that something strange was up. He was like one of those guys we used to see at Wash U, John, products of upper-class inbreeding: head like a rat, chinless and Roman-nosed and tiny-eyed, with curly blond hair, perfect self-assurance, and a skinny little body, lousy for digging ditches or bar fighting, but perfect for squash, looking good in a suit, or buggery. The kind of people that America exists to support.

This guy was probably a little bit of a miser, or maybe from the well-bred-but-not-rich cousins that go into academia, law, or medicine. His jacket was okay, but his shirt was high-end Penney's or low-end Bean, and the shoes were plain old Bass loafers.

Oh, yeah, John, all that matters. See, Hale fit into his setting like a clarinet in a gun rack. I told you he was like the Wash U old-money kids we went to school with. Well, that kind of family goes CIA or State, not DoD.

These last five years I've been flying to New Mexico, Utah, southern Cal, central Idaho, a lot, because people that do defense work refer you around and I'd been a good boy, gotten things done quick and cheap and discreet. So after a while you get to know what type guy to expect to find where. Normally, I'd expect to find a little hyper-high-tech defense company, especially its squarest-of-the-square offices like security, crawling with DoD types—Sunbelt state university, upscale fundie church, football and golf, calls his mother Mom, a Republican whose grandparents were Democrats.

And Hale was Ivy-Plus-Fifty, Episcopalian, baseball and tennis, calls his mom Mother, and either Republican back to Lincoln or Democrat back to Jefferson.

And yeah, that made Hale weird. Management guys at super-science companies listen to Tom Clancy audiobooks, have cathedral ceilings and barbecues, sing along with oldies on the car radio, and dress like they're trying to infiltrate Real Estate Professionals for Jesus. This old boy probably knew who Francine Prose is, had some third-world art on his walls, and could talk Monk and Bird and Trane. I couldn't figure how the hell he could've gotten past the interview to get hired, unless he was a fucking stone genius, and the geniuses at those companies don't work in security; they're the ones kept behind closed doors, with shitty haircuts, duct tape on their horn-rims, and obese Wiccan wives. Spend enough time in the territory, you get to know everyone's ethnic dress.

Hey, another Turkey-and-Evil? Yeah, I know I'm gulping them like milkshakes. I'm also avoiding the subject I wanted to talk about, because, being honest, John, I'm scared shitless.

All right. So, Hale was weird, maybe just his family's odd duck, but definitely one more weirdity among all the weirdiosity. They're words now. I used'em and you understood'em, they're words. Don't get me further off track than I already was, okay? Thanks. This better be my last Turkey and after that I'm into straight Evil.

Hale's office was a little white room, no pictures on the walls, no windows, just a large square closet with a totally bare desk without even a phone on it, a chair behind that desk, and a chair in front of it.

Hale sat down behind the desk and gestured for me to take the other chair. "We've got a leak. Probably a major one. We need to plug it quickly and discreetly. We know that it's in the Q-tip. From your past work with us, I presume you know what the Q-tip is?"

"Quantum Teleportation and Information Physics. They're the synthesis group that all your other research reports to. They work on some physics thing called simultaneity that I don't understand. Has to do with consequences of quantum events observed at large distances, so that you get an effect that looks something like information traveling faster than light, and something to do with this guy Wolf-something that has the idea that the universe is governed by algorithms and not equations. Is that what I need to know?"

"I'm impressed. You've remembered enough from your last couple of jobs so that we can skip the briefing." He nodded a couple of times like he was deciding that I was a good antique at the price, or maybe that he'd like to breed me to his prize Persian cat. I mean, if I'd been a Persian cat, myself. Though with some of those old money families, I'd believe anything—one time I was looking into an insurance fraud case up in Beaver Creek and—well, that's neither here nor there. Must be some good place in Gunnison to get drunk and tell stories, John; we'll go there sometime when I'm not working. Right, Mario's or the Cattleman. I'll remember.

Anyway, now that Hale had decided I was a good do-bee, he straightened his too-tightly knotted, too-loose-at-the-collar, skinny tie, like a shy high school principal who got his job too young. "We have a number of excellent reasons, which we'd rather not share with you, to think that the leaks are going mainly to Negon, who I know you've had run-ins with in the past—and you've never worked for them?"

"Never."

"Good. This needs to be done quickly, we have to be able to trust you completely, and, frankly, we think Negon might offer anyone working for us a great deal of money to drag his feet for a few crucial weeks. Let me add by way of incentive—and I realize your personal sense of honor is my real security—that if you get an offer from Negon, whatever they offer you to shaft us, we'll add fifty percent to it to keep you loyal, and double it if you can turn it against them. Not because we don't trust you but because at this point—I can tell you this, anyway—our upper management will pay just about anything to get even with those bastards.

"We are in a bidding struggle with Negon, regarding two different approaches to a phenomenon which is code-named 'Gaudeamus' and which I suggest you try to know as little as you can possibly manage about. Their thefts from us have put them far ahead of us, since in effect they have the benefits of an understanding derived from two radically different approaches. So first of all we need to be able to go to the relevant authorities and argue that we are entitled to an extension—or to Negon's temporary disqualification— due to the gross unfairness of the advantage they have gained by intellectual theft. Your work will provide much of the evidence for that.

"It is possible, of course, that the relevant authorities will not see things at all in that way. Should that prove true, then we will have to run this race at a spectacular disadvantage, but it will be all the more necessary to win it. So we also need to know exactly which documents Negon obtained, whose knowledge they were able to tap, which secure sites they had access to, and so forth— and on exactly which dates, ideally at what times. Bottom line, we need to know exactly how Negon stole exactly what aspects of Gaudeamus, and once we have that, we'll be figuring out what to do about it, and at that point there will be more work for you, probably even more lucrative than this."

"So that final report, then, it's got to document that they violated security to get the data, and it has to spell out the names of every-thing they got access to and the time and date when they did, with a complete explanation for how they got everything. But I'm not supposed to learn too much about Gaudeamus itself—not more than I already know from knowing that it's a Q-tip project. That about cover it?"

"That's it."

I wrote all that down on my steno pad, showed it to him, and he agreed that that was still what he meant. Then I asked the big question—"How much?"

"One hundred twenty thousand, plus expenses. Bonus of thirty thousand if you complete within this month."

I was blinking, John. And I swear, normally, I never let it show on my face when a client talks money and it's more than I expected—I mean, that's just business sense. But this time, before god and jesus and that whole crowd, I admit, I was blinking.

If I got done within that month, I'd get a check for three years of my gross. Now I know you and I both admire old Fast Eddy Ed-wards, four times the governor of Louisiana, for being the man who said, on *Sixty Minutes*, "I looked at it, and I seen it was money, so I took it." And in the spirit of our hero, that's what I did.

"I'll try to make you glad you hired me," I said, and I noticed my voice was a little deeper and my accent a little thicker. It gets that way whenever a client seems nervous, to make them think they hired the Lone Ranger, or Chuck Yeager, or Tommy Lee Jones. "So, then, you think—multiple sources? One guy spying on his coworkers? Some kind of ring?"

"No idea."

"Motive? Political, or pure money, or what?"

Hale raised an eyebrow like I'd conjugated a verb wrong. "You know, with the Sovs gone, we never even think about politicals anymore, but it's possible that some of our employees could be involved in some political movement, anti-American or maybe anti-government. For that matter, it could easily be organized crime, Mafia or drug gangs or something, branching out. It doesn't have to be a leak that was instigated by Negon for their purposes, at all; they might just be the buyer. But odds are it's just Negon getting an unfair advantage in the bidding."

I nodded. "Is there anyone you're already certain is involved?"

"Only managers have access to the whole array of what we know must have been stolen, but they wouldn't have understood it well enough to target the thefts so precisely, so at least some engineers have to be involved, and probably some of the Q-tip scientific team. At a guess, a manager to get the documents together, and two to five engineers and scientists—at least one engineer and at least one scientist—to explain to the other side what it means. At least three people, more likely more."

"Sounds like you're very on top of it," I said. "What do you need a detective for?"

"Ah, but, Mr. Bismarck—" (Honest to god, John, who else would begin a sentence with "ah, but . . ." except an upper-crust fourth-generation Ivy nitwit?) "We need to know the *structure* of how this is all being done; how Negon (or Negon and someone else) corrupted one whole section of a place that is entirely SCI. And we need to be able to act on the information. Not only are you much more apt than our own security to find out the things we need to know, but if we get the information from an outside source, that will allow us to make better use of it—better use meaning, possibly, just authorizing the outside source to take whatever steps are needed. To be as frank as I dare."

❖　　❖　　❖

"Now, John," Travis said, "I'm only about halfway to the weird part. Weird shit is like wilderness—you have to go through so much stuff that isn't it to get to it, nowadays. I guess. Or that might be a bourbon insight."

"It might be," I agreed, checking through my notes. "What's SCI?"

"Sensitive compartmented information—security clearances above top secret. 'Compartmented' means that supposedly each guy only gets exactly the information needed to do their job, though in fact there's usually a few big-picture guys around that you can't keep on strictly need-to-know because they're the only guys that know what it is that they need to know. Know what I mean?"

"Yeah, but I'm scared to admit it."

He ignored that, gestured grandly with his coffee cup, and said, "See, SCI's more an attitude than a designation; it's the level where you stop saying 'this guy is cleared to know secret stuff' and start saying 'this stuff is so secret, does anybody need to know it?' Like the default is to not tell anybody, see?"

"I guess I see I think." I looked at my notes again. "So Negon is the other company, the bad guys—"

"For all I know they're vegetarian saints who carry blankets to the homeless, John. Eventually I realized that for every Xegon secret Negon bought, Xegon bought one of theirs. I sometimes wonder whether anybody at either company even theoretically remembers that they are on the same side." He got up and went to look out the window. "Dawn comes up kind of pretty here, doesn't it? Sky so deep blue and the light glinting off the snow on the pine trees—"

"Yeah," I said. "Early mornings up here are great. They make you want to run right out and start doing . . . something. Then you remember it's Gunnison and there's nothing to do."

"Gotta be hunting and fishing and hiking, all that woods to go out and play in—"

"That's right," I said, to shut him up, because I didn't need to hear another lecture like the ones I got constantly from my healtho-outdoorsy neighbors. "There is nothing to do up here. Unless you're the sort of adult whose tastes in entertainment froze at the age of eight—and what you really want to do is ride your bicycle up and down hills, hang out in the woods, and never have any real use for good clothes, or even a bath."

"You must be looking forward to your Denver trip—"

I made a face. "It's a science fiction convention, Travis. Like being caught in a mass police roundup of geeks and your lawyer's out of town for the weekend."

"Wow, you're a lot of fun, these days, John. All right, I feel sorry for you, bud. I'm just dying for you, that you're forced to live in a place where people spend their life savings to get to live there, and that people who like your work invite you to come to big parties with them so they can meet you. My pity meter is on red-line overload and about to blow." He hooked a leg over the heavy wooden rail of the futon couch, wagging one red and white sock at me. "Stand by for pity detonation . . . Ten, nine, eight . . ."

The worst thing about having friends who are good at mocking you is that you have to be a good sport about it. "You *were* telling an interesting story."

"Oh, that. Sure. Got any more Pure Black Evil, no Turkey this time?"

"Hit your limit?"

"I want to stay up till the little—that is, till old Kara gets up. Maybe longer. Might not want to sack out till I get to a motel in Denver this evening. And as long as I'm awake I might as well stay coherent." He stretched and yawned, then woofed as Corner the

Cat, seeing a chance for somewhere warm to sleep, sprang with all eighteen pounds onto Trav's skinny belly. "Stupid cat. What if I'd spilled some of this good coffee and bourbon?" Corner purred loudly. "Better make sure it's safe," Travis added, draining the cup and holding it out. He scratched the big cat's blotchy black and white head. "What's your name, Rorschach?"

"Corner," I said. I took his cup. "Though Rorschach wouldn't be a bad name for him, either." Corner was now purring and kneading. "Stay right where you are and pet the oversize hairball, while I get you more coffee. If you get out from under Corner right now, he'll decide you don't love the cat enough, and make a nuisance of himself for the next half hour until he's had enough attention." I walked into the kitchen, filled Trav's cup. Normally I consumed about a pot and a half of coffee in a good working morning. Today the third pot was about to get started.

When I got back, Corner was stretched out on Travis, belly up, eyes closed, rumbling and slobbering in pure bliss.

"Corner because of Kitty Corner?" he asked.

"Yep, like that cat we had in St. Louis was named Astrophe," I said. "If I'd known Corner's habits I'd have named him Saliva. Then we could have said things like 'I've got eighteen pounds of Saliva on my lap,' 'Is Saliva on the couch?' and 'I was in the basement and I heard Saliva running down the stairs . . .'"

"The worst thing about that would be that you and Kara would get competitive about it," he said.

"True. If you've got that cat about smoothed out, how about getting on with the story?"

He took a deep, appreciative gulp, rubbed Corner's ecstatic head one more time, and said, "I was working on figuring out what the real first steps were going to be. Obviously this case was really about embarrassment."

"Embarrassment?"

"Yep. The lower level the case, the more it's about what they say it's about. This was a high-level case."

"Low and high—okay, Trav, I'm getting lost, and I'm not the one that's been drinking."

"Low level is ordinary people with garden variety problems that they sometimes need a detective for. Like finding a runaway teenager or proving that some deadbeat dad who says he can't work because of his bad back is lifting at a gym to impress his new girlfriend, and bouncing in the bar where she strips. In those kinds of cases, you don't have to worry about why people want you to do what they've hired you to do, because it's fucking obvious. But in a case that involves large amounts of money, or great power, or deep secrecy, or more likely all of the above—what I call a high-level case—your first job is figuring out what the real job is—because they won't tell you."

"Like?"

"Well, maybe it's easier to see at a middle level. Suppose some guy and his wife are the biggest couple at the country club, maybe he's a banker and she's an officer in the DAR, and their daughter goes to Vassar and collectively they are the hottest shit ever shat in the little town of East Buttfuck, Wyoming. Their fame reaches as far up I-90 as Possum Droppings, Montana, and maybe as far down I-25 as Jesus Junction. They are major regional players. And she is divorcing him because she has finally realized that her parents were right and he is a moron, and furthermore a moron who treats her with no respect at all.

"So her lawyer thinks he's getting some on the side, and hires me.

"Now, does the lady want material for some discreet pressure about settlement or custody? Then she wants evidence that the mistress is getting a hundred grand a year in this-and-thats while the wife drives a '95 Explorer that doesn't even have leather seats. Or is it that the wife is good and mad and wants the sonofabitch too humiliated to ever show his face at the country club again? Then what they really want is some nice clear shots that show his wrinkled old face and his hairy huge old fishbelly and a bored-looking trailer-trash girl half his age with her hand on his tiny dick. Or is the mistress the wife's onetime best friend, and does she want them both shamed? Then you want flattering photos of the candlelight dinners, and financial records of the trip to the hideaway at some beach in the Quintana Roo, and a bunch of stuff that looks like travel brochure things, because what she wants to do is take all the fun they had and make them feel so guilty that they'd rather roll over and die."

"Nice line of work you're in."

He grinned in the way that always creeped me out. "I see people acting just like I expect them to, and it confirms my view of the world. Like the phrase goes, it works for me.

"Now, when you get up to the Xegon level, you've got theft of important stuff from an above-top-secret lab. Normally that's a federal problem; quiet guys in black suits who never take off their sunglasses show up for that. So instead they're hiring a one-man operation out of Billings, Montana, a guy who spends most of his time on employee drug cases, adultery, runaways, and guys faking bad backs?

"No way. They ought't've called in the Men in Black right away. Whatever the whole story was, they wanted it all wrapped up before the high-end secret-government types even knew there was a problem. So it had to be worse than just losing something big they were supposed to be careful with. This was going to be the equivalent of finding a cocaine ring inside the Manhattan Project or a circle of pederasts inside Stealth."

I was starting to think he was being creepy deliberately, enjoying it for some reason. "Which is the kind of case you dream about."

"Yeah, in my good dreams and in my nightmares, bud." He took another slurp from his coffee cup.

CHAPTER FOUR

Yeah, you're right, I'm not getting any nearer to the story, am I?

Well, the job started off the way they always do, pure algebra.
What I did was, I got the dates for when Xegon was *sure* that Negon had one of their tricks. Along the way of doing that, noticing
how much Xegon knew about Negon's internal operations, I figured
out that Xegon had a pretty good industrial espionage op of its own
going. (It was none off mine, though, since I knew which one wrote
my checks.) The more I looked at the way the two companies re-
lated, the more it looked like Xegon and Negon were like twin
brothers that hated each other so much they couldn't leave each
other alone.

So, you worked in some R&D shops a long time ago, right, John?
Back when you were in New Orleans? You know about how they
log ideas going through the chutes, partly for patent and partly so
they know the creative types aren't sloughing? So they record all the
dates from the first rough idea memo, to discussion summaries, to
a seminar memo, to a paper, to when they put the done-and-ready
cookbook version into the manual. They treat every idea the way

a high-end Dallas sorority girl treats her first marriage and her first baby—every time it crawls forward a little bit or heaves up something gooey, they shoot pictures and date them and file them. I was thinking of the baby, but of course you're right, that could be the marriage too. I got cousins and I've seen that whole story, plenty.

So, anyway, you have this nice neat who-thunk-what-when for every little equation and bit of theory and algorithm and experiment—not just what they did and what they recorded, but who they talked to when, who put it on paper when, who read the paper and attached comments, who could've read the paper and might've spilled coffee on it, all the way till they blue-stamp it PCK, Project Common Knowledge—the point where everyone has access and it's pretty much just known to be true. Plenty of it never goes that far and stays SCI forever, of course.

So I took the concept history logs, and the schedule for reporting upstairs, and my list of the dates when Xegon's people had first suspected that Negon had the same thing, and worked up a chart on a few big sheets of layout paper, taped together, hanging on my hotel-room wall. Four days later, that wall was covered, and I'd boiled the list of all the engineers, technicians, managers, and scientists in the Q-tip down to a list of about thirty maybes, a list of seven probablies, and one for-sure.

My for-sure was the senior technical guy, the one in charge of explaining things to management, in the Q-tip, a guy named Calvin Durango. They couldn't be doing what they were doing without his being aware of it, but if he was in on it, then everything else was possible. Therefore he was, and if I could find out what old Calvin was doing, and how he was doing it, the rest of the solution ought to just tumble out, the way one of those logic puzzles does when you realize that the Swede lives in the blue house and drinks beer. In particular, old Calvin was the only single point they passed four areas through—qubits, subnucleonics, QT (which I figured was probably Quantum Teleportation), and something called QN or Core Gaudeamus that apparently was the hottest of the hot and the thing they were most worried about. He was the point guy for subnucleonic qubits, which I suspect means computing with quarks, and for studies of QT-qubit interaction, which I'm almost certain was a matter of having massively parallel processors that weren't limited by how fast light could get across the box, from one side of the computer to the other. And all that seemed to be part of the problem of explaining QN, or Core Gaudeamus, or what one young physicist (who wasn't security conscious enough) referred to as the "What the Fuck? Effect."

But I already knew enough about the science side—more than they wanted me to know. What I needed to learn was something more in my area of specialty—Calvin Durango's bad habit.

Trav was stretched out at full length on that huge old futon couch, one arm thrown over his eyes; I guess the increasing morning light was bothering him. "It would be okay with me if you caught a nap and filled me in later," I added.

"But it wouldn't be okay with me. I'll explain why in a little bit. You won't believe it, John, but at least it'll make sense." He sat up, sighing. "I'm not kidding. I could probably get away with sleeping some this afternoon, but it would be safer if I didn't, and I gotta make it awake through at least lunchtime. If you could pour some more Pure Black Evil into me—"

"I'll need to start another pot," I said. "Follow me on out to the kitchen and keep talking." I rinsed the pot and basket, scrubbed them with a few swipes of 409 and a paper towel, rinsed them again, and checked to make sure they were really clean—the coffee

I make for writing leaves a residue you could pave a road with. I pulled out a bag of my standard heavy African coffee, dark roasted till the beans drip oil. I ground it down to molecules, filled the basket about a third beyond what the directions would say, added deonized water just above freezing to the reservoir, and switched it on. "It'll take a bit," I said.

"You don't have the pot in there."

"It has one of those steal a cup features. I don't put the pot in till the basket's about to overflow. That way the coffee spends more time soaking in the hot water. Now, you were saying you wanted to know about Calvin Durango's bad habits."

"Well, that's where you're going to find a spy, normally. Drugs, gambling, pussy on the side. People don't betray their country for political causes or for high moral purposes nearly as often as they do for the crazy hot love of a streetwalker, or to cover a quarter million in football bets, or because they need to fix their noses every three hours. Besides, I had another reason to be sure it wasn't going to be political or ideological. Calvin Durango was Hispano— you had any of those in your classes here?"

"Lots," I said. Hispanos are people whose ancestors were already here when the border moved abruptly in the 1840s; they didn't come to America, it came to them.

"Well, then you know. Pretty conservative lot. Durango stayed in touch with all his big family, out to second cousins, and they were old money, at least by the standards of Hidalgo County, New Mexico. So chances were Calvin wouldn't be plotting revolution, planning ecoterror, or trying to start a race war. Almost for sure he just needed money for something that went into his bloodstream or bounced on his weenie."

❖　❖　❖

So I started following my man Calvin, and the third day I was tailing him, he didn't go right home to his wife (Angelina, also thirty-six like him, dark hair, blue eyes from contacts, nice body she worked out to maintain) and kiddies (Joe, seven, very serious kid with messy hair and huge eyes, and Wendiann, eight months old, and thanks to a totally illegal phone tap I knew, exhaustively, that both her grandmothers thought she was the cutest thing ever born. Thank God for voice recognition scanning, you know what I mean, John?).

This particular day, Calvin Durango left work about twenty minutes early—R&D shops are flexy about things like that—and drove to a run-down older strip mall out to the west, most of the way to I-25. He got out of his BMW, walked across the parking lots of two neighboring strip malls, and got into another car. Right there I knew that was pay dirt, because the other car was a perfect don't-look-at-me-mobile, a gray '92 Sable. He headed back east on Montgomery, the way he'd come.

I'd had enough experience to recognize the two-car trick—it's Old Reliable for well-off adulterers—so when he'd started walking along through those adjoining strip-mall parking lots, I'd started moving left, and as soon as I saw him open the door on that Sable, I swung through the next opening in traffic into a parking lot not far from his. When he took off, I took off, and I was on his tail again. He probably hadn't noticed me the first time, and rental cars tend to be chosen to be visually bland because it increases their resale value, so my ride was nearly as invisible as his.

He drove that old Sable over to a great big block of apartment buildings out on Mongomery, only about a half mile from Xegon's offices, across the street and a block or so from a Christian conservatory and into the parking lot of a cheap little seventies-vintage apartment complex.

I pulled into the next parking lot and went around behind, same as he did; I shot a few pictures with my digital camera of what apartment he went into, catching one not-great shot of a slim, dark-haired young woman in a little bitty miniskirt and great big clunko boots.

After about ten minutes I walked up to the second-floor gallery where the entrance was, and took a walk by the big picture window. The curtains were pulled, of course, but as I went by I planted a keen little electronic gadget that it might not be strictly legal for me to have. It picks up vibrations off the windows, so along with passing trucks and whatever's on the stereo and all that, you hear what's said in the room because a big old sheet of plate glass is just about the most perfect antenna for sound you could want.

I walked back to my rental car, put on my headphones, and jacked in to listen; my receiving station was also making an mp3 out of the whole thing.

A woman's voice said, "So, you want to? I'm kind of up for it. No charge or anything."

"It would be all right," Calvin Durango said. "But we don't have to . . ."

"No, it would feel good, I think," she said. "That is, if you have the time."

Some rustling. He breathed fast for a minute or so. She said "Easy" and then "Lighter." The bed rocked and creaked the way it does. He asked "Now?" The rocking got hard and fast for a while and then there were a couple of sighs. More rustling and scraping sounds as they put clothes and bedclothes back into position.

"That was okay," Durango said.

"I like to do that now and then," the woman said.

"Thanks," Durango said. "Regular time next week."

I was thinking that maybe in the movie it would be kind of overkill to have them played by Tom Hanks and Meg Ryan.

He came out the door, carrying a Tupperware bowl, and walked straight to his Sable. A moment later he had pulled out and away.

I got out of my car, looked around, and threw one of my special Frisbees onto the roof of her building.

It's my signal relay; it works with my bug. I start with a regular old Frisbee. Cover the upper surface with some photoelectric film I get from a client that I did a big favor for. Antennas run around the circumference, just hairline wires. Underneath, inside the flat bubble at the center, there's some micro storage batteries and a little radio-to-cell phone translator. Whenever it picks up the signal from the bug, it phones up that cell number and leaves whatever it hears as a huge voice mail.

The whole thing doesn't weigh four ounces more than a regular Frisbee, and it flies almost as good, and what looks more natural on a roof than a Frisbee? So I can throw it right where it'll get the most sunlight and have the best line of sight to a cell tower. If it gets knocked down it usually just gets thrown away, or some kid carries it off to play with and thinks, since he can't get the electronics to do anything, that it's broken, and then *he* throws it away. Chances of anyone realizing what it is, and connecting it to my surveillance, are about zip.

So after it landed up there, I put my cell-phone earpiece in, confirmed I had signal from the bug, and then zoomed off to catch up with that mud-colored Sable. Durango did just what I expected and drove back to that wilderness of strip malls, parked a few lots from his BMW, and walked back to it. I trailed him on home and shot my last pictures of the day as he loaded a stuffed tiger into his trunk at the Target on the way home. Sometimes these guys are predictable.

Now, back at the hotel room, with my laptop able to talk to the Frisbee over the modem, I could use some of its other cute capabilities. Like I said, I don't think that bug was ever really intended to be civilian equipment, but I'd been lucky enough to get a few boxes of them as a little favor from a company I'd done some work for before, and the Frisbees I could homebuild. So first of all, I worked with the scanner and found the frequency on her cordless phone.

Over the next few days, I hung out in Xegon's snack bar, appearing to write reports, and taped some conversations at the Denny's a few doors up from Xegon's office, and it became pretty clear that the lady, who everyone called Wendy, was a very open secret. Guys who had a Wendy habit were very eager to hook everyone else on her, and talked pretty openly about who had given Wendy the best ride in the rack or who she'd done something special for. Pretty much the only guys nobody tried to recruit into the Wendy Club were the very religious and the hopelessly geeky.

I'd seen circles of men form around an available woman or an economical prostitute before, in some other investigations. Once it was most of the male teachers in a high school and the soprano section of the glee club, all taking turns and swapping around in a mop closet, and trust me, John, that made for some real weird listening, and made me real glad that it was a little bitty town down south of Midland, where they settled it all real quiet and I didn't have to go play those tapes in court.

After three days, most of my list of possibly-involveds had been to Wendy. Every one that had, had also paid some extra money and left with a Tupperware bowl.

I truly thought that I had cracked it, and would be done within a week. Wendy and the drugs she was selling were both expensive habits, and most likely she was accepting secret documents in trade. I told Hale we could either bust them all now, or leave things up a little longer and find out exactly how they were doing it. I recommended the latter. Hale agreed.

But there were still some problems with my perfect case, and one of them bugged the shit out of me. I had burned scads of mp3s of Wendy talking to scientists and engineers, but not a single second when anyone said anything other than what you'd expect if she were just a hooker and drug dealer. And it bugged me that the drugs were called "God" or "goddies," terms I'd never heard before; usually I'm more current than that. Whatever they were, she was selling them in batches of twenty, packed in that Tupperware, and typically a guy with a goddy habit would consume about one a day.

And still absolutely nobody talked one minute of physics with her, except for a couple nice older PhDs that would help her with her homework—

Oh, yeah, John, she's a grad student in physics at UNM. Her real name is Lena Logan. Although they don't exactly put it in the college catalogs, there's usually some of the high-priced end of prostitution near college campuses. Textbooks and tuition are expensive, the culture says younger girls are more attractive, and there's not too many other ways for a college girl to make a few hundred in one night, so you got supply; colleges always have men with money coming by without the wife—visiting scholars, alums, coaches, politicians—so there's a demand. Deans and campus pigs and so forth do their best to keep it all quiet, which they can do, rather than to try to shut it down, which they can't. But having done divorce work, I can tell you that when a middle-aged biz guy starts heading for a hotel near a campus, or for one of the student ghettos, there's a real good chance he's not taking night classes.

Lena Logan is the kind of gal that makes money at that: late twenties, very thick very black hair, just slightly wavy, big eyes— dark blue, probably contacts over brown would be my guess— and thin lips that stuck out just a little so you'd wonder what she kissed like and how much her mouth moved around and what those would feel like brushing your dick. She was tall—five eight by her

DMV records—and slim—she claimed 125 and it was believable, but she was probably more 140 or 145. Round taut ass. Those kind of long, long go-on-forever legs with really long thighbones. Nice rack of high hard ones, straight off the collarbone and big and round and close together. She wore tight little tops, usually white or something pale, that showed the dark bra through, and sprayed-on Daisy Dukes with big old clunky wicker heels. In other words, old Lena looked just like what every younger male programmer, engineer, or scientist is always wishing he could have.

She only took appointments Monday, Wednesday, and Friday, because she had to TA a Tuesday morning lab, and she was taking seminars that met Tuesday and Thursday afternoons. She also had some independent study project or other with a Doctor Charles Ogden, but I never did detect any work she did on that. Which could either be normal grad student procrastination (early October and she hadn't started on something that was due in December yet), or maybe she was trading some fun to Ogden for an A that she wouldn't have to study for—if so, I kind of liked the two of them for titling that project "Chaos in Brief Contacts Between Deformable Bodies."

I moved into an old-fashioned motel off of Montgomery, about a block and a half away, took my room by the month and bribed the help generously to tell me whatever they happened to see around the place, and to not see anything around my room. I was close enough to replace the Frisbee relay with a simple wire antenna that I strung around the bathroom ceiling, so the listening was good, and if anything started to happen I could be over at Lena's on foot in five minutes.

It couldn't have sounded less like high-tech industrial espionage. On her working days, she picked up messages from her voice mail, called the men back, and made appointments; they'd come by.

With regulars, she'd have sex and sell them a Tupperware bowl full of goddies. If they were new, she'd sit down on the couch, do the "touch my boob" thing before she'd let the guy talk about money to make sure the guy wasn't an undercover pig, and then it would proceed according to script. They came to her for pretty normal stuff (at least normal to me after years of peeking and eavesdropping). They wanted to suck her toes, or for her to wear her hair in pigtails, or she had a latex cutout bra that some of them liked, or they liked her to call them "Dad."

Just once, a new guy asked about goddies. She invited him to try them while they got it on. There was *loud* noise for an unusually long time, and she told him that goddies were two thousand dollars a box, and he came back later that night with the cash and seemed to be glad to pay it.

A hundred dollars a pill. Must be a hell of a ride.

Anyway, if they were passing copies of Xegon's high-end secret research to Wendy/Lena Logan, I wasn't getting any evidence of it. Besides, she wasn't making any contacts with Negon that I could see. I shadowed her for a week. Absolutely nothing.

CHAPTER FIVE

"Hell, John," Travis said, sitting up and pushing the inert mass of Corner the cat off his lap and onto the floor ("Thud-grunt," Corner commented, before rolling over onto his back and waving his legs to have his tummy scratched), "it was all so normal that I was starting to wonder if maybe I'd just jumped at the wrong lead. It wasn't even unusual to find a grad student doing that. School is expensive, grad school even more so, and grad school in the sciences is amazingly expensive since it takes so long to get that degree, not to mention that you need to give your classes so much attention. A job that requires just a few hours of work for a substantial off-the-books income can make solid sense, if you can stand the icky side of things. So it was not at all unusual. I've often wondered how many professors I've known, over the years, who cocksucked their way through all that schooling."

"I wonder the same thing at every faculty committee meeting. It helps me stay awake." The sun was full up now and the room had a warm glow that I always liked; it faced south and west, with the neighbors' house in the way, so the sunlight coming in was mostly reflected and when it played on the big thick twelve-inch logs and the maple floors, it got a great amber glow that I was forever trying to copy with stage lights.

"Nice in here," Travis said, looking around. "You did all right for yourself."

"So it sounds like Lena Logan was turning out to be a dead end," I said.

"That was what I was most afraid of. Maybe she was just an unusually successful ho, who just happened to have a few dozen clients all at one business that had a totally unrelated industrial espionage problem. Maybe I'd just jumped into the wrong end of the pool and that was why I kept swimming against the wall. But no matter how much rethinking I did, I still thought it was more likely that she was just too smart to catch by ordinary means. You have a bunch of married guys at a secure facility, all seeing a hooker, who's also a dealer, and since she's a grad student in physics, just possibly she's capable of understanding whatever she hears from them. Start with those facts. And she's distributing something to them that they'll pay a lot for and go to great lengths to get. Man, John, if that isn't a place for secrets to leak, I don't know what would be, you know? So the hypothesis that she was too smart to catch by ordinary means seemed like the best bet, which meant it was time for some un-ordinary means. I know several of those, but unfortunately, I didn't know which ones to use, or what I'd be looking for if I did. So things went right on being ordinary, and I waited for something weird, to give me a hint."

"So we're not to the weird part yet," I said, "but maybe we're getting there?"

"Just going to start getting there, but yeah."

❖　❖　❖

One night I was working on an email to Hale, trying to figure out a new way to say "I still don't have a goddam thing" in corporatese, and, kind of in background, I was listening, live, to the audio from the bug on her window.

I wasn't listening real hard, because it was Jason. I'd been running down everything I could about all of Lena's non-Xegon customers, hoping to find the courier for the Xegon documents, and I'd have to say that Jason was pretty far down the list as anybody anyone would use for that job. The only way he'd be off the bottom was if she got a pet, and it would have to be a pretty dumb pet.

Compared to Jason, a rock by a park bench would be a better thing to entrust high-priced stolen documents to. Jason was a thirty-six-year-old owner of a pool-maintenance business, with a new baby girl three months old, two more kids under five, and a wife in treatment for depression, barely smart enough to be aware that he was unhappily married. (Amazing what you can find out once you get someone's social.)

No, there wasn't a web page that said his marriage was unhappy, John. He was a regular with a hooker, his credit cards were maxxing every month, his wife was in treatment for depression, and he had MasterCard slips late night at a titty bar a couple nights a week. I kind of figured from that. Sometimes, for a prof, you're a real idiot, you know?

So I was sitting there typing and listening to Jason get his usual when old Lena said, "Can I call you Calvin?"

"What? My name is Jason."

"I know that, Jason, but, baby, it's like this—" She drew a long breath, and sighed deeply, and I could almost imagine her lowering her eyes and showing him what a difficult confession this all was. "There was this guy, Calvin, once. He made me cum better than anybody ever before or ever since. Probably cause he had such a good big one, like yours. So I was thinking . . . um, you kind of got to me the last couple times . . . and if I could just call you Calvin . . . you know, to kind of remind me . . . just for me, just this once? I mean, it *will* turn me into an *animal* for you. That is guar-an-*teed*. C'mon, you gotta let me call you Calvin."

He wasn't what you call super happy about it, but she wheedled a little more, and he finally said okay.

A couple minutes later she started with "Oh, Calvin, squeeze my tits" and "Oh, Calvin, I want your big, big dick so bad," and all this raunchy rape-talk about her hot hole and his massive meat. Honestly, John, I've been eavesdropping for more than fifteen years, and I have to say, ever since pornography became easy to get, the quality of most people's bedroom dialogue has gone straight into the toilet, you know what I mean?

The funniest thing to me—I mean, honest to god and jesus and that whole crowd, John, I was sitting there and laughing fit to bust a gut while I listened—was that she sounded like she meant it. Which was pretty funny because by then I'd heard her boinking old Calvin a couple more times and you know that bed barely moved.

I just didn't think Lena Logan could be getting off fantasizing about Calvin Durango, because despite his high income, the man was a little rat of a person, losing his hair young, major acne scars, stick-outy ears and a potato nose, and no taste in clothes. Front view, Karl Malden doing a "before" shot for Stridex. Side view, a goblin in a kids' book. Top view, a very messy nest with one big egg and handles.

Anyway, so Lena got Jason out the door. By then the pure weirdness had pulled me out of my room at the No-Tell Motel and I was listening to the bug on my cell phone's earpieces while I watched through an infrared sniper scope, from under a bridge over a concrete arroyo.

No, the arroyos are a basic feature of Albuquerque, which is built on a desert floodplain—flash flood territory, in other words. So they're not much like the arroyos you have to cope with in desert hiking, though some of them must have started out that way. What they are is concrete ditches that cut all through Albuquerque. They give the flash flood water a quick, harmless route to the river on the rare days when it rains. Nobody goes into an arroyo if they have any sense or any choice, since they can go from bone dry to nothing-can-live-in-that in a few seconds, but us detectives are always short on choices and even shorter on sense. And if you work Albuquerque at all, you get to know your arroyos. Throw something under the bridge in an arroyo and the next rainstorm will take it way away—very likely right on down to the Rio Grande, and who knows how far after that. Half the murdered bodies in that town turn up under arroyo bridges.

Okay, so now are you picturing me squatting in that concrete ditch, and watching Lena Logan's door with an infrared sniper scope, and listening to Jason the unhappily married moron pool cleaner get his last little cuddle after having sex with "Wendy" who was insisting on calling him Calvin? Got all that?

Well, when he finally came out, it sure looked like she hadn't lied about showing him an extra good time. Jason was *bouncing* down the steps to the parking lot, from sheer pure joy, like Barney on crack. He looked like he'd been run over while dressing, and he more or less fell into his car, but he was radiating enough happy to be seen by the naked eye from Santa Fe. If they had a car that could detect when you're emotionally unfit to drive, old Jason'd've set off every alarm.

As soon as Jason left, Lena made two phone calls. The first one was to an engineer from subnucleonics section, a guy named Rod Johnson (indicating that God or his parents had a strong sense of irony, if one could judge by his past performance). She said, "Baby, I'm so sorry, but my mom is just coming into town tonight, and she didn't tell me she was coming, and she'll be here in an hour, so I gotta cancel with you. Can you forgive your little Wendy? I promise you the next one's free if you just forgive me this time."

Well, naturally, being an engineer, he was probably a shitload more excited about getting it free than he would have been about having sex, so he agreed right away. She thanked him gratefully and hung up.

Then there was a long, long silence. There is no longer silence than when you're surveilling somebody who leads a dull, repetitive life, and they finally do something interesting, and now they've stopped doing the interesting thing and you're waiting for them to start again. Trust me, John, they don't make silences longer than that.

Than the silence while you wait for something to happen again.

That silence.

They don't make them any longer—hey, don't throw your cat. I was just shitting with you, bud.

I climbed out of the arroyo and moved in closer, keeping an eye out for anyone who might notice a guy sneaking between parked cars with a scope in the middle of the night. Wouldn't do to get busted for a perv.

She picked up the phone and dialed. She didn't say hello and nobody said hello at the other end of the line. She just started. Her voice was flat and dull, not like a machine, just like she was real tired and trying to concentrate, as she said, "Xegon Tech Memo One Five Four One Oh Oh Two Nine Seven. Date October Two Nineteen Ninety-seven. Subj entropy increase with distance negative result. From Paula Carson To Ned Vernal Exec Sum Experiments with STS package reveal that the Gaudeamus phenomenon neither increases nor decreases entropy in response to changes of distance on the order of three to five orders of magnitude of difference in potential energy with respect to the Earth's siffergraf."

"Subj?" I asked. "Like the abbreviation for subject on memos?"

"That's what she said," he agreed. "She pronounced it, just like that. And like I said, in a weird tired voice, all flat and everything, like she'd spent the day running wind sprints and just gotten her breath back, and with no more expression than those reader programs on a desktop computer."

"And what's a siffergraf?"

"My best guess, after I did some searching in my special accounts, is that it's a pronunciation of SIFoR GraF"—he spelled it out, capitals and all—"which stands for Standard Inertial Frame of Reference Gravitational Field, which is what the crowd at Xegon seems to call the everyday world we all live in. To differentiate it from experiments conducted in orbit by a couple of robots on the space station or the shuttle, or out in interplanetary space on probes that aren't supposed to be there, or maybe on the moon. No question, though, that there are at least four alternative test sites to SIFoR GraF, so I'd say they're doing more in space than either of us would believe offhand. One of those other places is AFoR ISNc, and I'm curious as all shit about where that is. Now—on to the weirdness! We're almost there.

"So she recited physics and even rattled off very elaborate descriptions of graphs, giving all the points and every place where a curve intersected a gridline, and that went on for almost an hour, which meant she was transmitting maybe a thirty-page typewritten double-spaced paper, footnotes and all. Then she hung up, and I heard teeth brushing and clothes sloughing off, and her lights went out. After a while she was snoring.

"I went back to my room and checked; I'd gotten it all in the mp3, and recorded the number she'd dialed, which was a number in Negon's private exchange.

"So I burned a CD of that, and the next day I handed the CD over to Mr. Hale at Xegon. I suggested that we do the absolutely conventional thing: since it had already been outside the company and no longer secure, the thing to do was to transcribe it, say we'd picked it up on a cointel intercept, and post it for identification."

"I don't follow you," I said.

"And I only follow you if someone pays me," Travis said. "Maybe old Kara'd be interested, but only if she was going to try to catch you at something, and she's not the type."

"She's not," I agreed, "and you stole that joke from Groucho Marx. 'You follow me? Well, stop following me, I'll have you arrested.' *A Night at the Opera,* I do believe."

"Hey, all the best material is stolen," Travis said, "especially including the book you're gonna get out of this, someday, and you're stealing that from me and I'm stealing it from life."

"Life never sues," I pointed out. "That's what I love about it. So, now, explain what you were doing."

"Well," Travis said, "we had a transcript made. That was an ordeal in its own right, for me, and I think that evil bastard Hale was laughing his lipless little laugh at me the whole time. See, I knew I'd be needing transcripts of a lot of what had gone on in that apartment, and I asked Hale if we could get them all made—rush this one out and then have the rest done as soon as possible afterwards. And the Incredible Iguana-Faced Preppy said yes.

"See, I was expecting they'd send me some fast-typing engineer or some old court reporter with tech training, to get filled in on nonstandard and unfamiliar words he or she might hear. Instead they sent me this girl Lynn, who was probably twenty-five but looked fifteen, so besides transcribing all that physics, I was getting this little angel-face girl to type out a bunch of major heavy-duty fuck scenes. She wore her red-blonde hair in pigtails, didn't wear makeup, and every time I saw her she was wearing a different color sweatshirt with a different Disney Winnie the Pooh character on it. She looked like Heidi meets Pippi Longstocking without looking as jaded or decadent as either."

I told her what I needed transcribed and what parts I needed timings on (when you go to court, which we might have needed that for, you need things like how long the heavy breathing went or what times the screams and moans came, sometimes), and she took notes with complete seriousness, and as far as I could tell I was the only one embarrassed.

"Sorry this is such rough stuff," I said to Lynn, when she said she thought her notes were complete and she was ready to start.

"Where'd you get this stuff, anyway?"

"From a bug I planted in a prostitute's apartment," I said, seeing no way that she wouldn't figure that out anyway. "Somebody that some Xegon employees go to. That's what I do for a living. I mean I'm a detective and I follow them around, not that I'm a Xegon employee or a prostitute. This is all part of a security investigation."

"So there's only that one hour of protons and gravity and all that?"

"Yeah, but I need a transcript of the whole thing, and with sounds like snoring and squeaking springs and stuff like that, I need start and stop marks, and timings."

"Sure, I can do that, it will be interesting to type something with no science and a lot of entertainment value."

"I'm glad you see it that way."

"I'm just bored stiff with tech transcription. I got my AA's degree in tech transcription so I could support my son and me, but nothing in the world can make it interesting, you know?" .

Great. I was doing this to somebody's mother.

"Your son?"

"Neddy is two. At least I can do transcriptions at home, so we get more time together. I don't think I'll ever quit because the job's too perfect for what I need. But I'm *so* tired of typing about gravity and energy and teleportation. A few pages of 'oh baby' is going to be *such* a relief. Do you ever need this kind of thing done for places other than Xegon?"

"Actually I need transcripts all the time."

"Let me give you my card. I'd love to transcribe some sex and violence instead of all this science shit. They let me moonlight as long as it's for an approved firm and I promise not to share secrets between them but the only moonlighting work I've gotten has been transcribing more science papers for scientists at other companies, or for papers the guys here are going to publish. It would be cool to have a little variety."

So we traded cards, and filled out nondisclosure forms so that it would be okay with Xegon for her to work for me, and I promised I'd think of her when I had work. What the hell, I can always use a good transcriptionist. I just tried not to picture her typing the part where Lena was screaming "Oh Calvin, you're so big it hurts my fucking cunt" in her sunrise-yellow Tigger sweatshirt while a little boy played with Tickle Me Elmo at her fuzzy slippered feet.

Lynn got it done in a day, and we sent the transcript to everyone in the Q-tip with a note saying that our spook spotters had found this in a hostile location, and asking if any of them could identify it. We expected that almost all of them could but we'd only hear from a couple of them. That was okay, those were the ones we needed to hear from.

When you've got one rotten apple in the barrel, you want to find it and isolate it. But if the whole barrel is rotten—if you're just riddled, and you got more crooks than honest people, you don't want to isolate the few bad guys and pull them out; you want to find the few good guys, and use them as informers while you wipe out the bad-guy operation, before setting up a whole new organization.

So Hale put out the transcript with a note claiming it was a cointel pickup. If anyone recognized it they were supposed to contact him at once, and set up an interview (it didn't mention I'd be there). And it very strongly said not to tell anyone else that you'd recognized it.

We figured the authors of the paper would probably call in, even though we suspected that they were probably guilty as all shit, because they could hardly pretend not to recognize their own work and they'd have to at least try to bluff their way out by pretending to be innocent dupes. Other than that, though, we weren't expecting to hear from much of anybody, except maybe a couple of religious nuts and a couple of ubergeeks that probably had never been invited to share the Wendy Experience.

But three hours after he sent out the transcript, Hale called me. "*Everyone* on your list of suspects called in, and the very first was Calvin Durango, who appears to be quite distraught and wants to meet right away. He and I are both at the facility today—can you come down?"

The facility is what they called the labs where they actually tried out all the weird things that they worked out on blackboards in that nondescript little strip mall up in the northeast. If you head east on 40, past Kirtland AFB, you eventually pass a bunch of pricey gated community-type places that contain a pretty surprising number of majors-and-up—what's going on at Kirtland, at any given time, tends to be a hot area for getting promoted, and guys want to be

standing next to it, and it's been that way ever since they were figuring out how to get an atom bomb into a B-29 and then get the B-
29 off the ground. It's not quite as general-and-colonel-heavy there
as it is in some developments around Groom Lake or Vandenberg,
but close enough.

Past the super-high-end subdivision, you run through a bunch of
strip-mallish stuff that caters to the lower ranks, places where a
bored guy can get drunk, hunt pussy, get his motorcycle tuned, and
so on, and then it trails off into hills and desert. All that long way, as
you drive east, off to your right, it's still Kirtland, which is a hell of
a big place. And every so often, there's a road south, that leads to a
guarded gate, and then a road beyond that through more and more
guarded checkpoints, and finally there will be some little building
in the middle of nowhere, where brainy guys are playing around
with stuff that nobody will admit to.

The facility is one of those buildings, and considering that it
might change the whole world, and there's a danger that someday it
might be famous, I wish it looked a little less like a standard light-
assembly plant, or at least had something other than "Operated by
Xegon in cooperation with the Departments of Energy and Defense" over the door. It took me a little time to get there because
they crawled all over my car at each checkpoint, and while I was
driving along the gravel road a jeep full of guys in unmarked uni-
forms came up and they searched me too, as well as waving some
gadgets over the rental car that presumably were good-guy gadgets
used for detecting bad-guy gadgets, but the equipment itself looked
like R2D2 with an old-style vacuum-cleaner hose coming out his
butt, hooked to a supermarket price scanner.

Finally I got to the facility, and it was a nothing-special building
like I've described—see'em in any industrial part of any big city. I
went in the square, double-doored glass front entrance, which,

since it faced west, was already turning into an oven. Beyond the second set of glass walls and doors, they had bone-chilling air-conditioning, and a nice, thirtyish, plump receptionist. I wondered what her life was like when she wasn't sitting at a counter, taking calls and visibly wearing a big old honking nine-millimeter—she seemed like the type that goes to church and volunteers for Habitat for Humanity, and there was a picture of her with a little boy (but no man in sight) on her desk.

She found my name on a list, gave me a badge, and called in a guard who walked me through the corridors swiftly, with an air that suggested he'd rather have blindfolded me, stuffed me into a box, and wheeled me there on a dolly. I did my looking around just as discreetly as I could.

The windowless white office was absolutely bare; just two desks with phones, three chairs, Mr. Hale, and Mr. Calvin Durango. Old Calvin was acting and sounding like the most innocent man that ever breathed (even if his face still looked like a troll with a live wriggling gerbil stuck in its butt). He wanted to help to the max. He knew the leak had to be coming out of the Q-tip, and he was the senior engineer-manager of the Q-tip, and he was *screaming*— I mean, literally, his voice was high and loud and not in control, these big high-pitched emotional shrieks of "I want something done and I want it done now!" I think he might have actually screamed those exact words, but even if he didn't, it was sure as fuck what he meant.

Not one word of his screaming was about suddenly discovering that there was a detective prowling around his group. So I figured it wouldn't be a real good icebreaker to say that although we'd never met, officially, I'd listened to him fuck several times. I'd have to save that to start some other conversation, some other time.

As Durango's scream level declined, mostly because Hale kept interrupting him and trying to focus him, it became clear just what Calvin Durango wanted. He wanted me to jump on that case and bust it wide open and arrest everyone within a hundred miles, right now. "Don't you understand?" he shrieked at Hale. "If this leaks out at this stage in the research, we're all dead one way or another. It's either like the atom bomb but a hundred times worse, because you could build this in any well-equipped high school anywhere in the world, or it's suddenly as public domain as the wheel and the whole world gets rich but we don't, or . . . for god's sake, Hale, try to at least look a little concerned! This is a disaster, to have this outside the company anywhere."

"Mr. Durango," I said, "we have no way to compel you to do this, but it might help for me to put you under a polygraph. Would you be willing?"

Durango nodded emphatically. "I have nothing to hide. How soon can we do it?"

"I need to see some other people and formulate my questions, based on what they say," I said. "I'll need your permission to talk to everyone in your group."

"I'll order full and complete cooperation, and then stay away from them so that they don't shade the truth. And in this environment I can order them all to take a polygraph test at any time. Just let me know who and I'll issue the order." Being able to say that he was taking drastic action seemed to calm him considerably.

"All right, well, what I ask during the polygraph sessions will depend on what I find out while questioning. So it might be a day or two before I start that. But I'm on it, and I'm busy about it. You can at least count on that."

Durango nodded and finally caught his breath, beginning to seem almost human. "Are you cleared at a high enough level to know what a disaster this is?"

"I believe so, yes, sir, though it's always possible that there's more I don't know about."

After he left, Hale looked like a poisoned fish, but not so cheerful. "All right, I know you've been in the security business a long time. So have I. Wasn't that the best innocent act you've ever seen?"

"Damn straight it was. Yeah. But on the other hand—"

"I know the evidence. I just don't see how it all adds up. If Calvin Durango is guilty, how can he be carrying off an act like the one we just saw? I can believe he could give us that performance but not of that story; he'd have to know that we might have the goods on him. And why would he immediately agree to everything you asked?"

I gave him my best Bruce-Willis-style cocky, irritating grin, and said, "Because he's not guilty of anything serious. Not to his knowledge, I mean. He's not stealing the information, but it's being stolen *through* him. He didn't know that till now, and he doesn't really know it yet, but he suspects it, probably because he himself knows some way that it could be happening, which means he'll be trying to find out if his horrible suspicions are true. So I gotta go track him for a spell; and chances are that as he tries to find out if the worst is happening, he'll lead me to what I want to know. So, if you don't mind— I got things to do."

Hale nodded, tugging at his lower lip. "I am not in the habit of second-guessing; sorry I asked."

"Naw, you needed to know I wasn't crazy."

Hale and I got the schedule of interviews set up—he really wasn't a bad guy, for a pickle-butted Yankee—and I got out of there. I had another idea, and good guy or not, Hale was one person I shouldn't discuss it with.

CHAPTER SIX

One thing that just gnawed at my intuition was the spooky flatness of Lena Logan's voice when she had relayed that paper over the phone, and the methodical way she went about every bit of description. You picked up on it, a little, John, when you noticed that she pronounced "Subj" rather than saying "Subject."

My brain just wouldn't leave that alone. Now, if I'd been law enforcement, some lawyer would have been telling me I had to convince a judge enough to get a warrant. Or if I'd told Hale about it and made him see how weird it was—she has sex with Jason, calls him Calvin, and somehow that causes something on Calvin's desk to download verbatim into Lena—well, even if he'd had the imagination to say, yeah, that must be happening, he's corporate security, and he'd have to think about what might happen if company employers or contractors got caught.

Whereas I could just figure, it was Tuesday night. She had her seminar. Perfect time for a very low-profile burglary.

So that evening, I walked by her apartment's front door on that second-floor gallery, real slow, and looked through the gaps in the drapes; a few minutes later I did the same thing, coming from the other direction. Of course I needed to look like I belonged, which was why I wore a bland brown uniform and carried a clipboard.

She had her drapes drawn, but I could catch glimpses of her living room through the openings. It looked like the model apartments that managers show you if you're thinking about moving into a fancy complex.

She had a lot of hardware on that door. And the door itself was visible from many angles. So I headed around to the back side, which turned out friendlier—darker, fewer angles it could be seen from, time and space to get a good look. She had a "model" bedroom, her own messy bedroom, and an office, which was nearest the kitchen. So she'd actually rented a big three-bedroom, but with its layout and all, her student friends, if she ever had them over, wouldn't notice that her apartment should have been out of her price range.

There was quite the array of locks on the back door too, but with privacy, I could work confidently and quickly. Two minutes later I walked into her office and sat down at her computer.

I'd modem-watched her enter her mom's birthday as a password for three different subscriber web sites. Sure enough, all the password-protected stuff on her hard drive took the same password.

All she had was password protection, and very simple off-the-rack commercial password protection at that, for her money-related files, which are the first things somebody like me goes after. She had a plain old Excel spreadsheet with her business records, and from those records, I learned a hundred times what I had learned from that bug on her window—and became at least a thousand times as baffled.

Now, a good-looking young incall hooker in a high-tech area makes *money*. Affording a nice three-bedroom apartment at the high end of student living, all to herself, was no doubt a breeze, and she probably had other nice extras and luxuries too, especially since the income tends to be in cash and therefore easy to hide from the IRS. Even the stuff that was on the books was a nice little chunk of change. But then I saw the rest of her books.

All that prostitution income was chump change compared to what she was getting from selling goddies—she was turning maybe eight tricks a week, but every goddy she sold—just the individual pills, and she sold'em in boxes of twenty—was almost as much as half a trick, and she was selling about two hundred pills a week. That was the point where I found out that goddies were yet another thing named Gaudeamus, a registered trademark of the Krygon Corporation, according to an image of one label that she'd scanned and stored for no reason I knew.

Yeah, I thought that too. Xegon, Negon, Krygon—three names that were kind of but not quite the names of the inert gases—and . . . well, anyway, I still don't know what that's about. Logically I'm gonna run into Argon, Hegon, and Ragon before this is over, eh? But here's one thought that would make some of our old Wash U profs proud of us, John. Suppose that -gon is like in polygon and hexagon and pentagon, it's *side*. Then you stick other roots on, and shrink things for English tongues that don't like jammed-together consonants, and you get Xegon, the Strange Side, Negon, the Anti-Side, and Krygon, the Hidden Side. What's that mean? Fuck if I know. But, like one English professor used to yell at us, "it doesn't matter if anyone *meant* it, it matters if it's *there*, and if you can see it, it must be *there!*"

"You do a pretty good impression of him even now," I said, "or at least our memories faded the same way. He was sure a character. He died last year, it was in the alum news, which you don't get because you were a slacker dropout who went off to kill babies—"

"That's what he would have thought, for sure. Well, say nothing bad about the dead, because they get all eternity to make fun of us, eh?"

"And you'll never guess who did the 'I remember Old Yellow-fang' article in the alum mag. A name I bet you haven't thought in twenty years."

"Wallace the Waffle Whiffer."

"More obscure than that. Hint. What genius was nearly seven feet tall and looked like a dirty haystack and smelled like a laundry bag that got forgotten and was going to save the Earth—and was the only student that Old Yellowfang ever acted like he liked?"

"Not Brown Pierre! I thought he had to be dead! He was gonna chain himself to a moose to save it from hunters or something, wasn't he?"

I shrugged. "People change. I didn't want to be confined to an office and now most of the time my offices, here and at school, are the only places I feel comfortable."

"People don't change *that* much. Brown Pierre . . . wow, yeah. The man who wrote a thirty-page paper, in one night, about how *Black Beauty* was a better book than *Huckleberry Finn* because horses had it rougher than slaves, and got a black Twain scholar to give him an A on it. The man who wrote about *The Last of the Mohicans* from the viewpoint of the trees, and got an intervarsity prize for it. And it wasn't just that all those English profs were a bunch of woo woo nutbags, either. Damn that man-mountain hippie dirtbag could argue. I always figured that if I'd been trapped on an elevator with the Giant Envirohippie Walking Compost Pile for three hours, I'd have come out a Quaker vegetarian."

"If you hadn't asphyxiated in the first ten minutes," I agreed. "Yeah, when I'm teaching rhetoric, I sort of understand why our profs were that way about him. Very few undergrads can really argue anything; when you meet one that can, you almost don't care if he's a creationist or a cannibal, it's just so nice to see that. Anyway, he wrote about just what you were making fun of, that the big thing he learned from Old Yellowfang was that it wasn't what was meant but what was said, and that that was a lodestone in his life, and had made him the vagrant pile of laundry and literary genius that he was today, and like that. Same structure as Biff Oldbux's memoir in which he says some biz professor's inspirational example led directly to Biff's deciding to become head of Oldbux Corporation (after he inherited it). Anyway the article finished up saying 'Brown Pierre is a writer and lives in Colorado most of the time.' So I guess it could've been him instead of you at my door. Here to hold a funeral for the chicken in my freezer, perhaps."

"Yeah—hey, I have to ask—when the Unabomber stuff was getting all that publicity, and the manifesto came out . . . did you think of Brown Pierre?"

"Um, I thought real hard, about how much the Unabomber Manifesto sounded like Brown Pierre, and then I called the FBI and turned him in."

"So did I, old son. And I still think I was right—I don't mean that Brown Pierre was the Unabomber, I mean I was right to turn him in, because the manifesto and Brown Pierre sure did sound alike, and if I'd kept silent, and it had been Brown Pierre, I'd feel like there was blood on my hands when he hit again. Wonder if Brown Pierre is one of those people that writes fan letters to Kaszcynski? They'd have a lot to agree about, you know."

"Yeah. Well, anyway, I just thought it was interesting that we had an old buddy in the neighborhood, and you made me think of it. So, you were reading through this hooker's biz records—"

"Oh, yeah." He looked up at the ceiling. "Well, if what you are is the main thing you do, and everything else is a hobby, then old Lena isn't exactly a hooker. What she is, is a real conundrum, and I got no idea how to solve it."

Lena's earnings from selling goddies were about an order of magnitude bigger than her earnings from being an incall. Figure she didn't work year round, most of 'em don't, then she had a fifty k a year or so prostitution business but she had a more than half a million a year coming in from goddies—that's net. Her supplier was charging her something, but her sales were about three times her cost of supply. And like I said, that was all chump change compared to her *large* business.

Yeah, her large business. The one that dwarfed hooking and pills—the one that came in at at least ten million a year. Industrial espionage. She wasn't just selling Xegon secrets to Negon. Through a separate line, she was doing the reverse—probably many of the reports I'd seen from Xegon's intel op had in fact come from old Lena. Besides those two companies, she'd been stealing from and selling to just over a dozen high-tech companies, defense, computers, aerospace, nukes, robotics, name it . . . if you wanted tech reports from a lab that the public wasn't even supposed to know existed, Lena Logan was your gal. She had a neat little file naming every technical paper she'd sold or acquired, all of them mp3 voice files, with who'd paid how much for it.

Turning tricks must be her cover, in case some tax authority noticed that she had bales of unreported income. I mean, nobody really likes having sex for money, or at least in all the years I've been interviewing and hiring—to get the goods on wandering-eyed husbands, smartass—in all those years I never met a girl who really liked what she did. Not enough to keep doing it as a hobby.

Even selling goddies looked like a hobby compared to the industrial espionage work.

But why pick two highly illegal activities that are a lot more work, and don't make as much money, as covers for a quasi-legal one that makes orders of magnitude more money?

And incidentally, she wasn't just making enough to pay for grad school. She was making enough to have put three or four good physicists on the payroll, if there was really something she wanted to know. So why the hell would she want a masters in physics? It's employable and all that good stuff, but this girl didn't need a job. She was already getting paid like a ballplayer, and working shorter hours than a preacher. The only purpose of the incalls and the drug deals had to be to get her the access for the espionage.

But that was dwarfed by another fact: her records showed that she was writing checks to the business, every now and then. It wasn't feeding her; she was subsidizing it—or more likely it was shell for buying things she wanted, for whatever her real purposes were.

Imagine that you've got Rockefeller-class money, either inherited or earned. So you use that to set up an incredibly lucrative spying business that could get it all sued away from you and maybe land you in a federal pen, which you then hide behind a massive drug-smuggling operation, except that, to keep all of the above concealed, you turn tricks. Now, why do you do that?

I didn't have any idea either, so I just popped a copy over to my laptop, and looked for more things, and finally saw one of the most obvious.

Lena Logan was using an off-the-rack commercial hidden partition program, one of those things that makes your hundred-gig hard drive look like it's a sixty, so you can hide forty gig of whatever, with a secret key combo to get in. Once I booted her machine up from a CD, and saw that the hard drive was actually a hundred, I restarted again, held down the four keys for the numbers of her mom's birthday, and tried hitting alt and control and so forth, singly and in combination—a little routine I've made up for that, because the trick is so common. Sure enough, shift-alt-mom's-birthday got me onto the hidden part of the hard drive.

It held a single ten-gig file called GAUDEAMUS CONTROL. I brought it up—it was an application—and of course the first screen was an enter button with a password—Mama's birthday worked again (you know, if I ever marry old Lena, I'm gonna so impress her mother with the way I remember her birthday). I clicked on it and it felt like the furnace came on—a weird low thrum in the floor. I opened some doors, and found the next weird part of the weird part.

Lena Logan had a big old refrigerator sitting where her dryer ought to be, and it had come on with a whump. That was my first thought. But it had obviously been messed with, and not neatly—there were holes patched with plywood and duct tape, and things running through the plywood covers, cables and hoses and pipes. On the back of the fridge, the hot-side coils were covered by an oven hood and the exhaust of the oven hood had been connected with an aluminum duct to the dryer vent.

Down lower, beside the freezer compartment, two thick cables came in; she had both her dryer 220 and her stove 220 jumpered over to something inside that fridge. That at least made sense of the hood and fan; she had up to 17,600 watts going into there, enough to heat her big apartment and then some, and she needed a way to get rid of the waste heat. The fridge itself was running, moving the heat out onto the hot side coils, but that wasn't the humming I'd noticed; a fridge running is one of those sounds that no modern person can focus attention on. The deeper, more resonant bass hum I heard was coming from the freezer compartment.

I opened it and saw a big old mother of a transformer, the kind of thing that normally you'd have in a metal housing outside a decent-sized machine shop. She was using the freezer to cool it enough to keep it running.

There was a set of leads as thick as my wrist running up into the fridge compartment. I wrapped two bandanas around the fridge compartment door handle—I really didn't want to grab on to that much power, and remember I had no idea what might be inside that door—and pulled it open.

There was rack on rack of old computer motherboards, every one I could see a Pentium. She had a homebuilt Beowulf. I didn't take time to count exactly, but since there's architectural advantages to using powers of two, and she had way over a hundred, my guess is she had 256 processors in there. All that power—as much as the dryer, oven, and range together would use to run flat out—was just barely enough to keep that homemade monster running.

"A Beowulf," I said. "Jesus. You're really not kidding, are you?"

He shook his head solemnly. "That's what I mean, bud. A massively parallel processor like they use for animation. Or flight test simulations. Or designing atom bombs. Or cryptography. Or molecular design of drugs. The poor man's do-it-yourself supercomputer. Yeah, one of those. Well, I closed that door real careful and tiptoed back to her office, and then took a deep breath and booted up GAUDEAMUS CONTROL. A data entry screen came up, and it was a list of twenty-two blanks starting with x, y, z, t, and e, and continuing into Greek and I think some Hebrew. Below it was the note 'Place test object on plate before beginning.'

"Now from here on out, we're at the weird part, and it just gets weirder."

❖   ❖   ❖

So I looked around and there was a metal box, topped with a flat steel plate, lying on the desk, and a USB cable led to it from a hole in the wall. Another peek around the corner, and, sure enough, it was plugged to a USB jack on the back of the Beowulf-refrigerator. Another USB lead went discreetly down by the floor, hidden under duct tape; it connected to a ten-port USB dock way back under the desk. So the desktop computer was the terminal for the super, and the Gaudeamus program was the driver. And the supercomputer controlled Gaudeamus, which apparently was that little box with the circular metal plate, like a crude model of a hot plate, via the USB cable.

Well, maybe Mama Bismarck did raise one idiot. I figured, I've come this far, I gotta try it.

I took a quarter out of my pocket and set it on the plate. Then I entered twenty-two numbers, just alternating ones and zeroes, onto the screen. In some fields it wouldn't take a zero, in others it wouldn't take a one, but if it wouldn't take one, it would always take zero, and vice versa. When I was all done a little red box with the blinking white word "GO?" appeared at the bottom of the screen, ringed with a blue line—which made me suspect that if I hit RETURN, it would go. Whatever that might mean.

My finger was poised over the the return key when something went off about two feet behind my head, with a bang as loud as a thirty ought six and a flash like a flashbulb going off. I jumped, and my finger came down on RETURN.

With a soft little pop, like the way a bubble in a sheet of bubble wrap pops when you squeeze it, the quarter vanished from the plate.

I stared at that for a second, and then my disoriented mind

realized that something much bigger had happened behind me just before the quarter vanished.

I turned around and the quarter was lying on the carpet, a wisp of smoke curling up from around it. It was burning the carpet. I darted into the bathroom, got a handful of water, and splashed it on the quarter; it sizzled and boiled, and the stale stench of boiled student carpet came up.

After waiting a few seconds, I put my hand over it, not touching it, and it felt hot. I timed off a full minute, and gingerly touched it; it was warm but not enough to burn my skin anymore. I picked it up and pocketed it. There was a quarter-sized seared circle on the carpet.

I decided that whatever GAUDEAMUS CONTROL was, I didn't need to fuck with it any more that night. The Gaudeamus experimental results files she had, and her lists of stuff to get for her Gaudeamus laboratory, were all referenced to case numbers in the industrial espionage notes, which were cross-referenced, several different ways, to the prostitution and drug records. Oh, and in a small U-Haul moving box beside the terminal, the size they used to make for albums, she had two small butane torch cylinders, a package of those blank cartridges they use for those gunpowder-driven hammers that you use for setting a bolt, and a paper bag containing about a quarter pound of loose black powder. So maybe the real secret to it all is that she's Brown Pierre's girlfriend and she needs all the money to go bombing with him.

Three interwoven businesses, her own weird whatever-it-was gadget attached to that Beowulf, a bomb-making kit right next to where she worked, and every goddam thing in the goddam universe seemed to be named goddam Gaudeamus.

✧　　✧　　✧

"Spelled like Gaudeamus igitur?" I asked.

"Yep. Or like that web cartoon."

"I was just looking at it when you rang my door."

"Well, there, that's another 'gaudeamus' into the mix, hunh?" He slurped down more of that fierce coffee; I think by then I was equally puzzled as to how he could still be staying awake, now that the morning light was showing me the grayness of his skin and the bags under his eyes, and how he would ever be able to go to sleep, given that he'd had so much of my writing coffee. He sipped again and sighed. "If you're wondering how I'm staying awake, bud, it's half caffeine, half fear. But what I'm afraid of can't hurt you. I'm getting to why not. Meanwhile, I just got to stay awake. So, anyway, hell, yeah, all the 'gaudeamuses' I was running into were spelled like *that* 'gaudeamus.' That is the 'gaudeamus' we are gaudeamusing here. Latin for 'let us rejoice,' 'let's all get happy,' or more loosely, 'whoopty ding dong.'"

"I kind of like 'whoopty ding dong,'" I admitted, "but the most conventional translation would be 'let us rejoice.'"

He nodded seriously, as if accepting my expertise, and I felt stupid for interfering with his telling the story when he was already very tired and confused.

"Anyway, anyway," he went on, "probably the way 'gaudeamus' keeps popping up as the name for things is not really a mystery or even a connection. It's just that everything really trendy and really cutting edge has been getting named after the trendiest thing on the Internet, which happens to be that web cartoon."

"If you can call anything that's that complex a cartoon."

"You said it, John." Trav rolled over and took a sip of his coffee, making a face. "Need to get a warm-up." He headed out to my already overworked coffeemaker, his thin bony shoulders hunched in his denim jacket so that from the back he looked like a tall eighth-grader with a bad case of eighth-grade attitude. But when he came back with his steaming cup of coffee, and shoved Corner (who had leapt onto the couch and curled up the instant that Travis got up) over to the side, above the rising steam from the Pure Black Evil, his eyes looked a million and ten years old.

"Anyways," he said, "I had one stray thought that I couldn't dismiss till later—I was wondering if Lena Logan might be the real author of *Gaudeamus*. That would explain why she had a Beowulf—everyone knows you need a super of some kind to put *Gaudeamus* together—and her other occupations might help explain why whoever wrote *Gaudeamus* could be in on so much stuff that nobody else was in no position to know, or not know, or whatever. Damn, I'm tired. But then it got a whole lot weirder." He sat back and sighed. "Nice to be here. And I know from my visit to Pittsburgh that this old futon couch is about the most comfortable thing ever developed for a human being. A night sleeping on it took ten years off my pathetic old-man back. But I gotta hang in and stay awake. And you're still listening, so on with the story."

I had never seen Travis Bismarck look this tired.

So, anyway, John, since I didn't understand a thing I was looking at, I went back and looked at all the shit I did understand. Lena Logan had forty-three regulars, most of them scientists and engineers at high-tech companies, but six of them just ordinary working joes—and she was giving all kinds of price breaks to the ordinary working joes so they could come see her more. She had these elaborate files on all the scientists and engineers, but on the pool cleaners and contractors and so on, just some notes about what they were into in bed. New clients went into the group of thirty-seven scientists or the group of six studs, or—almost all of them—into the "tell him

I'm busy" list. Like she needed big stupid horny guys that knew what they were doing, and she needed all these tech geniuses, and that was all she needed—if you weren't one or the other, she didn't want your business.

Well, I recorded everything I could record, shut down everything I had started up, and got out of there well before she got back, leaving everything as I'd found it, except for a damp spot on her carpet with a darkened, scorched circle in its center. It was still forty minutes till she'd be back from her night seminar, but there was nothing that would make me push my luck to stay longer and learn more. The plain fact of the whole business was that I knew much less than when I had started.

Maybe they were all bringing secret documents, or covertly emailing them to her—but almost forty men, all with ultra-high security clearances? Sure, the system screws up now and then and lets some bozoid have a clearance, but that many, mostly cleared to SCI, at the same few companies and labs? You can believe a professional spy recruiting one or two or maybe even five sources—but thirty-seven? Without getting caught? Somehow she had to be getting it from them without their knowing about it.

At least that much was completely consistent with Calvin Durango's reaction to the stolen material.

Well, I'd tried going in the back. Time to try the front.

I unpacked one of my fake IDs, as Evan Gardenaire, tech sales rep and amiable moron for a high-tech firm whose products he didn't understand. I called one of her "Wendy" numbers using Evan's cell phone, said I'd be in town on Wednesday and I'd seen her ad in the Santa Fe arts paper, would she like to get together for a good time?

It seemed like the one way to find out what she actually did. And besides, after all that time looking at Lena, I wasn't exactly thinking it was gonna be unpleasant. My biggest worry was that Hale might get pissy about putting it on the expense account. But when the worst that can happen is not getting any information, getting stuck for a lousy $250, and getting laid by a nice hardworking ho with big old high hard ones and a round little butt, well, what the hell.

She got home half an hour after I left the message, returned my call, and set me up to be her first date of tomorrow night—not that she told me that I was her first date of the evening, but by then I had a calendar taped up over my desk in that shabby little motel room, with probably a more accurate layout of her schedule than she had.

And knowing I had something to look forward to, hopefully a break in the case, but at least something I'd enjoy, I went to bed early and slept better than I had in a while, even slept in the next morning. Which was a good thing, because I haven't slept since; like I said, I'm running on about thirty-five hours of caffeine and fear.

CHAPTER SEVEN

Wednesday night, just as the sun was setting, everything all golden and in sharp relief the way it gets in the fall in the desert, I was standing up on that board-floor gallery, knocking on Lena Logan's door. For purposes of the evening I was Evan Gardenaire, from my repertoire of identities. Oh, yeah, John, I usually carry five or six ready-to-go identities with me, especially when I'm out on a long-term case that's at all complicated. For each identity, I have a prepacked appropriate wallet, plus cell phone, keys, hotel guide, whatever else goes with it.

Evan Gardenaire traveled in transfer-of-tech deals for a little bitty obscure instrument company out of Coeur d'Alene. I'd developed him a few years before for an industrial espionage case; Gardenaire looked like a guy who might have information worth stealing but almost for sure didn't understand a lick of it. I always played him as eager to please and just a little dumb, which, if someone was looking to buy trade or tech secrets, made him look like pure solid gold left lying out on the counter.

She did the whole old-fashioned thing of calling me "Mr.

Gardenaire" a couple times till I said "Evan" was okay. Then she made a little twisty smile of a face—something to let me know she didn't like what she was doing but what could she do, these were the rules, and all that—and pulled up her t-shirt and bra, whipped out a titty, and asked me to touch her. Lots of hos think that if they do that before money or specific acts get discussed, the guy can't be a pig. It's sort of true, but only because the average vice cop doesn't want to sit in the witness box with a defense attorney asking him to describe every detail of getting a feel. So when they decide to really entrap a girl, they just do it and then lie about it.

You'd think that anyone in an illegal business would realize that cops do lie, and often.

So I gave her nice big firm boob a good grope, and she slid her hand down me and tugged on Mr. Joyboy, just one long easy stroke, and said, "I really like touching your cock, it feels so good in my hand," I guess so it would be recorded if I was wearing a wire.

Once we had established that I wasn't a pig, we got down to real business. We sat down on the couch and talked for a few minutes, and she found out what Evan Gardenaire did, and as soon as she knew, she started a cutesy lead-in of explaining that she was a grad student in science and she wanted to work for a high-tech company someday, and soon we were off the clock and just the bestest buddies, besides being about to have unbelievably hot sex, because she wanted Evan Gardenaire to know that—drop gaze, flutter eyelashes, smile a shy little "please don't hurt me like other men do" smile—*she really liked him!*

Which of course meant that poor dumb Evan blurted out more about his business. I gotta say, John, I never did see a working girl quite that excited before, especially not from just talking to her. And most especially not from just talking to her about using colored laser light to carve nanoscale steps and ramps onto a silicon surface and then using an atom laser process to dope individual nanoplanes with single-atom-wide lines of semiconductors. I think if I'd mentioned that the resulting chips were biocompatible, she might have come right then.

Anyway, now that she was good and excited, she decided to get me good and excited about a more traditional subject, so she started talking about what we were going to do. And that naturally segued into the main pitch. "Let me tell you about something. I think you might like it." She reached into a drawer in the end table, and came up with three aquamarine capsules. Each was marked with a big whirly G quite a bit like the old General Mills logo on cereal boxes. "These are called Gaudeamus, but most people call them god pills or just goddies."

"Hey, no, no, Wendy, I'm not into that kind of stuff at all." I put on my best real moron trying to act supersexy boyish grin, which looks a little like a steer that needs a finishing whack from the sledge-hammer, and added, "I just want your sweet pussy, babe. And besides I gotta take a urine test on a real regular schedule and it's only two days till my next one."

She smiled; it was all cute and flirty like a seventeen-year-old talking to a college guy and impressed with herself. "Gaudeamus is *much* too new for there to be a urine test for it. It's not an upper or a downer, and you can eat a fistful of it and it won't change the way you drive, or get you into fights, or put imaginary bugs in your shorts. What it will do is enhance sex and give you awesome sex dreams."

"Well, uh, I don't think anything in the world could make me like it any better than I already do." I needed to keep her talking about it, and get everything she would say about it.

"I have never once had any side effects, and I've taken it hundreds of times. And I went into this, um, line of work, because I like sex too—what a surprise, eh, baby?—and you know, it's even better with goddies. But no matter how many times you take the god pill, sex without it doesn't get one bit worse or less interesting. Very not like cocaine, for example."

"Well, I don't know—"

She let her hand slide up my thigh and gave my dick a nice squeeze. "That's right, sweetie, you don't know, but I can tell you, and you can try it. Like the old expression goes, the first time is free. *Then* you'll know. And then you can decide whether you want it again. Now . . . let's try one."

I planned to acquire about ten, so I could take a few to a lady I know that does some lab work for me out the back of a biochem lab in Bozeman. And I figured I'd strung this out long enough to make it believable, and I'd heard about all she was likely to volunteer. It was time we got down to what I came for.

Oh, stop giggling, John, you fat old pervert.

So I said all right, I'd give it a try, and she said now you're sure you want to—like setting the hook you know—and she even said I didn't have to if I was afraid (just like in all those after-school don't take drugs movies). So naturally I got all huffy and demanded to take a god pill. And by then it all looked right, good and natural, nothing to make it suspicious.

I paid her, and we each took a goddy, and she said it would take maybe ten minutes to hit, let's get undressed and make out while we waited for that. That was weird, most of the time they won't kiss, and the few that do charge extra for it.

Okay, now this is going to sound weird, it's relevant, you'll see why a little later in the story: *damn* that girl could kiss. And for that matter she could sure everything-else too.

Then the goddies hit. God and jesus and that whole crowd, John, you wouldn't believe how those fuckers hit when they fucking hit.

❈   ❈   ❈

"Good?" I asked, feeling like an old creep, but I wanted him to keep talking about it.

"Like my whole skin was the underside of my dick. It was like I was going to come through my *pores*, man. And that was just the *start*, like the first little tingly-tingle. She did totally exactly completely the right thing every goddam second, and I could feel that she was every bit as sensitized as I was and I was doing the right thing for her, even before I would feel what the right thing would be."

"They're good at fooling you that way, aren't they?" I said, glad that Kara wasn't awake and out here to hear me say that.

"How do you mean?"

"You sound like you were actually feeling her enjoy it," I said. "Like you could know. You can't know that even when it's *not* a whore. And since she *was* a whore, and working, besides, you can't—"

"Well, now, see, that's going to be kind of the point of the story, John." He got up from the couch and wandered over to the big front window, opening the curtains to the west, to let the bright mountain morning daylight bounce in off the row of big white houses across the street. "What I mean is, it felt like—oh, I don't know—like having porn-style sex while you're in a Vulcan mind-meld. Like having a whole human heart, body, and soul, all perfectly responsive, that you could use like a soft rag to beat off with, a whole human being just as responsive as your own hand. Like what you hoped sex was going to be just before you lost your virginity—if you lost it to someone you were crazy-mad in love with—only getting the whole experience from both sides at once. And one more weird detail, John, before we get to the weird part. She called me 'Norman' the whole time she was doing it."

"Well," I said, leaning back in the papasan chair and putting my hands behind my head, "she called that pool-cleaner guy 'Calvin.'"

Travis nodded vigorously and tapped his nose with his forefinger. "Exactly, just exactly." He glanced at the clock on the wall. "Two hours, still, till the earliest that I'm sure it would be okay for me to go to sleep. I guess, like it or not, I *am* going to get to the weird part."

"After all this buildup," I asked him, "don't you think you owe it to me?"

"Guess I do, at that."

"Well, that was great," I said, "and I see what you mean about the god pills. I don't suppose a fella could buy some from you?"

It turned out a fella could. "A hundred twenty-five a pill," she said, "or twenty for two thousand."

"Pricey, but I got it," I said. "Can I get ten? It's my whole sex on the road budget but it's worth it."

"Sure, if you want. You take that much money to a new incall? I mean, I'm pretty ethical, but you don't worry about getting robbed or anything?"

"Well, I can afford to lose it—it's about a day's commissions—and you never know when something special might be offered." I calculated that that was just stupid enough to sound exactly like Evan Gardenaire, as I'd built him up.

Lena Logan pulled out the big bottle and counted out ten, carefully, putting them in a little plastic prescription vial, one that was too dark to see into. "This vial isn't much in the way of conceal-ment, by the way," she said. "If you get stopped and they look in-side they'll know it's not Viagra. But they usually won't look inside a vial with that label, if it's a middle-aged man. You might want to move them to a better hiding place, though, soon as you can."

"Good idea! That's what I'll do, yep."

"Now, if you take one just before bed, you'll have a whole night of vivid sex dreams, full sensory detailed hallucination, different every time, usually involving people you don't know. If you take it before sex, and your partner does too, you'll have an experience like you and I had. There's no side effects and the pill's good for about three days—some guys get only two days to a pill, some get five— and after that you have to take another one if you want the same effect. The fading is very unpredictable. A pill every night will give you very high intensity, which just keeps building. Don't take more than that—you'll just pee it away without it doing you any extra good. If you don't have the money to take it nightly, taking it twice a week, spaced a few days apart, will still make most of your nights really nice.

"And that's about all there is to it.

"You've got my number so call anytime. We can do goddies together, or I can supply you, or we can just do plain old sex. Whatever you have cash and time for." She kissed me again, firmly and well, but not trying to start anything. "Love you, baby."

So I drove out of her parking lot and went the long way round, in the car I had rented on the Evan Gardenaire MasterCard. I knew her next appointment was in an hour and a half, so I didn't want to come back into the neighborhood in less than two hours—didn't want her to spot the car I had come to her place in, if she went out to get milk or something.

Evan had rented his car for pickup and dropoff at a downtown hotel. While I'd been in their lobby to pick up the car, I'd quietly lifted a key card out of the express checkout at the front desk, and slipped that into my Evan-wallet. I was carrying nothing he wouldn't have.

I drove the rental car back down Montgomery—the way an

out-of-towner would do to not get lost. And on the way—hey, re-member the old dorm room poster about not getting a blow job while driving? "Coming and Going Don't Mix?" Well, I found out one drawback to goddies right then. I was driving on a busy main traffic artery, early evening, maybe eight o'clock, on a week night, all stop-and-go and lights and lane changes, and suddenly I was having vivid hallucinatory sex, better than some real sex I've had, sort of like when a fantasy crosses your mind—I didn't stop seeing the road or anything—but overwhelming, and full sensory, and all. And it was about sex with Lena.

At first it just felt like I was having sex with Lena, wild and good and totally different from what I had just done an hour ago. I felt myself having a flabby, out of shape, overfed goopy-doughy body, the kind that a guy always thinks is basically okay and is basically not. On the other hand, my flabbier body was younger than I was, and it had a bigger dick. It was less vigorous and if I do say so my-self less imaginative.

I was also having sex *as* Lena, not just with her, and she wasn't comparing, she was just enjoying. I could feel my pussy squeezing around that big thing of his, and the way his chest brushed my nip-ples was great—while I was trying to stay in my lane and deal with a stop-and-start geezer driver in front of me while a bunch of Harleys roared by on my left. And I had a stray brain cell to think that Lena had something else going on entirely. I could feel her thinking that this was nice enough and *for a soft pasty-skinned guy with that funny fat clean white boy smell he isn't bad, but I really need to get him out the door*. All those feelings and thoughts were ghosting over my irritation, as I drove west and south, at some ass-hole who kept speeding up and slowing down to stay in my blind spot.

Then the sex hallucination stopped like a light switching off.

All that was left was a vague feeling that somebody, somewhere, was really pissed off at me. Swear to god, John, I looked around but didn't see any drivers I'd cut off or anything; that was my first thought.

I got onto 25, took it south to the downtown, hooked over onto 40, and headed east into the area where all the big chain hotels cluster, the kind of place that not only would old Evan stay, but where if I had a tail I hadn't spotted, and shook him, he'd go nuts trying to cover all the possible places I might be headed. I deliberately got off onto the wrong frontage road and wound through a few streets like a little lost businessman, and finally made a sudden, unsignaled turn into the Marriott parking lot.

Evan Gardenaire was definitely the kind of traveling man who sees the ho before he checks in at his hotel, so I'd picked up three moderately worn bags at the Salvation Army earlier, stuffed them with rags, crazy-glued them shut, and left them in my trunk. They were untouched, so probably nobody had messed with the car while I was in Lena's parking lot. Anyway, I hadn't talked to myself, and if they'd put a bug in the car, all it had picked up was NPR news, which I had playing really loud because that's the kind of thing an affluent loser who wants to feel hip plays.

I walked into the Marriott, grabbed one of the rental car return folders, scribbled an incoherent note about not being able to find the rental car return and just leaving it in a parking slot on the side of the building, and dropped the key in the folder into the express return. They'd come up with a bunch of charges, but "Evan" was being covered by Xegon's expense account, so it didn't matter to me, and this way, it would probably be hours before they got around to retrieving that rental car. Anyone staking it out was going to be watching that car for a while.

Then I walked into the bag check and checked those faked-up

102 · JOHN BARNES

suitcases, which are very likely still there and might be for a few more months if you need a glued shut suitcase full of rags. I went into the bathroom, took a pee, caught the rhythm at the bag check counter so that I got a different attendant, and claimed the gym bag that contained my own wallet and keys and so on. I flipped the key card back into the front desk's express checkout, swapped Evan's wallet and cell phone for my own in the gym bag, and Evan Gardenaire was gone again till the next time he needed to appear. I caught the elevator down to the parking garage where I'd left my rental car.

At least if I'd been shadowing me, I'd've lost me.

As I was pulling out onto Louisiana, my phone beeped with a voice-mail message. It was only fifteen minutes or so old, so I figured I was still on top of things.

It was Hale. "I don't know where you are, but I need to talk to you as soon as you get this. We have an urgent job for you, over and above what you've been doing for us. Call me back at this number—it's my private cell."

I called him. "We can't talk about this over the phone," he said. "Go to where you've met me before, not the office but the facility. You will be let through at every checkpoint, but they might hassle you a little, if they haven't received the word yet. If they give you any more than a *little* hassle, call me and get it straightened out. I'll meet you there."

"Right, I'm on my way."

"Thank you, Mr. Bismarck."

Well, I got out to the Xegon test facility as quick as I could—I didn't break any traffic laws, and I didn't even bend any very far, since getting stopped would've been a disaster, but I stayed focused and efficient and I did it quick.

Things were no different than the last time at the general test area guard booth, just over the hill from the highway. They looked at my ID and sent me through, reminding me which turn to take for Xegon's area.

Under the glaring sodium lights the white gravel road might have been the only thing that existed in the universe. For a few timeless minutes, there was only the crunch under the tires; then the guard booth and fence seemed to leap out of the dark at me. I hadn't realized how fast I was driving, and braked hard to slow down. Probably not the smartest thing to do around nervous men with guns.

I pulled up to the Xegon guard booth, and instead of one nice guy leaning in my window like last time, I had a very serious guy standing in front of the car, holding a Spectre M4. He wasn't pointing it at me, but he cradled it like it was definitely more his friend than anyone coming in the gate would be, and it's a brutal-looking weapon, makes you think about holes blown in your body no matter where it's pointed.

Another guard leaned in my window. "Open your door please sir." His delivery was more emphatic than "Open the fucking door" ever could be.

I opened it. He moved in to where he could shine a light on my face and look me over from head to toe.

"Identify yourself please sir."

"Travis Bismarck. I'm a private investigator under contract to Xegon."

The guard with the M4 came around and peered in at me; I recognized him from the time I'd been there before. "It's him."

"Unlock all doors, Mr. Bismarck."

I hit the button. The guard standing by me shut the driver's side door just as a guy in a suit slid into my passenger seat, picked up my gym bag, peered into it with a flashlight, and said, "What's in here?"

"Materials for a false identity—wallet, cell phone. A recording from a wire I was wearing while I was with a prostitute. A probably-illegal drug, not yet identified, that I bought from her."

"Okay, just so it's nothing to worry about. I'll give it back to you when you come out." So he took my bag and waved me through.

CHAPTER EIGHT

My stop at the guard station had been just long enough for other people at Xegon to get their act together, and a nice young woman wearing a stewardess suit, referee shoes, a shoulder holster, and an ear dingus met me in the parking lot to walk me through the building to Hale's office.

Hale was wearing a Dickey Pocket-T with tiny dots of paint on it and a small hole in one armpit. It hung untucked over his chinos, which slumped over his Bass moccasins. He seemed to have thrown on whatever was handy; there were so many different colors of paint, in such small spots, that I wondered if he painted for a hobby. Maybe he was regretting having stayed up an extra hour to finish a landscape.

Before he spoke, he poured a gigantic mug of coffee from the thermos on the sideboard, and drank about half of it straight down. "Any for you?" he asked.

"There won't be at that rate. Sure, I'll take a cup."

He filled another mug and set it down in front of me. On one side of it, O. B. Joyful was holding up a middle finger (out of three), and on the other side, Monique from *Sinfest* was also giving the finger. Around the bottom, it said "Coincidence? How did you happen to think of that?"

"We have Bad Attitude Friday once a month," Hale said. "People bring in things to work out their hostilities." He held up his own giant cup, which read "COFFEE consumes FIFTEEN TIMES its weight in Excess BULLSHIT!!!"

"Very cool. I've worked a lot of places that should've had that," I said. I dumped in three teaspoons of sugar and stirred so that the coffee cup tinkled like a dinner bell. "And it holds coffee, too. Now, what's up, what do you need me for, and what will you pay?"

Hale tented his fingers in front of his face. "We've had something vital stolen." Then he made himself rest his hands flat on the desk—probably practicing for something unpleasant he was going to have to say to people who were going to be much less pleasant than me. "For all practical purposes, with a little reverse engineering, whoever has it, has *all* of Gaudeamus. We certainly know how they *stole* it—the actual theft was a pure brute force job. I need you to find out who they are, how they knew as much as they did about our security system, and where they took it. ASAP."

He set a number that would have seemed impossible a couple of weeks ago, with a bonus if I got all the information within seventy-two hours. "This is probably beyond hope, but if you recover the object itself, we'll come up with some reward—it will be considerably more than that, but I don't have any idea how much more. Enough that we'd have to do some kind of special budget thing to pay you even remotely adequately."

"Why me?"

"You already know just about everything I would be allowed to tell you. *And* you've already got as much clearance as I can give you. And you don't have to keep the kind of idiotic records that my own people do, or report to superiors six times an hour, or waste all the time they're going to make me and my people waste." He sighed. "I was private for some years before I took this job, and there are times when I'd give anything to be private again. I used to specialize in child recovery. And as far as I can see, the problem I have here is sort of like a stranger abduction—what's really essential is going to be moving fast, before they get it too far away or too well hidden."

"I've done some child recovery too," I said. "So I know what you mean. There's no chance they'd destroy it?"

Hale shook his head. "They'd be about as likely to burn the Mona Lisa, if they'd stolen that. A Gaudeamus machine—that's the object—is only of value to them intact. And they have to keep it long enough to get it to a real heavy-lifter of a physics lab, and work on it for a while, before they'll be able to copy it, which is when all the payoffs come in. So it's only extremely unlikely that you'll recover it, but not impossible. Let's get you out working on it. Here's what you're looking for."

Hale turned around and opened up a big black briefcase, one of those hard-sided rectangular boxes that's designed to get a computer through airline baggage check. He pulled out a flat white enameled-metal box, the kind of thing you get at an electronics shop to build your own stuff into, the same height and about twice the area of a cable box. It had three buttons, labeled X, Y, and Z, each with an LED above the button. There was a red button labeled "ACT" on the left, and a white Edison 3-prong socket on the right. Across the top of the white box, along the edge, a thin black strip with silver letters read XEGON CORP at one end and GAUDEAMUS at the other. It sat on small black rubber feet.

I stood up and looked it over. There were eight USB ports and two big multipin ports along the back.

"Those back ports are for instrumentation and telemetry," he said, which told me exactly nothing.

The top of the box was marked with two red arrows that bled slightly, like they'd been done with a Sharpie and a steel rule; one pointing to the back was labeled Z, and one to the right was labeled X, scrawled in the same red ink. On the right side, as it faced me, there was another arrow, labeled Y. At the base of each arrow was a more carefully applied tiny black dot—no, a hole. I leaned over and saw the shiny, melted beading around the holes—laser-drilled.

The whole thing was put together with ordinary recessed Philips screws. Except for the incongruously precise tiny holes, it was a standard piece of shopwork that any proficient Heathkit builder might have done to finish off something he wanted to keep. In the reflected glare of the fluorescent lights I could see some smudgy gray fingerprints, and it was stained a little with ink and pencil dust; this little machine worked for a living.

When I got to that stage of detail, I figured I'd seen enough to be able to tell a Gaudeamus machine from a washing machine, and looked up.

Hale said, "We had ten of these, and now we have nine. We also have a senior engineer who's had a terrible beating, and fifty security people who keep trying to tell me that since this couldn't have happened it must not have and therefore it didn't."

Hale carefully positioned the box on the corner of the desk nearest me and said, "All right, now let me show you what it does." He pushed the X, Y, and Z buttons, and all the LEDs lit up with zeros. Then he pushed the ACT button once. "That tells it to mark its present position as zero," he said.

Then he got out a tape measure and measured from one tiny hole along the arrow and out onto the desk. "Nineteen centimeters this way," he said, and entered "19" by holding the Z button down, same way you set an alarm clock. Then he measured across the front of the desk, from the other top hole, and said, "Sixty this way," and entered "60" into X.

He handed me a set of protective phones, just the regular things that you use on the pistol range, but with an extra pad of Swedish wool inside each. Then he handed me super-dark shades—welding-goggle, solar-eclipse dark.

"You will want all of these. Are you armed?"

"No, why?"

"Because, once, when I demoed this thing to one of my security people, he was startled and drew his weapon. He didn't fire. I was grateful for that, as, when he drew it, he pointed it at me. Since then I make a habit of telling armed people what they will see, first. It spoils the surprise but on the whole I think it's better. But since you're not armed, you get to have the full experience. Now, put the glasses and the earphones on. Watch this space." He pointed to the empty spot he'd run his steel tape out to.

In the dark blur of my peripheral vision, I saw him push the ACT button.

It's kind of hard to tell you what it was like, John. Put it this way: I once knew a guy, from a bar in Billings, who we all called Ed-the-Gun-Nut, like it was one word. Being known as "the Gun Nut" in Billings is kind of like being known as "the Village Idiot" in New York City; you really have to overachieve.

Of course Ed hand-loaded, and had a dozen cute little insanely dangerous tricks that he'd made up, all of them things that would make any engineer or tech rep wet himself to see Ed doing. He was very proud of one he called the "blinder," which was one of his already-*way*-overloaded rounds doped with powdered aluminum and a powdered oxidizer, to goose the temperature and pressure way up. It made a really hot, bright flash coming out of a .357

Desert Eagle, and Ed thought it would add to the terror of the guy you were shooting at. Plus, he said, the flash would blind him so that if you missed with your first shot, he wouldn't get a shot at you.

The few times I saw him fire one, it surely was blinding and deafening.

As for terror, well, one day Ed the Gun Nut really terrified two buddies of mine when he was out plinking with them. Ed's .357 Desert Eagle, having coped with all that extra heat and pressure one too many times, blew up and tore his hand apart on its way backward into his face. It got him a change of nickname, though, from Ed-the-Gun-Nut to "Clawhand Ed With No Teeth."

This flash and bang in the office at Xegon was about as loud and bright as one of Ed's juiced .357 rounds—about like a welding arc for brightness, and maybe as loud as four or five simultaneous pistol shots. I jumped and yelled "Jesus!" and even Hale, who knew what was coming, lurched away.

The flash had come from that space of empty desk, but it wasn't empty anymore. The Gaudeamus box had appeared there.

I could barely see Hale take off his goggles and phones—the tint on my goggles was that dark. I took mine off. "Touch the box, carefully," he said.

I did. It was hot, not kitchen-stove hot, but definitely hot enough to be uncomfortable.

"So you set the position in centimeters and it goes there," I said. "How fast does it actually go?"

"Instantaneous," he said. "True zero time. And it doesn't go to anywhere in between; we've shown visiting generals and bureaucrats that it will go right out of a concrete box into a closed wall safe. It's true teleportation.

"When the Gaudeamus machine arrives in a space, no matter what is occupying that space, it all counter-teleports to the nearest point outside the teleported volume. So all the air that was in the volume of the box was instantaneously jammed into a one-molecule thick layer of extremely compressed air on its surface. The flash is what happens as that layer expands, and the bang is partly from that and partly from the implosion where the Gaudeamus machine was before."

"Can people ride on those?"

"Probably. If we had a bigger one. Box number five has an interior capsule for biological specimens. So far two mice, about twenty goldfish, hundreds of bugs, and billions of germs have made the trip. No apparent harm, except that if you're a germ on the surface of the box the heat is enough to sterilize it. So I guess so far it hasn't killed anything bigger than a single-celled organism."

"So far?"

"Well, one use for it is as a weapon, obviously. Send it into something denser than air and you get a huge explosion—we disposed of box eleven by teleporting it into rock under the Nevada Test Range, and the next day the arms control people were all over Livermore and Los Alamos, accusing them of conducting a nuclear test in violation of the moratorium.

"For that matter, send it into the world leader of your choice's head or chest and you get flying stew. Theoretically if you jump it into the core of a neutron star, all those trillions of tons of neutronium that would take up the same volume would end up as an even thicker film of neutronium on the surface and you'd have a major starquake. Right now the reason we can't try that out is that we'd have to wait decades or centuries for the light to get here so that we could see the starquake happen.

"No doubt you can see how many uses there are for this, militarily. As long as your rangefinder is good enough, you could teleport a block of explosives into a tank, a plane, an ammo dump—or an incoming missile. A miniaturized Gaudeamus bullet could have a proximity fuse so that when it sensed something a meter away, it would teleport one-point-oh-oh-five meters forward, and reappear on the other side of armor or blow a meter-wide hole in a bunker wall. Or you could send Army Rangers into a hostage situation on an airliner with an unbelievable flash and bang to cover their arrival— you'd probably want them in thermal suits for that."

"This thing is bigger than the bomb," I said.

Hale nodded and ran a hand through the hopeless blond curly mess of his hair; he really looked like he needed to be home in bed. "And for all the spy scandals the Manhattan Project had, nobody ever actually knocked down Oppenheimer and walked out of Los Alamos with an atomic bomb on his shoulder. But that's what just happened to us."

He unplugged his desk lamp from the wall and said, "Now let me show you something less dramatic but probably more important." He plugged the lamp into the socket on the front of the Gaudeamus machine and turned it on. The lamp lit, fully as bright as it had been from the wall plug.

"That's some battery," I said. "How long does it last? How far can it jump on one charge?"

"Not a battery," he said. "You can't charge a battery fast enough. Huge, very fast capacitors—that's what most of the space in this box is—to capture the energy every time it jumps. The process of making a jump produces much more energy than it consumes. This lamp would stay lighted for many hours, basically till the charge leaked out of the capacitors, just on the energy from that thing jumping two feet. If we didn't capture all that energy into the capacitors, the machine itself would have melted—actually some of it might have boiled. Set one of these to vibrate in place, for a few seconds every hour, and you can pull enough power out of that plug to run the whole Xegon facility. We did just that, recently, as a demo. You're looking at the thing that replaces every motor in every form of transport from Segways to submarines, eliminates nearly all pollution, and probably takes the human race to the stars."

My first thought was trivial. "Can I take half my pay in stock options?" Hale grinned and was about to answer when suddenly an entirely different thought hit me. I realized why that flash and bang—and the box being hot—had seemed so familiar. "Uh—" I said, not sure how to ask this "—uh, do you think that you're the only company that has the Gaudeamus technology?"

Hale looked shocked. "Do you have a reason to think we're not?"

"Can Gaudeamus be used to send objects somewhere, rather than just sending itself?"

"That's a theoretical possibility, or so the scientists say. There's a group working on it."

"And—this might be a really stupid question—can it be used for time travel?"

"Have *those* documents leaked out?" Hale seemed to be in a near panic, so I figured he had just answered the question, and didn't make him formulate his answer into complete sentences.

I told him about my burglary of Lena Logan's place. I figured if he'd been private, for a while, himself, especially in a shades-of-gray area like child recovery, he wouldn't be too shocked that I'd done a little breaking and entering.

If he was, he didn't show it, anyway. He listened to my story the whole way through without saying anything, and at the end, he said, "Well, it's certainly consistent with the idea that someone else has Gaudeamus, and they've been penetrating us, not to steal it, but to see how far we go—or maybe to send us barking up the wrong tree."

I nodded. "Look, here's what I think. I think they've got a probably more advanced, definitely different version of Gaudeamus

technology, which they use for purposes of their own. That flash
and bang from your Gaudeamus box was like a bigger, slower version of the one from what their machine did to my quarter.

"What I think is that there was a mini causal loop right then.
That quarter went back one second in time—because one of the
variables I set was a one, probably—and one meter up, and one
meter behind me. When it reappeared it was carrying a big old load
of energy, because Lena Logan's team, whoever they are, don't
have your energy-absorbing system, so it popped out way hotter
than that box did. Or maybe backwards time travel releases more
energy. Where's the energy come from anyway? Does this thing re-
peal the laws of thermodynamics?"

"I have tried asking every scientist in the Q-tip that question,
from time to time. I have a degree in physics, so you would think
they'd be able to explain it. I am always lost after five minutes. They
talk about Casimir power and zero point and neuroquantumistic
effects interacting with neuroquantumological effects. And wave
their hands. A lot. Would you understand more of it than I do?"

"Only if they were quoting comic books or sci fi novels," I admitted. "I've heard of Casimir and zero point. Some idea that
plain old vacuum contains all kinds of untapped energy that can
do a bunch of very weird things. And I never heard of anyone
making a distinction between '-istics' and '-ologies' before and
then saying they interact. All I can tell you is, I think the bang
from the quarter reappearing startled me, one second later, into
pushing the button that sent it back in time, and to me that looks
like there's some kind of conservation law operating. The bang and
flash and heat are all consistent with the idea that the process
makes more energy than it uses. Though why Lena Logan needed
a supercomputer to control her Gaudeamus, and you just have a
box—"

"A lot of what's in the box is hard-coded and not reprogramma-
ble," Hale said, "as a safety measure. My guess would be that it's an
engineer's choice—allowing three inputs, instead of twenty-two,
is a pretty good way to keep people from hurting themselves."
He rubbed his face; it seemed to me that every few minutes he
looked grayer and older. "Look, at this point, you have already been
worth your weight in gold; there's so much you've picked up we
wouldn't have gotten any other way. Keep it up and—are you all
right?"

I wasn't. I was having a feeling like that strange sexual hallucination I'd had while I was driving—well, except without the sex. And
without the hallucination. This wasn't the hallucination, but it felt
like a hallucination trying to arrive. I didn't know quite what it was,
but I also figured I had already told Hale enough strange stories
about me bending the rules, at least for the moment. "Uh, I'm fine,
and I'll explain later, but I just realized we absolutely totally got to
get me out there working, as soon as possible," I said. "Real quick,
tell me how they took it." The strange, itchy feeling in my head
grew more intense. I had visions of a man stumbling around in the
dark, mad at everyone, especially mad at Lena Logan, because they
had made him leave the car so far away and he had gotten lost walking to it in the dark—

I made myself concentrate on Hale's story.

As I listened, I thought that the job had been done by some very
professional amateurs, or possibly professionals freelancing with no
resources or backup. The whole operation didn't absolutely require
more than three people, maybe four or five would be useful but
any more would be in each other's way. Expenses were probably
less than two grand, and the whole thing had run slicker than snot
on a brass doorknob.

According to Hale, here's what happened:

Norman Lawton, a senior NQ physics engineer in the headquarters section of the Q-tip, was working late, alone in the lab, planning to sleep on the bed in his office. This was not unusual. Some Gaudeamus experiments take as long as fifteen hours to run, and since they weren't well understood, often an engineer or physicist would elect to sleep near it, with a bunch of detectors and alarms set, just in case something interesting happened.

I recognized Norman Lawton's name from his two visits to Lena Logan's place during the time I was listening in. He was fifty-five years old and had bulgey toad-eyes, a petulant expression, irregular shaving habits, and one of those hanging bellies that looks like he's hiding a giant spare brain under his navel. He had the manner and personal style of one of those janitors that reads the encyclopedia and the almanac constantly and will follow you down the hall late at night telling you all about the braided rings of Saturn or exactly how much the federal government spent on the designs for a nuclear dirigible, the kind you can only get rid of by taking a really long dump or asking them about their emotions.

But maybe he *was* hiding a giant spare brain in that belly. Instead of being an eccentric janitor, Norman Lawton was taking up his space in the universe as a brilliant engineer with triple phuds, physics, chem E, and neurology. People in his shop called him "Always Right Norman."

He had four marriages in his past, none of them more than two years from license to final decree. What I could gather from my bug was that he was one of those very businesslike engineers that treats it as "the job of sex" and doesn't seem to want to waste any time on irrelevancies like enjoying himself. Both times I had listened in on him with Lena Logan, he did what he was going to do (not much, very briefly), bought forty goddies, and left. That might have had a thing or two to do with his marriage record.

His large frequent buys of goddies made me suspect that he was a low-level pusher for goddies someplace, but now that I knew they were sex enhancers, I was inclined to think that he just needed a lot more than most people.

In midevening, about the time that I was buying my goddies from Lena, Norman Lawton had been sitting watch over a long-running Gaudeamus experiment, while typing up a technical paper about what happened to excited barium nuclei when they made a Gaudeamus jump. He was hungry and tired, and it was going to be a long night, so he ordered a pizza, something they allowed them to do because, as Hale explained, "it's better to have a pizza wagon you can search come into the secured area, driven by someone who has no idea of what's going on, than it is to have employees start developing smuggling routes, which anything or anyone might travel along." He sounded like he really wanted me to say that's the way to do things (after all just now he had every reason to be worried about his job), so I assured him it was what I would have set up if I'd had his responsibilities. He seemed to draw comfort from that.

So old Norman lay down to take a nap till the pizza got there, since he knew it would be at least forty minutes—the facility is a ways out, even though the pizza parlor is in the just-off-base noncom strip. Also, it takes some time to get through security. Atom Bomb Pizza did it because Xegon will pay them a huge surcharge to do it; that was another advantage Hale derived from that arrangement— there was only one pizza place that would actually deliver to the facility, and only three approved drivers.

The bad guys had some kind of surveillance on the connections between Xegon and the outside world, obviously. Nobody could possibly have had timing as good as theirs without that. And they had been watching the facility a long time, with people in place, because there wasn't much of a crack to slip in through, and they went in and out mighty goddam fast, and without touching the sides. If they hadn't committed a murder along the way, I might even have kind of admired them, in a purely professional way.

There's about seven hundred feet of access road, after the guard station and before the lab building, that's not under constant observation. That seven-hundred-foot stretch is seen at irregular intervals, for maybe five minutes at a time, two to four times an hour, by an armed patrol in an off-road vehicle. There are three patrols, crew of two each, out at all times.

Each armed patrol takes a randomized route through the open land around the facility, checking all the guardposts along the way and surveilling various blind spots like that seven hundred feet of gravel road. They are also supposed to provide backup for any emergencies at the facility itself, so "they've got a little more to cover than they should have, ideally," Hale said.

I agreed that he was right about that too. So far he'd been a smart, supportive guy to work for, old money Yankee or no, and I didn't want to trade him in on an unknown, especially not right after he'd made me a verbal contract for more money than I'd seen on any six jobs put together before.

The pizza car cleared the guard checkpoint just as it always did. Cheryl Tusson, the twenty-four-year-old single mother of two who was driving the car, stopped and kidded with the guard at the checkpoint (Paul San Luis, age forty-nine, a longtime reliable Xegon employee, who knew her from church) for her usual minute or two.

Exactly one minute and fifteen seconds before the pizza car entered that hidden area, several widely scattered strings of firecrackers went off on the far side of the sandy hills to the west of the road, all at least a few feet off the ground. Two patrols were close enough to hear the bursts and roared over the low sandy hills to investigate. Just as Cheryl's Celica, with its little Atom Bomb Pizza flag, slowed on a curve in the hidden area, a flash bomb, like the bright concussion bursts in an aerial fireworks show, went off one more ridgeline to the west. Both patrols headed in that direction.

As Cheryl was coming out of that turn, which had a good deal of loose gravel and was poorly banked, she slowed to about twenty-five miles per hour. She saw a man in a Xegon guard's uniform flagging her down. She pulled to a stop in the middle of the road—traffic was uncommon and would see her hazard flashers in plenty of time, and besides the shoulder was soft.

Then the man in the guard's uniform killed her and took the car.

Her death was probably not entirely deliberate; probably, whoever they were, they just didn't care very much what happened to bystanders. Cheryl was about five feet tall and more than a hundred pounds overweight, a quiet lady whose main recreations were AA and church, so she wouldn't have put up much of a fight if they had just ordered her out of the car. I sure as hell don't think she would have risked her life and her children's future to save one Godzilla Size El Garbago Thick Crust, and two two-liter bottles of Mountain Dew, for a rude engineer.

But she didn't get a choice. The phony guard had a bear tranquilizer dart in a little handheld gadget he could conceal in his palm. When she opened her door he reached in and jammed the dart-head against her skin and fired it straight into her neck. The little pop from the dart gadget was no doubt totally lost in the third round of fireworks now detonating out on the hills.

Cheryl Tusson took most of the tranquilizer right into the carotid. The attacker stripped off the guard uniform jacket and put Cheryl's Atom Bomb Pizza smock on over his t-shirt. He left her in the gravel road, where she'd fallen after he'd opened the car door. Somewhere in the next few minutes she stopped breathing, or went into cardiac arrest, or choked on vomit, and died.

They found her next to a guard uniform jacket, lying on her side, her clothing undisturbed except for the missing smock. Probably the guard jacket was the one that had been stolen from the dry cleaner's three months before, about which they'd never been able to find a thing.

Police were out there right now with Xegon and Kirtland security.

"It happens," Hale said, "that I met Cheryl a few times, and she was a very nice young woman who always had a pleasant word for everyone, getting her life back together after a really bad start—when I cleared her to be our regular delivery person out here, I read her record, and she was just one of those women who finds Mr. Wrong in high school and doesn't get rid of him for a while. I'd talked with her a few times when I was working late, and she'd shown me pictures of her children. So although (unfortunately), Mr. Bismarck, I can't authorize company money for you to find Cheryl's killer, I can mention that the people you are being paid to find are the ones who killed her, and that it is my personal and unprofessional opinion that if you do find the son of a whore, and anything bad happens to his worthless ass, I will probably believe and corroborate anything you later tell the authorities."

I was getting to like Hale better and better.

Wearing that pizza smock, our boy drove straight to the lab. Norman Lawton opened the door and caught a face full of Mace and the end of a softball bat, then about twenty hard ones, real systematic, like a pro who is trying not to kill you but wants to make sure you wish he had. The fake pizza guy gave Lawton some damage to his tailbone, floating ribs, forearms, shins, ankles, and soles of the feet, finishing off with a hard one in the nads probably just out of pure meanness. Old Norm wasn't going to be getting around much, for research or anything else, for weeks or months.

That was interesting too. They didn't kill him; they wanted him to keep working, I would guess, but they didn't want him to be doing it quickly or soon. And they didn't want a guy who would make too good a witness.

Then the guy in the pizza smock grabbed the Gaudeamus box, leaving the leads to the recording computer lying on the table (so he knew which of several pieces of apparatus on that table to take). He also took the paper copy of the research paper from the printer. He got back into that pizza wagon and drove it out a road pizza drivers usually didn't take, one that led east, away from Albuquerque and into the boondocks.

Meanwhile someone else hack-spoofed the security switchboard and told the guard post on the end of that road that the pizza car would be leaving by a different route because there was a major security breach on the usual road and they were sealing it off. (That much was even true—at the time of the fake call, they were just in process of figuring out that all the flashes and bangs had been a diversion, but they hadn't found Cheryl's body yet.)

My boy sailed right through the guard point onto a ranch access that goes through to I-40. Three miles up that, he left the pizza car by the roadside, and picked up whatever vehicle had been left for him.

Ten minutes later, when the whole Xegon facility was in an uproar and Kirtland base security, and every other test facility's security, were all getting into one big honking commotion, a helicopter spotted the pizza car's warm engine on IR, circled in, and ID'd it with a spotlight. A team rushed out there and made a careful approach, but the guy had left a little bitty thermite pipe bomb jammed down into the gas fill pipe, probably triggered by a motion detector. As soon as the security team got close, the vibrations set that little bomb off, and the gas tank blew while everyone was still backpedaling. Casualties there were three guys shaken up badly, with minor burns; one of them, who had fallen or been knocked over backwards, maybe had a broken rib. They weren't going to get much evidence out of what was left of the car.

Just then, that was about as far as they knew. Everyone was pretty much assuming that the on-the-scene bad guy had escaped in another car, but he might be out there on foot, still making his rendezvous with someone, or he could even have been picked up by a light plane that flew in under radar or got very lucky with not getting detected; that access road was paved and there were no tracks. Anyway, the sonofabitch had an almost-two-hour head start on me. He could even have dashed to the Albuquerque airport, boarded a flight to Mexico City, and already be out of the country, maybe just boarding a flight to Havana.

Now, that weird about-to-have-a-vivid-sex-hallucination feeling, which I figured was an aftereffect of the goddies, got more and more intense as I was listening to Hale, and then got more and more focused. I was getting a picture in my mind. Of a guy throwing a pizza uniform smock into an arroyo.

Anyway, the funny thing was, I wasn't picturing my boy doing it, I was like, being him, in my head. I felt the cold sweat and the feeling that he didn't want to take one second extra and the nervousness about something he had heard on the police scanner. I felt that he knew he was supposed to bring the smock along to be destroyed, and not delay to do this, and he was so afraid of being seen dropping it into the arroyo, but he was real afraid of being caught with it, and he didn't want the others to see the blood on the collar because he had been supposed to shoot her in the thigh, but hell any dumbass knew a tranquilizer in the neck would—he didn't want them mad at him, he really wanted them to understand—fuckin' fuckers had no business judging him at all. At all. Fuckin' at all. He really had to get out to someplace just off Montgomery Avenue, near the Christian conservatory.

He was visualizing Lena Logan's place. He hadn't been there very often and the Christian conservatory, which has a distinctive modernist bell tower, was his landmark.

I knew where he was and how long he expected to take and I knew that if I whipped out of Xegon and got back onto 40 and floored it, and luck was with me, I could meet up with him just before he got there—I saw all the paths in my head.

Now, I've had hunches before—half my business is having hunches—but this was more like the hunch having me, like it totally took over my head, John, I'm not fucking kidding it was weird.

Well, hell with it, I'd played hunches that weren't half that strong before, so I said to Hale that I had an idea and thought I should act on it right away, and that if he could have the guard at the gate have my bag ready—

"Of course," Hale said. "I'll walk you out to the lot." He got up, and we walked, and he talked on his cell and set me up with an escort guard car.

"Hey," I said, "thought. Maybe useful thought. Send a blank round via Lena Logan's Gaudeamus machine, and what happens when it arrives? It arrives white-hot and blows up, right? And there was a box of those blanks beside her computer, right by her Gaudeamus platform. And for a bigger boom—put two butane torch cylinders into a paper bag with some black powder, and send the whole works—"

"Boom," Hale agreed. "I'll tell them to look for bits of fused and melted metal out there, for analysis. But I would bet you're right."

As we walked out the front door into the sodium-glare parking lot that held back the vast dark night around it, the escort car was just pulling up.

Hale walked with me to my car. He hadn't asked me a single question. Right then I decided he was the best guy at Xegon, even if he was a lipless inbred Yankee child of wealth. You can forgive a lot of a guy who doesn't ask stupid questions when the clock's running and you don't have answers anyway.

CHAPTER NINE

"Good luck," he said. "As long as you get that box back, no one will care what you did on the way, and I can promise the money will be good."

I had that rental car in gear before I had my belt fastened or my hands on the wheel. The escort took off ahead of me, siren and lights on, and he put on brights plus a front spotlight, so that gravel highway was plain as day and I went along it at about ninety, leaving my lights off so as not to annoy my friend in front. We were waved through all the guard posts except the one where I'd left my bag; as I passed through that one, I hit the window button, slammed on brakes, and slowed down, and my buddy the guard—the one who was so cool about what was in the bag before—just tossed it into the passenger seat, like I was the fucking pony express.

That guard car rode me all the way out to the base guardpost, where the road joined blacktop, and from there I floored it up onto 40 and was finally—maybe seven minutes after getting my hunch—seriously open for business. I knew where my boy was going from having been inside his head—I just didn't know how I'd been inside his head. I could work that out later.

So I went west on 40, back up towards town, with the pedal held down the whole way, slowed to make the turnoff, and then slammed it north on Tramway Boulevard as fast as I could. Tramway Boulevard connects the little tech start-ups in the northeast part of the city with the older, high-security stuff around Kirtland, basically a big traffic artery that they built because they figured sooner or later there'd be growth enough out at the end of it to justify its existence. Looking at the growth they got you had to say it was a dubious kind of justification.

You can make good time on a main traffic artery in light traffic, as long as you know what you're doing and the pigs aren't out. I switched up my radar detector and my police scanner, kept my ears on, and duck-and-popped my way along, staying to the right when I could, keeping big trucks between me and anything that might be watching from up ahead, beating every yellow and careful of every red. It's nerve-wracking and challenging and frankly I think it's fun, but because of what it does to your brakes and clutch, you'd never do it with your own car, or if your renter didn't have pretty decent brakes.

And the whole time the hunch kept getting stronger. My boy had taken 40 practically the whole way to the downtown and then cut back up, the long way round to go, but I knew that he didn't know Albuquerque even as well as I did (which wasn't all that well).

The big problem was that I knew he was meeting somebody at Lena Logan's, and I knew he would feel safe when he got there. I had a sense that there might be a lot of them, too, and that they were all set to pick up the white box and whisk it away; I had a real sense that it was a biggish operation about to fold down, that there was going to be nothing left after tonight, and that this guy was just ticking off the seconds as he drove, slowly and carefully, towards Lena's.

Then he recognized the turnoff to 25 and saw the cemeteries down beyond, and checked his clock.

It was clear as a bell. I mean—*as a bell*. It actually rang inside my head for a second, John, like imagine thinking of a bell, now imagine that your thought of the bell, inside your head, could be loud enough to deafen you, and you got what it felt like.

That landmark told him that he had shaved about six minutes off his time, and he was happy as a pig in shit. I sure wasn't.

That was six minutes I didn't have. Not if I was going to get into the lane next to his car, cut him off, push him into a side street, take him from there, and hold him long enough to call up Hale and get some reinforcements from Xegon security. Especially because I wanted to do that somewhere a long way from any reinforcements *he* might have.

Well, no chance for that now. If I pushed it, I might get to him a few blocks short of Lena's, but I was not gonna do any better than that, and I'd be headed the wrong way.

I put the pedal to the metal, stopped worrying about not running reds, and just prayed for a pork-free environment for a few minutes. And to my deep surprise—hell, I'd've thought, based on all past experience, that Murphy is my copilot—I got clear sailing. I made the turn onto Montgomery, up where there's miles of those new El Cheapo condos that look like the man who is trying to invent the habitable Taco Bell has some work left to do.

I took that turn on two wheels but I was on the track. And the funny thing was that at the same time I could feel my boy on Montgomery, breathing easier and easier, looking for an address—Lena's address, I realized—and annoyed in the dark by how hard it was to read street addresses, wanting to slow down and go way too slow in the right lane to look for a readable number, but afraid to be that conspicuous.

I passed Lena's. I could feel him out there, would see him in a second. I had won the race. Now if I could just maybe think of something to *do,* I'd be in great shape.

Then I ran out of thinking time.

My target was in a small brown pickup truck, a late-eighties Datsun with an old lawnmower, a paint-spattered ladder, and a messy tarp in the back, the kind of thing that wouldn't draw ten nanoseconds of cop interest anywhere in America, especially considering it was driven by a man with a mop of gray hair surrounding a deep brown face, wearing old clothes. He was headed towards me in the far lane, half a block away. I was six lanes away from him laterally.

Sometimes you just go with an idea and allow your idea to be a little stupid, and it still works out better than if you'd put any thought into it. Montgomery is a big, wide urban street lined with strip malls, and it's divided with many breaks. There was a left turn lane for the other side of the road that I could get to if I floored it, so I did, shot across traffic, and went through it the wrong way. A car and a truck slammed on their brakes and gave me a tiny bit more room; my guy was still looking at addresses as I threw the wheel hard to the right, yanked my emergency brake, and put my car into a flat spin that slapped my trunk up against his front bumper.

I was belted in, and I tucked up good too, fists to my forehead, elbows against my ribs, and head shoved back against the headrest. Momentum was pretty close to zero—I was on the side of the car that was spinning away from the direction of overall motion—so I just got thrown side-to-side for an instant, and then everything ground to a stop as the front of his little truck tried to climb up over the back of my rental car,

But he wasn't belted in and never had time to put on his brakes; somehow I knew he was looking to his right, trying to read the address, right until my rear lights flashed for an instant in his peripheral vision, a split second before his left front fender crunched.

He thunked his face on the windshield and slammed his thighs against the steering wheel. The windshield cracked but didn't break and the wheel and dash were padded, so he was hurt plenty but he would live. I could feel the agony in his head as I opened his door and let him fall onto the street; I stepped over him, reached across the bench seat, and sure enough, my hand grasped the cool enameled metal surface of a Gaudeamus machine.

You know, John, I didn't think of it at the time, but if that old Gaudeamus machine had not been right where I knew it would be, I'd sure be a nut with a lot of explaining to do, now wouldn't I?

I pulled the Gaudeamus box out, grabbed my bag from my rental car, and took off at a trot. A couple people who had stopped were yelling at me in Spanish. (I don't know Spanish but I suspect it was something like "Come back here, you son of a bitch! I saw what you did and I'm calling the cops!")

I ducked down a breezeway between two stores in a strip mall, jumped a fence, and went down into an arroyo. Could be a good way to get killed but I wasn't planning to stay long, and if it flash-flooded in the next minute, well, I guess Murphy would just be claiming his own.

I ran three blocks, popped back up at a vacant lot where neighborhood kids had broken down the fence, and doubled around to get back to my hotel. As soon as I was there, I used the pay phone in the lobby (just in case the opposition was scanning for cell phones) and let Hale know that I had the package and I needed a pickup, ASAP. I told him to send the pickup team to my hotel room, figuring that I was better off taking the chance that they might know about this place than being out on the street where they would be looking for me.

Hale was amazed—I guess I had just become super-detective in his eyes—and promised to have an armed team out there in less than twenty minutes.

I stopped at the Coke machine and got three cans of Mountain Dew; I was exhausted and figured I would need all the sugar and caffeine I could get. I got back to my room, hung out the DO NOT DISTURB tag, took a leak, and settled back into my chair. As I was gulping the first Mountain Dew the utter weirdness of the whole thing hit me. That I was sitting here with a machine that did at least two things that were supposed to be impossible. Which I had re-captured from bad guys. About whom I knew nothing. Using— ESP? In which I had never believed.

Hell, my head was still ringing in sympathy with that poor bas-tard Elvis's head—

All right, how did I know his name was Elvis? Or that right now he was staggering up the stairs to Lena Logan's apartment?

I reached for my laptop, started monitoring my bugs, put the signal up on live audio. I heard Lena's door open. "Elvis! Are you hurt? Come in here, right now." She seemed really worried about him, like she knew him rather than that they just worked together.

Now, luckily, the most distinctive thing that people remember about me is the combination of black hair and blue eyes, and it was way too dark for Elvis to have seen my eye color. And I had switched rental cars. So I wasn't too worried about him describing me accu-rately enough for her to realize that the guy who had attacked Elvis was Evan Gardenaire.

Allowing for lousy light and no training, old Elvis did an okay job of describing, but if he'd been talking to the cops they'd never've had enough to look for me seriously. Meanwhile, while I waited for

Hale, I pulled out the recordings the bugs had been making in my absence.

Sure enough, I remembered right when I compared—she had said and done exactly the things that Norm the engineer liked, with me, and she had called me Norm. The fact that within an hour he'd taken a beating and been robbed of the white box that sat beside me now had to be more than a coincidence.

Furthermore, while I'd been driving downtown, less than ten minutes after I'd left, Lena had taken a last-minute call about a possible quickie, and it was from Jason the pool cleaner. He wanted to just stop by for a blow job and some goddies. While he was on his way over to her place, she put a blob of dark lipstick onto one lip, and told him it was a cold sore when he arrived; she offered to fuck him for free since she couldn't do what he wanted without giving him herpes. She called him Norman for a while, and then switched to calling him Evan.

My blood froze. I couldn't think what to do, knew this was important but didn't know what to think. I sat there and listened as she finished fucking him, sold him six goddies, threw in two for an extra-special bonus, whisked him out the door, and called Elvis to tell him that Norman Lawton had just ordered a pizza at the facility.

Then she phoned Negon and started dictating the paper that Norman had just finished; the only copy of which at that moment resided on an unnetworked computer on his desk at the lab, and in the printer basket next to it.

And that was the precise, exact, dead–on moment when dawn came up over Marblehead.

The Gaudeamus pill was not just a mildly addictive sex-enhancer. If anything, it was more remarkable than the Gaudeamus machine. It was some kind of induced, not perfect, worked-strange-but-*worked,* telepathy.

Jason was one of her big dumb studs. Basically a stimulant . . . so she had called him Calvin, and then Norman, and then Evan . . . my alias—

I got up and put the dead bolt and chain on the door. You know how a room feels when it's just your room, and nobody should ever be in it, but you walk in and suddenly you just know someone has been in it? That's what my *mind* felt like.

I slipped the Gaudeamus machine into my laptop case (since the laptop was out on the desk in the room), and hung the case on the back of the bathroom door, against the wall. Then I grabbed up the laptop and tucked it onto the shelf in the closet. For a one-minute job of hiding things, not bad, I thought, as I closed the closet door.

My cell phone rang. "Yeah."

"Bismarck, it's Hale. The pickup team coming out for you was just run off the road by a big, aggressively driven bread truck. Which the police tell us had just been reported stolen. We're trying to get cops out to you, and there's another pickup team on the way, but—"

A sledgehammer blow shattered the upper hinge on the door to my room. The door rocked back into place.

"Tell the police to hurry," I said, calling them "police" instead of pigs, which tells you how bad the situation was and how much I wanted them. "The other team just got here."

"Are you—"

"Gotta go," I said, dropping the phone but leaving it on and moving toward the door, hoping to jump whatever came through.

Whoever was on the other side of the door took a setting-up tap. I took a deep breath and held it.

The next blow broke the middle hinge. Then a very muscular three-hundred-pound Indian, still holding the sledgehammer, kicked the door down. It fell into the room, and the wind from its top edge fanned my face as I jumped back. The broken door shattered the lamp and television in its path.

The big Indian flipped it out of the way with his foot, letting it crash across the little round table by the heater under the window.

He didn't seem to be in a real good mood.

He was this huge Indian, darkish brown, and maybe a bit more than six-five, *big* across the shoulders and I mean even for his height. Hell, it's hard to believe they *make* people as big as that.

He had just the little stubby start of braids, not seriously reaching for his shoulders yet, like he had only, maybe, started growing his hair out about two years ago. He was in greasy jeans, tucked into scuffed-up old work boots, and he had on that black t-shirt you see on so many kids nowadays, the one with O. B. Joyful holding the dead Merle the Killer Squirrel by the tail, with that famous caption "No town is big enough for the two of some people."

Actually, John, I didn't think till now to wonder if he'd put that shirt on special for this occasion.

He set down a big ass old boom box that he was carrying and turned it on as he did. The loudest, nastiest punk rock in the history of the universe filled my room.

I closed the distance with a sidestep and kicked hard at one of his knees. That's when I found out that besides being big and strong and all that stuff I already had figured out, he was also fast and knew his shit. He whipped an arm around and nearly trapped that foot; I fell back into a T-stance and grabbed the floor lamp beside me—you remember that rule we all learn, John, "The most important thing in unarmed combat is not to stay unarmed."

I whipped that lamp over my head, using it like you would a boken in a martial-arts class, trying to brain him with the base. He popped a roof block so fast that I felt it whiff by my face, an instant before that flimsy old floor lamp broke in two; that left me with one arm stinging so bad that I couldn't do much of anything with it, and I was back to unarmed.

He did a tight, quick back flip of his wrist, so that the backs of his fingers slid around my still-numb arm, caught my sleeve, and whipped my arm around. I somersaulted and landed at his feet, definitely not by my choice. He stretched me up by the arm, picking me right up off the floor, pivoted and snap-kicked. The toe of his boot thumped the bridge of my nose. I ragdollied onto the floor. The whole time he was yelling like a nut.

He let go of me and walked back out of the hotel room, maybe seven seconds after he'd knocked the door down. I didn't seem to be able to move, or even to tense a muscle, though my eyes were open and I could see. He came back in with two milk crates, pulled a bottle out of one, and poured it all over me. Cheap gin. Stunk like hell.

Then he pulled about ten more bottles out of those crates, set some of them out (sloshing booze around as he did), threw a couple against the wall, and threw the last one through the window— between my ringing head and the screaming punk rock, I couldn't even hear the window break. I still couldn't do more than drag my hands in little circles on the carpet in front of me, so I watched as he threw a handful of mixed pills onto the floor and bed, then pulled out a little brown paper lunch bag, set that into an ashtray, and lit it; after it blazed up, I smelled rope. No doubt by the time the pigs got here, which was scheduled for any second now, this would all look like a real serious party.

He grabbed the remaining lamp in the place, and threw it into the mirror, and walked into the bathroom. He turned on the light, which darkened for an instant as the door swung closed; he would be grabbing my laptop bag from the back of the door. The door reopened in a spill of fluorescent light as he came out with my laptop bag, which contained the Gaudeamus machine. He'd just gone straight to where it was. Hell, I doubted he'd even looked inside the bag, or needed to.

That suck-dog awful punk rock was still shrieking as he went out the door with the key to my employability slung over his shoulder like a big purse. He left the boom box on.

On his way out I heard him pound on the door next to mine and yell, "Wake up, bitch, come out and suck my cock!" A second later he was pounding on a more distant door yelling, "Hey, if you call the cops, I'm gonna come in there and cut your ass dead!"

It's always nice to know you're dealing with a professional who knows how to put the finishing touches on a job.

I was not feeling good at all.

Honest to god and Jesus and that whole crowd, John, I think I might've just passed out there, and let things get sorted when I woke up in jail or the hospital, except I so purely hated that fucking music. But I dragged myself over to turn that off, couldn't find the switch, battered it till the batteries flew around and there was a silence like a choir of blessed angels. By the time I did all that, I knew I wasn't dying or even passing out.

A flashing red glow from the open doorway might be the cops that Xegon had sent, but more likely they'd been called by the hotel. If they were like most pigs, they'd be approaching slowly. I sucked in a deep breath, and my head cleared a little, and I looked around.

Thing I learned early: live packed, and always have extra room in your bag. I always put clothes and toiletries and all that back into my bag as soon as I'm done with them. So I staggered up to the closet, took my laptop, and threw it into the duffel bag. I grabbed that little case with my fake ID materials and my supply of goddies, and tossed that in. I zipped it up, and everything I had was all packed and ready to go. *Semper paratus*, beep repaired, Mrs. Bismarck's boy was ready to win the ready camper award.

I lurched for the door; normally there's nothing heavy in my duffel bag but this time I seemed to have accidentally packed a small Buick in there somewhere.

I got my balance at the railing, pushed back and stood up straight. There were six pigmobiles in the lot, and a confused mob of milling cops. I lurched down the gallery about twenty steps, and no spotlight hit me. They were still getting organized.

I was already on the stairs down when I had a close encounter of the porcine kind—two cops came running up. "I am never staying in one of these motels again," I said. "Never, never, never. This chain is never getting my business again."

One pig looked and saw a messed-up man who looked like he'd just grabbed a bag and walked out of a hotel room.

"We might need you for a witness, sir—" he began.

"Right, now you Albuquerque assholes want me to do your work for you. Like I can afford the kind of time to go to court. Your Chamber of Commerce is going to get a *serious* letter from me," I said, and staggered on down the stairs.

"Sir, if you've been drinking, you shouldn't drive—"

I turned the corner at the bottom of the stairs and hustled through a breezeway; ducked into the little hotel's public laundry, down the hallway through their restaurant kitchen, where I startled the dishwasher into dropping a plate, went out the back door, and was on my way.

After I had staggered for about a block and a half, and found a nice dark shadow on the back side of a drive-through bank, I fished around in my duffel bag till I found that gym bag, and messed around in it till I found the cell phone. I hit the last number dialed, and got Hale. "They beat me up and got the Gaudeamus machine," I said. "And I need pickup."

"Fuck," Hale said. "Fuck fuck fuck." The boy was becoming

goddam nearly human, John. I was thinking to myself, next thing you know, he'll be growing lips and maybe a chin. "We've got to get you out of there and right now I don't have a thing to do it with. My pickup team is still fifteen minutes from you and our communications are penetrated. We've got to risk something somewhere—let me think a moment—"

He was managing to sound concerned—might even have been for all I know—so give him credit for being pretty human in a bad spot, which is more than most guys would be when they're dealing with danger to the hired help in the middle of a national security disaster (and probable bankruptcy) that is all going to be blamed on them.

"Okay," Hale said, "I don't really like it, but here's the plan. I need you to—"

This was the third time in my life I've heard a silenced pistol make its weird little *splott!* over the phone. I told you the other two stories, long ago, eh, John? And you only need to hear it once to recognize it forever. Whoever it was fired once, maybe three feet from Hale's phone.

Hale coughed hard, made a sick little gurgle, and said, "Don't come." The line went dead. I didn't figure I should call back.

CHAPTER TEN

"And there you got it, John. I don't know who the other side is but Hale and me, sure as god and Jesus and that whole crowd, we pissed them off bad. And anybody that's had a god pill, they can read your mind, sometimes, a little, like a very spotty radio with a lot of static and the batteries dying pretty fast, but you never know when they'll get some clear channel signal like I did when I nailed that bastard Elvis. And they've got old Lena and I bet with her practice, she's the big mama bear of all telepaths, and if she, or someone like her, gets close, I better not be asleep, because that seems to be when they get strong signal most easily. I got telepaths with guns after me, and I don't know what their range is, but since they obviously got all the way inside Xegon, which is like a fortress, and shot Hale while he was talking to me—what I gotta do is duck and weave for a while till I get myself clear of them, and then head back towards them, since there's probably nowhere on Earth far enough to run. Better to be closing in and fighting, anyway, than spend the rest of my time hiding from them—whoever the fuck they are, other than 'Lena Logan's team.'"

"Was Hale *killed*?" I asked.

"I don't know, John, that was the last contact I dared have with Xegon, night before last. They have my number and if it's safe they'll call me." Travis stretched and groaned. "Needed to get myself as clear as I could of every connection, before I make a careful approach. Figure, though, if Hale is dead, and maybe some others—besides Cheryl the pizza driver—then they'll have a hell of a time sweeping it under the rug, even if the other side *can*—maybe—wave around a 'national security' magic wand. So I need to let about two news cycles go by to see what gets reported."

"And you came *here*," I said, "with people trying to kill you on your trail—" I hate it when I can hear my own voice getting whiny, but I guess by my mid-forties the most likely thing is that I'll never get it under control.

"I don't think they're out to do that," Travis said, "and, buddy, have a little faith. I shook 'em hard and I've been watching my back. They ain't on my trail anymore."

"If you were being extra reassuring, you'd make that Texas accent thicker and say 'they ain't on my trail no more,'" I said, overcompensating. "I know you're actually a prep-school trust-funder who just enjoys going slumming—"

"Going trailer-parking," he corrected me. "Yeah, I know, every so often I slip up and use the subjunctive. I wouldn't do that if I were a real redneck." He sighed. "John, I didn't have much choice. And to know about any connection between us two, they'd have to have busted into my office in Montana and read an email file marked 'Christmas letters' and traced your address from the college, since I wrote to you at your college email. They ain't going to do that. If they were going to go to that much trouble, they'd never have let me slip off their screens like they did down in Alamosa. And so far as we can tell that telepathy comes and goes, and we haven't seen it work more than ten miles away. Hell, there was no trace of the bad guys in Alamosa; I think they just chased me out of Santa Fe because there were a few of them there and they spotted me, so they had the chance to look busy. I don't think I was really any kind of priority, you know what I mean? Just something to do to impress the boss."

"I wouldn't know a thing about that," I said, "being a college professor trying to suck up enough to get tenure."

"Yeah. Well, it was pretty much your textbook evasion of guys who don't intend to shoot you. They came up from behind—you know what US 285 is like in that stretch, you can see three miles ahead and four back because you're climbing a gradual rise that goes for so many miles. Besides the road and an occasional fence, you'd never know there were people on the planet. Just road and empty, with a far-off frame of sky and mountains.

"That time of midafternoon, when everybody's already where they need to be to work, you can go a solid hour without seeing another car. So I had a car in my rearview for a long time—huge old black Cherokee, took him a long time to close up with me, they should've got the V-8 model. I suppose even bad guys worry about fuel economy, nowadays, or more likely it was a renter.

"In the twenty minutes while the black Cherokee was closing up, I got buzzed twice by a helicopter, also black, no markings, probably just shooting pictures. Second time I waved at him, but he didn't wave back that I could see. Then the Cherokee closed up, and I whipped a J-turn, and the stupid sonofabitch tried to get turned around that fast himself—"

"Hey, how about a note on what a J-turn is for those of us who write adventures for a living?" I asked, fascinated by Travis, as always, despite whatever passes for judgment in me (mostly middle age and physical cowardice).

"Don't try this one in your SUV, John, for sure, and really not in *any* car, but if you have a nice little low-to-the-ground Jap roller-skate like I was driving, and a really empty road, that's about the safest situation you can do it in. You slam on the brakes—you're aiming for a skid—and tick that old wheel just far enough to do most of a 180 spin, or a little over, as you get down to stopping speed. If you're not a Hollywood stunt driver or haven't practiced forever, you're gonna go all over the fucking road and maybe into the ditch on either side, doing that, so it helps to be on a forgiving stretch of road, but like I said, 285 from Alamosa south is about as empty as they make it, and as it happened I stayed on the road.

"Then you pop it into reverse—which is now the direction you're going—for about a second or two, with your foot *off* the gas. In a front-wheel-drive car, that straightens it out and gives you back your control. Hit the brakes one more time to get to zero speed, while you're slapping it into first, and then stand on it. I hand-shifted my way up through the 1 and 2 on that automatic, giving me more acceleration than it was ever supposed to have, and when I popped it back to D, it *wailed*. All that was a couple of seconds.

"So now we were accelerating towards each other. I was probably doing fifty, back the way I had come, and he was coming on at seventy or so, in a good old-fashioned game of chicken.

"I had to hope he didn't want to collide with me, and luckily I was right. I got over to my side of the road and crouched down, driving Florida-style—"

"Which is?"

"Hands over my head and looking through the wheel. Scared shitless might be part of it too, come to think of it. Anyway, there were no shots, and they didn't swerve to collide.

"Now, my plan was to take advantage of the head start I would get from the time they took to turn around, run back a long enough ways to get the horizon between me and them, look for one of the little crossroads-gas-station-church-and-bar towns that show up every twenty miles or so, and see if I could find a road off 285 that went somewhere over the mountains, either way, and get out of the San Luis Valley, since trying to hide there, especially when the other side has a helicopter, is kind of like a tarantula trying to hide on a birthday cake.

"But I was watching that Cherokee in the rearview, and son of a bitch if the poor stupid idiot didn't try to U-turn to come after me. SUVs do not U-turn in two lanes at seventy miles per hour. They do about a third of a U and then they tumble.

"My road to Alamosa had just reopened, so I slid into the next pullout for a ranch gate, three-pointed out, and floored it back towards them. Two old boys all dressed up like Mormon missionaries with sunglasses were just climbing out of the overturned Cherokee, in the ditch, when I went by. I managed to refrain from shooting them the finger, but I did notice that I was in reach of a cell-phone tower—must've been up on one of the distant mountains, you get spotty moments of beautiful reception every now and then—so I phoned up the staties and reported a wrecked Cherokee there, said they had been weaving and driving real fast and I thought maybe they were drunk, and that they had shouted and waved guns at me as I went by. Just trying to make sure my friends in the bear hats would arrive with a trunk full of questions, a back seat full of unpleasant attitude, and a roof rack carrier full of red tape to go with it, and therefore those particular mibs would stay out of the game for a while."

"Mibs—Men in Black?"

"Yeah. Commoner than deer out there in the San Luis Valley. There's so much weird shit for them to keep hushed up—so many experimental aircraft tests and operations rehearsals and all that, and maybe other stuff that ain't all ours, as well. They never say who they work for, but I've never thought they were all government. So those old boys could've been Negon, or working for the same outfit as Elvis and Lena and that giant ass-kicking Indian (whatever outfit that was), or any old third player in the game you want. My thought was that they were probably some third player; Negon and Lena's boys both knew I didn't have the Gaudeamus box anymore, and I don't think I could possibly have had any information they wanted. So it had to be someone who wanted the box, or wanted to hurt Xegon, and didn't know that I was out of the game myself.

"Which might also be why they haven't followed me since I dumped that renter in Alamosa, bought a ticket to Denver, went into the secure area with one long line and came back out in a crowd of arriving passengers, and then hitched this way. The home office might have called them and told them that the Gaudeamus box was elsewhere, anyway."

The strangest thought was beginning to creep up on me. "Tell me, one more time, what the Gaudeamus box looks like," I said. "I'm thinking of something."

"All right, it's just a white enameled-metal case, like you used to get from Heathkit or Edmund for do-it-yourself projects. Maybe a bit bigger than a cable box. On the front there's an Edison socket, three-pronged, one-ten comes out of that. Three LED readouts, each with a cycler button under it. A button all by itself marked ACT. XYZ axes marked with red Sharpie, coming off little laser-drilled pinholes. Little rubber feet. Eight USB and two serial jacks on the back. Why, you got one in your basement?"

"I couldn't tell you about the back side," I said, "but I bet you didn't see *Gaudeamus* today—the web animation thingie, I mean—being busy fleeing for your life and so forth."

"Thingie," he said. "You've been around college students too much, John. You're not going to tell me that—"

"Maybe you'd better look for yourself."

So a few minutes later Trav was standing over my shoulder next to that old orange throne I used to write on. A very long time back, I'd worked for the U-City Children's Theatre in St. Louis, and there had been a rummage sale/junk dump for Halloween, and I'd needed a desk chair. What I got, for three dollars, was a vis-orange throne, from god knows what long-forgotten children's show, which happened to be exactly the right height and shape for my slightly dinged-up back, ass, and legs to sit in for many hours comfortably. At one time or another, as a joke (I hope one without too much point), each of my wives, and one girlfriend, had given me a crown to go with it, but I never found a comfortable crown. Eventually, nineteen or twenty books wore that throne to pieces, and toward the end it was at least as much made up of angle iron, t-plates, and corner braces as it was of its original materials. I still have my collection of crowns in a box somewhere.

I don't think sitting in that relic of a kid's show ever really affected the writing, though now and then, especially when working late, I would look around for my henchsquirrels, intending to stand up and sing about controlling all the acorns in the forest.

Okay, not really, but it makes a better story. I'll take it out in later revisions. I did promise Travis, and some other people, that I'd try to stick to facts.

Anyway, Travis was leaning on my orange throne, and I popped up the day's unpacked *Gaudeamus*—I usually let them hang on my hard drive for a few days before erasing them—and connected to the web, since sometimes a link was updated after the original main cartoon was posted.

He watched in silence until he saw the Gaudeamus machine on Ower Gyro's nightstand; then he reached over my shoulder, grabbed the mouse, and stopped it. "That's the machine, John, no question about it at all." He clicked on the picture of the device.

Before, I had found myself facing a computer screen asking for a password. This time, there was a connection to a picture of a very pretty brunette woman in red see-through lingerie. Below it, in blue letters:

> Wanna fuck Wendy? It's cheap, and you better do it soon, before somebody shoots her right through her pretty left tit.

> Fuck you, Lena, it's always been about you. But now it's not. You're not fucking up the best thing that has ever happened in my life.

> Huggies for my mostest special-est buddy-boo, Susan.

Travis said, "That's Lena Logan, all right." He swung the cursor arrow around the screen, but only the photograph indicated a link. He clicked on it, and we were at "Fun in Albuquerque! Meet Wendy for the time of your life!" a perfectly ordinary escort's webpage that doesn't quite mention prostitution, and has a small-print disclaimer saying that it's not about prostitution. There were several more pictures of Lena Logan.

"Uh, I don't remember a 'Susan' from your story," I said.

"Me either," Travis agreed. "Okay, maybe *I'm* not all the way to the weird part, either."

"Am I too late for the weird part?" Kara asked, coming in. She was in the usual array of jeans, sweater, slightly blurry expression, and huge coffee mug, indicating that it was 10:30 in the morning. "Hey, Travis. When am I going to dump John and run off to France with you?"

"I gotta work this week."

"Yeah, and I'm playing a gig at a roadhouse up in Almont. I guess some other time."

"Hey," I said, which was at least not as feeble a retort as "ummm" would have been.

CHAPTER ELEVEN

"So who's this chick you're trying to set me up with?" Travis asked as we walked downtown, about an hour and a half later.

"You can only be a chick up through ABD, and Melody finished her dissertation, accepted and all, last month," I pointed out. "She's *Doctor* Chick. Especially to a college dropout like you."

It was one of those gorgeous days when even I could sort of understand the attractions of Gunnison; big white fluffy clouds drifting below a deep blue dome, bright sunlight that made everything stand out in sharp detail, nothing moving on the wide, quiet streets. "Nice little town, isn't it?" Travis commented.

"Be sure to tell 'em you're a Texan and you want to move here," Kara said. "That always delights the locals."

Travis chuckled. "I was just noticing that it must be a pleasant place for a guy who likes the outdoors and has the time and money to enjoy it."

"It takes more time than money," Kara said. "If you're going to be around a couple of days, I could take you hiking—John never wants to go. It's great up in the mountains right now. And we have a week to go till regular hunting season—the bow hunters are out, but they don't shoot hikers."

"It's an old joke here that bow hunters are the smart ones," I explained to Travis. "One, they don't shoot hikers, two, they don't shoot cows, three, when was the last time you heard about a guy getting killed because he was cleaning his bow and didn't realize it was loaded?"

"And I can guess just what part of the country contributes the old boys that do shoot cows and hikers and each other, which is why my accent is so popular locally," Travis said. "Never said my home state was perfect. That's why I was required to go into exile. To live there you're required to think that. Anyway, I'd love to go hiking around here—even though a certain out-of-shape guy who likes to live in the basement tells me there's nothing to see—but unfortunately I'm catching a ride with John into Denver this evening."

"Always assuming he goes," Kara said. "John has a gift for missing cons."

"I have to meet with my co-author," I said. That's how you get used to referring to them when they're celebrities; it doesn't sound like you're dropping a name, and it doesn't cause people who don't know you to burst into silly questions. "So I'm at least going to get to Denver tonight. I was only going to make it to the convention for a couple hours tomorrow morning and on Sunday afternoon."

"And just incidentally and by the way, Melody is nice, Travis," Kara said. "You'll like her. We're not fixing her up with you, we have a standing Friday lunch date with her to eat white trash cookin' at the W anyway, and you're just joining the fun."

The W Café is a Gunnison institution; for whatever reason, location or food or its various owners, practically everyone eats there, even people who say they hate it. For not much, you can get a big plate of just about anything that's vaguely Tex Mex, sort of

Oklahoma Truck Stop, or approximately Down Home. Something about the place just feels comfortable and homey—the naugahyde booths, or the old-style glass case counter at the register station, or the odd artifacts of the past hanging from the walls (farm implements, a toy Howdy Doody, a Boy Scout uniform shirt of the type that they had back before I was a scout, various wise sayings carved onto wood).

When Melody Wallace had come out to Western State, in my department, a year before, she'd quickly become friends with both me and Kara; she had now been here long enough to stop telling us how "authentic" the W was, so we no longer had to swat her with a rolled-up newspaper every few minutes. I suppose that anyone with a masters in pop culture was doomed to use expressions like "authentic," but she was now almost trained and could be allowed out in public, even around authentic-looking people, with hardly any danger at all.

I was just explaining all that to Travis when we walked from the bright glare of the street into the cool dim of the W and there was Melody, already at the corner booth. "And here she is," I said.

She was thirty-six and had hit her peak of attractiveness so late that she wasn't exactly used to it. She was thick-thighed, busty, big-assed, firm and muscular. She could hike most people into the ground; she still had puppy fat in her round, unlined face. She had fabulous long thick chestnut hair that she usually clipped to the top of her head in a pile, big vivid green eyes that she hid behind horn-rims, and a goofy grin that she couldn't conceal. She was much given to slightly ridiculous hats and to bright-colored vests; she and Kara could talk vests for at least twenty-six minutes at a time (I timed it once).

I could practically hear Travis's "charm module" activating beside me as I introduced them. Once Melody got a good look at him and found out he did something romantic for a living, Kara and I were pretty much spectators for a while. As practiced professional writers, we read and write upside down pretty easily, so we spent a while scribbling notes on napkins and grinning at each other as Melody and Travis conversed—for some weird reason I still have both napkins, and I can still trace the progression, my handwriting alternating with Kara's, from "Cute . . ." to "Way too cute . . ." to "Cute enough to make me heave . . ." to "Okay, let's heave together."

We didn't actually heave. I'd never waste the chicken-fried steak and eggs breakfast plate (served all day, with a gallon or two of fresh coffee—when you pass through Gunnison remember you want the home fries, not the hash browns, and you want gravy on them) at the W. You can gain about a pound and a half at lunch there, without even thinking about dessert.

After a while, though, since Melody was especially fascinated with this being a real private eye, she got onto the question of his current case, about which he couldn't talk much, which just seemed to add to the charm, but also put a shaft or two into the spokes of the conversation wheel, so Kara and I began to be invited into the conversation peripherally, mainly Kara supplying footnotes to Melody's stories about playing bar gigs (now and then they did folk duos, since Melody played banjo, and they enjoyed singing old-timey close harmony), and me supplying corroboration for Travis's stories of his younger days. (I've never ceased being grateful to Kara for not being the sort of spouse subject to retroactive jealousy.)

Sometime after the plates had been cleared, well before we'd all had enough coffee or Melody had to run back for the Friday afternoon office hours that no one ever came to, Travis's cell phone rang. "Yeah . . . Hey! You're not dead! Are you okay? . . . Well, that sucks . . . I was going to be there anyway, getting there tonight . . . cool. Hey, did you look at this morning's *Gaudeamus* online—no, the webtoon. I'd say Xegon has more security problems even than either of us thought—so you did see it. Cool. Okay, talk in Denver, bye."

He looked up at me as he holstered his cell phone. "Hale. Alive. Meeting him early tomorrow."

"Did you say 'gaudeamus'?" Melody asked.

"Yeah, a little Latin word that just keeps showing up all over my current case," Travis said, his voice touching the words "my current case" with the same caress that other guys administer to "my BMW," "my med school days," or "my horses," when talking to a pretty woman. (I guess you use what you have.) "I don't know why but that word shows up in all sorts of ways that don't quite seem like they should be connected, but always turn out to be."

Melody sat up as if Travis had groped her thigh. Kara and I both glared at him. Then my colleague said, "Gee, I might actually, sort of, know why. How many different things are called 'gaudeamus' that you've encountered?"

"Well, the webtoon, a physical effect, an experimental machine, and a probably-soon-to-be-illegal drug," Travis said.

"Hmm." She pulled out one of those spiral-bound packs of notecards from her purse. "Can you tell me anything about any of those? It happens I'm doing a project about 'gaudeamus,' aiming toward a paper."

"Which one is your paper about?" I asked.

"About the word, or the idea." She pushed her glasses up her nose and did what all professors do—and resent when others do it—in conversation: launched into a lecture. Like most experienced professors, and especially communications professors who have had to make up lots of ex temp examples while teaching public speaking, she laid it out quickly and efficiently. (Kara always said that when Melody got rolling you knew exactly what was going to be on the quiz.) "Every now and then, a few times a decade, a word goes from ordinary or occasional use, in a dictionary sense, to universal use to mean 'good' or just 'extremely positive,' to cliché and datedness. No one knows why, but it happens. I'm spending a good deal of my time online, scanning everything I can, because I'm trying to get a handle on the word fad for 'gaudeamus.' Because I think, while it's happening, I might be able to observe some things that I think happened previous times."

"Such as?" Travis asked. If the answer had been in Melody's eyes, he'd already have had it.

"Well . . . let's see. There was a big fad around 1922 for 'acme,' a previously obscure term, for example. The early 80's saw big waves for 'excellent' and 'fresh'; just recently, 'extreme' was that way. The fad words pop up as brand names for dozens or hundreds of products and services. There's usually a spirit that gets associated with it, too—you might have noticed that 'acme' didn't really denote things that were the absolute best and the utter peak of perfection, that 'excellent' only rarely meant 'standing out above the rest'— remember how berserk that drove some of our older colleagues when the local school board declared that its goal was 'universal excellence'?"

" 'And all of the children are above average,' " I said. "It annoyed the shit out of me, too, and I'm not that old."

"But anyway, a fad word usually means something specifically— though vaguely—different from plain old good. Good in a particular way. Twenties 'acme' does not translate into forties 'atomic' does not translate into nineties 'extreme.' They're all different kinds of goodness—which sounds like a slogan for a breakfast cereal company—see, there's an example of how things have very precise overtones, goodness is something a breakfast cereal can have but it's different from tasting good or being good for you (though it implies both) and it works for food but not for an ISP or a washing machine, which, instead, would have, um—"

"Gooditude?" I suggested.

"Goodiosity, maybe. Anyway, whatever it is, each fad word names a particular flavor or type of gooditudiositousness."

"You can say that again," Kara said.

"Not on a bet. Now, the odd thing is"—Melody adjusted her glasses again and rested a pointing finger on the table beside her coffee cup—this next point was going to be on the test for sure—"whenever one of those words becomes a fad, there's a placebo effect associated with it, which persists and continues to work for things named during the fad period, but can't be successfully deployed on anything named afterwards. Don't groan, John, it's not nice, and you know I'm serious."

"I'm groaning because I know you're serious," I said.

Very few of us at Western State had any reputation at all as scholars, and the few of us who did didn't get much reward for it; Western is proudly, even obsessively, a teaching institution, and research is if anything devalued there. That was another way that Melody didn't fit in and was probably headed elsewhere soon. She'd made quite a stir with her paper on the semiotics of placebo, which I'd read and given her notes on before she submitted it; she hadn't liked my notes much so she'd made little use of what I'd said.

I thought about seventy percent of it was brilliant, ten percent the sort of grease needed to slip a paper past some of our colleagues, and twenty percent utter crap, and said so; the notes and comments columns in the semiotics journals were alive with people arguing about it, some having the good sense to agree with me and others trying to push Melody into endorsing positions that would be about eighty percent utter crap, that being the preferred ratio in communications and performance theory.

"Catch me up here," Travis asked.

"I'm going to go take a very long time in the bathroom," Kara said, "I've seen enough reruns of this show." She went back toward the kitchen, where the W's bathrooms were, stopping at a couple of tables to talk to people on the way.

"It's probably my uncanny powers of deduction but I believe your wife has heard some of this before," Travis observed. "Let me direct here; I'm used to asking people nosy questions. I know what a placebo effect is. So using a word that's currently going through a word fad does what?" He looked at Melody and held a hand up at me.

"Well, anything with that name will tend to work slightly better than it otherwise would," she said. "So giving your project a trendy name is a pretty good way to give yourself some extra luck with getting it to work. Sometimes I wonder if I'm not just duplicating the work of some top-secret researcher many decades ago—after all, 'Manhattan' was a big word just before World War Two, and 'atomic' and 'rocket' were big just after, and look how well all that stuff worked."

"Okay," Travis said. "And John, you are turning purple with desire to say that—"

"Oh, I think Melody's two-thirds right. She gives three reasons for that. Two of them make great sense. One, it's the semiotic process of framing or de-framing. Like, cut out a piece of canvas that's been used for brush wiping when we're painting scenery, so that it has lots of big smears and blobs of different colors, plus students work paint out of a brush by practicing lettering (mainly insults at each other), and smiley faces and cartoons, and sometimes someone will do a quick pencil diagram or sketch to make clear what the designer wants, all on that old piece of shot canvas. Put it in a frame and you can sell it as art. Or the way that some Christies will pull ordinary Romantic adolescent rebellion—'I am Satan' and pentangle jewelry and all that—out of the frame of bored teenagers in some suburban gulag-for-the-would-be-hip, and put 'I Long to Be the Bride of Satan' into the frame of a secret underground, thereby creating that whole fantasy that there's a vast Satanic underground out there eating babies and having sex and whatever else it is that a vast Satanic underground does (generally whatever parents moved to the suburbs to avoid)."

"I know *my* folks moved to the suburbs to avoid having *me* eating babies. So 'frame' is the fad word for 'context.'"

"Hey, don't blow our gig," Melody said.

Too much time as a prof, and you learn to ride right over heckling; it's an occupational hazard, at least as severe as drinking is for writers. I rolled on. "So Melody points out that one reason placebos work so well in medicine is that they create a frame of 'I am being cared for and I am getting better.' The patient starts looking for signs of getting better—which, of course, occur randomly and naturally in most illness and injury—and finds them, and responds to them, and, ba-wunga, they get better. So, sure, if something was 'atomic' in 1948, it probably got extra attention paid to its experimental results, and if it worked at all, people poured effort and money into making it work better. That argument, I got no problem with."

"Now, argument two," Melody said. "People getting a placebo want to be good patients. And 'the patient is getting better' is the signifier that signifies 'the patient is a good patient.' So many of them tell the doctor they're feeling better, whether they are or not. Reinforced, of course, by the framing effect, which makes them believe it themselves. So it's not that people get better as much as it's that they report getting better.

"Now, the place where John and I get into a fight would be argument number three, which is this. Logically, a placebo is a contradiction in terms—it's a beneficial medication or procedure that has no effect. 'The pill isn't doing anything but it is making me feel better.' So if a pill or a touch or a beam of light doesn't work, it's not a placebo because it's not beneficial, but if it does work, it's not a placebo because it has an effect. Since, from the patient standpoint and the doctor standpoint, the thing either works or it doesn't, there can't be any such thing as a placebo.

"Well, I said that what resolves the question is that there's always a who-decides about whether it works or not. If you experience a sugar pill making your headache go away, hey, you're the only person who can say your head aches in the first place, or that it stops. 'I took the pill and the headache went away'—if you get the same report for a sugar pill and an aspirin, then the only difference is that a guy in a white coat says that the aspirin is blocking those pain thingies in your brain, whereas the effect of the sugar pill is all in your head. Well, duh. Then the difference isn't in the brain cells, it's in the guy in the white coat."

"I can see where this would set old John off," Travis said, diplomatically.

"Well, because logically, it means there's no falsifiable effect," I said. "Waving crystals over a broken leg—or over a broken radio—is just as appropriate as a splint or checking the connections. Look, Trav—Melody and I go around about this one a lot, you don't need to be caught in the middle. Suffice it to say that Melody thinks—"

"That she's still present, and she ought to say what she thinks for herself," she said.

"Uh, right. I was just about to say that."

"Did you ever tell him he's all right for a narrow-minded pompous old fossil?" Melody asked Travis, who glanced at me with an expression that said "Don't say a word about my age" just about as clearly as a kick in the shins could have. *More than one signifier can signify any given signified, and the choice of signifier signifies in and of itself,* I mentally quoted. "Anyway, I think there's an un-dismissable, unassimilable third factor: name something after a fad word and it just works better. And no matter how many individual cases you are able to reduce to physical or psychological causes, or to contamination of the reporting, you always end up with an irre-ducible remnant that work for no known physical cause—which are the only cases that everyone will agree are placebos. So by logical definition, when you study placebos, you're looking for something that works without having any reason to work, and the fact that there's anything to study means such things exist. There's a little bit of magic that's always just over the frontier, you see? That's what re-ally drives John crazy."

"But is the effect *real?*" Travis dropped a hand on my forearm while I was taking a deep breath. "I know you don't think so and I can see why, John, so let Melody answer, you sexist pig."

She winked at me, bless her. "You mean, really real, whatever re-ally means? Well, I say it's really real and John says it only looks real to every real observer, and we disagree about whether or not that's really the same 'real' or two different 'reals' or a 'real' and a 'not real.'"

"That's three sides and there's only two of you," Travis pointed out.

"We trade off. Like playing round-up baseball when you were a kid and didn't have enough players," I explained. "Anyway, that's the argument, and as usual Melody has put it better than I would have."

"And 'gaudeamus' is a fad word? Right now?"

Melody nodded so hard that the pile of brown hair on top of her head wobbled and threatened to spill down over her face. "'Gaudea-mus' is *exploding* as a fad word right now. I don't know why a mildly obscure one-word Latin sentence, meaning approximately 'Party on, dude,' has suddenly become the it-word, but web-search it, and you'll find hundreds and hundreds of references on the web, and thousands on Usenet, almost none of them older than six months. Everything and its brother—anything or its brother?—is being named 'gaudeamus.' "

"Except for me," I said. "I am being called a sexist pig by a redneck Texan."

"There are more things in heaven and Earth, Horatio . . ." Travis said. "Now prove you're really a theatre professor, and finish the quote."

CHAPTER TWELVE

I guess if the timing had anything to do with it, it was my fault. I kept finding ways to delay departing; since Kara had always liked Travis, and hated cooking, it wasn't too difficult to get her to come along for a late lunch-early dinner at Mario's, which is Gunnison's version of that good college pizza joint that every college town is legally required to have at least one of, before we finally departed. As we headed east, toward the massive swell of Tomichi Dome beyond the golden arches of the McDonald's, Travis said, "You really don't like science fiction conventions."

I shrugged. "Most sf writers complain about them. I'm just one of the few who actually avoid them. It's not easy because so many writers, and especially editors, used to be fans and they don't want to hear that you don't like fan stuff—the same way your favorite aunt or cousin doesn't want to know that you aren't coming to the family reunion because you hate most of your family, but you try not to mention it around your favorites." We were beyond the Gunnison town speed trap but we had to get through some miles of the favorite hunting grounds of Colorado state troopers, so I pushed it into fifth gear and sat back, letting gas mileage be merely crappy instead of execrable, hanging within a mile or two, give or take, of the speed limit. Besides, this valley was lousy with deer and elk—that's why we got a Texan infestation every fall—and early evening was their favorite time to be out.

"Aren't fans the ones who buy your books?"

"Not if you're doing well. Almost everyone who reads sci fi just *reads* it—heck, most of the readers don't even know that there are people in the world who get snotty about anybody calling it sci fi. I *love* those folks that just read it—or maybe occasionally drop me a note telling me that I'm a genius, I changed their life, and they'd like to have my babies. But those are the ones that call it sci fi and leave the paperback lying on the airplane seat when they're done, or dump all their city bus books at the Goodwill a couple times a year, and let it go at that. Fans means something different. Fans are the maybe one or two percent of sci fi readership that ever goes to a con or reads some online fannish thing. And fans are *weird*."

"No!" Travis started laughing, and I joined him.

"All right," I said. "I don't mean that. They aren't weird *enough*, in that sense—most of them have completely reactionary tastes in everything, haven't caught up with the painting of 1910 or the poetry of 1930, and many of them lead very circumscribed lives, like any suburbanite that belongs to a strange little church or anyone in a dead-end job who puts most of their attention into some all-consuming hobby. It would be good for most fans to get weirder, in that sense, and heck, a lot of them do. I *like* many of the ones that are genuinely weird. But I meant weird in that they're a weird demographic; their tastes are different from general readers. Not totally different, but different enough that they can skew your market sense. Fans read the stuff for different reasons than most readers, and if you start to write for fans . . . well, it's like what would happen if McDonald's started doing all their customer surveys along a hundred miles of the Rio Grande."

"They'd serve food with flavor?"

"They'd lose sales."

"Those aren't mutually exclusive, bud." He leaned back and said, "Damn pretty up here. Half a mile higher than Denver, you said? And two hundred miles away—"

"And fifty years into the past. Yeah. Drives me crazy every second that I don't love it, and I love it every second it doesn't drive me crazy."

"I think I'll add this place to my list of places to go out of my way to pass through," Travis said.

Dead ahead of us, Jupiter was coming up over the distant mountains; in the rearview I saw the very last glint of red sunlight flashing out across the West Elk, pursued down the sky by an unusually gold Venus. I remember thinking that it would have been nice to have more of a moon for this drive, but at least the pavement was dry and there wouldn't be fog to cope with. In the dim light, the cattle and horses in the fields might as well have been lawn ornaments on the biggest lawn you ever saw.

"How come that creek's so twisty?" Travis pointed to our right, to the winding tangles of curves that the ribbon of dark silver made on the mountain meadow.

"Tomichi Creek," I said. "A geologist friend drew me up a diagram of that once, when I asked him that question. I guess the short answer is that it's old and the ground doesn't slope much through here. You'll be all wrinkled too when you're old. Something like that."

"For a guy who puts that much science into books, you don't remember it very well."

"Actually the problem is I always remember more than I ever knew."

We roared past the little crossroads towns, Parlin and Doyleville, and it was full dark by the time we passed the Dome, which I knew was there only by the dark absence in the stars in my left peripheral vision. "Lot of stars out here," Travis said.

"We keep the extras that they don't want in the cities anymore."

The valley narrowed to a steep-walled canyon. Rock walls bounced in and out of my headlights between black voids. We came to the last broad part before the pass, the patch of soggy flat ground, mostly horse pasture, around Sargents. "This light coming up is your last chance for a pee or a candy bar till we're over Monarch," I said. "Twenty-three miles to the next anything."

"I'm good."

The truck started the long climb, roaring as if it were trying to intimidate the pass in front of us. Monarch is awesome in the sense that kids never mean anymore—a place that induces pure awe—with high peaks, steep dropoffs, bare rock faces, deep snow far into the summer, the kind of place that Christmas card painters and poster makers mean when they say "Colorado." It's also a frightening series of hairpin curves with very steep and far dropoffs, and one of several contributing factors to one of the less-pleasant aspects of life in Gunnison—everyone knows some people who died young. Monarch is dotted with numerous makeshift monuments, usually wooden or metal crosses surrounded by plastic flowers, bits of outdoor gear, teddy bears, that kind of thing, on both sides of the narrow two lanes of US 50, either along the steep stone wall, or just the other side of the guardrail, by the edge that drops off anywhere from fifty to two hundred feet. I had known three of the people that the crosses represented. There were many more than three crosses.

Tonight, though, we had the road almost to ourselves, till I saw a gray-brown mass ahead, for just an instant, in my bouncing hi-beams, and downshifted and braked, well short of a young bull elk, who was just wandering along the road, in my lane, with the usual expression of ruminant stupidity. He stopped to look back at us for an instant, as if to say, "Well, are you coming?"

"Can you imagine," I said as we followed at about five miles an hour, "that there are hunters who can't tell one of these guys from a deer? Grown men who can't distinguish between something this big, with a completely different head, and an ordinary deer? And that said grown men are allowed to run loose in the woods with liquor and guns?"

"Hell, John, I'm a Texan. I can imagine things that would blow your mind. But yeah. Uh, just out of curiosity, think we could pass this old boy?"

I shrugged. "We will when there's a good place to do it, and here is not one. Anyway, they don't stay on roads very long—they don't like them—so he'll probably move off soon. It's narrow here and a truck could come around that curve—"

I saw the glow of headlights and flashed mine rapidly and repeatedly until a big semi, pulling a City Market trailer, appeared. He had slowed to about ten, and crept by the elk and then me slowly; you can never tell what elk are going to do, and everyone has seen them just casually walk from the shoulder into the lane with a moving car almost on top of them. You just kind of have to hope that you won't be in that moving car at the time.

I could barely see the trucker waving through his windshield at me. I waved back. The elk had stopped to watch the truck pass, and so I stopped, and now I was about ten feet behind the elk. I drove slowly up to him, at about a mile an hour. He resumed walking in my lane.

"Maybe he's going to Denver too," Travis said. "Not in a hurry, though. Feels the same way as you do about sci fi conventions."

"Well, the summit tourist store is closed by this time of night, and Monarch ski area won't open for another few weeks, so he can't be headed this way to get a cap that says 'WORLD'S BEST GRANDMA' or a lift ticket. Maybe he's headed over to the roadhouse in Poncha Springs to grab a beer. But we've got a solution available now."

I pulled right and Travis grabbed the holy-shit handle above his window; as dark as it was out there, and as unfamiliar, for an instant it must have seemed that I was driving over a cliff, instead of into a wide truck pullout. I sped up slightly, cruised on around the elk, got back onto the road, and went on at a speed a little more appropriate to the twentieth, almost twenty-first, century.

"You couldn't have just crowded him till he got out of your way?"

"If I was driving an ambulance and lives were at stake, sure, I'd take a chance on that. Not when it's about just getting me to the geekfest. You can usually crowd them, but there's a little risk because now and then they get mad about that. And you saw how big they are. A deer will wreck your car by getting in front of it, if you're going fast enough; an angry elk can do a pretty good number on your car, with both of you starting from standing still. And when it comes to colliding at speed, well, a deer will wreck your car but an elk will kill you, especially if he goes up onto the hood, which they tend to do. So, call me a wimp—"

"Wimp."

"Call me a coward—"

"Coward."

"Oh, god, call me a cheap slut sex poodle, that's my favorite."

"Yuck."

A few miles later, as we wound down from Garfield to Maysville, Travis said, "So, um . . . your colleague, Melody Wallace . . . is she attached?"

"Not that I know of. And Gunnison is hell on the single. Once you've dated both the people in your age range there's not a lot of alternatives left. That have anything to do with your idea that you might be visiting more often?"

"Uh, everything."

"Well, she kind of obviously likes you too, you idiot."

We rolled past the yellow haunted house in Maysville, and on through Poncha Springs, the few streetlights at that crossroads suddenly blinding after all the long darkness, made the left turn onto 24, and headed up towards Johnson Village.

"So," he said, "it doesn't seem to me like skewing your market sense is really grounds for you to do more than avoid the fans, or politely decline invitations."

"Okay," I admitted, "so, they remind me of the guys I had to hang around with in high school because I couldn't find any better friends than that. Now that I'm allowed to sit down the table from the cool kids' clique, I don't want to spend time with the nerds anymore."

"Life is high school with money."

"Who said that?"

"Me, just now. Lots of other people before I think."

As we topped a rise, I was doing about eighty, taking a small risk of a ticket at that time of day—that area between Salida and Buena Vista is a notorious speed trap, because it's so dull that people try to get through it as fast as they can, there are lots of good places for cops to hide, and there are many short stretches where the limit is suddenly, unexpectedly lower.

Down the hill in front of my truck, a deer was running straight at me, in my lane.

The road was empty. I downshifted, let the engine howl up close to the red line, changed lanes, switched off the headlights so I wouldn't blind and hypnotize him. He was still plainly visible as a dark silhouette on the light blue of the road.

He changed lanes to match me, and he was getting much closer, still running full tilt.

I switched lanes back and braked, sounding the horn.

He switched lanes again to head straight for the middle of my bumper.

I switched lanes again and pushed the brake to the edge of skidding. The buck hesitated, then darted into my lane.

I locked the tires—not what you should do, just a pure tension reaction—and we skidded into him, doing about thirty or so, hitting him with the right front corner of the SUV.

The steering wheel kicked against the heels of my hands with a single, hard slam that I controlled with effort; crunch-bang of metal breaking around an empty space, over on Travis's side of the truck.

The deer bounced back in front of us, crossed the road in a sick cartwheel, and flopped and tumbled onto the shoulder to the left, neck obviously broken. I pulled the truck over onto the right shoulder, set the parking brake, put it in neutral, and left it running.

"Why are you—"

"Sometimes when they go partway under, especially on that side, they smash the starter," I explained. "I might be able to get this thing to a gas station on its own power if I don't turn it off." I grabbed the flashlight from the glove compartment and got out to take a look.

"Got a spare flashlight? I ought to take a look at the deer."

"In the glove compartment. Need a hunting knife for him, there's one there." If you drive in the mountains much, you get in the habit of carrying something of the kind.

"Thanks."

It was cold but dry that night, the kind of weather people hope for in hunting season. I had just an instant to note that without headlights, the sky was ablaze with stars, enough, even without the moon, to silver the snow on the Collegiate Peaks.

I was in an old sweatshirt and jeans, so I just got down on my belly and shone the flashlight upwards to get a good look. There wasn't much blood on the bumper, but it was partway off; the starter was half-buried in a tangle of bent metal, the radiator was leaking, and so many little braces and supports were broken and twisted that I wouldn't have bet on the battery not dropping onto the road sometime in the next few miles. "No good," I said. I got up, dusted myself off, reached into the car, and turned off the engine. "Have to call Triple A from here. Thank god for cell phones and the towers being all over around here."

"What will Triple A do?" Travis said, coming back from the deer.

"Tow it back to Gunnison. I can't afford to spend half a week in Salida or Buena Vista getting it fixed and I don't have any way to get to Denver now. Trip canceled. I'm sorry, Trav."

"Hmm." Travis grabbed up his bag; with our flashlights off, the lighter parts of his features glowed like dim, disconnected nebulae in the dark shape he cut out of the stars behind him. "Listen, John, how far is it to the nearest twenty-four-hour gas station?"

"Probably that would be either the Amoco in Poncha Springs or the Texaco up in Nathrop. Both of those are dot-on-the-map places with fewer than a hundred people. Just let me call a tow with the cell, Travis, there's no point in you heroically walking for help."

"I wasn't planning to be a hero," he said, "it's just that . . . hmm. Well, here's the thing, John. That old deer was dead. Like you'd figure, way he tumbled. But he was wearing a collar with a radio thing on it—"

"Oh, shoot," I said. "Must be a wildlife research project. There's going to be paperwork too."

"Would a Department of Wildlife collar have a lead going up from that collar to a metal jack that went straight into the back of his head? Or would Fish and Game collars carry an acid self-destruct, so that by the time that I looked that collar was melting and smoking?"

"What are you saying?"

"That deer was steered into us with that gadget which is now burning away on its neck. Officially such things don't exist but I've heard plenty about them in the black world."

I didn't know what to say.

"The other side found me again, John. I don't know why they haven't moved in yet, but they haven't, so I should get running before they show up. For your safety too, you know, bud. So which way's my nearest gas station? I should start moving quietly, one direction or the other. We closer to Poncha or to Nathrop?"

"Nathrop," I said. "Keep going the way we were going."

His hand fumbled at my right wrist for a moment, then gripped my hand and shook it. "Later," he said, and an instant later, I was alone by the road.

I called Triple A and got them headed out toward me; they said they'd take care of calling the staties.

It took an hour for the tow to get there, since the nearest available truck was actually the one at my favorite garage in Gunnison. While I waited, I got my flashlight and went to look at the mysterious cyber-deer that Travis had described, but found no deer there at all. Some blood and hair in spots where he'd touched down in his deadly tumble; a big bloody patch on the gravel. But nothing led away from there, no deer tracks, no trace of a vehicle, no footprints. And yet the deer was gone.

CHAPTER THIRTEEN

The day after Christmas, I'd gotten up at five-thirty in the morning, though it hadn't snowed. It had snowed, and heavily, a couple days before Christmas—if you want to be assured of having a white Christmas with icicles on the eaves, all the houses looking like melted cakes, all the trees holding big armfuls of snow, all the emergency rooms full of heart attacks and thrown-out backs, and all the streets full of nasty gray slush, you could do worse than move to Gunnison, Colorado (though you'd do even better in Crested Butte, a bit farther up the road). The town looks like Christmas looks on television and in most people's childhood memories (which, nowadays, are mostly of television).

Kara was going to see her family for the holidays, on a cheap flight at 6:35, Gunnison to Montrose to Tucson, where her sister was going to pick her up and they'd drive to LA together. It's a great flight—a glorious view of the "America's Switzerland" area around Telluride, and it nicks a corner of the Grand Canyon, and those are just the high points, on the way down to the soft warmth of the winter desert.

"Don't be jealous," Kara said when I kissed her good-bye at the airport. "You're the one that decided the book had to get done."

"One British publisher, the IRS, a bunch of doctors, and the credit card companies are the ones deciding that," I said. "I'm outnumbered. Have a good trip, hunh?"

"I'll try."

I stuck around the airport long enough to watch her plane take off and to start feeling sorry for myself; kicked myself in my mental butt for that; and drove home, about a three-minute drive. On the way I saw that the W Café was closed, so I went around the block, back onto Tomichi, and saw that the Quarter Circle, the other good breakfast place in Gunnison, was open. It was even a shorter walk from my house.

I parked, went inside, and fed the cats. They were all wandering around mewing, the way they did when they were disappointed by my having allowed Kara to escape, which they regarded as very poor management. Since I hadn't bothered to take off my coat, I walked right out the door and down Colorado Street, the packed snow crunching under my boots; it's easier to walk in the street than on those sidewalks, where the city plow trucks leave head-high mountains of snow, and fresh sheets of ice form every afternoon.

If you like it quiet, you owe it to yourself to try Gunnison, Colorado, just before dawn on December 26th. It seemed as if I could hear the bits of carbon banging against each other in the smoke rising in slow, perfectly vertical columns from every chimney, and the crackle of my breath freezing onto my beard. I could hear the occasional crunch or squeal of my duck galoshes on the snow, my own breathing, and almost, it seemed, the slow soft beat of my heart. Between the blinding pools of the streetlights, I could see that the sky was just beginning to creep from black to deep blue, and the dusty haze of dimmer stars was being cleared out, leaving just the bright ones shining.

The Quarter Circle has been rebuilt and remodeled so much that only the center part of the outside facade reveals its origins as a just-post-WWII hamburger stand. Inside, it's what you're always hoping for when you stop in a family restaurant in a small town— scrupulously clean, neat, decorated with some pencil sketches and watercolors, rungbacked hardwood chairs, and those tough modern unstainable tables. Big windows let in all that mountain sunlight. It's where the ranch guys come to sit and have coffee during the off season, when most of the day's work is done by 7:00 A.M.; there's a senior-citizen crowd, a college faculty crowd, and usually a prayer group of townspeople on any given morning, plus whoever drifts over from the hotels across the street or just wanders in because they like the place. If you've been there a few times, you'll have shaken the owner's hand and you'll be greeted by name; it's the kind of place that is more common in the movies than in real life, which indicates that real life could use some fixing.

On the day after Christmas, it was as close to deserted as I'd ever seen it in the morning—only about half full. Cattle don't know it's the day after Christmas and neither do the stomachs of the men who feed and tend them; old people get lonelier even than usual on that day; so those crowds were a bit overrepresented, compensating for the people who were sleeping in, or still stuck at home putting up with family and holiday stuff.

I vaguely wished I'd brought a book, but service was so fast that it hardly mattered. I was just sprinkling Tabasco and ketchup on the eggs when a familiar voice said, "Well, hey, I was gonna walk up to your house, but I was hungry, and here you are."

"Travis!"

"Right on the first guess." He was standing by my table, his old duffel bag slung over his shoulder, wearing a couple of raggwool sweaters, a heavy denim jacket, a hunter's flap-eared hat, and Bean snowsneakers, which is to say, dressed like half the local population. "It's the accent that gives me away, isn't it?"

"Have a seat. Get some breakfast. This place is good. How have you been?"

"Well," he said, "most recently, I've been freaking cold, but I got lucky and got a ride with a trucker all the way from Cañon City, and decided I'd rather come here where there was likely to be a warm place, than stay there and hope for a ride to Saguache, which was less likely, especially day after Christmas. So that's the recent history. In the longer run, it's been a tale or two. Or six. Several of which got to the weird part and then just kept going. The story as a whole is kind of a long one."

"How much coffee, and how long have you been up?"

"There's a twenty-four-hour truck stop right outside Cañon City," he said, "which is about the only place you can get a ride there, since the prison's right there and right near the highway. Got into Cañon real early last night and had been up for twenty-four then. So I went to bed about seven, couldn't sleep no later than four, got up, slung up the bag, sat and drank coffee and looked for a ride till one came through. That old trucker was filling up two one-gallon thermoses to keep himself going, and we drank it pretty much continuous all the way here. So I guess I'm a little wired; a nine-hour nap followed by maybe a half gallon of coffee. I'll try to pause for breath now and then. Where's old Kara?"

"With her family—or actually, she's landing in Montrose, right now, on her way to visit her family," I said. "Are you still working for Xegon? How did that case come out?"

"I'm still working for Xegon, and it *hasn't* come out, yet. With a good pot of coffee or three, you could hear at least a little more of the story, and then if you like, maybe even go see a tiny bit of it—might involve a little driving, this evening."

"What a surprise," I said.

"Aw, don't be that way. If it wasn't for me, you'd never go anywhere." He reached into his wallet and pulled out a check. "This is what the guy at the Standard station told the Xegon folks that repairs to your truck cost."

He handed me a check; it was made out to me and drawn on a Xegon account at a First Interstate in Albuquerque, and it was accurate to the penny, if you counted an exact $250 lagniappe thrown in.

"Well," I said, tucking it into my wallet, "it certainly does improve a guy's mood. I thought for sure I'd get a note from you or something when *Gaudeamus* did the series about 'Robodeer, Enemy of the 4Runner.' I mean, Harris McParris even had Triple A, and Robodeer's real name was Poncha. How could there be that many details?"

"Actually, I wasn't reading *Gaudeamus* right then—if you've saved it, I'd like to. I was kind of busy *living* a pretty good story, all that time."

I didn't really want to be grouchy with an old friend, and besides my life had just improved drastically in the last few minutes—I wouldn't be moping around the house all by myself, I had an unexpected windfall (since I'd already paid to have the truck fixed), and besides there was apparently going to be a good story in this one. So I gave up trying to be crabby, and my old friend sat down and we carried on like old friends.

Presently I asked him, "Can you tell me any part of the story here in public, or is this another wild one?"

"Oh, I can get started. Fill the rest in later. And like that. What were you going to do today, though?"

"Sit around, read books I'd already read, play with the cats, try to get up the ambition to do some housework. Same things I always do the first day that Kara's away. That place feels so big without her."

"And how about this evening and tonight? You up for a drive?"

"Where to?"

"Down to Saguache. To a roadhouse called 'The Mutilated Cow.' Where we're going to see a band called Skin2Skin. Or rather they're playing, and I'm going there to see their manager, Jenapha Lee."

"Jennifer—"

"She's respelled it, J-E-N-A-P-H-A, and she makes a point of that final A. Like nigga or sista. And if you call her Jennifer, she acts like a nigga that's been called a nigger. Anyway, she's Skin2Skin's manager, I'm mad-dog-bugfuck in love with her, and it's all thanks to that goddam guided deer that wrecked your truck. And they're playing at the Mutilated Cow tonight. Now, you want to go soak up some weirdness?"

"I have the weirdest feeling that I don't really have any choice."

Travis called the waitress over and basically ordered one of everything. I reflected on the unfairness of the fact that he was still wearing his college pants size.

When he'd acquired a coffee cup of his own, and begun to chase his morning load of coffee with more coffee, he said, "Actually, John, you're welcome to just hang back here in Gunnison if you like. And I'll still tell you the story. But I kind of thought you might like to get an actual look at some of the participants. And it does get pretty strange here and there, so maybe you can treat it as research or something."

"Well," I admitted, "it has to be more fun than sitting on the couch, re-reading a Lawrence Block mystery and wondering why I can't get myself into motion enough to clean the cat box. Almost for sure. Is the band any good?"

"They suck, but they suck in a very important way. Jenapha Lee, or one of the band, will explain that part tonight."

So I listened, and Travis talked, through his gigantic breakfast, which he washed down with another half gallon of coffee. I always wondered why moths didn't fly at his eyes.

Well, to begin with, John, I really wanted to do something about that dead deer. I could hear you back there talking to yourself, mad as hell about everything, and on flat land in a mountain valley, on a clear night like that, sound carries a long way. I figured that, excuse my saying it, but it's true, you'd be even less able to defend yourself than usual, and right then, mad as you were and noisy as you were being, probably a company of infantry could sneak up on you. So I wanted to make sure that whatever it was that was after me didn't accidentally get you. And I figured they'd home in on a transponder or something on our friend Buck Cyborg, so the thing to do about that dead deer was to get him moved.

I was just thinking about that, real hard, standing there beside the deer and still hearing you cuss up a storm at the universe. Trouble was, I was also thinking about not wanting to take a long walk with both a duffel bag and a dead deer on my shoulders in the middle of the night.

Then a beat-up old pickup came along, going the other way, with just his parking lights on and real slow. I stuck out my thumb and the guy stopped—one thing I like about your part of the country, people will stop to pick up a guy who might be in trouble, rather than let him freeze his ass off. As he pulled onto the shoulder, the ass end of that dead deer was right in those parking lights.

And he got out, and said, "Hey, Travis, Travis Bismarck? Wash U's best-known Nazi redneck baby killer?"

Well, wet my shorts if it wasn't Brown Pierre.

He was pretty much the same guy as he'd been twenty-some years ago, when you and I used to watch him pick fights with the world on behalf of all the little furry woodland animals. Hell, you know. I hadn't seen him since 1978, I'd guess, and here he was, probably still going on the same shirt, pants, haircut, and maybe bath. He fit in pretty well out here, your basic mountain hippie redneck, except for being gigantic, and even that kind of worked. Nowadays he wears wire-rimmed glasses, and ties that hair back in a long gray greasy ponytail that looks like fifty well-oiled house-rat pelts sewn together, and so many shredded-out flannel shirts that I kind of think he must just put fresh ones on as the outer layers wear down. He also had on a pair of greasy old jeans, those dumb-ass tire-tread sandals that never wear out, trucker wallet on a chain, and a cell-phone holster.

We listened to you being rude to the Triple A lady—aw, shit, John, don't argue, I *heard* you and I got a witness—and decided that maybe this wasn't the time for reunion week. I didn't explain everything because he grinned and said, "Well, damn, it's nice to find a guy with some muscles, that I happen to know. Look, I'm not going as far as Salida, but I'm going most of the way, and you wouldn't have too bad a walk to Poncha Springs from where I *am* going. I have sort of a, uh, delivery route for a man who has a little old pharmaceutical business—just herbal if you know what I mean—and I usually stay the night with a real nice lady that's about to be my last stop, right up by Poncha Springs. Save you a lot of walking. Now, I'm still vegan, but this is good meat, and it's no-body's fault that it's dead, and she and those kids are *not* vegan—and frankly a little protein in the diet would be a good thing in that house. And otherwise this will just end up being picked up by the highway patrol and thrown in a landfill—they don't leave 'em out for coyotes anymore. Now, a ride from me will save you a good two hours—you want to help me get that deer into the back of my truck?"

"Sure," I said. "I'll even take the heavy end." That's the head, of course, and in the dark, I kept that Brown Pierre from seeing the funny collar, which was way up on the neck. If anybody was using a locator or something to track it, the trail would head back for a while, then end up in the backyard, among the other trash, behind some ganja-mama's hippie shack.

Well, we only took maybe three minutes between talking, deciding, and heaving that deer up—oh, so you did look, later on, and you saw no traces that we'd taken it? Just out of curiosity, John, are you any kind of tracker? And that shoulder was dry hard-packed gravel, and we didn't drag him since we wanted to preserve that meat and didn't want to get any more blood around than we had to—so of course there wasn't much sign, except for that splash of blood, that we'd been there.

Anyway, Brown Pierre had quite a bit of good quality dope in a little metal box under the chassis, and getting stopped with roadkill in the truck bed would get him searched, so he needed to be careful. He drove exactly the limit and obeyed every law, but he didn't turn his lights on till we were over the hill from you, because he didn't want anyone marking a place where his truck had stopped for a while and coming down to see what that was about.

It was maybe a ten-minute ride to Leslie-Sue's place, and once we got away from the scene of the bambicide, he launched into one of his enviro lectures just like there hadn't been a twenty-year interruption in it, everything about the intrinsic destructiveness of human beings and all that. I don't know if he breathed once in the whole time.

But despite all that, getting a little deer blood on me and doing a little work, it was worth it. We went on by you, and the net effect was that I had doubled back and taken that possibly traceable deer with me, a win all around. When we got there, Leslie-Sue, the predictable big soft fat lady, came running out to hug him, and about three thousand kids all ran out to jump up and down and tell him everything in the world. I was invited for the night, with a suggestion of threesies, but since I like my ladies bathed, I kind of said duty was calling me, and took off. Besides, there might be a few questions I didn't want to answer, if it should happen that they got a good look at that radio collar and the wire leading into the thing's brain.

I slung up my bag and trotted back to 24, like I intended to walk the fifteen minutes to Poncha Springs and work from there, then doubled back in the dark and headed north again. This time I needed to get thoroughly lost, so I was going to take the first road that wasn't just a ranch access, off to either side, and go from there.

As it turned out, the first road I came to was to the left, and said it led to the Mount Shavano ski area, which was kind of perfect—it was a warm enough night, so if I kept moving I wouldn't freeze, and that time of year, there'd be setup crew already up there and probably I could beg a floor to sleep on and a ride in the morning. Had my jogging shoes on, so it was just a matter of picking'em up and putting'em down till I got there.

After about a mile I saw something off to the side, just a ribbon of smooth darkness beside the road, and realized how much I was in modern Colorado. This was a barely-paved road leading up to a ski area, running mostly through cattle pastures, but there was a brand-new smooth modern bicycle trail down there beside it. I dropped down the next low point at a bank and started jogging on that; less risk of being seen, and a better, safer surface. It was getting truly late, and I'd been up forever, so I kept breaking into a run for a while, to help stay awake.

Probably about two in the morning, when pasture had given way to mountain passes and if I didn't keep moving I'd feel how chilly it was, the sign said I was only three miles from the Shavano ski area, which meant if I just kept moving it was all going to work out fine. Orion was just rising, coming up over the mountains bow-first like he was on a commando raid across the sky, and my eyes had become so starlight-adjusted that I could pick out most of the shapes I needed to easily, especially with nice bright Jupiter bang overhead.

The bicycle trail swung away from the road to switchback its way down a ravine to a bridge; in daylight I might have chanced cutting off some switchbacks, but here in the dark I really didn't want to turn an ankle a long way from help, and then have to wait till somebody came along in the morning.

I was rounding the right turn around the end of the third switchback, just starting to notice how dark it was getting down here, when it got just a little brighter, as if a crescent moon had come out from behind the clouds—and yet there was no moon.

Just beyond and below the ridge, a bright light was moving around, apparently in the sky, without any sound. The road was the other way, so it wasn't just headlights, and anyway, I was hearing the gurgle of the creek a hundred yards away—those mountains are *quiet* late at night—and if there'd been an engine I'd've heard it. So I just quietly trotted back to see if I could see anything from the trail.

I was looking up the draw toward a low saddle, covered thick with pine trees. Right above it were fistfuls of bright stars flung all over the deep blue of the sky—and it was a real deep indigo-blue, not black, because something big was glowing and moving around back there. I looked down at my feet. In the light bouncing over the ridge from whatever the hidden, glowing object was, I could see a dirt trail that took off up towards the saddle so maybe it went there—you know how mountain trails are, who knew what it might do when it bent into the trees a dozen yards away?

You know me, John, the Bismarck family motto is "What the hell." I figured I'd follow the trail till it wasn't going where I wanted to go, then turn back. That light in the sky, and that trail pointed that way, were just too interesting to walk on by.

It was dark and stumbly as I went up out of the draw, and I about kissed a couple of trees that I hadn't been introduced to, and one part of me kept expecting to do something truly lame-ass dumb, trip over a mama bear or something, but instead, once it was further from the bike trail, the trail straightened out and became smoother; by the skyglow I could see it had been graveled, and maybe even tarred a little. I could've ridden a bike on it.

Now that I knew I was onto something, and that I was unlikely to lose my way back, I put my rear in gear and charged on up that saddle to see what I could see. And unlike the bear that went over the mountain, I found a lot to see.

I left the trail just before it summited, and went up between two trees, over a big old freeze-ass cold boulder. And lying on top of that, and looking into the draw below, I saw a mountain cabin. Nothing rusticky and old-timey—this was one of those split-level lots-of-deck golden-varnished-wood things that rich people put up around here, the kind of thing that looks like it belongs in the tony suburbs of Rivendell. Light was glaring and flashing off all that glass in all those windows, and gleaming off the propane tank. No wonder it had been bright enough to be noticeable over the saddle.

The source of the light was a slowly descending flying saucer, about thirty feet across the flat cylindrical part, with a stick-out bevel that put maybe another six foot on the radius, the whole thing about seven foot thick. It was painted dull gray, like autobody primer, with no markings; if the dark squares on the upper surface of its beveled sides were windows, no light came from them. It had a single fin that rose from its center to about five feet above its rim, in a long smooth curve that was maybe parabolic or elliptical or one of them, I can't remember how you tell the difference anymore.

It was making no sound but there was light around it, gold-white flickering light like a hot campfire.

It set down on the grass. The flickering light couldn't be too awful hot because it didn't affect the grass at all. I slid down the rock in front of me and trotted down the trail to the next swichback turn, hoping to see better.

Two reasons why that was a mistake. One reason it was a mistake, I missed a lot in those few seconds of sneaking around. Next time I got a good look, the boarding ramp had already dropped, so I'd missed that part, and the flickering had gone out, so I wasn't seeing as well, but that was partly made up for by the bright ordinary light coming from inside. In that light, as it spilled across the cabin's yard, I could clearly see two clowns, in big baggy pajamas, orange hair, white face paint, and round red rubberball noses, but with strangely normal-sized feet, get out and run down the ramp with bags of something over their shoulders.

The second reason it was a mistake was that I'd already been spotted and I was moving into a more vulnerable position.

I found that out a minute later, while I was watching the ramp fold up after the two clowns had gone back and forth one more time. A guy behind me whipped a big old burlap sack over my head, followed by a loop of rope, and all of a sudden I was bagged up neat and clean. The rope tugged hard, once, while I was still yelling in surprise, and I fell backwards onto the trail, my hands pinned to my side and that bag over my head. I felt the cuffs going around my ankles even as I was kicking and yelling. Then they dragged me down to that cabin by the rope, bouncing and thumping all over the trail, like I was the coon and they were setting up coon dog trials, only I didn't think they'd let me just climb a tree and wait for the dog pack when we got to the end.

CHAPTER FOURTEEN

They chained the cuffs holding my feet to a post on the porch of that cabin, and told me that if I kicked around and ended up hanging head down over the side of the deck, from that chain, my arms crushed against my sides, they'd be just as happy. Then they cut a hole in that bag with a box knife, so I could breathe better, and then cut away some of the burlap around my hands and cuffed my wrists together before they undid the rope loop. I wasn't feeling great but at least I could breathe now, the bag had protected me from the worst of the scrapes if not from the bruises, and they were acting like, while they might not care if they hurt me, they weren't especially out to do it, either.

"Travis Bismarck," a voice I didn't recognize said. "This is Travis Bismarck. I just beat the fuck out of him the night before last, and here he is again."

The figure that swam into my field of view was very tall and dressed, like the others, as a clown, but something about the ready-to-go way he carried himself was familiar, and I said, "Umm, yeah, you'd be the guy that visited me in my hotel room, wouldn't you?"

He laughed. "'Visited.' I hope you don't 'visit' your mother in the hospital. Yeah, I looked a little different at the time. Shitfire, man, you get around. I think we've just decided you're a major nuisance. Which is not as bad as it might sound." The big clown turned to the three smaller clowns beside him. "This is the one that trashed Elvis and tried to take the Gaudeamus box back—the one I beat up at the hotel. Detective, based out of Billings, working for Xegon, reports to Hale there, and he's had a dose of the Gaudeamus pill so watch what you think."

The smallest clown said, in a woman's voice with a distinct Memphis twang, "Well, I'm impressed. What do we do with him?"

"Let's start off by taking him inside and making sure he doesn't get away," the big clown said. By now I was picking up that slight grunted enunciation that meant he grew up on the res, probably spent some time at boarding school, and then had lived among whites for a long time, since it was faint; one of the Northern Plains nations, I guessed. "Sorry, Travis Bismarck, but you've pretty well convinced me that you can put up a good fight, so we'll have to drag you, since I don't want to untie you."

I cooperated as much as I could, not seeing any reason to get my head bashed any more than it already was. They were less rough than they had been while dragging me down the trail. The living room they carried me into might have been any affluent Dallas or Atlanta family's "Christmas house," used only for a few weeks around the holidays—clunky-looking sorta-Southwest-Mission peeled-log furniture, godawful Bev Doolittle puzzle picture stuff on the walls, a bunch of dreamcatchers just in case anybody ever happened to have a dream, the whole thing suggesting that the residents liked being Westerners (for about three weeks out of the year) and felt real bad about the Indians. They set me down on a thick rubber-and-poly rug in a Taiwanese approximation to a Hopi pattern, which lay on the hardwood floor (of course there aren't many hardwoods in Colorado, but pine and fir are known to be cheap) that had been painted with polyurethane to make it shiny and golden yellow.

My mom would have loved that place, John, and here I was tied up on its floor. I felt like such a failure at life.

"Now what do we do with him?" the smallest, female clown asked.

"Hey, this was as far as I thought of," the big clown admitted. "Travis, are you uncomfortable? More than from just being tied up?"

"Can I squirm over to lie on my side?"

"Go ahead."

So I did. "The problem is," the big clown said, "we said no unnecessary killing before we started, and since we're going to be basically on the same side with Xegon and Hale and all, eventually, I'd think killing a hired gun working for Hale would be a very bad idea and we shouldn't do it."

I liked the way he thought.

"But we can't let him go," one of the medium-size clowns said. He took out one of those long, thin, extra-nasty-smelling cigaroids and lit it, absently pulling off his big red nose. "At least not till we have some kind of a deal with everyone involved, all the good guys on board and on the same side."

"Well, technically, we only need to talk to Hale," the other medium clown said. They were very hard to tell apart. Both of them had that faint trace of res in their accents, as well. "But he's not going to be very happy after Elvis killed that poor lady. And he's not going to believe that we tried to tell that whiskey-bum idiot stink to be careful and not to shoot it into her neck. Hale will look at that and say it was on purpose. Even if he does believe it was an accident, he's not going to be happy."

"It *was* on purpose," I said. "I was Gaudeamus-linked to him and he was mad at you for telling him not to."

"Yeah, Lena said that too," the big clown, who seemed to be the leader, said. "Let's face it. Elvis is a total fuckup and we should never have brought him in at all."

"We could let Hale have Elvis as a sign of good faith," the female clown said.

"He's our brother," the big one objected.

"And a total fuckup," the smoking clown said. "A stink total fuckup, that's our brother. And now that he's hurt, he'd be worth more traded off than he would on the team. In fact he was even before he got hurt. Every fuckup we've had was Elvis, at the root of it."

"Fuck you, cousin, I hate it when you're right," the big clown said. "Okay, he still listens to me. I'll square it with Elvis—which will take some squaring, since he's gonna be up on a murder rap—which one of us calls Hale?"

"Um," I said. "Considering you shot him, I don't know if Hale is going to be in a forgiving mood. I kind of doubt it. Even if you do let him have Cheryl's murderer, which he wants very much."

Even through the makeup I could see them wince at "murderer," which reminded me that it wasn't smart to irritate them, but at the same time it was sort of reassuring that they didn't like to hear the word.

After a long moment, the female clown said, "Hale's been shot? Is he hurt bad?"

I stared at her. "Are you trying to tell me that you all didn't do it?"

"If somebody did, it wasn't us. Most likely it was the Glasgow organization. Did they come in with a lot of armed force?"

"I don't know but they did it at the facility at Kirtland," I said. "Who are the Glasgow organization?"

"Oh, man," the big clown said, pulling off his round red nose.

"Oh, man, man, man. Yeah, if you don't even know who they are, you boys'll get chewed up like what happens when the dog eats cat puke. We gotta make contact and get you on board with us right away; if we wait there won't be much left of you. Is Hale hurt bad?"

"I've only talked to him on the phone since he got shot, not seen him. He sounded okay then, but not too all-fired cheerful. I'm supposed to meet him in Denver in about, oh, five and a half hours if it's three o'clock A.M. right now."

There was a very long pause.

"You know," the big clown said, obviously still thinking, "if we do this right, we could meet with Hale, with Travis here present as a witness and/or hostage (which might not be a bad thing to have). If we deal right with Hale, then we can also hand over Elvis and get him locked up where he can't fuck things up or get hurt himself. We've all said we wanted to get him some help, too. And if we do that we can get everybody on task on our side, because the fucking Glasgow people just whipped our ass for the, what, nth time in a row?" He scratched his head and flakes of clown white fell onto the sofa around him. "Of course we've pissed Hale off enough so that he might still show up with fifty soldiers and try to capture us. But I bet he won't if he thinks it might endanger Travis. You know how he is, he looks after his people, hey?" He looked down at me. "Will you cooperate enough to get released? Neither you nor Hale will be hurt, I can promise you. We'll even tell you who we are and let you see some of what we're doing, before we go meet Hale. Is it a deal?"

"I think so," I said. "It beats lying here on the floor for the next several hours, and besides, I really gotta pee. My cell phone has Hale's private cell number programmed—you can reach him there. Now can you allow me enough parole to let me get some relief, and then maybe we'll talk in more detail?"

✢   ✢   ✢

So they let me pee and even let me have a shower, and I persuaded them to call Hale and say they were going to release me to him, because I didn't want to be the one who lured him into a trap; if they were going to trap him I preferred to be innocent bait, not part of the scheme. Getting to like that overbred fishface, I guess.

They set up a meeting at some roadside rest outside Denver, out east where there's nothing but miles and miles of miles and miles, and they did all that while I got a long overdue deep nap on that sofa.

By the time I awakened, the sun was up, a very sulky Elvis was cuffed in a chair across the room from me, and they didn't look like clowns anymore.

Of course I had seen the big one without clown makeup, but this time I got a little more leisure to look him over. He was still big, and with more light and less anxiety (I knew he was capable of pounding the shit out of me but he wouldn't be doing it right then), I saw his face had a couple of small scars, and his arms were marked by old, fading, distorted tattoos. But he didn't have the skin damage or the worn expression of a guy who'd had a drinking problem, or lived on the street, or any of that. Actually he looked pretty healthy and prosperous, for a guy in his early thirties, who had obviously been down some hard roads.

His belly was flatter than not, and he moved like, if he needed to, he could really move. "Kermit Irwin," he said, sticking his hand out. I shook with him—if he wanted to be friendly, hey, I already knew how much it beat the alternative. "Professor of physics at Fort Lupton Lutheran College—in fact I'm the department—lead and only guitar in Skin2Skin, general purpose guy who can't stay out of trouble. I am sorry about beating you up like that. It seemed like a good idea at the time."

"No hard feelings unless I grow several inches and spend a while bodybuilding," I said, and we shook.

The younger of the middle-sized clowns was obviously Kermit's brother, with the same bronze-brown skin, and was smoking another one of those vile shitstrings that Hollywood always has the good sense to put in the mouths of villains. He was headed for pudgy already, despite being maybe twenty-four, and other than the fact that he was plastering his lungs with asphalt, looked healthy. He also looked angrier than the others, and was in process of finding his missing mirrorshades by pacing around, turning things over, and yelling at people that he couldn't find them. He only kind of grunted and said, "Yeah, yeah," when introductions were happening, so the other middle-sized clown said, "This is Jake Irwin. He's our brother, lead singer, and, when he's in a better mood, our best computationalist and programmer."

"Uh, I seemed to be getting a little confused about who you guys are," I said.

The older guy, who had been the other middle-sized clown, walked in, brushing his iron-gray hair, which fell to the middle of his back—he was brushing and braiding it as we talked—and said, "Man. Oh man. Confused about who we are. You really want to be careful. If you get confused *enough* about who we Irwin brothers are, you might *become* an Irwin brother. Based on the fact that the people *most* confused on the subject *always* turn out to be Irwin brothers."

He had that same over-emphasizing style you have, John, and your friend Melody does—another professor, sure as shit.

"Well, anyway, I'm Esau Irwin. I am also the twin of Elvis, who you beat up, and who is a jackass fuckup but our brother, so we always try to do something for him."

"Hey, fuck you, hey," Elvis said, from his chair.

"If you want to suck up to me tell me that we're nothing alike. The three of us, together, are Skin2Skin, sort of a band. Jake sings lead, and Kermit plays guitar—"

"Or tries," Kermit said.

"—because you can't have a band without a guitar, and I work an electronic drum-and-vibe-driven synthesizer that Kermit and I whacked together for fun one weekend. Whenever Elvis is sober we put him out front with an old drum, unamplified, and he helps the white middle-class kids in the dreads feel all tribal and native and Earthy-Earth and stuff, and we play so goddam loud that, thank god, nobody ever hears him."

"Hey," Elvis said. "Hey. I'm the only real Indian in the band. I am the only real Indian. How you like that?"

No need for Esau to tell me he was a professor, he also had that riding-over-hecklers thing that you and Melody and all your colleagues have, John, and he had it perfect. He just kept going. "Kermit and I are PhDs, him in physics, me in math, and if it weren't for having to save the world, we'd both be reasonably happy professors at godforsaken little dumps that they pass off for colleges."

"Fuckin' apples, there's only one *skin* in the room."

"Jake will get his Ph.D. as soon as we get the world saved, I think."

I was about to ask about that flying saucer, which struck me as being the one little detail that somehow seemed out of place—you know how us detectives watch out for details that are out of place, John, I'm sure you watch movies. But before I could ask, the voice of the female clown—a soft little-girl Memphis drawl—said, "And I'm Jenapha Lee. I'm the manager, agent, and accomplice for Skin2Skin."

I turned around and—oh, Lord, John. There's words like "thunderstruck" and "smitten" and they don't half cover what this was. She had that kind of mixed-blonde hair that grows in ash-blonde and finishes out, if it gets some sun, pale gold, and it rippled and tangled all the way down to her waist, like she'd been painted into existence by a pre-Raphaelite. She had a sweet little snub nose and huge green eyes (they turned out to be contacts, but at the time it just grabbed me), and she was just fat enough, like somebody had sat down and designed the woman that would most turn me on in the world, a comfy tummy roll that would feel so good against me but never get in the way, and big old sagging full *tits,* John, I mean, the girl had *tits,* and thighs that were made to be pillows—oh, all right, sure, on with the story. Anyway, she also had thin little pursey lips, the kind that twist all over the place when she's being ironic, and she was working them now, saying, "I keep trying to get these guys out of the saving the world business to concentrate on music and getting somewhere. I don't have much luck."

Mentally I checked. My mouth wasn't hanging open. I was doing about as well as I could.

She was wearing a soft white dress, one of those clingy-stretchy things that the catalogs are full of, and heeled sandals, and her toenails were freshly done in baby-pink—

Oh, all right, John, but I don't see why there can't be some interesting stuff in the story, besides all these facts.

"It's just that you know we don't share tastes in female bodies—"

"You munchkin-molesting leprechaun-jumper," Travis said.

"Well, we don't. I don't wish every woman in the world was drawn by R. Crumb. And I also know that once you start talking about someone to your taste, it runs a while. And I want to hear more of this story. Now, Esau Irwin?" I asked. "Wait a minute. I know Esau Irwin. He teaches math at Durango—Fort Lewis College."

"Well, yep, he's real," Travis said. "You didn't think I was making all this stuff up, did you? Everybody else in the story is real, too."

By now we'd walked back to my house and were hanging out in the living room, Corner securely curled up in Travis's lap and obviously intending to stay there forever. I'd made up a pot of coffee but neither of us had touched it yet.

"Now, look," I said. "Your average three brothers with math talent—even three brothers right off the res—what nation are they, anyway?"

"Well, I was wrong about them being right off the res. They grew up in Great Falls. Their mom was kind of unwelcome with the relatives, because she shacked up for twenty-five years with an *East* Indian—an engineer from India that had a little business in precision machining—has to have been one of the very few Indian-Indian marriages and god knows how all that worked out. She had twins, then Kermit twelve years later, then Jake almost ten years after that, so I gotta say, they were well-spaced from a paying-for-college standpoint, but that's sure a big chunk of your life. So far apart in age, though, that they basically raised each other, after she got the twins raised. Then that engineer died, right after Jake was born, and she died when he was about ten, and there you have it.

"The boys got tough like her, and smart like him, and raised each other. They fought their way through all the Indians that would pick on them because they were breeds, and through all the black and white kids who didn't know what they were but it was different and they knew they didn't like that, and they never did have any contact with their dad's family, and here they are, the best combination genius scientific team and suck-dog awful tech-punk band since *Buckaroo Banzai,* or at least the best Indian-Indian one to come out of Montana in the last ten years. If you want them to be the best (as a band) the one thing you've got to do is figure out some definition for which they're the only. Because if there are two bands in a category, and one of them is Skin2Skin, you can trust me, the other one will be better." Travis shifted his lap as Corner stretched and yawned; he rubbed the big idiot cat's head, and the cat settled back into bliss. "See, your cat knows the truth when he hears it."

"I'm just glad he has you to climb instead of the Christmas tree," I said.

"I wouldn't think this beached whale of a cat would move any more than between the couch and the food dish."

"He likes the tree," I said. "He likes to whack the balls."

Travis looked down at him; the cat looked up blurrily. "Do not think of me as a tree substitute, hairball."

Corner purred, curled, and went to sleep.

"Look," I said. "I know that this area is crawling with flying saucer stuff. Especially over Cochetopa Pass and down into the San Luis Valley. There've been sightings there for decades. But that's also the La Veta Military Operations Area, and they test all kinds of military aircraft, including the ones we test for our allies, down there. And I know lots of people who have seen lots of things. One buddy of mine looked up from a deer blind once and saw nothing but metal—a saucer, maybe three hundred feet across, sitting less than fifty feet above him. He got out of the blind, waved, gestured at his blind and his setup to tell them they were spoiling the hunting. Maybe they got it, maybe they hadn't known he was there and were supposed to avoid being seen, who knows, but they went from silently hovering at fifty feet to a dot in the sky—just as silently—in half a minute, then shot over the horizon. But *that* saucer had a great big USAF painted on its underside. Did those three guys build their saucer in the garage or something?"

"Naw, it was a lot easier to accept once I realized it was the standard model Air Force Boeing SR-8. Basic utility, training, or search-and-rescue saucer. There's two squadrons of them flying out of Twining AFB down in Kennedy County, Texas."

"I never heard of Twining—"

"And it will be at least another five years before anyone does, but it's been there since they set it up to play with captured foo-fighters in 1946. Anyway, the Irwins, plus Lena Logan and Jenapha Lee, *are* Negon Corporation, which has a research facility there, and they have some borrowing privileges when they need them."

"The only SR I ever heard of is the SR-71—"

"Oh, yeah, I built one of those models when I was a kid, too. They're cool-looking but not good for much; they go fast and high but they're not steady enough to make good camera platforms and anyway they'd be too easy to intercept. Basically the SR-71 Blackbirds supply the alibi for photos that obviously can't have come from a satellite, by going out over the ocean, turning around, and coming back. So they named that big fast plane the SR-71 because it helps to confuse the other side about what they are—like the way the British called armored fighting machines 'tanks' and radar 'carrots,' or we called the atomic bomb project the 'Manhattan Engineering District,' it's not just a code word, it actually helps to throw the other side off; there were German pilots pounding down beta-carotene and German spies crawling around Manhattan, which helped to keep them out of trouble. So they named it the SR-71 because that way, if a photo or a radio intercept accidentally got loose with 'from AF SR something' on it, people would assume it was a high-altitude reconnaissance plane.

"But actually SR is the Air Force designation for a flying saucer, like FB for fighter-bomber. All those supposed SR-71 photographs they always wave around in the media, whenever they're trying to get money for a war with the Raghead of the Week?—those are all actually taken by saucers."

"I notice you don't say UFO."

"UFOs are Unidentified, by-def, old son. Some UFOs are saucers but most are other shapes. But this is getting ahead of the story."

"So do flying saucers work on the Gaudeamus principle?"

"They could use it for a power source, and they're talking about doing that for the eventual civilian models, but it makes them way too easy to track to be any good in a military application. This is where it gets complicated and weird, John."

"Like it's been simple and normal up till now?"

"Right. Hey, how about not disturbing your cat, 'cause I don't want him remembering that he likes to whack balls, and pouring some coffee?"

"Hold him, Corner, guard," I said, taking Travis's cup. Out in the kitchen I kept trying to think of questions, but the bright sunlight on the backyard, and the swarms of birds around Kara's feeder—I reminded myself again that I had to keep reloading that stupid thing while she was gone, the birds weren't going on vacation with her—and the general quiet, quickly lulled me into a near-trance.

Still, when I returned with the coffee, I did say, "Uh, I've checked in my desk sources, and there is not now and never has been a Twining AFB, in fact the Air Force has no presence in Kennedy County. All that's there is a lot of empty space and a thin scattering of people who work too hard and don't make enough money."

"Kennedy County is very far south in the panhandle, and it adjoins the Gulf, in the direction you'd want to fly if you were headed up to orbit, since spacecraft always take off west-to-east if they can. So it would be a perfect place for covert space launch, or covert anything, now wouldn't it? Besides, you didn't show that there's no

Twining—only that there's no acknowledgment and no public record."

"Um, yeah, right. Did they say anything about how those flying saucers fly?"

"Now and then. Nothing I remember. And you read more science than I do, but you're just as rusty. You know as well as I do that if you can't follow the math, you don't know the physics, and it's all hand-waving, and you were never all that good at the math, so why do you want an explanation?"

"Habit," I said. "Most science fiction readers can't read the math but they appreciate good hand-waving. And they want to feel like, if they could follow the math, my hand-waving is what the math would say. I'm used to pleasing that audience."

"Have you looked at your online reviews?"

"I'm used to pleasing *some* of that audience."

"That's better. A good liar like you should stick close to the truth."

My first flying saucer ride felt very much like an elevator ride, except that there was more of a view—but the view might as well be a film shot from a helicopter flying over Colorado, or better yet from a steadicam on a cherry picker on top of a mountain, because it's that steady and there's that little sense of motion. They gave me some story about how inside the saucer there was gravitation relative to the Earth but no inertia relative to the universe, whatever that meant. It was sort of a light, easy feeling, and for a few minutes, until I learned to do what they did and "pull" every nonvertical movement, my hands would fly out from my body and then slap back at me, every time I gestured. Thank god I didn't try to itch my nads; it was like the brakes were off on all my motion, and yet I sat as comfortably there as I'm sitting here, my weight holding me into a chair. It wasn't near as dramatic an experience as that stuff you imagine for money all the time, John.

It's also a little peculiar when you realize that the pilot has about ten controls, total, more or less just telling it to go somewhere and then watching it while it does; and a pilot smoking while he flies is a strange thing to see nowadays; but maybe strangest of all was that his main control was a plain old Mac optical mouse. I commented on that and Kermit shrugged. "Secret projects don't get forced to buy from high markup suppliers, the way public defense projects do, and besides, you can't expect the Air Force to use PC parts in something has to work right, with lives depending on it. Of course it's a Mac mouse."

I watched as Jake selected a destination from a list, clicked on it, and told the saucer to go there "usual way," as the pull down menu put it. Then he sat back and faced the rest of us. Now that he had found his mirrorshades, he looked like an angry bug. They'd been in his jacket pocket all along, by the way.

Another disconcerting feature of the saucer was that it was all cabin; there was no equivalent of an engine compartment, or a transmission hump, or anything at all that suggested "a volume of space containing working parts." And still another disconcerting feature was the old beat-up Ford Explorer parked in the cabin with us. The word "disconcerting" kept coming up; I tell you, John, if I'd boarded that flying saucer totally concerted, my concertment would still have hit zero in less than a minute. Yes, that's a word too. You understood it.

At takeoff, we went straight up, very fast, to about sixty thousand feet, way above airliner altitudes, and then, as the landscape crept by far below, went at just below sonic, to avoid the boom, to a point directly over the landing area, and made another very high speed descent. Apparently the inertialess business meant that we could comfortably take turns, starts, and stops that would have been twenty g's or more without it. I started to hope that gadget never happened to need a reboot in mid-turn, but nobody else looked nervous, so I wasn't going to, particularly not in front of Jenapha Lee.

From just west of Salida to about fifty miles east of Denver took maybe an hour and ten minutes; the Front Range from the air was as gorgeous as ever, but farther away, so it went by slower, even with our greater-than-airliner speed.

On the way I asked a couple of questions. "Why the clown suits?"

"Hmm. Let's see if you can figure it out, Mr. Detective. If you saw three Indians and a white chick get out of a flying saucer, and they were messing around someplace connected to the Gaudeamus effect, how many suspects would match that profile, assuming you had any other information?"

"Uh, that would be you guys."

"Unhunh. Now suppose you see a UFO and a bunch of circus clowns get out of it."

"I'd keep my mouth shut."

"Remarkable, Holmes, how do you do it?"

We flew on, silent as a cloud, swift as an arrow, mixed as a metaphor, and I couldn't think of anything else to say for a while, which annoyed the shit out of me because I wanted to start a conversation with Jenapha Lee, who was standing there smoking very importantly, in her perfect white dress and perfect heels and perfect her, and I felt like a gob of phlegm on the sidewalk by comparison. Yeah, I know, smokers are no fun to kiss. I know she'd taste like an ashtray. But she'd taste like an ashtray with style.

John, how does someone so unromantic get to be a writer? Just go with it. I was crazy fucking in love with her.

We crossed the mountains far below, and kept going; we came to a stop that was visually abrupt, but I felt nothing in my feet or body. There was a funny swirl in the air as we descended.

"Cloaking," Kermit explained, standing beside me. "Doesn't work perfectly but basically it causes most of the light coming at the saucer, in all directions, to travel about 180 degrees around it. It's not precise, so on a city street or in a forest this thing would have a shimmer like something projected off a drop of mercury, and you'd see through it only about as well as you see through a clear shower curtain with the water going. But as long as the background is the sky, it hides us till we're almost down."

"You're going to land this thing at a roadside rest stop?" I asked.

"Naw, we picked that rest stop because it's only six miles from one of our concealed hangars. We'll drive the Explorer over."

The seeming abandoned barn below us retracted its roof, and we settled inside; as the roof closed over us, Jake touched a button and that weird flamelike glow surrounded the saucer; as it had the night before. "What is that?"

"One of the atmospheric effects we get by tweaking the fields around this thing," Kermit said. "If you want to know more, call me after you finish your master's in physics, and I'll give you a reading list, and you can start applying for security clearances—"

"We do have regular headlights—hell, we buy'em at Sears—but this is just way cooler," Jake added.

"Thank you for an explanation I understand."

The saucer extended its tripod of legs and sat on the floor of the converted old barn. Jake selected a command, and a door opened and a ramp dropped, right behind the Explorer. We all got in. Esau grumped at Jenapha Lee until she fastened her seat belt. And in a minute or so, we were rolling down an old farm road in that bright October daylight.

And a week before I'd thought I had an ordinary industrial espionage, prostitution, and drugs case here.

It was a nice day, like you get, very unpredictably, on Colorado's eastern plains at that time of year; the skies were clear, the air was warm, and there was that fall smell that it's impolite to like anymore, plowed dirt and burning waste and all the other things that tell you that this land works instead of just looking pretty. We all rolled windows down even for the short drive.

Hale was sitting in a t-shirt and jeans at a picnic table at the rest area; it was kind of early in the day for anyone to be there, except maybe to pee or have their dog take a dump. He had an arm sling and a great big bunch of pads and things on both sides of his left shoulder.

That must suck, since I was pretty sure he was left-handed.

We got out of the car and approached Hale; I felt Kermit's big hand close on my wrist in the light way that a chef holds an egg that he's going to break but not yet. Esau and Jake each had one of Elvis's arms, and Elvis was calling them stinks, over and over, and bringing up their mother constantly.

I stayed with Kermit like a good boy. The Irwins and Jenapha sat down all around Hale; he didn't seem worried about that. He did check me over for a moment, visually, confirming that I looked like hell but not unfixable.

"All right," Hale said. "As far as I can tell, you not only have all the good cards, I don't even have a hand. So, why don't you begin by telling me what you want and why you think I might do it for you, or get it for you?"

"Well—" Jenapha Lee said, but Esau cleared his throat.

Kermit nodded. "We think the time has come to let Xegon as a company, and you in particular, know what's going on. We hadn't planned to do that anytime soon but our hand has been forced;

you're making such rapid progress on the Gaudeamus Effect." He reached down into a black case he had been carrying and pulled out the Gaudeamus box that he'd taken back from me just three nights before. "We've taken your Gaudeamus box apart, measured its performance, and it confirms that you have come very far very fast, which means we know now that you're going to have the full panoply of Gaudeamus tools within a few months at most, and be conducting large-scale experiments. Go ahead, take the box back, we've seen it, and if we want one we can make a better one, at least for right now. Oh, and we do think your energy-absorbing system is a great idea and you're way ahead on that."

Hale dragged the box closer to himself; he seemed pretty shocked and bewildered. I guess he hadn't envisioned the meeting going like this. Neither had I, of course. "Who are you?" Hale asked.

"You'd know us best as Negon Corporation. Your rival, I guess. I've written all the reports to you that you thought were coming from industrial espionage on Negon, so you know me that way too. A much better question might be *what* we are, so I'm going to pretend you asked that one."

Kermit let go of my wrist and said, "Now, I'm trusting you to be a smart guy, Mr. Hale. I've been tracking you for a long time and I know a lot about you, and I don't expect you to rashly kick the board over before you know what the game is. Am I justified in that trust in you?"

"That and no more. The moment something smells bad I'm bolting."

"Fair enough. All right, here's what I want. You'll have no reason to doubt that. Then I will tell you why I want it. I'm going to have a hard time persuading you that I'm telling the truth, but I have a few very persuasive arguments at my disposal—arguments of evidence, not of force."

I noticed that the less rough stuff was involved, the more Kermit talked like a professor. I wondered if he thought of himself as bilingual, with his two languages being academese and goon.

"Finally, if you agree with me about what I want and why it's desirable, we can talk about how you will help—which, if you believe me and understand me, I think you will want to do. You'll forgive my being an old college prof who tends to deliver everything in lecture? I hope you're not one of those students who's good at sleeping with the eyes open? All right, then, this will take a little explaining. Let me know if you need a bathroom break."

CHAPTER FIFTEEN

"That sounds like a good idea to me, too," I said, "now that the coffee is hitting."

"Hmm. Must be contagious. Come on, Corner, let's go pee."

Damn if that weird cat didn't follow him into the guest bathroom, as if he understood.

"So you want me to drive you over to Saguache," I said, returning to my living room. "To a place called the Mutilated Cow. And Skin2Skin is playing there. And I take it your real purpose is to see Jenapha Lee?"

"Oh, it's a real purpose, but there's some work-related stuff. And, like I said, it might be your chance to meet some of the people that come up in this story. For some reason, I want you to know it. I guess because you're likely to be the guy who writes it down, if anyone ever does, and I kind of think it might be important, someday, somewhere, somehow, that it gets written down, if you see what I mean."

"No, I don't."

"Sometimes a case just feels important, how's that?"

"It'll do. So what exactly did Kermit tell Hale, and how did that lead to your showing up here?"

He got up, walked to the phone, picked up the phone book—in Gunnison, that's a thin little thing the shape but half the thickness of a trade paperback—flipped in the yellow pages for an instant, and then asked, "Who's the decent pizza place in this town—decent local, I mean? We ate there—"

"Mario's."

"Good. Let me get one headed this way—it's been some hours since we ate, bud. My treat. And then I'll pick up the story. Got any beer or red wine?"

"More Fat Tire than both of us together ought to have in the fridge," I said. "I teach. It's a necessity."

"Will a Buddhist order come out okay?"

"They have about forty ingredients. 'One with everything' will come out pretty soggy. Order their veggie combo and add meat to it."

"Awright." He phoned in the order. After he hung up, he asked, "Frozen glasses in the freezer?"

"Mais c'est de rigueur, mon vieux."

"Either that means your answer is yes, or else my answer is I'd have to be drunker and you'd have to be prettier, and as far as I can tell, we can only fix one of those things." He emerged with two chilled glasses full of Fat Tire, handed me one, and then said, "Look, I can't remember exactly how Kermit told it all, okay? And Hale is one weird case—turns out he's actually a Ph.D. in physics and quit it to be a detective, which makes him the weirdest physicist since Bud Grace. Though not nearly as funny. So the things that most convinced Hale are exactly the things I can't remember, and the whole story is pretty goddam strange no matter how you slice it, bud, so—how about the capsule version? And you want to do me a real favor, you'll take notes, and give me a copy, because

I've been carrying all this in my head and I know I'm getting parts of it more and more screwed up, and other parts of it are getting so faded in that I can't really remember not knowing them before, and I tend to leave them out of the telling. So—"

I rolled to my right, grabbed at my work bag on an end table, and pulled out the tape recorder. "Fresh tape, fresh batteries, I'm good to go for an interview," I said. I slid my thumb back and forth, hitting the fast forward and then the rewind to rack-and-pack the first few inches and make sure it would start smooth. "Ready when you are."

Travis's story was like a fusion of the weirdest, nuttiest possible explanations for every page three news story going on at the time, and I'm not sure whether the incoherence I find here is in my notes or was there in Travis's narration or what. Tammy, the girl I hired to do transcripts for me that year, is the only reason why there is any of this. She recovered her rough draft transcript from her crashed hard drive, which was quite a feat, but things that are quite a feat are not unusual for Tammy.

She was one of those brainy types that Western State sometimes gets due to family financial crises that hit right in their senior years of high school, or because their family has no college graduates and therefore can't recognize a feeble college, or lack of confidence, or any of a dozen accidents that will send a could-go-anywhere student to WSC—the faculty were just grateful every time it happened.

I never quite knew what Tammy's story was, but most such stories had something to do with poverty. I first got to know her because she applied to work in the theatre and turned out to be a tech wiz, keeping lighting gear running way past any time when it should have—she might be the youngest person on Earth ever to have correctly rebuilt a ceramic resistance coil, a kind of dimmer that was officially "obsolete" according to textbooks published in 1960. Tammy also wrote and installed software fixes in the main board, since we couldn't afford upgrades, which is to say she learned and wrote in an embedded control language.

All that might have gone into a letter of reference for her, but she never needed one. When she graduated, she enlisted in the Marines, made it through flight training, and nowadays she ferries Harriers. (She claims that when she retires she wants to spend her time at horse tracks, following the veterinarians around, calling them names, and urging them to work faster, so that she can then say that she also harried farriers. Certain things cannot be fixed by even the best teaching, mentoring, or advising.) Whenever we're in the same town I have a beer with her and she tells me stories at least as wild as Travis's. But Tammy is for another book, another time.

Anyway, she'd done transcriptions for me many times—she understood tech terms, spelled well, and got stuff done fast—and this time, she'd just finished transcribing on the first pass and gone for a weekend visit to her boyfriend over in the Springs. Tammy's new roommate threw a party, which received three separate visits from sheriff's deputies, and when Tammy came back, the tape of Travis had been erased, her backup floppy was in an ashtray melted into a puddle, and her hard drive had been wiped, except they didn't realize that she was far better at this stuff than they were, and she managed an almost full recovery.

But she had only gotten as far as doing a first pass. First passes contain great swaths of gibberish and confusion that has to get corrected in the second and third pass transcription, and it never got the additional passes. This is what I could assemble from my beer-sozzled memory, Tammy's first pass transcription, and some phone calls to Travis, who doesn't like to talk about this stuff over the phone and gets cryptic right when I need clarification. So, if it makes no sense, well, it makes no sense.

Once upon a time, in 1987, there were seven women, and they all were at Moloch College in southern Indiana, in a lab which they had formed by pooling the *laboratoire du chair* funds for three of them. Moloch was one of those little places that the Midwest is littered with, well-endowed experimental colleges that contain a mixture of bright and talented kids with rich eccentric kids. They're good places to find yourself if you're eighteen and mentally or emotionally missing; interesting places to party if you like smart people and if your idea of partying isn't standing around in an alcoholic haze and wishing you were attractive to people more attractive than yourself; and every so often they are just what they were intended to be, incubators of wild and interesting talents. There are maybe a hundred of them—Kenyon, Oberlin, Hillsdale, Ringlebury, Earlham, Carleton, Waverly, Chatham, Otterbein . . . each with its odd mix of missionary zeal, eccentric joy, and obsessive focus on something or other that noplace else is interested in . . . they're among the best things in American education and they're also where many "crazy professor" stories in the tabloids come out of. They were among the first fully coeducational colleges, among the first to admit black students, among the first to drop the Jewish quota . . . the cradles of every extremist political movement in American politics, right and left, for a century . . . places about which many American academics, hearing a story of some craziness at one or another, say, "Go figure," and shake our heads, and secretly wish that we were there.

Every so often I let myself think about applying for a faculty position at one of them. I'm afraid I might not be crazy enough, and I'm also afraid that I might be, after teaching at one of them for a while.

Now, Moloch was no more and no less eccentric than all the others. It had started out liberal Congregationalist, as the Quid Volumus Scriptural College. In 1889, a family of Tidewater tobacco barons had bought it and renamed it Moloch, setting it up with a mission to preach free market capitalism to young men in all fields. It flourished in the thirties and forties, supplying the country with young male Republicans, but by the 1960s, the bottom was falling out of free market poetics and free market chemistry, or at least the market was collapsing for colleges with five required economics courses in all majors, and no girls. The college had been taken co-ed, co-op, and co-curricular (with various programs at neighboring colleges) in 1972, and after most of the old faculty voted to sell their stock to new, incoming faculty, Moloch had redefined its mission, setting itself to train students in a "New Magickality for the Aquarian Age."

In practice that meant it was a place for every real scientist who wigged out and got interested in crystals, astrology, homeopathy, pyramid power, and all the rest of that sorry lot, and for every religious studies-semiotics-ethnic-studies-comp-litter who got fascinated with the language of science. It was where people with doctorates who had come a little loose from their intellectual moorings—or perhaps floated right down the intellectual river and over the intellectual falls—went to get all cosmic, and they'd do all these strange experiments that didn't work too terribly well, and argue about whether they worked or not and what it would mean for them to work and whether "worked" meant "worked," or only "like it worked," or whether "it worked" and "it was like it worked" were the same thing, and like that.

They'd had the idea that one thing that was wrong with "non-Aquarian" science was the German laboratory system in which faculty scientists had to apply for lab time and convince other scientists that their use of resources would be productive; they decided that they would set things up as *laboratoires des chairs,* which is the old French system (now abandoned even in France) where you give every scientist a tiny little lab and a tiny little budget and a couple of assistants and tell them to go play. "It's the system that enabled the French to invent penicillin and computers, create the theories of relativity and quantum mechanics, and of course to land on the moon," Travis remarked. "I'm sorry, John, but you got to understand this lame-ass *laboratoire du chair* system that Moloch College had, or you're not going to understand how all this happened."

"I do understand it," I said. "Because of what I do I read history of science. And, hey, it was common in English institutions a hundred years ago, too. And people like Pasteur and Darwin, Madame Curie, Lord Kelvin, they all had *laboratoires des chairs.*"

"Unhhunh. And the Wright brothers had a bicycle shop, but I don't think we'd speed up the pace of aerospace research if we disbanded all the big labs and gave every engineer his own bicycle shop. For that matter I don't think we'd find more new continents if we started looking for them with sailing ships. Anyway, there's one thing, and just one thing, that that system has going for it; every idea that can be investigated cheaply—no matter how stupid—eventually gets investigated."

And, according to Travis, just that once, in the pooled lab space of Doctors Susan Glasgow, Brenda Johnston, and Annabeth Trinidad, something had actually worked, and it had worked in a spectacular fashion; they had accidentally created the first Gaudeamus machine, sometime around 1987. Those women had had two senior assistants, Candy Peggoty and Melinda Belgrade, basically work-study students doing what would be done by low-level grad students in a place that had a grad program, and also two typists, Heart Reno and her work-study helper, a freshman girl named Lena Logan.

If I remember right, that was the point where I was floundering in the alcoholic haze—I drank too fast and was starting my third beer when the pizza got there—trying to remember where I'd heard those names before.

"The Hardware Store Killer," Travis said. "That's why some of the papers are now calling him the Moloch College killer."

"Oh, yeah, you're right," I said. "Except of course Lena Logan is still in your stories, and the Hardware Store Killer has only had five victims, so one of them—"

"Susan Glasgow. She's about to get into the story here. She's the other one that's still alive."

"Do you ever worry about Stacy and Traci, I mean, did you, once the papers realized that everyone who had been killed by the Hardware Store Killer was connected somehow to Moloch College in the late seventies or early eighties?"

Stacy and Traci had been two witches, or witches-in-training, roommates at Moloch College; I could never remember which one was which, but one was short and pixieish and the other was huge, and Travis had known Traci (I think)'s brother in MP school, and Trav had set us up for some glorious weekends at Moloch, some real trips to Redneck Paradise.

During those weekends, we'd gotten hooked on Richard Reno's *Gaudeamus* panel in the Moloch student paper, and for about a year afterwards either Stacy or Traci—the fat one, anyway—had faithfully mailed a copy of it every week to Travis, who had then photocopied it and sent me one, making us among the elite few who had read it before it was on the web, people who knew all about the mutual vow of battle to the death between O. B. Joyful and Merle the Killer Squirrel back while Reagan was president and paisley was hip and hip was non-ironic.

One little detail made me sad, when Travis told me. Heart Reno was Richard's older sister. Considering she'd been the third victim of the Hardware Store Killer, this certainly explained why *Gaudeamus* so often contained pointers to the ongoing investigation. I wondered why Richard Reno didn't just post an explanation somewhere—many fans just hated the constant references to the Hardware Store Killer case, and perhaps if they knew of his personal connection, they'd cut him more slack on the point.

"Yeah, I guess that's sad, but I'm not as sad about it as you are," Travis said, "and I'm getting to why."

"So the Hardware Store Killer isn't just the Moloch College Killer," I said. "He's the Gaudeamus Effect killer. Jeez, I can see why Lena Logan is sort of desperate and crazy. Does anyone know what's happening to Susan—Glasgow, was it?"

"Well, yeah. We know a fuckload. And we wish we knew more. Remember that nasty message that you got by clicking on the Gaudeamus machine on Ower Gyro's shelf, in that episode of *Gaudeamus* on the day I turned up here? That nasty message was from Susan and that's about as nice as she gets. And incidentally all those mibs that were chasing me were hers too. I'm getting to this. Let me continue the story. Here's the hard part to accept, and I might as well get it over with."

I so wish I hadn't been drunk. I know in the middle of it the pizza arrived, delivered by a former student who thought it was very entertaining that Professor Barnes was very drunk, and kept looking at Travis funny until I realized it was because I was a theatre teacher and Travis was good-looking.

I know that as he explained and I objected, Travis had to repeat some of the same evidence three and four times. I know I don't remember large parts of the evidence. But I do remember, eventually, being forced to concede that I had to agree, that yes, that was what it added up to, that if Travis (frequently accompanied by Hale, who didn't sound the least bit like a man inclined to stretch the truth) had seen and heard what he said he had seen and heard, then he was right to believe what he did.

I just wish I remembered enough of it.

Our voices slurred, and we interrupted each other and argued constantly, and talked over each other. Poor Tammy only got scattered words of it; she might not have been able to recover much more even if she had had a chance to go over it a couple more times, and as it was she did her best, probably the best anyone could have done.

But here's as much as I remember of what Travis tried to persuade me of:

Gaudeamus technology is one of the eight basic technologies for all intelligent species in the universe. The others are cutting edges, fire, boats, agriculture, heat engines, electricity, and recombinant DNA. And that's pretty much the order that most civilizations get them in, with minor variations.

Once you have Gaudeamus, you need almost nothing else. Gaudeamus translates any basic physical property into any other— temperature into distance, charge into mass, time into energy, whatever you like—in a way that is outside space and time. It's an unlimited power source and a starship drive and for that matter it allows you to always hang wallpaper correctly on the first try. Every civilization in all the galaxies that finds it, within a generation, uses almost nothing else.

Gaudeamus puts out a characteristic signature, a pulse or a beep or whatever you want to call it, that is easily modulated—Travis was pretty sure it wasn't usually a wave so it couldn't very well be amplitude or frequency modulated, but whatever it was that it was, whatever characteristics that had, they are easy to modulate. And modulated Gaudeamus pulses are the basic communications media for every advanced civilization in the universe.

There is no such thing as natural Gaudeamus. Not the least trace of it happens in any exploding star, or in the tiniest reaches within a neutron, or to a single particle of dark matter, unless some process—designed by an intelligent being and caused deliberately—makes it happen.

And thus, when a new civilization first discovers Gaudeamus, it's as conspicuous as dropping an anvil into a punch bowl. It's as if everyone in a dark forest first learns to make light, and only later discovers they have eyes. So that first Gaudeamus experiment at Moloch College had lighted up the galaxy, and beyond, with the news that there was a new species on the block—which also had to mean that there was a new habitable planet out here. And from that had come all our sorrows.

The code name used among the seven women who first found Gaudeamus was "Experiment 198 phenomenon." Which was one of those understated phrases that scientists seem to be so fond of.

While they were performing Experiment 198, the block of steel that they were heating to incandescence, to demonstrate how much power Gaudeamus could draw from the universe, began to pulsate, alternating between white-hot and liquid-helium cold at intervals of exactly one second, then two seconds, then four. Then it began to pulse in dots and dashes; Lena Logan and Heart Reno had both been Girl Scouts, and they read the message:

pulse machine on off

acknowledge please

request permission make contact

The aliens had popped stealthed satellites into Earth orbit, probably putting them in decades before, maybe listening to all the radio traffic since the 1930s radar experiments, analyzed it, gotten the hang of our languages, spotted Moloch College's lab as being in an English-speaking area . . . it's remarkable what you can do when you have time travel, especially what a computer can do when it can have its conclusion before computing it.

The seven women took a quick vote, and agreed unanimously. They invited the aliens to make contact. And one second after sending that message (which they had carefully worked out by referring to the Morse code chart in the back of an old desk dictionary), they had jumped back from a glowing golden square above the lab table. A rope ladder had fallen through the square, and down it had climbed something that Lena Logan, much later, had said looked like a four-foot-tall cricket, walking on its hind legs, with a lobster's legs and a raccoon's head (if you imagine a cyclops raccoon), covered with pink shag carpet—except that it all worked together, somehow, so that the thing looked natural.

In Arthur C. Clarke's *Childhood's End,* Earth is visited by aliens who look like Christian devils; it turns out that they are the end of our species, not because they are our enemies, but because they are here to help us fulfill our destiny, and the image of the devil was a kind of sense of the collective unconscious of what the end of the world would look like. Well, if ever there were a species that ought to have looked like Satan, the pTh'tong n'Wi—as close as

Travis could get to pronouncing them—should have been it, for they arrived contracts in hand, with a deal for human souls that would be almost impossible for us to resist.

Basically, Travis said, the deal was twenty-four dollars in beads and blankets.

"Melody Wallace would give you a dissertation on that one," I said.

"Thought she was a semiotician or a sosh-of-com type, not a historian."

"Twenty-four. It's amazing how often that number shows up in legends and stories. Doctor Faustus gets twenty-four years of unlimited power. The Indians sell Manhattan for twenty-four dollars in beads and blankets. She'd have ten more examples."

"Wednesday morning three A.M." Travis nodded solemnly.

"What?"

"Early Paul Simon song. Or was that twenty-five?"

"Never mind, there's twenty-four beers in one of those cases in my basement—"

"Good, that's twenty-four too." Travis raised his bottle; when had we given up on the glasses? I raised mine in return, we both drank, and then he asked, "Uh, so why does twenty-four come up so often?"

"It's *your* story."

"No, I mean . . . Melody Wallace had some idea about how so many twenty-fours come up in stories?"

"Oh, yeah. Twenty-four hours in a day. So it stands for 'a single day.' Or brings up the idea. So the idea is that people always sell out too cheap, see? They'd hand over everything really worthwhile in their lives to get twenty-four hours or years or whatever—one little day—of everything they want, and the twenty-four is over too soon and then they have nothing. Like that. So whatever the actual value of the trade goods that were used to buy Manhattan, once somebody came up with a way that it worked out to twenty-four dollars, bingo! That stuck. Because it was such a good symbol."

"Jesus, it sure is," he said, leaning back and staring at the ceiling.

According to Travis, the seven women at Moloch College had been confronted with a blunt, straightforward deal: in exchange for signing over the rights to the entire planet, each of them would receive seven metric tons per year of pure platinum. It took them a few days to confirm that there were ways of selling it without drawing attention, and to confirm that the samples they had been given were pure platinum. But once they knew those two things for sure, they jumped at the deal. After all, who wouldn't? Clearly the silly aliens didn't know that the Earth had no single owner and no one had the power to sell it.

"Remember that old frat brother of yours, John, the one that used to say that he figured the Indians that sold Manhattan probably thought buying land was like buying the sky or the ocean? So these guys in funny clothes with cool stuff, which they obviously have plenty of, and don't know the value of, show up and offer to—*giggle!*—buy land. 'No shit, man, they wanted to—*snort*—buy land. So, we go, oh yeah, buddy, we're all like, we'll *take* all those blankets and stuff. Oh yeah. You ever want to—giggle some more—*buy more land,* you get in touch, know what I mean? Hey, watch your funny hats, going back through the trees there. Buh-bye. Boy, did we take *them* for a ride . . . ' As I recall the point of the story was, you can't cheat an honest man, and a dishonest one will cheat himself, eh? Well, it happened again."

Most of the rest of the group of seven women had rushed off to newly invented identities—a covert income of around a hundred million a year *will* change the average professor or student's lifestyle—but Lena Logan had let the curiosity bug bite her, and kept playing with Gaudeamus, since she hadn't been told not to.

Every couple of days she met a new group of aliens, who immediately lost interest in her when they discovered that she had already sold the Earth. For a while, the lab floor of her new mansion in Switzerland looked like the best sideshow she'd ever seen, as one bizarre creature after another paraded through.

And then she met the cop.

The cop from the galactic-multispecies-entity-that-would-be-the-galactic-government-if-there-were-such-a-thing-as-a-galactic-government-and-if-the-concept-were-meaningful didn't look very much like the short little grays that people down in the San Luis Valley say they have been anally probed by. But he didn't *not* look like them, either. He shrugged and said he'd had Earth as his beat for a long time, and not all of his native assistants and deputies had been discreet.

His head was as flat as if he were in *The Family Circus*, and hairless, with a small triangular mouth that served as his breathing, eating, and excreting hole, and large bulging ovoid eyes that worked like a Newtonian reflector telescope. On his floor-length arms there were three-fingered hands on which every finger opposed every other, which was why Lena nicknamed him All Thumbs (she couldn't make several of the sounds in his actual name). His legs, which had an extra knee or ankle (depending on what you counted as what) ended in gripping four-toed feet a bit like a lizard's, with the toes pointing to the corners. Normally he carried his body-length tail in a gentle curl up his back, and most of it was muscular and relatively inflexible like a python, but the last ten centimeters was a delicate, prehensile structure that gave him, in effect, a third hand.

"Kermit must have really spent a while describing that one," I said.

"Naw, he didn't have to. We looked around, nobody was coming, so we went behind the rest rooms and All Thumbs got out of the back of the Explorer. I had no idea he'd been back there; I guess he can sleep or rest perfectly still for hours, under a blanket, in a box, whatever.

"Since I have promised to tell the strict truth here, I really should admit that Hale was far cooler than I was about All Thumbs. Maybe because he's always worked on the good side of the law, and really who this guy was, was *Marshal* All Thumbs. Galactic Marshal All Thumbs. Something like that. The Galactic law on this barbarian planet."

When Lena Logan met All Thumbs, he had explained just how awkward (but not at all unusual) humanity's situation now was. Like law anywhere on Earth, particularly law among a diverse population, the law for the galaxy's 89,000 (and increasing) registered civilized species was a series of compromises. Many species liked their laws altruistic and generous; many liked their laws property-oriented and market-driven; many liked law to foster cooperation, and many others to satisfy honor. The great majority were like human beings— they wanted the law to do all that, and make everyone else be moral, too.

For a while Lena Logan thought that All Thumbs was essentially a commerce regulator dealing with primitives; then that he might be sort of a game warden whose special area was intelligent game; then that he was sort of like a BIA agent; then the equivalent of a Peace Corps volunteer; or a very pro-chicken chicken inspector. Finally it was most comforting to think of him as the marshal, and that didn't seem to displease him. His job was to make local regulations to enforce Galactic law, and enforce those regulations, and somehow or other cause the judges who reviewed him, the species on whom he enforced the law (human and alien), and anybody who might look over his shoulder, to agree that he had done the fair thing. "Sort of like a U.S. Marshal given a copy of the Ten Commandments, the Endangered Species Act, and the Scout Law, sent west and told to make this happen and not violate the Bill of Rights while he does it, subject to review about every twenty years."

And what he explained to her was this. For a period corresponding to about twenty-four of our years, beginning from the first agreement to communicate, aliens making contact with a new species could buy the planet from them. Planets were bought for several different reasons. Organizations that were the equivalent of the Nature Conservancy bought planets to protect them, which sounded nice until you realized that they usually intended to exterminate most of the intelligent technological species, put the survivors permanently back into the Stone Age, and set up the planet as an eternal nature park. Other organizations bought planets to provide slaves, or to be converted into tourist spots, or sometimes just to strip for scrap—essentially they'd take all the finished and refined metal off the planet in a few seconds, which could be rough on anybody in a skyscraper or airliner at the time, but not as rough as the species that bought the planet to take all the protein.

Unfortunately, the seven Moloch College women had sold the planet to the pTh'tong n'Wi, who were devoted to nature and wildlife—but only to the nature and wildlife of their own homeworld. If their purchase held up in court, they would irradiate the Earth with enough hard gamma to wipe out everything right down to the microbes in the deepest hot springs under the oceans. They would then reseed the Earth with the full ecology of the pTh'tong n'Wi homeworld. In about three thousand years, Earth would be one among the hundreds of copies of the pTh'tong n'Wi homeworld.

But, Lena had protested, she and the other six women had no actual authority to sell the planet. Surely All Thumbs could just arrest the seven of them for fraud, make them pay whatever the penalty for that was (even if it were death), and announce that the contract was void?

Well, no.

During that first-contact period, which corresponded to around twenty-four Earth years (or am I only remembering its being that number because Trav and I had already talked about significance?), every alien species that could find Earth people to talk to could buy the planet from any of them that hadn't already sold it. This was regarded as permitting and yet controlling the natural tendency of advanced sophisticated societies to bilk and cheat more primitive ones.

The rule that each individual could only sell the planet once was why all the freak-show aliens contacting Lena Logan were disappearing as soon as they found out she already had a contract.

Sometime in early 2011, there would be a gigantic multi-sided lawsuit that might take eons in the courtroom but would be settled within four seconds from the perspective of our common consensus universe. At the end of those four seconds, it would be decided which of the many sales, if any, was actually valid. Human behavior and custom would be part of the evidence, but were not determining factors; the pTh'tong n'Wi's having secured the very first contract would weigh heavily in their favor.

Furthermore, "remember that thing that Marshall McLuhan is supposed to have said, John, that it steam engines when it's steam engine time? Lena Logan's monitoring system, right now, is showing that there's about two to three re-inventions of Gaudeamus every month all over the world. People are getting the basic idea and building those damned machines out of parts from hobby stores, or things they pry off of old junked TVs, or parts from old PlayStations, nearly everywhere. And every time they do, the alien freak show comes rushing in. The pTh'tong n'Wi alone have bought the Earth more than eighty times, which All Thumbs says is actually pretty much in our favor because it can be taken as evidence that they didn't think the first sale was valid all by itself."

"Can't we just . . . keep the planet ourselves?"

"That's what All Thumbs is working on. Either that, or we end up as a Galactic protectorate, which I guess isn't so bad except they send a police force to keep order, missionaries to straighten us out, and sanitation engineers to clean up the planet. Which isn't all that good a deal when you consider that there's thousands of things that are illegal in a Galactic protectorate that we've never thought about one way or another, and that we'd be getting envoys of about nine thousand religions, all of them empowered to suppress our local religions and compel everyone in the neighborhood to go to one of the alien temples or churches or whatever they called'em, and that the first thing the sanitation engineers would do is sterilize everyone that they thought was unfit to breed, turn off all fossil fuel consumption even if it resulted in a couple winters of people freezing to death, and build a few thousand nuclear reactors. Then at whatever time in the future ninety-nine percent or so of our descendants all agree that this was the right thing to do, we get to join as full citizens. For whatever strange reason, All Thumbs kind of likes us, and he'd like to see us come in as junior members, but full-fledged citizens right from the start."

In typical cautious government research contractor fashion, the Xegon project had been doing Gaudeamus at such low power that it hadn't been spotted yet; thus only the U.S. government, as far as anyone could tell, had operated Gaudeamus without getting a chance to negotiate the sale of the planet with aliens. And that had made it - immensely valuable; Xegon and Negon were the only two projects going on the planet that were actually learning anything about Gaudeamus.

The problem was that as soon as anyone turned on a working Gaudeamus experiment, aliens showed up to offer everything the experimenter ever could want. The happy inventor or scientist then sold the planet to the obviously advanced-yet-dim aliens, and took off to enjoy the proceeds.

"Now, the problem with this, John—and it's a big one—is that we can't afford *not* to have Gaudeamus up and working by February 4, 2011, just about twenty-four years with some Tennessee windage from when the pTh'tong n'Wi first contacted the seven women at Moloch. Because once there is one big mother of a suit, everybody except one lucky planet-seller is going to have to give the stuff, or equivalent value, back. That's a few million tons of gems and precious metals, I'd guess, and god knows how many priceless artifacts time-traveled up to here, and a bunch of stuff like patentable cancer cures. And mostly it was given to people who did not have the right to sell the planet—"

"None of them had the right to sell the planet." I thumped each word out on the floor with my empty beer bottle. Corner watched the bottle go up and down with samurai concentration.

"Right. None of them did. You're totally right. That's why I come here, because I need to talk to a guy who's right. Another Fat Tire?"

"Do I have to give you the planet for it?"

"It's your beer, bud, I'm just helping you drink it."

"Well, thank god somebody is, or I could be drunk. Now, so, everybody is going to have to pay back—"

"Except whoever the Galactic Court decides had the right to sell the planet, which they decide based on cafeteria—criberia—clitoria—aw, they got rules for deciding who owned the planet and who sold it. Then that deal stands and everyone else just fucks off. Except. If you sold the planet and you didn't have the right to do that, you have to pay it back. Whatever you got from the aliens."

"How do you pay back a cancer cure?"

"Not easily. Railroad cars full of diamonds, that's bad enough. But eternal energy sources, very advanced tech . . . well, there's just a lot. Now, the thing is, if everyone would just pay them back right now, that would indicate we never wanted to make a deal in the first place, and the court would say they had to go away and leave us alone. So Lena . . . she's pretty cool, John, if she'd gain some weight she'd be damn sexy . . ."

"You had sex with her—"

"Not with enough of her. She's not like Jenapha Lee though. Jenapha Lee has the most—"

"Tell me more about paying back the aliens. Or about pissing up a rope, for that matter. Just tell me about something that isn't Jenapha Lee and her mongous bazongas."

"'Kay. So those are the two sides."

"What are?"

"Lena Logan and Susan Glasgow." He got very serious and breathed deep. "Got to get this one out, clearly, so you remember. Big part of the story. Now, Lena Logan learned a list of legal loopholes . . ." I was fascinated by the alliteration for a moment and missed everything he said next, but the short summary seemed to be that if enough of the human race paid back on those contracts ahead of time—returned whatever the aliens had given in exchange for the planet—it would be taken as very strong evidence that no one should have been selling the planet, and therefore all the deals would be voided, and the planet would be as safe as it ever was, at least in a universe where asteroids wander around randomly, supernovae go off every now and then, and so on.

"Well, then, yay Lena," I said. "Nice of her to save us all."

"But that's the thing, it's just her, and Negon, and now Xegon, and that's about it. Everybody else stops doing Gaudeamus research as soon as somebody with three heads and an orange toupee shows up and offers them all their dreams come true in exchange for strip mining rights to the planet. And we have to have Gaudeamus because with it we can make all that stuff ourselves, eventually, and buy up all the contracts, and save the Earth . . ."

I asked him what the Susan Glasgow side was about, and I thought he was too drunk to tell me. He just muttered "bitch" a couple of times, and then finally said, "She's about keeping the stuff. Like the lottery. Most people lose in it but they vote for it cause they know that most people lose but they figure they themselves will win. So they all give Susan a little money to make sure things don't get paid back because they want to keep their deals, even if it costs the planet—"

"Won't they die with the human race?"

"All but one will. That one gets to check into the Hilton Galactic and spend the rest of eternity shopping, I guess. Or playing guitar in front of adoring crowds. Or whatever . . ."

Tammy swears that Travis said "Check into the Hilton Galactic." He swears it must have been something else because he has no idea what that could mean. I asked him if the successful planet-sellers ended up like wives of Third World strongmen, living in the best hotels with nothing to do but shop, and he said he'd ask All Thumbs, who—if Travis isn't just making All Thumbs up—said that hotels was the wrong concept, and suggested either zoos or quilting bees, "except when it's not." So maybe we got it and maybe we didn't. Anyway, it was midafternoon and time for a long nap. I knew now that Lena Logan was trying to buy back the planet, and Susan Glasgow was trying to keep it sold, and I had grown up on Saturday morning cartoons, so I knew which side the good guys were on.

CHAPTER SIXTEEN

Somewhere in the middle of all that, I fell asleep, or Travis did, and when we woke up, there in my living room, we both had hangovers and it was dark outside. Luckily, though, Skin2Skin's gig at the Mutilated Cow started at ten P.M.—time enough for us to shower, shave, put on half-ass decent clothes (in the mountain West, sweatpants are suitable for anything short of a wedding or funeral, so getting dressed up isn't much of a production), fill travel mugs with coffee, and get going. We stopped to pick up a sack of a dozen McDonald's hamburgers and a big box of McMaggots and gobbled those as we went.

Eight miles west of Gunnison, there's a turnoff to C114, which is a narrow two-lane road that winds up through Cochetopa Pass, through all kinds of gorgeous scenery, and eventually descends to the even smaller town of Saguache, which is how the Spanish explorers spelled the same Ute word (probably meaning "green") that American settlers spelled Sawatch. I seriously doubt that any Utes would recognize either the Spanish or the English pronunciation of the word, today.

It's dark and lonesome and about an hour and ten minutes, but I didn't especially feel like talking. It seemed to me that either Travis had just told me his biggest bullshit story ever, bigger than the transvestite rodeo queens festival, bigger even than the All Naked Girls Marching Band for Gun Rights, and he had done it by the unfair use of one of America's most popular and legal drugs. My head hurt, I was concentrating on the road, and I really didn't want to talk.

So after a while the son of a bitch went and fell asleep, and I might as well have been doing this stupid night drive over a mountain pass in midwinter all by myself, for my own reasons, if I had any.

I had worked myself into one *fine* mood by the time I got to Saguache.

"John," Travis said quietly, "I tossed my bag in your back seat. I can get a ride with someone else if you just want to go home. I can tell you're pissed off and I guess you have a right. I wouldn't have believed me either."

"Shit," I said. "If I stay, I'm going to watch you moon all over this woman Jennifer—"

"Jena*pha*."

"That's the one, and listen to a band that you already say sucks, and hang around for hours with nothing to do and get depressed and bored and keep thinking that I could have just gone with Kara and enjoyed some warmth and sunlight and company. So that will suck. But if I turn around and go home now, afterwards you're going to tell me some insane story about what happens tonight, and I'll wish I'd been here, and always wonder whether you told me the truth about what happened here tonight. And that will suck even more. All right, I'll try to cheer up."

The Mutilated Cow might have been the name of a very avant-garde steakhouse, or maybe an animal-rights coffeehouse, but in fact it took its name from the strange condition that dead cattle had been found in, all over the San Luis Valley, for decades. If you drive up and down that valley, from Saguache or Moffat down to the New Mexico line, and talk to ranchers, you'll hear twenty cattle mutilation stories—their own and all their neighbors—and what was done to the cow will be different every time.

The cow is always found dead. Sometimes all the blood is gone, with no puddles or pools anywhere. Sometimes internal organs are stacked neatly beside it, or have been removed through neat holes apparently cut with a scalpel or laser. Sometimes parts like the face or udder or the skin on the back have been slit partly away and folded back to expose what's underneath, sometimes some distinct set of parts is missing. Cuts into the body are almost always made in a very sharp straight cutoff, not the sort of thing a coyote's or a cougar's teeth or claws could do (though there are people who contend it's actually being done by a few surviving, unknown grizzlies, which can sometimes make very precise cuts with their great strength and razor-sharp claws. If so, the San Luis grizzlies would be almost a thousand miles south of any other grizzlies that are known to survive—but if there were going to be unseen grizzlies anyplace in the Rockies, it would have to be somewhere like the San Luis Valley).

Now, a funny thing—every cattle mutilation has a reasonable explanation, which you can usually hear from the rancher next door. It's only the mutilations that an individual rancher encounters personally that mystify them. The guy over the next hill will be able to tell you just how a teenage thrill killer, or rustling by organized crime, or a coyote, or a freak accident with barbed wire or glass in the windows of an abandoned building, could have led to that weird feature of the death. The guy who saw it is never convinced by that.

And of course, since there's such an abundance of saucer sightings and so forth in the San Luis Valley (or the La Veta Military

Operations Area), there are plenty of people ready to tell you that aliens, or the armed forces, or aliens working for the armed forces, are doing it for reasons all their own.

Now, confronted by constant weirdness, people eventually just shrug and live with it, which explains Manhattan, New Orleans, Silicon Valley, and Kalispell, Montana, just to mention the examples with which I'm most familiar. The Colorado ranch population might have been a little freaked at first, but "at first" was back in the 1940s or earlier. We've got third-generation abductees out here. So the men and women in cowboy hats, stopping in the cafés of the tiny crossroads towns that are such a long way apart and surrounded by so much empty land, are not exactly superstitious, terrified peasants, clutching pitchforks and torches to storm the house full of queer folk on the hill and put things back to the way that the Lord intended. They get used to pretty much everything, and once it's been there for a while, it becomes part of what's always been, and then they get proud of it. Alferd Packer, the Colorado cannibal, could probably run for governor if he were still alive (he'd be around 150 years old, of course), just because gawdammit, he's *our* cannibal. The Mutilated Cow is just one of dozens of businesses named after the weird goings-on in the valley, and while nobody likes finding a cattle mutilation, at least when you find one, you know you're at home.

Up in the mountains "cultural attractions" get cheap; nobody will pay much to be entertained. The cover was just three bucks and that included a little orange ticket for half off on my first beer. Which was a Coors Light because the other beer they usually had was Coors, and they were out.

The place was basically a big room with a bar at one end, rest rooms at the other, some four-by-eight platforms legged up to make a stage in front of the rest rooms, and a few busted-up old formica tables huddling back against the bar as if they were afraid of the music. (If so, I was shortly to hear, they had a point.) The place stank of old cigarettes and beer-soaked plywood and the thousand kinds of oil and grit that get onto people who mostly work outside all day in all weather.

There were dozens of photos, some glossies and some ripped out of magazines or newspapers, framed on the walls, the glass in front of them smeared yellow-gray with old smoke. Posters covered most of the wall, anything with an alien theme—a couple old posters for *E.T.*, some variations on The Truth Is Out There, a couple of the old UFO Map of Colorado, a big chart labeled The Truth on one side and The Cover Up on the other with the standard alien face in the center, that sort of thing. Several inflatable aliens hung from the rafters by ropes under their armpits, and over the rest rooms hung a fairly crude painting, which made up for its artistic execution by being nine feet wide and five high, of aliens squatting on toilets, with the caption THE PORTAL POTTY.

"We get all that stuff from Judy Messoline's ranch, down by Hooper," the bartender told me. "You're Doctor Barnes, aren't you?"

"I am." I squinted at her and said, "Western student?"

"For three terms. I wasn't going to take no classes from no hard cases, I was there to party, it's a party school, that's the *point*, you know?" She held up a hand for a high five, so I stuck mine up and she slapped it. "I mean, party, that's what it's about. So I bailed out after Christmas of my sophomore year, moved up to the Butte to ride my board and smoke the rasta, got pregnant, the guy was from here, moved down here with his folks, he took off and joined the Army, but I get along real good with his mom, and she owns this place, so now I tend bar here. You probably didn't recognize me because my freshman year, when you saw me a lot, I was like all Christian girl and stuff. I grew my dreads since."

"Oh, right. You used to come by because your roommate worked in the scene shop."

"Yeah. She said you were okay but she was afraid of you. She said you were like a nice hardcase, like you were always all 'build to plan' but then you'd have everyone over at your house for dinner. She got real Christian and now she's got two kids and sends me pamphlets about it. For joining her church, I mean. Not for having two kids. I got one and he's plenty." She held up her hand, so I slapped it. There is no polite way to decline a high five.

"This was—Molly?"

"No, I'm Molly. She was Jennifer."

The band was setting up by the time-honored method of several people standing around watching one person wrestle with some small artifact and swear at it. I recognized Esau and waved, but he was locked in a life or death struggle with a mike stand. I figured that the plump, thirty-something blonde woman in the black silk blouse, black leather mini, narrow wraparound sunglasses, and stilettos had to be Jenapha Lee, basing this on the fact that she kept pacing over to tell Esau something or other. He seemed to be ignoring her, but then Travis would ask her something about it, and she'd give him a very long explanation.

The costumer in me figured she was wearing between seven and nine hundred dollars, not counting jewelry, which meant the total cost of the clothes on her must be about equal to the total cost of the clothes on the other twenty people in the room, combined.

"Have you heard them, Molly?" I asked the bartender.

"Naw, but I hear they suck."

"That's what I hear too."

"Friends of yours?"

"Friends of a friend—that skinny guy in the denim jacket is the friend. And actually he's more friends with their manager."

"I hope it ain't nothing big to say this but she's a real bitch. If that's okay to say, Doctor Barnes."

"More than okay with me. 'Real bitch' tends to be what Travis likes."

"Another Coors Light?"

"Sure." I knew the rhythm of mountain roadhouses. My next beer wouldn't be getting to me any time soon—she'd have to visit with everyone at the bar, going both ways, and spend a certain amount of time just staring into space and chilling before getting around to the stressful job of opening a bottle and collecting my money.

The band started up then, and it was every bit as bad as Travis had threatened. Esau was as close to a musician as they had, and as a musician, he was an adequate engineer. He'd rigged up a system through MIDI and a couple old computers so that it picked up pitches coming off Kermit's guitar and produced thirds, fourths, or fifths, above or below, actuated by Esau's drumsticks on the oddly mixed drum set (looked like one snare and two cymbals too many to me) or on the vibes. The drums and vibes themselves were amplified, so what you got were these weird chords in time with the pounding drums, and Kermit's three chords and some slides up and down the frets, all backing up Jake, in mirrorshades, tight tee, and black jeans (a bad combination on a guy who was already turning to pudge), who was yelling something or other into the microphone, whenever he remembered to hold it near his face. I wasn't able to follow the exact text but the basic message was that he was Indian, we stole his land, and he was pissed off.

Everybody at the bar (except me, Molly, and three old-timers who sat with each other and never moved) got up and sort of jumped around to it. At least Esau gave them enough of a beat to jump consistently. In the middle of it all I could see Travis and Jenapha Lee dancing sort of with each other; that is, he had his hands on her waist and was bumping back and forth, and she was simultaneously grinding on him and looking around the room. She looked incredibly bored, like she was looking around to see if there was anything to do while she danced. Well, every time I'd known Travis to fall hard, it had been for someone who ignored him, and I had to admit this was the most thorough job of ignoring him I'd ever seen.

After about half an hour Molly came by with my beer, and I paid her. "I'd promise to give Jake his land back if he'd skip the rest of his sets," I shouted into her ear.

"Dude!" She high-fived me.

At last the set ended, and everyone piled off the dance floor and up along the bar to grab drinks. They all seemed to be white kids who felt like they were having a major spiritual experience, though the ones who had seen the band before were complaining because they didn't have that "real totally spiritual guy, that shaman, with them this time. He's awesome."

"Hey," the girl next to me said, pointing with her cigarette, "that one there. That one."

She was pointing at Travis.

"Yeah," the guy beside her asked.

"Dude, you got to look at his eyes when you get a chance. Alien for sure. At least three quarter blood alien. I can smell it on them but the eyes are like the total giveaway. Fuck, he's like coming this way. Don't look at him. They can smell fear."

"John, I'd like you to come on over and join us at the band table, and get acquainted," Travis said. I followed him.

Seen up close, Jenapha Lee was a recognizable type; the mountains are full of people who live there because it's nice, and can afford to because their money comes from somewhere else. Very often the somewhere else is a trust fund or a supportive family. It's not unusual to meet someone who is waiting tables but living in a paid-for half-million-dollar house, whose pocket money comes out of that part-time job but who flies to ski and sun areas, all over North America and Europe, a few times a year, and who can't touch the principal but has a few hundred grand in the bank. Some of them turn into the peculiar lifetime potheads known as trustifarians, some become perpetual imitators of venture capitalists who are forever on the brink of a good deal but don't have the capital (because their parents won't let them play with the real money), a few become activists for the more radical environmental groups or the more dedicated Christian rightists, but most just sort of drift, year to year, from one pointless activity to another, unable to forget that finally what they do isn't going to matter.

Jenapha Lee had a number of gifts as far as I could see. She could smoke with an air of deep thought. She wore expensive clothes very well. And she could talk artsy, though not art theory. She was explaining Skin2Skin to me. "The thing is, that even though Skin2Skin totally sucks, it totally sucks in a way that's really important, so we gotta keep playing, especially because there's no reason to."

"Why?" I asked, feeling sillier than usual.

"I just told you. Because there's no reason. Like, people are always doing things for reasons, and if they weigh out the pros and cons and all those, then the reasons will add up to doing just one thing, and they don't have any choice, they have to do that one thing, so not having choice, they're not free. I mean, I know all this stuff. I had a second major in philosophy for a while and I know it, and the instructor said my final paper in this one class was really good. So I know that I know what I'm talking about, and it's just as plain as it gets, you know, that when people let their reason run their lives, they aren't free. See, like, why are people of the First

Nations free, you know like they are so free that they are *symbols* of freedom?"

I glanced sideways at Kermit. Coors Light and having a reasonably sane, ordinary conversation with Molly had mellowed me, so I didn't want to start pointing out just what kind of "freedom" the native/Indian/First Nations people had, which would merely have been a case of spitefully picking a fight with Travis's girlfriend, but on the other hand, I didn't want an educated person of color to think I bought into this kind of bullshit, because I'm an academic and most of us would rather die than know that anyone with darker skin than us thinks we're full of shit. Kermit shrugged, like a man who did not want to be an example but couldn't get out of the room. While I was still thinking about whether or not to interrupt her, Jenapha Lee went on. "They're free because there's *no reason* for them to be here, see, it's the same thing as no place in the modern world, only they're really free, because with no reason, they can't be controlled by the reason, see?"

"We're fucking lucky to get invited to a fucking UN Conference on fucking genocide," Jake put in. He hadn't taken his mirror-shades off yet. Travis was right; he did look like an angry bug. "If we go white and learn to fit in we vanish, and if we don't we just fold up and die. We're about the most unnecessary people on the Earth. We're the victims of a crime so big that all the law is inside the crime."

"I'll buy that much," I said.

"You're white. You'll steal that much."

"So," Jenapha Lee said, "the thing that makes Skin2Skin so necessary, so totally necessary, is okay, maybe, like musically, they suck, suck bigtime, you know? That makes them a band without a reason, which is a comment on a people without a reason, which means that it's about free people. So it's all about freedom."

By now I was seriously considering arguing. I didn't want to get along too well with her and let Travis think I approved of his taste, and having him think that might mean I would have this conversation repeatedly for the next several years, because he was acting and talking pretty smitten. So I needed to establish a boundary or twelve—

Melody Wallace walked in.

Feeling a deep evil impulse, I waved at her to get her over to our table. She came over, grinning to find me here, and her eyes lit up to see Travis.

Glances bounced around between Travis, Melody, and Jenapha Lee, about as fast and about as numerous as photons around three charged balls, but the interactions were more complex. It did have one beneficial effect; Jenapha Lee stopped looking bored and started to get lively. Introductions zoomed around the table, and I generously scooted sideways to let Melody in between me and Travis. He had the patient expression of a man who has broken a tooth on a Friday at three in the afternoon, cannot get down to town before six, and knows that the local dentist is due back on a late Tuesday flight.

I went to take a leak, and as I was standing at the middle urinal in the Portal Potty, someone huge stood next to me. I looked up to see a big, ragged hippie type, who I could smell even over the stench of a roadhouse bathroom, and then realized. "Brown Pierre," I said.

"Hey, John, Travis said you were up here in this part of the country now."

Well, one of the strangest things about the Ivy Plus Fifty, that circuit of hyper-endowed colleges that much of the American ruling class goes to, is that no matter who you were in school, or who you are now, if you run into someone from the same place, or especially a classmate, you can hardly stop comparing notes and establishing that you're both part of the group. We went up and had a beer at the bar, and then shouted stuff in each other's ears during the next Skin2Skin set. It was kind of like having a casual beer with the Unabomber, except that as far as I knew Brown hadn't actually blown anyone up, and kind of like old home week on Mars, exchanging information about ". . . what happened to that girl who used to whirl around every dance floor all by herself and never talked? Did she really marry a senator?" and ". . . so did those two get married and have their optimal three little tax deductions, a boy athlete, a girl scientist, and a troubled but talented gay composer, and retire at forty-five like they planned, or by any chance did something mess up the plan?" and the perennially popular "no shit, Billy the Goon is a federal judge now."

He had to leave early—turned out that he lived up in Crestone, about thirty miles away, and had things to do in the morning, so Brown only stayed for one set. He and Molly and I decided we had bonded by agreeing that Skin2Skin were really terrible but it was very wrong of us to notice.

So I shook Brown's hand and we laughed and said we should step up the frequency of our meetings, to maybe once every ten years, and he took off at the band break. I went back to rejoin Melody, Travis, and Jenapha at the band table.

The tension could have been cut with an ax, barely. It was one more thing for me to not like about Jenapha—she was the sort who acts indifferent until someone else wants what she has, and then really switches up the bright-and-charming girl act, which I think is about as tacky a way to treat someone you care about as there is. Melody was making sure we all knew which one was the Ph.D., which was equally tacky, really, but I'm more used to it. Travis was trying not to look spineless or like a jackass and was failing in all directions at once.

The Irwin brothers peed, drank some cold water, and decided to do the sensible thing, chicken out, and start their next set ASAP. Jenapha more or less grabbed Travis and dragged him onto the dance floor. The white kids in dreads followed immediately and soon they were all hopping around in the same sort of controlled spasm as before.

"Not much like dancing, is it?" Melody bellowed in my ear.

"Is that what they're doing?"

Jake was again shouting about how he was an Indian and he was mad. It occurred to me that there was an interesting feedback problem in that Kermit's guitar was getting more out of tune, so a wider range of noises coming out of it were generating thirds, fourths, and fifths on Esau's wired percussion system, which meant that the melody (if any) must be vanishing more and more. Jake didn't seem like the guy to track it down and find it, either.

"What are you doing here?" I hollered to Melody.

"Bored, nothing in Gunny, and doing research officially," she shouted back.

"On what?"

"You didn't know? This is an abductee bar."

It took me a moment to process that; once I did, I shook my head in admiration. "So everyone here has been abducted on a UFO? Or thinks they have?"

"Yeah. I've got an interest in the narratology of the abduction construct. I think there's a potential way to deconstruct it with respect to the urban-rural power relation."

Which is what a semiotician says when she means she's looking for patterns in the way people put together stories about being kidnapped by flying saucers, and she thinks that if you remove the elements from the structure, and look at how they were fitted into it, you'll see something that reveals how people in rural areas feel about

being under the political domination of cities. One thing I liked
about Melody, when you got to the bottom of her short pronouncements, there were long pronouncements that meant something.

"What's Travis doing here?"

"He's got a *major* thing for Jenapha," I said, seeing no way to
soften it. "By the way, he's an idiot."

"You said that about him before. Are they serious?"

"He is. I doubt she's ever serious about anything."

We sat and watched the band for a while, and they maintained a
pretty constant level; nothing was any worse or any better. I visual-
ized them as following an isosuckage plane in suck space. I leaned
forward and said, "Hey, let's go out in the parking lot for a second.
I have an idea for how I can be a treacherous bastard."

Melody followed me out, and I said, "You know, I've enjoyed
about as much of this band as I can stand. And I got up at five
freakin' thirty to put Kara on a plane, and then sat and drank with
Trav all afternoon, and drove over the mountains, and you know
what? I'm really tired. And they have another set after this one.
And then Travis will want to spend some more time following
Jenapha Lee around. So here's my idea. Let me give you his pack to
put in your car. Then I'm going to take off and drive home while I
can still do it awake; there's cliffs, turns, and dropoffs that I'd rather
be able to react to. And then his way back to Gunnison is either
you, or else he'll have to stick with the band."

"You *are* a treacherous bastard," Melody said. "I'm nominating
you to go back on Faculty Senate when you get back from sabbatical."

"I'm just betraying a friend," I said, "it's not like I'm fixing up
roast baby sandwiches or anything."

"But you're betraying a friend with such style. It's the essence of
faculty self-governance. Okay, let's do it."

I handed her his pack, gingerly because with Travis you never know what might be in there, and said, "Careful with that—you never know what that maniac may be toting around."

"Hey, John?"

"Yeah."

She gave me a hug; there was a lot of Melody, though she carried it all well, and my hands didn't quite touch comfortably as they closed over the rough red wool of the back of her coat. Into my shoulder, she said, "From the way he's looking at her, I don't think I really have a chance, but thanks for trying to give me one, okay?"

"You're welcome. I should start driving before the set finishes out—it'll spare some awkward explaining, and leave your story more credible."

I watched her go back into the Mutilated Cow, and felt like I might be missing something, but I turned the engine over, flipped up the headlights, and pulled out. The 4Runner's lights swept over a long row of huge battered pickups and tiny even more battered granolamobiles; one old Land Cruiser had a bumper sticker I liked: "Carpe Callosum."

Really, it had probably been better than staying at home and being depressed, but it was time to go home now. I spent most of that long winding drive, up and over the pass, explaining that to myself repeatedly, and when I finally got home at two in the morning, I just took out my contacts, fed the cats, and fell into bed.

CHAPTER SEVENTEEN

"It's really not your fault," Kara said, as we sat in the W and waited for Melody. "And you weren't there—you worked hard not to be there—and you don't even know what happened. The Gunnison paper isn't very good for finding out what happened, you know?"

"I just can't believe I left no more than an hour before it happened," I said. "I have such a talent for not being there."

"Don't worry, Travis will show up when it's most inconvenient, and he'll tell you something better than what really happened." She had that silly crooked grin that had probably induced me to propose in the first place, and as always, as soon as I saw it, I felt worlds better.

I glanced down at the Gunnison paper in front of me. Normally it was a very thin paper anyway, about the size of a college paper at a medium-sized college with no j-school. The first issue of the New Year was even thinner than usual, since pretty much everybody was either down somewhere sunny, up the mountain skiing, or at least at home doing as little as possible.

"Nowadays I get all my news from reading *Gaudeamus* on the

web," I said. "I think I believe in Ower Gyro more than I do in our mayor. Did you see it this morning? There was an icon of a pill, with a glass of water, on O. B. Joyful's desk, and if you clicked on the pill, you got a magnifying glass to look at it, and on the pill it said 'Thinkenfuk.' And the glass of water said 'From Saguache Springs.' You know, I've told you that Travis and I have some connections with Richard Reno—"

"Often," Kara said.

"Okay, but it's a cool story."

"Even in reruns. Which always dwell on Traci and Stacy."

"Okay. I'll skip all the stuff you've heard. I'm just wondering if maybe Travis hasn't told me but is still in touch with Richard Reno, and is telling him the same stories he's been telling me. It would explain how *Gaudeamus* keeps referring to things in Travis's stories, and it would also mean that Travis's stories didn't necessarily have to be true."

"I would think you'd want your friend to be telling you the truth."

"If he is, I'm an old fat lazy coward, passing up the best chance I'll ever have to see something, and write about it, that could make me rich and famous. If he's just a crazy liar with a taste for tall tales, and really bad timing, then I can feel okay about myself."

"Uh," she said, "uh." She was doing her little double-take thing that meant she thought I'd stopped making sense. "And exactly how does that follow logically?"

"I'm on sabbatical. I don't have to think logically till I go back."

"Is that it?"

There was an edge in Kara's voice that made me nervous, like we might have one of the fights we rarely had, or like she wanted to talk about something more serious than I wanted to talk about, so I looked down at the paper in front of me again, a bad choice for somewhere to hide.

Kara's finger pointed to the headline that had started the conversation: DRUG BUST IS TOTAL BUST.

About an hour after I'd left the Mutilated Cow, the Saguache County sheriff's department had raided the place, confiscating large quantities of a pill variously called "God" and "good moss." Which I suspected was the *Times* reporters doing their usual job of writing what they thought they heard and not checking afterwards. On various occasions I had been reported as the author of *Original Residence, One Four Morning Glory* (presumably the address of the Original Residence), and *Encounter with Fiber*, about which I refused to think. It was probably unrelated to my being introduced as the writer of *Encounter with Timber* on local radio.

"So Travis Bismarck dropped by the *Timely* and told them the same outrageous story and got them to corroborate it?" Kara asked. "Is that really what you think?"

"All right," I said, "Point taken. But like you just said, given where the story is running, there's really no telling what actually happened. And even if it's miraculously accurate, the whole point of the story is that no one was arrested or charged and the whole thing was a big mistake. But, okay, okay, okay, you're right, it's the closest thing to a confirmation that I've had that any of this wild stuff Travis is telling me is true. And I have the strangest feeling about the other headline—the giant sinkhole."

"Oh, according to the news this morning, they've definitely ruled out a sinkhole, which means it's really unexplained," Kara said. "It's going to be in all the Ripley's and Strange and Unknown books for decades to come. And it made the national news, anyway, and the Denver stations sent camera crews down there. Though how you can get footage of one million cubic meters of sand not being there is beyond me."

The other above-the-fold headline in the paper was the freakish event at Great Sand Dunes National Monument, at the foot of the mountains on the eastern side of the San Luis Valley. It's one of those awe-inspiring places that the West abounds in that seem to get no press or public awareness even a few hundred miles away— an immense high-altitude dune field piled up against the western face of the Sangre de Cristos. Satellites and survey crews had confirmed that sometime during Christmas night, in an area exactly one kilometer square, a meter of top sand had disappeared from all the dunes. As Kara pointed out, it was a very exact one million cubic meters, and round numbers are naturally suspicious. (Trust a mathematician's daughter to notice that.)

Now, the dunes shift all the time, but the sand goes *somewhere,* and the scientists are used to being able to figure out where. This time, a million cubic meters had vanished, and there was no evidence that it had blown, washed, or sunk anywhere. That, plus the exactitude of the kilometer square by one meter deep—its sides lined up perfectly north, south, east, and west—had brought many of the strange-phenomena people out, and they in turn had drawn the news media with them, because any good station manager knows that a Bigfoot sighting or a UFO is ten times easier to cover than foreign policy or biotechnology. So the TV screens in Colorado and the neighboring states had been filled with images of people with rigid hair and huge teeth standing in front of sand dunes with high, snow-covered peaks in the background, reporting that before the mysterious incident, this place had looked just like this but a meter higher.

"Betcha dinner at the Cattlemen's that Travis works that one into his story," Kara said.

"The sand dunes story? No bet. I'm just wondering if he'll work in 'First Graders Make Giant Christmas Tree from All Recycled Materials.'" That was the other front-page story.

Melody still wasn't there, so we flagged down the waitress and got coffee. "Take your time and wait for your friend," she said. "Without idle people sitting around it'll look like my job is unnecessary."

After she'd gone, Kara said, "You know, somewhere back there, you made a good point—I'll try not to faint. The drug story is the closest thing to confirmation you've had for any of this wild stuff Travis has been telling you. At least the name sounds like 'gaudeamus', and it *was* a drug, and then a 'Mr. Hale from a federal agency' showed up and revealed that all the drugs were part of some mysterious government project and in fact it was fine for them to be in that pickup truck. Can you imagine someone getting a local cop, out here where they're used to being authority and making decisions, to back off on half a ton of pills, especially when he's busting a bunch of strange people that the neighbors don't like, *and* the primary is only a few months away? Hale must have really had weight to throw around. Which gives me the feeling that Travis must be telling some approximation to the truth, doesn't it you?"

"If Travis Bismarck is telling the truth about anything, I'll eat both my boots, composite soles first, without A-1," Melody said, sliding into the booth beside Kara. "Sorry I'm late. So you guys saw the paper too."

"Did you get caught in that?" I asked.

"Naw. The instant that Travis realized you had gone and left his backpack with me, he suddenly remembered he had to go somewhere, with that rich nitwit, right after the show. So he got his bag from my car and that was the last I saw of him, except catching a glimpse, now and then, of him out on the dance floor grinding with the Former Debutante Most Likely To Have Been Dropped On Her Head."

"She doesn't impress me much, either," I said. "Pure poser. It's funny how even the worst bands have one or two of those around.

And the worse the band, the more likely it is that their hanger-on is going to be somebody rich."

"Sure, they'll never make the money to pay her. She has to do it out of charity. On the other hand, she gets that band all to herself—poor thing. So over time the successful bands get beautiful hangers-on, and the sucky bands get rich hangers-on. Pure market-driven evolution." Melody sighed. "Okay, I'm bitter. And I'm not over it. Damn it, John, your old friend is *hot*. A jackass and a deep-seated loser, but hot. And cool. And I could so use to have someone cool come through town to see me now and then. I'm starting to think about looking for love in all the wrong places."

Kara sighed. "When you start quoting country songs, you're pretty far gone already."

Melody nodded. "Well, that song in particular."

"I always wondered—if you're looking for love, what *are* the wrong places?" Kara asked.

"Under cowboy hats, above cowboy boots, and behind cowboy belt buckles," our waitress said, coming up behind me. "Shit, Professor Wallace, I've been single in this town for ten years, and I've already done the research. Don't you start. We don't gotta verify or confirm no results."

CHAPTER EIGHTEEN

"Hey, thanks for letting me ride along with you," Melody said, as
we roared across Kansas in the bright noon of early January. Wheat
stubble, broken here and there by a fencerow or ditchrow of trees,
stretched right out to the soft white sky at the horizon. We'd been
going steadily since leaving at five-thirty in the morning, and the
whole way we'd had the Western State van in front of us. "I
couldn't quite believe it. Three hours in the van and I wanted to
scream. But those two actually seem to enjoy it."

"They like theatre students," I said, "and they're used to coping
with a two-year-old, which is very valuable experience if you're going to deal with theatre students. And the students can tell they like
them—which is part of why they're such fun people to have as faculty, but also why all kinds of against-the-rules stuff tends to erupt
around them. I like theatre students too, actually, but for some reason they behave fairly well around me."

"Because you're gruff and mean and a brutal hard case?"
Melody suggested.

"Must be. I find if I kill and eat the dumbest kid in each class, right on the table at the front of the room, at the beginning of the term, the rest of them behave pretty well afterwards."

Melody snorted. "Yeah. Right. Doctor Teddy Bear."

I shrugged. "Well, half of them think that, the other half think Doctor Ogre, and they all think I'm strange. Which is probably the real reason why so many of them behave—they can't predict how I'll react. Anyway, compared to past years, this trip is a breeze. It's only maybe eleven or twelve hours, total, to Kansas City. You should see what it's like when the regionals are in Minnesota."

As a science fiction writer, creating fictional societies, I find it very hard to capture one observation about real societies—that a big, free, rich society will have hundreds or thousands of interesting things going on that no one outside each little world has ever heard of. Science fiction conventions, which might not interest me but obviously amuse thousands of people. Limerick championships. Minor league baseball. Bar stool races. Recaptioning *The Family Circus*. The Burning Man. Bloomsday.

And in this particular case, KC-ACTF Regionals. The KC in question is the Kennedy Center, in Washington, the national headquarters of the whole thing. The ACTF is the American College Theatre Festival, which is an immense competition in, and celebration of, all the dozens of crafts that go into theatre production and therefore must be learned and practiced at the college level. I've been a volunteer respondent (the politest and most nonthreatening word for "judge") for it for many years, and it's one of the most interesting things going on in either American academia or American theatre. And of all the aspects of it, the most charming and interesting is the regional festival—six days during which students compete in acting, directing, all forms of design, playwriting, and technical areas; every theatre faculty member who can get there gets a chance to schmooze about every aspect of college theatre programs (and about what jobs might be opening up and who got into what kind of censorship trouble how and so on); and several of the best college productions from the past year in the region are remounted for everyone to see. (I've always admired the courage of anyone taking a show to regionals—imagine reviving a show that has been mothballed for months in order to perform it in front of an entire audience that is sitting there muttering, "Why didn't *our* show get invited instead of *this*?")

While I was at Western, it was also an occasion for finding out why I was glad I didn't have teenage children, since temporarily I had anywhere from four to fourteen of them, in an environment where there were also several hundred temptations in the form of other theatre students.

I had talked Melody into coming along because over in her end of communications, she'd never seen anything like this, and it was the kind of place where her keen eye might pick up fifty or a hundred ideas and observations for papers and books. Also because I knew the noise in the van would swiftly drive her crazy, she'd move over to my truck, none of the students would want to go to a vehicle where they'd be outnumbered by faculty, and thus I'd get either pleasant conversation or comfortable, friendly silent company for that eternal drive across Kansas.

It was about ten days after we'd met at the W Café, and though I hadn't heard from Travis, I'd talked to a couple of cops who were former students, and/or friends, and asked for the behind-the-scenes story; the whole thing had been weird enough that practically every city and county cop in Gunnison County, and all the other counties that adjoined Saguache, had called some cop or other over in Saguache to get the straight poop.

It had started with an anonymous phone tip to the Saguache County sheriff's office that a large white pickup with a distinctive camper back contained several crates of experimental pills, possibly stolen but certainly misappropriated, which were only supposed to be in the first stages of human testing, and said pills were supposedly being sold for more than a hundred dollars each.

Common sense should have told them that no one would be bringing a load like that to a place like that to sell it. If you looked over the crowd in the Mutilated Cow, perhaps a few of them were trustifarians who might have afforded a drug that expensive. But the great majority were classic wandered-in-and-stuck types who you find in every small town in the Rockies; people who'd found a niche and never had one before, and therefore didn't want to live anywhere else. Brown Pierre was almost typical.

Most of the hit-and-stick residents scrape by on odd jobs, part-time employment, and a little help from their friends, and probably half the crowd had had a little trouble coming up with a three-dollar cover. But major drug busts don't fall into the laps of small county departments very often, so Saguache County's Finest came in like they were busting Jack the Ripper, Al Capone, and Hitler, all at once, blocked all the exits, and hauled everyone down to the jail, all about twenty minutes after Melody left.

"I'm not sure how I got home," she told me and Kara. "It's a good thing driving while crying isn't a crime." Later Kara turned that phrase into a song, and still later she got so many requests (it was a pretty good song, I'd have to say) that she got sick of it. Now she won't sing "Driving While Crying" no matter how much you ask her. She'll even try to convince you there was never any such song. Melody does it well, though, so if you're ever passing near Gunnison and you catch her act at a roadhouse, you can hear it then.

After they had all been shuffled around from room to room in the Saguache County Jail, while everyone figured out what to do with them, the whole crowd from the Mutilated Cow was suddenly released. A mysterious Mr. Hale, with all kinds of federal authority and "confirmation out the wazoo from FBI and BATF and CIA and I swear to god even Fish and Game," as one Gunnison cop had quoted the Saguache County dispatcher to me, had shown up at the jail, everything had been declared one big mistake, and they'd all been let go, with no one even questioned. And there the matter rested, everything undone, as vanished as the one million cubic meters of sand from Great Sand Dunes.

I had told Melody Travis's story, omitting the whole way-too-bizarre business about Earth being sold multiple times to aliens and all of us being pawns in a chess game between Susan Glasgow and Lena Logan. Melody had been delighted to find an enormous number of mythic motifs and shared elements with urban legends and paranoid structures in all of it. "What you'd expect from a real good liar," she said. "Your friend is a remarkable creative artist who prefers audiences of just a few. There are lots of such people in the world—every little town has a Medal of Honor winner who in fact was never in any uniform after leaving the safety patrol, and a guy whose great-grandfather was the real inventor of television, and a couple of cannibals and one or two hidden European royalty in its past."

"Gunnison's cannibal was real," I pointed out.

"Gunnison's cannibal was *documented.*" She leaned back and played with her long hair; I thought again that Travis was a real idiot, but then I'd been thinking that for decades, and it had never done either me or Travis one bit of good. "You'll probably enjoy getting away from the weirdness for a while," she said.

"At ACTF Regionals? Oh, there will still be plenty of weirdness. It just won't be *weird* weirdness."

The sun crawled down the sky behind us, and our shadow ran

out in front across the stone cold road, and the tires ground away, pushing more of Kansas back behind us. Hours clicked by as we drove and stopped, drove and stopped, pausing only now and then to take on gas and Whoppers. I realized Melody was right; this conference would help get my head back into its normal shape, and I was looking forward to the chance for that.

One problem with ACTF, for which there is really no solution, is that schools vary enormously in size and budget and extent of drama programs. There are universities that spend, on a show, as much as some others spend on a season, and though talent and training can compensate, and a hundred-dollar set can look like ten thousand, when it's sitting next to a ten-thousand-dollar set that was designed by someone just as talented and better trained, and built by a professional shop staff, that hundred-dollar set is still not going to look like much. And when one school offers two acting classes—a non-majors class and a beginner class, and that's it—in the English department, and another offers two different acting classes plus voice and movement every term, in a conservatory, well, sometimes it's the equivalent of your high school football team playing in the NFL; the most important thing is that everyone be kind, refined, and totally blind.

As a tiny school with only three faculty who did theatre at all, Western was painfully aware of this, but, for us, we were having a great year. Not only did our lighting people do well—that was usually our strength—but one of our costume designs had gotten a rave critique, and one of our guys made it all the way to semifinals in the Irene Ryan Acting Competition, so all the kids were tense about that. Then he didn't make finals, so after semis everyone went out to get drunk, and I got back to my room late.

There was a flashing light on the phone. I picked it up, followed directions and punched buttons until it played my voice mail, and nearly dropped the stupid thing when I heard Travis's voice say, "So, you got any time to talk to an old friend, in between putting the wood to all these little coeds?"

Other friends might have said, for example, "Hi." Or "John, this is Travis," if that was who they were.

He said he had a room in the hotel, and to call no matter how late it was. I looked at the clock and my schedule and realized I didn't have to meet anyone, or be anywhere, till one the next afternoon. I thought for maybe a minute. I considered calling Kara, who was usually awake late, to have her talk me out of this.

Then I called Travis. He was still awake and dressed, and only two floors away.

Two minutes later, I opened my door, and there he was. "I suppose you're wondering why—"

"I'm trying to give up wondering why for the New Year, Trav, it's a resolution. Come on in."

He set a sixpack of Fat Tire into my room fridge, pulling one for himself. "Want one?"

"Better not."

"Well, then." He opened his. "John, I have to say, bud, you've got a knack for not being there. It took me a while to get over being pissed about that, because if you'd stuck around just a little more, instead of going home to sit in a basement and type your damn book, you could've seen stuff that would've kept you in book material for the rest of your life. So let me start off just saying that I was mad, but I made myself think it all through from your viewpoint, and by the time I got done with that, I wasn't mad anymore, okay?"

"I'm glad you're not mad at me for having not cooperated in having my life disrupted."

"I'm sure there's meaning in that sentence somewhere."

"I have a life, Travis, one I like. You used to be entertaining. The uproars are getting kind of frequent and really tiresome. And, like I said, I have a life."

"You have a *dull* life, John, and if you like it, how come you're blowing up like a balloon and turning a funny shade of gray and look halfway to the grave? But suit yourself. Like it or not, life or not, you're the guy I'm going to tell all this to." He took another pull at his beer, and began.

It seemed as if the universe blinked once, and there I was, stretched out on my bed, listening, while Travis sat in the armchair facing me, and told me another preposterous story. I used to think that Travis's visits indicated something good I'd done in a previous life; then for a while I thought they indicated something bad. Upon reflection, if there is actually any connection between Travis Bismarck's visits and my actions in a past life, I think it must be that I was some kind of horrible practical joker, or maybe an experimental psychologist or a professional saboteur.

I settled back deeper into the bed, thinking that perhaps if I fell asleep while he talked, he'd just leave. To my dismay, his story became interesting.

"Okay. So, you left the Mutilated Cow to go home and write and sulk, and you left my pack with Melody, and if you'd talked to me for half a second you'd've found out that Hale called and we had a meeting with him in Albuquerque the next day, he was coming that night to pick us up in an SR-8—yes, Mr. Sci Fi Guy, you missed seeing a flying saucer—so there was no way I was going back to sleep on your couch, or going back to bounce on Melody, or any such, I had work to do, and so did the Irwins and Jenapha. Of course, because we both got bombed and then you got sulky and didn't want to talk, I never did finish filling you in about what all was going on."

"Well, I got the part that it's all an epic struggle with one side being Lena Logan, Call Girl for Truth Justice and the American Way, working for All Thumbs, who is sort of a cross between the Lone Ranger and E.T. And the other side being Susan Glasgow, Evil Capitalist Scientist, backed by the—let me try to pronounce this now that I'm sober—the pTh'tong n'Wi, who are sort of like insane gardeners and con men, with a property-rights fixation . . ."

"Hey, not bad, you remember. Did I tell you about the Third Force?"

"Uh, no," I said, being in no shape to lie well.

"Oh, man. And that's where the Hardware Store Killer gets into it, don't you see?"

"Um. I'm sure I'll see if you tell me." It is seldom a good sign when I'm starting a lot of sentences with "um."

"See, the problem is, when you're working with the good guys, you gotta be noble. At least I think that's the problem. And besides, Lena Logan is sentimental and a nice person, whatever she may like to do when she's loaded up on Gaudeamus pills. That's where it all starts, is that problem that Lena Logan is a nice person."

You remember that poster you used to have on your wall in the frat house, John, the one with the picture of the gorilla holding a ball bat, and the caption "Physical brutality is the sincerest form of criticism?" Well, that seems to be a guiding principle in Galactic law. If somebody sells their planet, and their own people then kill them, that's taken to be convincing evidence that it was disapproved of, and that therefore the deal might not have been valid. So when the court is looking at the behavior of individuals within an individualist species, trying to figure out which individuals actually had the power to make contracts that could bind the species as a whole, they often look at whether the natives were killed or punished by their own people. Just the way it is.

Instigating the killing of the people who sell the planet, however, is not something All Thumbs, or any other marshal, is allowed to do; they can mention that it strengthens your case, but you're highly subject to challenge if your species doesn't usually settle matters by killing each other. Now, of course, when I heard about that, I said right away that I think we could win that challenge, if our history was admissible in that court. But Lena felt strongly that she didn't want to kill her old friends, and for a long time she was the senior native leader of our little organization, and All Thumbs thought her feelings should be respected. I guess I agree with Lena that the good guys ought to win with their hands as clean as can be managed, at least as long as they win. But that might just be that what-would-roy-rogers-do side of my nature.

And that's how we know there's a Third Force in the game, besides Susan Glasgow and Lena Logan. We just don't know quite who. But clearly they know the rules too, because when the Hardware Store Killer murdered those five women from Moloch College, it strongly reinforced the case that we, the people of Earth, did not agree to sell our planet so that those seven women could be rich. So the way to put it, John, is that the unknown Third Force is basically bad guys on the side of the good guys.

Best guess I can make is that they don't want the feds or any cops figuring out anything about why the murders are happening, so they try to make it look like a serial killer did it. And it kind of worked—it wasn't till the third one, Heart Reno, that the papers even noticed the Moloch College connection.

As a matter of fact, we're the only side that doesn't do much killing, though obviously, if you think about that poor pizza girl, our hands aren't spotless either. But the real heavy-duty killers are Susan

Glasgow's outfit. Because the problem gets worse every month that more and more people keep inventing Gaudeamus, on their own. Everything is fine with Susan's group if the pTh'tong n'Wi or any of a dozen other species gets to the inventor to offer platinum and diamonds, or all the knowledge in the world, or whatever they want, for the same deal—sell the Earth. And most of the inventors do get all clever-stupid and crafty-dumb and realize that they had someone begging to buy the Brooklyn Bridge and offering the Hope Diamond to do it, and cut the deal. See, every time the Earth is sold again, it reinforces the record that that's something we would do and that you can buy the Earth from any old individual human.

But now and then, someone tries to go to the government about it. When they try, Susan's little group just gaudeamuses an air bubble into their brains, then gaudeamuses it back out after it has destroyed enough tissue, so it just looks like a freak stroke.

Now, they don't fuck with me 'cause somebody real good's got my back. I'm hooked in with All Thumbs, like Hale and all of Xegon and the Irwins, and if they mess with me, just on the general principle that they never let anybody fuck with their native help, All Thumbs and the marshals will be all over them. It's like being Tonto, you know, old Kemo Sabe might treat you like a servant but when the bad guys whomp your ass, he's all over them. And All Thumbs himself is even more secure, being what he is. Apparently hurting or threatening a Galactic Marshal is, cubed and squared, like shooting a Texas Ranger.

I really had meant to fall asleep, but I had to ask. "Do you like him?"

"All Thumbs? Interesting question. You like your cat, right? And maybe the neighbor's dog? But you probably don't like some random shark in the Atlantic and you could give a shit about the bacteria in your yogurt, right? And yet all of those are less alien than All Thumbs; in some ways you've got more in common with that old coleus plant on your windowsill than I do with him. He explained something, once, as Lena was trying to learn to communicate with him, and she passed it on to us. Vertebrates have two basic axes, pleasure-pain and distress-eustress, so you like something in the pleasure and eustress quadrant, you're brave about something in the pain-eustress quadrant, you feel guilt or shame about things in the pleasure-distress quadrant, and you hate and fear things in the pain-distress quadrant. With all kinds of twinks and mods on that, of course. Well, All Thumbs doesn't have axes, he has hexagons, and four, not two. So our like, don't like, can live with, all that stuff, is like the gray scale in a dog's vision; what he has emotionally is like full-color vision plus UV and X-ray. One of us can have friendship with him about as easily as Corner the cat can play Scrabble with you." He tilted his chair back and stretched. "Eventually this story is also going to explain why I'm here, bud. I mean in your hotel room, not about Dad being too lazy to get to the drugstore."

"That joke's still old."

"We're all getting old, compadre." He took another sip. "So the case went on getting more complicated, but at least All Thumbs was now a step closer, via Xegon, to getting respectable contact with a genuine government, and since he couldn't officially teach us anything about Gaudeamus, it also meant we had some research that might give us that technology in time for us to pay off a lot of the contracts, maybe all of them. Lena and the Irwins and Jenapha worked pretty long and hard to make that happen; it had been the focus of most of their activity for about a year and a half, just steering and borrowing Xegon's research, and importing whatever other companies' research would help Xegon, and back-door distributing all the ideas that lead to better and more Gaudeamus. Because we need to really understand it and have it working by February 4, 2011, and that old clock keeps ticking. And meanwhile Susan Glasgow was buying out or killing most of the good talent. And the unknown Third Force was killing the Moloch women, which was good news as far as our case went, and frankly I had to admit I thought it would be great if they bagged Susan, but we also had to worry about whether they might go after Lena, since killing Lena would make the case just as thoroughly. So we had a lot of players on the field, and no exact count of teams, and that's when the whole works got kicked over, and it all went into the soup."

"You mean it gets *more* complicated?"

"Getting there, getting there. Good stories have some twists and turns, and the best stories are *all* twists and turns."

"Bullshit."

"You'd be the authority on that," he said. He threw his empty bottle, straight and hard, into the wastebasket across the room, knocking it over. "On bullshit, I mean. Make your living making it up. Me, I got to live it."

CHAPTER NINETEEN

So, anyway, John, you left, and then Melody left—I was sorry to have hurt her feelings, but what can I say, sometimes my own feelings surprise me, and I was never going to be interested in anyone else while Jenapha Lee's around, and I can tell you don't like her much so let's not talk about that right now, 'kay?

All right. Now, while you all were in there, somebody drove a Ford Ranger full of Gaudeamus pills right into the parking spot where you'd been, spiked its tires so it would just sit there, and phoned the Saguache County Sheriff's Department. Since we'd just been fucked over but didn't know it yet, and Susan Glasgow's organization had been *really* fucked over too, it's a tossup whether that truckload of goddies was the Glasgow group's trick, or the Third Force. I'm betting the Third Force because of two things—first of all, it involved distributing something new and creating a demand for it, and that's something Glasgow's people hardly ever do, and secondly because it was subtle, almost like a practical joke, and everything I had seen of Glasgow's folk, from storming the facility and shooting Hale to that completely clumsy, stupid attempt on me, by those two mibs on US285, had been crude and dumb and overdone.

So the cleverness of this little prank argued that it wasn't Susan's group at all.

We were just finishing up the set and I had those funny aches you get in your leg muscles when you dance to a bad drummer, because you're always doing all these little jolts to compensate for him not being quite on the beat. Still, being merely a bad drummer, and a good programmer, Esau Irwin was the musical talent in the family, compared to the suck-dog awful guitar, lyrics, and vocals supplied by his brothers.

I was looking forward to Hale getting here with that SR-8, because Jenapha Lee had me all worked up, and going to Albuquerque by flying saucer, we'd be able to get in some quality time in our room before we absolutely had to sleep. The meeting with Hale wasn't till ten A.M. the next day.

The lights came on, kerbang, and they chopped the band sound, zip, and all the local piggery swarmed in, plod plod plod. In their best body armor, with the attitude to match. They lined us all up and shouted questions at us. None of us acted really afraid like we were supposed to—after all, these were mostly people who had been one kind of druggie or another, currently or in the past, and they knew the drill. Pretty soon we were all being shoved onto a commandeered school bus to be dragged down to the county pokey, and that good mood I had had while I was dancing with Jenapha Lee was pretty much gone.

Since I was with somebody who was with the band, I was in the first group they questioned. For about forty minutes we had to keep saying "never heard of it" and "I don't know" whenever they asked about the Gaudeamus pill. It was kind of fun, though, to listen to the real innocents, the club owner and the bartender and so forth. They didn't want anyone to know that there was a drug they'd never heard of, so they were either real vague or made stuff up, and that caused more questions, and the testimony got so far away from the truth so fast that I figured we were never getting caught.

Then Hale showed up, waving all kinds of federal authority, and we all got out at about three in the morning. He'd brought an SR-8 out of Kirtland, and he took us back to Albuquerque in one big swoop over the dark San Luis Valley. Probably we were so high up that no one spotted us that time; I wondered how many times, though, the saucers had been seen.

"Actually," Hale said, "as saucers, not all that often. At least that's what they told me while I was learning to drive one of these things— one more reason why I ought to thank you all, because these are really fun. But anyway, mostly saucers don't fly low enough to be recognized as such. There's a few big SR-17s and SR-6s, the things that make about half the bombing raids that people attribute to the Stealth, that practice low over the La Veta MOA, so they get seen. These SR-8s seldom have any reason to fly low. So we don't get seen as saucers.

"What we do get seen as is weird lights in the sky. The cloaking system is very imperfect, it just sets things up so the average path of light is around the ship and back out of the distorted air at a point about in line with where it went in. But some light doesn't go on the average path and much of that off-track light gets diffracted. So people are always seeing oval shapes that have rainbow colors smeared along them, in bright sunlight, way up in the sky; it's the sun refracted into a rainbow by our invisibility equipment. Not long ago we had a real dumb student pilot—uh, me, to be precise—on his first solo flight, get it locked into hover mode up by Salida, broad daylight, and some guy shot a whole videotape of this elongated oval with rainbow colors washing over it. Took me almost an hour to get it out of hover, so they got a lot of shots. Tonight, though, we're only going to be seen if someone points binoculars right at us."

With all the delay from getting arrested and released, we didn't get to our hotel rooms till past five A.M., so we rescheduled to meet late the following afternoon. Then at nine-thirty the phone rang, and it was Hale, and he said a limo was coming out for us, we had to meet right away. Jenapha Lee and me got dressed in about two, and the van was already sitting there in the hotel drive when we got down there. The Irwins came tumbling out a minute later, and we were on our way. Naturally the driver wouldn't have a clue what was up, and all of us were exhausted, so we all got some extra sleep—not near enough—while he drove us out to the facility.

So far on this long-running job, the pay was consistently good, the work was consistently interesting, and what it really was, was murder on your sleep.

As soon as we had gathered, All Thumbs set down his cigar—

Hell, yeah. Do you know how many of the chemical compounds in tobacco are neurologically active, and how many are immunologically active, and how many are both? Anything that's had its biology re-engineered to eat Earth food is going to respond to Earth tobacco, and apparently All Thumbs's species, or maybe every species from his planet, is cancer-proof, or they can fix cancer, or for all I could tell from the one explanation he ever gave me, maybe they do get cancer but they enjoy it.

Anyway, he sure likes big old stinking cigars, the kind that guys smoke when they're trying to compensate, that go with bleached blondes, Harleys, and tailored black suits. So, like I was saying, All Thumbs set down his cigar and said it was good of us all to come, and like that.

He's got a weird little voice that he makes with a bladder like a bagpipe with a slot-whistle in it, totally separate from his lungs and his digestor (which is something different from a digestive tract or an esophagus-stomach-and-intestines, but he hasn't quite explained it to me in a way I can picture yet). So he can eat, smoke, drink, and excrete one of those weird little balls that he has instead of shit, all while still talking. You'd love being in his species, John. You'd never have to shut up.

I'm doing all the talking, this time, because I'm the one that knows everything. Same argument you use with your students, bud.

So. Okay, the story's gotten up to where All Thumbs meets with the Irwins, Jenapha, me, and Hale. You got anything else to stick in, or can I let the guy set his cigar down and start talking? Cool.

He started off with saying that he appreciated our being there and then said he wanted to give us some news, starting with some from Hale, and then moving on to more surprising things that he knew. We were going to take the evidence in order of rising dramatism, to promote clear thinking—I gather his species thinks that you start with the dullest stuff first and work your way to the most shocking because, somehow, that's supposed to result in the best ideas. Maybe like something Melody told me in an email, the more surprising information is, the more it changes your thinking. Oh, yeah, we're friends again, John, she's a classy forgiving lady and I like her a lot, just not that way. So anyway I think what it is, if I get it right, is that All Thumbs's people try to make their changes bigger and bigger with each new piece of information, which seems backwards to me—I believe in closing in on an answer—but maybe that's why he's the Ranger and I'm Tonto, you know? I guess it would mean they keep innovating further into the process, you know?

So even in an emergency meeting, with All Thumbs, he always starts with the *smallest* and least-surprisingest piece of news (yeah, it's a word *now*), and that was why, apart from it being a big shock, I think we all about shit our pants when he said, "Lena Logan has vanished. Disappeared completely. Even with my resources, I can't find her. Anything that killed her, even if she had been instantaneously vaporized at high temperature, should have resulted in a signal my equipment would have detected, and there has been no signal since she went up to Crestone on a special mission. Yet if she's alive, it's even more mysterious. She has a microscopic implanted transponder, which signals in radio, Gaudeamus-pulse, neutrino, and graviton. The device could be disabled, but I don't believe that she herself would know how, and no other human would know to look for it, I don't think. To find it, they would have to take her apart and look at each piece under a microscope, and in that case, they'd have killed her and I'd have received a signal. Improbable as it is, the most likely thing is that she is being held in a pocket universe, or has been taken into one and then killed.

"Now, human beings don't have the technology for small, controlled pocket universes yet, and that technology is very strictly off-limits for a primitive/candidate world like this one, so something very serious is going on, no matter how we look at it. Almost certainly some organization from off your world is taking direct measures against my work here.

"Let me sketch my feelings as I believe they are relevant to this." He went to the whiteboard, grasped a drymarker between the three thumbs on his left hand, and lettered rapidly, changing colors as needed. He does that a lot; his people process a lot more in the emotions and a lot less in logic than we do, but they have very precise emotions, and their emotions are more parallel and less series than our thoughts, so to translate what he's feeling to how we're thinking, he draws matrices and graphs. You get used to it.

He puffed a small cloud of smoke, drew on the cigar, puffed again, placed the tip of the green marker to the board. "I see Lena Logan's disappearance and its most probable cause as change with two major opposed directions and a host of minor directions":

changing the situation in our favor	if we catch them, that's a serious violation which will allow me to use my full powers to take them out of the game permanently.
changing the situation against us	1. they clearly think they can kidnap key native personnel with impunity 2. and so far they are right and 3. they may well be right because 4. they know more than we do, so that it may 5. either be 5a. a potential real negative change or 5b. at least a temporary perceptual negative change, altering our judgment in inaccurate directions.
changing in four directions orthogonal to our desires	1. after so long a period working with Lena Logan, her welfare affects my emotional balance 1a. negative for clarity 1b. but positive for determination.

2. Several of you also have personal attachment to Lena Logan which will affect you emotionally

3. all of us feel empathy toward her and may think unclearly if we learn she is

3a. being tortured

3b. frightened or anxious

3c. seriously injured.

4. It is necessary to consider the possibility of betrayal by Lena Logan and I find this extremely distressing to imagine due to long association and close emotional bonds; therefore

4a. I shall not consider the idea adequately, leaving me with

4b. a nagging concern that I am not really considering all possibilities as I should.

All Thumbs puffed out a cloud of smoke and stared at the ceiling. "I'm approximating the major emotional trends on this matter," he added. "My feelings are actually much more complex. While I recover my composure, perhaps, Mr. Hale, you could . . ."

"Sure." Hale clicked on a big screen and showed us two episodes of *Gaudeamus* I had missed, both from the last week. In one of them, there was a Xegon Gaudeamus machine, again, perched in the crook of a tree above Harris McParris and O. B. Joyful as they jogged by. When you clicked on it, the whole screen flashed white, a big red word KAPOP! appeared, and below it there was CRE-STONE . . . LAST RECORDED LOCATION . . . A.T. PHONE HOME!

In the other, a list on a bulletin board, when you clicked on it, was a list of seven short entries. Lena Logan was the only one still readable; next to her name, it said, "And then there was one."

"But Susan Glasgow is still alive," Kermit said, sounding deeply bewildered.

"She was until a couple of hours ago," Hale said grimly. "Living in that penthouse in Manhattan. But at eight o'clock A.M. Eastern time this morning, she fell, probably from her penthouse window, possibly from its balcony, to the sidewalk in front of her building. Her body was naked, with hedge clippers, twelve-inch carbide hacksaw blade, two-pound rubber mallet, five-eighths-inch case-hardened cold chisel, and toilet plunger all driven into or through her body in the same ritually significant places as in the other victims of the Hardware Store Killer. Also like the other victims, autopsy revealed that she was shot in the head first, with some very small caliber very high velocity weapon—as always, something that approximates a BB shot moving at Mach 8 entered her right eye and exited through her brain stem, cratering the back of the office chair in her penthouse, presumably where she was sitting when killed. And as before, no bullet was found, leading to speculation that it may have been made of ammonia ice, since traces of ammonia were found in its path.

"Everything was exactly the way the Hardware Store Killer has done it in the past. Her clothes were cut off her in irregular swatches with a box knife or something similar, and stuffed into her toilet, again exactly like all the other victims, who were also killed at home, and whose clothing was also stuffed into the toilet in the master bedroom. After the ritual mutilations, all of which were after her death, as in all other cases, she was thrown out the window or off the balcony—both possible places are close together and both were left open, and from such a great height, they can't calculate the path of her fall. She seems to have been carried to the place from which she was thrown, rather than dragged. She was a small woman, about a hundred five pounds, and we know that the Hardware Store Killer must be a very large man and quite strong; chances are he just grabbed her up, ran with her across the room, and threw her."

"So the Third Force strikes again," Jake said. "Shit, I hated her, but what an awful way to go—"

"The Third Force," Kermit said dully.

"Who else?" I asked.

He looked utterly bewildered. "I guess you're right. A Third Force, though. Jesus, hey." He looked around, and finally said, "Yeah, it has to be a Third Force."

"Why is this so important to you?" Hale asked.

"Because up till a few seconds ago I would have said there's no such thing as the Third Force. Or rather because up till now, I was the Third Force." He bent forward, as if looking at the table, and said, "I haven't been strictly following our agreements. I *was* the Hardware Store Killer. The first five Hardware Store murders were all mine."

Everyone was staring at him blankly.

"When All Thumbs explained the rules to me, I thought, well, fuck, I know Lena doesn't want them killed, but they're her friends, not mine, and if it would make a stronger case to save the Earth—besides, I was just fuckin' pissed—I mean, shit, *I'd've* knocked off Squanto and every other 'white man's friend me-good-Indian,' too, way back, if I'd had the chance. So I just used some of our special equipment in an unauthorized way now and then. I still wouldn't have told you, except that I'm *not* the one that killed Susan Glasgow. And I have no idea who did, or whether he might go gunning for Lena, or maybe he already has her."

While we were still stunned, Kermit explained pretty much what I had guessed before about the Hardware Store Killer. If you're going to kill several women, and you want the FBI and police to chase wild geese instead of you, you might as well pretend to be a serial killer. And if you want to be the world's most effective one, borrow yourself one of All Thumbs's transporter-booth style Gaudeamus machines, find out exactly where and when each target will be all alone, and blink into existence in each time and place.

The murder weapon was a gadget Kermit built himself, a little midget rail gun that kicked a frozen ammonia pellet up to very high speeds. Kermit had used that purposely weird weapon, not because he thought it would be undetectable, but because he was sure it would kill instantly, so that all they'd feel was a moment's surprise when a very large Indian materialized in the room. And it was a bonus that trying to find out who made the weapon would keep the police busy.

Before Kermit killed the first one, Annabeth Trinidad, he went to thirty different hardware stores in several different cities, buying his list; he had produced the list by stabbing his finger at random into tool catalogs. "It's not that hard to come up with stuff that's very symbolic if you think about it," he said. "The average skinny white boy that becomes a serial killer is acting out a code built around real common obsessions from his whitebread culture. Toilet, clothes, psychologically loaded spots on the body. So I just worked up a mix and match and figured a few man years would go into trying to interpret it. Not too different from letting a chimp throw paint on canvas and then giving it to art critics. They think it's intended to be meaningful, so they're going to see things there."

I got to tell you, John, it froze my blood, the way Kermit smirked when he said that "Someplace out there some poor profiler is going totally nuts."

But now someone had imitated the Hardware Store Killer, getting the details so right—according to Hale's copy of the FBI report—that no one seemed to even faintly suspect that it was anyone different.

Of course, since Annabeth Trinidad had been killed more than two years before, and media attention had begun to focus after Heart Reno's death, both the cops and the media had traced the Hardware Store Killer's victims back to Moloch College—it was now common knowledge for every newspaper reader that most of the women had worked together—but a narrow focus of victims was not unusual in serial killers. "I'm sure Susan Glasgow had more than figured it out," Kermit said. "She was incredibly careful about not letting anyone know exactly where she was, and she only rarely slept alone or in any predictable place. There were bodyguards all around her, both human and pTh'tong n'Wi, all the time. I'd been trying for nine months to get a clear shot at her. So I suppose I gotta give props to whoever did. I sure didn't manage it."

Jake had been sitting and brooding; he looked up and said, "You know that you probably got Lena killed. They're gonna find her any minute with Hardware Store Killer shit done to her, because Lena being murdered will just make the case against the pTh'tong n'Wi contract better, and—"

"No." All Thumbs was decisive. "If she has been murdered, and her transponders have not notified me, it has to have been a non-human agent doing this to her. Which would *not* make the case. If someone had murdered her to make the case against the contract, they needed to use human hands alone."

Jake drew a long, shuddery breath. "So you think she's still alive?"

"I think that the evidence is much too thin for me to think anything. I feel in four ways that she is still alive and feel in two that she is dead and feel in one that she is in immediate danger, on the average, but they are not the strong clear feelings that one has rationally. But two more things seem relevant somehow. You are no doubt aware of the disappearance of a million cubic meters of sand from Great Sand Dunes? That would be characteristic pTh'tong n'Wi sampling, and perfectly legal, but extremely presumptuous, so normally they would refrain—so as not to irritate the judges—but they might do it if they feel very sure of winning the case. Perhaps that provoked the Third Force, which now exists, whatever it might have been before, into killing Susan Glasgow.

"Secondly, the appearance of vital clues in the *Gaudeamus* webtoon is consistent with certain other facts, which include the following. One, Brown Pierre makes the Gaudeamus sexual telepathy pill at his home and lab in Crestone, and two, it is not developed from any naturally occurring material on Earth, and three, your science of molecular design is far too rudimentary to have come up with such a molecular-level machine as the molecules of the Gaudeamus pill, so it must be concluded that Brown Pierre has access to alien technology, which leads us to four, he has or is close to someone with Gaudeamus technology, which leads to—"

"Shitfire," I said. "Sorry, All Thumbs, but here's the big thought,

I think. Brown Pierre is the Third Force. To be getting non-human tech in the quantities he does, he has to have sold the Earth, which means he built, or was one of the builders of, a Gaudeamus machine. And he wouldn't sell the Earth for personal advantage, and he wouldn't sell it to benefit humans either. He wants the Earth preserved, but he doesn't want it run by humans, either . . . which is sort of a third position between Lena's and Glasgow's, and why he never approached our side or joined theirs. Because he is his own side, see? And he's found some aliens who will go along with it." I whacked my forehead; thoughts were coming much too fast now. "And all the references to Xegon and to every other step we take, that we find in *Gaudeamus* the webtoon, are perfectly explainable if you assume the person talks to one of Lena's group— didn't Elvis make all the buys?"

"But it was Lena's original contact," Jake said. "She said she got Gaudeamus pills from the guy who introduced her to them, and then after that she sent Elvis up to make the buys, because she wasn't very attracted to the guy. So he might even have had a little telepathic connection to Lena . . ."

"Plus knowing me . . . jesus, he's probably followed everything we've done for years."

"Oh, wow," Kermit said, which might have been as smart as any of us was sounding right then.

"Oh wow you said it, and god and jesus and that whole crowd besides. No wonder Brown Pierre showed up right after that accident with Robodeer. And you know what Lena Logan is doing right now? She's helping produce *Gaudeamus*—the webtoon I mean— and that's how she tucked in that little message. Brown Pierre must know Richard Reno—"

"He might have *known* him," Hale said, "but according to a report I had done after the Robodeer story ran, not lately. It didn't seem important at the time that Richard Reno wasn't the actual author of the webtoon—"

"How do you know that?" I asked.

"Because once we started looking seriously, the Richard Reno who drew the college paper panel cartoon at Moloch College was surprisingly easy to find; the Richard Reno that signs the webtoon, and uses many of the same characters and some of the same settings, isn't him. The real Richard Reno was killed in a motorcycle crash four days after he graduated, in 1981, oddly not far from an Air Force test area in Nevada, while riding cross-country to take a job as a political cartoonist at a small north California paper where he was also going to cover high school sports and write obituaries. Whoever is producing *Gaudeamus*, it's not him."

All Thumbs said, "It's Brown Pierre. He would need considerable computing capacity to do the *Gaudeamus* webtoon, and a very large amount to operate the micromachines required to make the Gaudeamus drug . . . and Lena Logan was going to his house in Crestone at the time that she disappeared. I'm officially requesting Travis Bismarck and Nathan Hale, our two experienced human detectives, to go to Crestone and find out what's going on."

"All we need is to identify a good place nearby to land a flying saucer," Hale said.

"I've been to Crestone," I said, "and you can probably park it in front of Curt's gas station without anybody saying a thing."

"One last thought," All Thumbs said. "Or feeling. If we are right, and Brown Pierre is actually 'Richard Reno' and the Gaudeamus pill maker and the Third Force—be very careful. Don't forget that when we were looking at Susan Glasgow's murder, one reason that it looked like the work of the Hardware Store Killer was that the murderer must have been exceptionally large and strong."

CHAPTER TWENTY

"Nathan Hale?" I asked, as our flying saucer lifted off from behind the Xegon facility at Kirkland. We had a nice loaded Range Rover in it, the safari package that's intended to get you to and from an African war on dirt roads, the sort of thing that the people who actually write and photograph the news, as opposed to reading it aloud on TV, would love to have if anyone would spend that much money on people who don't appear on camera. Ours was pre-splashed with mud and came with tinted windows plus one huge guard dog, Beeper, a big-ass Rhodesian ridgeback with more training than the Army had ever given me and Hale combined. Possibly more brains, too.

"Nathan Hale," Hale agreed. "No middle name, either, so I had nothing else to fall back on. Unfortunately my grandfather was a China Hand, one of the ones that had to leave even though he didn't get caught out as a comsymp. Getting bounced that way and seeing what happened to all his old friends turned him even more progressive, and he sent my father to a very progressive private school. Dad knows lots about building things with popsicle sticks, and probably knows every union song Pete Seeger ever wrote, saw Allen Ginsberg recite *Howl* three different times, knew where to get marijuana in Vermont before 1960, and gets every joke on Elaine May and Mike Nichols albums. But he doesn't know when the War of 1812 was or who the Washington Monument is named after.

"Dad met Mother at that little private school, and she was the daughter of Hollywood people, producers I mean, so she'd been raised in the kind of world where if marketing needs Krakatoa to be east of Java, it is. So neither of them knew there had ever been a Hale that said 'I regret that I have but one life to give for my country,' or that the original Nathan Hale had been a spy. Given that Mother grew up culturally Jewish in Beverly Hills, among girls whose idea of cultural attainment was a British boyfriend, I'm not sure she was even aware that there'd been an American Revolution, and I'm *sure* she wouldn't have approved. Dad had less of an excuse, because according to a huge history in the library at Grandpa's house, that first Nathan Hale apparently was some kind of blood relative. But then so are half the white people in northern New England, Yankee inbreeding being what it is."

Well, John, I couldn't help laughing, and the sonofabitch grinned back at me, and annoying as it was, I was friends with chinless New England old money. Despite whatever the fuck he might think about Texans.

"How do two old progressives feel about your line of work?"

"I spent a lot of time with Grandpa when I was young. And really, as far as my parents are concerned, I just went into the family business. Like being a Bush or a Kennedy, you know—what other kind of job could I get anyway?"

"Must've been hell going to a real school as Nathan Hale."

"Not really. I was known as Sparky. A fact which you will now forget . . ."

"Old Jedi mind trick," I said, "I can't remember a thing you just said. So, what do you think about all this business, aliens and flying saucers and all?"

"Well, I like my planet, I like humans, I've got a wife I love and a child on the way, and after so much talk with All Thumbs, I guess I trust him. And Lena Logan is not a bad sort once you get to know her, though I don't think I'll be introducing her to my family. Besides, I did swear an oath to preserve and defend the Constitution of the United States, which, to my way of thinking, does extend to cover saving the planet that the United States is located on. And since all this happened and the guys in the black suits took over Xegon, I know my paycheck, coming as it does direct from the Treasury, is more secure. So, uh, it's a job. How do you feel about it?"

"It's a job," I agreed. "There's a serious crush and some personal revenge involved, too, but I'm always glad to have work."

We had waited till after dark, and now we flew high above the Front Range, the crumpled-newspaper topography of the mountains to our left, the long flat smear of eastern Colorado and Kansas to our right. Directly below us there were swarms of bright dots winding through the pools of dark—traffic on I-25.

Beside Hale, Beeper whined and growled softly to himself. "Hey, it's okay, fella," I said.

The huge dog looked up at Hale, who solemnly said, "It's okay."

"He checked with you."

"We've worked together before. And yes, he's that smart. Until he knows you a little better, you're only a *provisional* good guy, or member of the pack, or however Beeper thinks of you. That's why he keeps checking—to get you placed in his scheme of things."

Beeper made a little contented grunt, as if agreeing, and curled up beside Hale to sleep.

Anyone who has ever heard of Crestone usually pictures something different from what it is. In fact you can go there a lot of
times, John, and you'll still picture something different from what it
is. It's never going to have that kind of Christmas-card quaint that
ski towns like Aspen or even Crested Butte do, which they get from
their World War One railroad-and-mine-town architecture, because
Crestone doesn't have much that's all that old left standing. It's not
going to look all Norman Rockwelly and small-town Christmas-card
pretty like the older parts of Gunnison or Montrose or Salida, because those were built back in the picket-fence days, when there
was some money in those towns, and when you mostly filled up your
lot with house. Naw, the best thing that snow does for Crestone is
hide most of it, because what it is, is a scattering of houses and
buildings, most of them trying to hide away from the dirt streets—
most of them needing to hide. The houses are usually surrounded
by collections of gear, stuff, and junk that would look right at home
around a Houston mobile home park. Crestone is really just a scattering of houses, not too laid out, around a few rectangles of dirt
streets, way, way up in the mountains, looking out west across the
San Luis Valley. It's real pretty, with those long views of the valley
and breathtaking sweeps of the mountains, as long as you never look
anywhere near where you're standing.

And yet if you just think of it as a collection of just-above-shacks
among the pines and aspens, way high up, you'll totally miss what
the place is all about—the fact that Curt's, besides being the gas
station, is an art gallery and a bookstore, or that right out back of it
there's a New Age and Third World art store, or all the Buddhist
flags and New Age symbols and the fact that that town has a couple
liquor stores but probably twenty places you can buy crystals, more
people who think they can levitate than people who think they can
golf (and trust me, John, since you don't golf, the percentage of

people who are right about either, no matter where you are, is pretty much the same).

It's the kind of place where everyone is spiritual and where nobody has a religion, where all the churches seat fewer than a hundred but there are big new Buddhist and New Age worship centers up any dirt road you care to take into the hills. Good luck finding a guy to fix your truck—and if you do, it'll be some nice old hippie who does the work under a tree, back of his house, while ten kids run around him and scream—but if you need work on your aura, you can shop all day and still not cover all the possibilities.

Probably two-thirds of the folks who were at that Skin2Skin performance in Saguache that I dragged you to had driven down from Crestone.

We came in over the high peaks, still in the dark, about four miles south of town and up the slope to the east. We were displaying no lights, and the nearest human lights, visible in the valley below, were twenty miles away, but the stars were so bright and numerous that everything was in clear deep blue light.

As we topped the peaks and descended westward over the mountain, we were almost skimming the treetops, and Hale had the cloaking effect turned on, so at distances of more than a couple hundred yards, to anyone on the ground, we were just a blur in the stars. Up closer they might pick out the saucer shape, so it was always possible that someone was sitting cross-legged on the floor of her mountain cabin (which she and twenty friends would have built—some unearthly contraption clinging to a mountainside by a few big logs and the beneficence of the goddess) and happened to see us, but if so, she was no doubt working real hard at calmly accepting everything she saw, and didn't call anyone about it, except maybe one of her spirit guardians.

Of course, she only existed hypothetically, but I hoped we seemed like a good omen to her, and made her think the day would be a nice one.

We set down in a bitty turnaround among tall trees, at the end of a dirt road from town that was pretty far and snaky but unlikely to have any other traffic for a few hours. Beeper hopped into the Range Rover as soon as I opened the door, eyed me once, decided to be a good doggy and not call shotgun, and mashed between the bucket seats to get into the back.

"Does he like his ears scratched?" I asked.

Before Hale could answer, Beeper's head was resting on my shoulder. "That would be a yes," he said. I gave Beeper a good head-scratching and some special attention to the spots under the collar where it gets itchy. He made noises that I hoped were bliss, rather than contemplating taking me apart.

Hale lowered the ramp and drove onto the dirt road. He left the cloaking on as the door closed up behind us, so that in the dark, the saucer became an indistinct blob of gray-blue fog behind the bushes by the trailhead sign.

In the winter, those dirt roads are used mostly by people taking supplies to and from all those spiritual centers. The typical "center" is a big house somewhere back from the road, and usually contains about as many people as a big family; if All Thumbs or one of his cronies were passing through here, they might not notice it was any different from a road lined with affluent homes near any recreation-industry small town in Colorado.

Being a native Earthman and all, I noticed the differences—all the rings of stones, the wildly eclectic collections of religious statuary, the false gateways hung with symbols, and so on, to my right, and the vast sea of dark emptiness that was the San Luis Valley far below to my left. There were swarms of partial washouts and ice-filled spots in the road, and Hale drove carefully, but I could tell he was a good hand with a four-wheel and figured I shouldn't joggle him by making suggestions, not when his judgment was at least as good as mine.

The town of Crestone itself had a few lights on here and there, presumably people who were staying up late to find themselves or getting up early to go work in Salida or Alamosa. The nice folks that run the Shambala Coffee House, which is where everything and everybody meets, had just fired up their wood heat, and the dirty, not-yet-hot smoke was just oozing out their chimney and heading up towards the stars as if it really didn't care; there was one light on inside, and I saw a slim, pretty lady starting to load up an espresso machine.

We turned right, passed the laundry-lumber-grocery place, and headed up the badly rutted mud road, slipping a bit on the snow and ice. "You've been here before," I said to Hale.

"My sister Raynande does crystal healing. She was up here for three summers," he explained. "Given how much weirdness is happening here, I'm kind of glad that she'll be in Bhutan for the next two years, even if I do miss my little niece."

"Her name is Raynande Hale?"

"People pointed out how funny my name was to my parents, so they gave my kid sister a name to make it look like they'd done it to me on purpose. But no, Sis is not Raynande Hale anymore. As soon as she was sixteen, she quit high school, hitchhiked west to UCLA, found a nice grad student in chemistry who was obviously going to make a good living, and jumped his bones so devotedly that after a while he proposed. Her name is Raynande Dubrowski now. And my niece is Tei-shan Celeste Dubrowski, named after two of Grandpa's favorite colleagues. I occasionally feel sorry for the genealogists of AD 2100."

He hung a left. Even at about ten miles an hour, with all-wheel drive, the Range Rover's back end fishtailed a little. Hale turned off the lights; with the reflection of the town lights and the starlight off the snow-covered hillside above us, we didn't really need them anyway.

Half a mile further, and we were at the top of a ridge, looking at a typical Colorado sight: a long, steep-roofed log cabin (which had probably been modular to begin with), with a sheet metal addition on each end, and three satellite dishes in the yard. Hale pulled to a stop.

"Well," he said. "We're both wearing ducks, so walking shouldn't be uncomfortable, but that stuff is deep, so it will be hard work. Should I try to get closer, risk getting stuck but possibly make our getaway quicker, or should I leave the car sort-of concealed up here, so that we take a long slog both ways?"

I was looking it over with binoculars, and finally I said, "Hmm. I see no tracks—zero—anywhere near that place. Not even old lumpy fallen in ones. But the porch is swept. Nobody's gone in or out of there since the last big snowfall, but there's a good chance somebody's in there. Even if Lena Logan did vanish from there a few days ago, the snow must have fallen since. Which means the going will be extra hard, and no matter what, our tracks will give away that we were there, and anyway whoever's in there is going to hear us and see us coming if they're at all on alert, so there's no chance we'll surprise anybody. I vote we drive up and bang on the front door. There's two of us to rock the truck out of the snow if we get into something too deep."

"Sounds good to me," Hale said, put it in gear, and started us down the hill. As it turned out it was no worse than bad, and we got right up to that porch, which (now that we were close) was very obviously swept with the big push broom leaning against the wall. Tracks led back and forth to the woodpile at one side of the porch, clearly visible in the light of our headlights.

"Well," Hale said, "here goes. Stick your hand out to Beeper."

I did; Hale said, "*Friend,* Beeper. *Guard.*"

We got out and I said, "So that means he'll let me back in?"

"You or me or anyone that seems to be with us and okay. Anybody else is in real deep shit. Like I said, he's smart." He gestured toward the house, now just a few feet away. "Don't you hate that prickly about-to-be-shot feeling? I always get it when I knock on a front door on business."

"Yeah, I get it too."

We stood at the front door and knocked loudly. No sound came from inside. Peering in the windows revealed the usual clunky fake-Southwest furniture that's perfect if your friends routinely bring their plow horses on visits with them and insist on having them in their laps. There was a large woodstove along one wall; it was clearly completely out. From another window on the porch we could see into a small kitchen. Rough-cut door frames with cheap steel doors, the kind that institutions put on closets, led into the sheet-metal additions. Power must be coming from an underground line, because we didn't hear a generator and indicator lights were on all over the big computer rig sitting next to the woodstove by the back window. After a moment I realized, and said to Hale, "Hey, look. Either that's the world's highest tech refrigerator, or else that's another Beowulf like Lena's."

The heavy data and power cables ran up to the big old refrigerator, and a plywood box with a window fan mounted in it sat on top. A smaller, more modern refrigerator in the kitchen probably really *was* a refrigerator.

Then I banged my face on that hard plastic outer window—they don't break and they do bend, but not enough, trust me John. I did that because a voice behind me had said "Travis Bismarck," and it hadn't been Hale.

I wiped my face and turned around, trying to get combobulated enough to see, and the helpful voice said, "Don't do that. It hurts."

Blinking to clear my eyes, I recognized the figure in the multiple sweaters, old Army wool pants, and red hi-tops. "Hale," I said, "this fellow, holding the gun on us, is Brown Pierre, my old classmate, so I think we found part of what we're looking for, or it found us."

"In the circumstances, I am pleased to meet you, Mr. Hale, and I've known quite a lot about you for quite a long time," Brown Pierre said, "I think I'm going to have to keep the gun on you gentlemen while we have a conversation. The door is not locked. Travis, turn the knob slowly."

I did and the door swung a few inches inwards.

"Just put your hands above your heads, and walk in slowly."

We did. He got us cuffed to that big old monster of a log-frame sofa, and frisked us thoroughly pretty quickly, and I didn't think a pro could have done a better job, though I didn't think it would be wise to discuss it with Hale, the other pro in the room.

Then Brown Pierre piled a few full-sized logs into the woodstove, opened the damper, and pulled out an industrial welding laser and plugged it into a little metal box beside him. "Amazing what you can do with enough power," he said. "Can you imagine the hash that the Gaudeamus power source is going to make for the energy companies?"

With the bright spot of the laser he drew a slow line along each log, and flames billowed up from the laser spot. "Ever read Jerry Oltion's *Frame of Reference*?" Pierre asked. " 'Primitive man discovers fire.' Well, it will be warm in here shortly. Let me know when you want to take your coats off, or take a pee. I'll have coffee shortly."

He went into the kitchen, and then I heard him open another door and say "Get up and get dressed, we've got company," and then there was the sort of crashing and banging around in the kitchen that indicated he was throwing together a sizable breakfast. "You guys eaten yet?" he asked.

"No," Hale said, "what are you going to do with us?"

"You know that part of the story where the arch-villain explains his whole nefarious plan to the tied-up hero? We're at that part." He went back into the kitchen, whistling "When the Red Red Robin Goes Bob Bob Bobbin' Along," with about twice the volume and half the pitch control that would have been optimal.

"Please, God, let that be a joke," I muttered. Hale whispered an "Amen" next to me that couldn't have sounded more sincere if he'd been raised Baptist. It was looking like being a long, long morning.

CHAPTER TWENTY-ONE

While Brown Pierre cooked, and Hale seemed to be catching a nap, and whoever it was back there presumably was getting up and dressed, I looked around the room. If a big, elaborate house that's still a suburban tract house is a McMansion, this was a McLoghome. It had that high ceiling, due to the steep-pitched roof, that sensible people would use for attic space instead of somewhere to throw the heat away. I guessed if I needed to twit Brown Pierre, that would be the thing to twit a serious enviro about; then I thought that if the whole place was running on Gaudeamus power, that wouldn't be much of a twitting. So much for that; if I needed to twit the boy, I'd have to remind him about that blonde art student from New Orleans who wouldn't go out with him, back in college. I wished I could remember her name.

Below the high ceiling there were exposed log trusses big enough to hold up a four-lane highway bridge, though all they were really holding up was a regular steel roof; I guess they were supposed to make it look more antique-y, since the old-style log roofs were massive and really did need that kind of trussing, and thus having them in your house would imply that your house was old enough to have once had a log roof. I think that's how that works, John, we might need a semiotician in on the case.

The logs of the walls had all been covered with that clear plastic coating so you could clean them with a dust rag if you wanted, and the floor looked like they'd stolen a basketball court, and the furniture and rugs appeared to have been stolen from a Southwest-themed DoubleTree Inn.

It wasn't quite perfectly Colorado cliché. There were no stuffed animal heads on the walls, but then Brown Pierre was very enviro. No made-in-Taiwan Indian artifacts, but if he was the same guy he was in college, he was probably still an atheist and anti-spiritual. And no skis, snowboards, mountain bikes, or other grownup-toys, but maybe he just worked here, and he was a serious kind of guy, anyway.

While I had been thinking all of this, I'd been working away steadily, but with no effect at all. I couldn't get any grip on the locks of the handcuffs that held me on to one end of the couch, and Hale was cuffed to the other end, so we couldn't have helped each other much, even if he had been awake. I had to envy him his ability to catch a nap in the circumstances, because it was way more productive than anything I could do.

The sun came up further and I really hoped no one was doing an early-morning XC trip up that dirt road, because I just had a feeling that if they found a flying saucer and called the pigs or something, Hale and me'd be the ones to get blamed for it, on top of everything else that was going wrong. "Hale, old bud," I said, more to have something to say than anything else, "this really sucks."

He snored, John. The sonofabitch snored. If you can keep your head when all about you are losing theirs, you ain't gonna have many friends after a while, you know?

After a few thousand years (that took only about fifteen minutes to pass, by the clock on the wall), things started to smell kind of wonderful from the kitchen, and Brown Pierre stuck his head out and said, "Hope you all can stand vegan food for a while. It's what there's going to be. I'm a good cook but you're going to be here for a long time."

Another eon, of about ten minutes, went by, and the room reeked of good Mexican food; I guess if you're avoiding eggs, meat, and milk, that's about as good a cuisine to approximate as any, since the one big change that you got to make is you do it without the cheese, and there's lots of bean-and-grain dishes to give you protein. Then a female voice hollered something, and Brown Pierre said, "Okay, just a sec, got to take this off the burner," and I heard a door creak again.

In another minute, he led Lena Logan in; she was wearing a sweatsuit that was a bit too big for her slim body. She wasn't hand-cuffed and she was holding his hand. I did my best to look all jealous and furious, figuring that it wouldn't have any effect if she was really with him, but it would help her cover if she was with us. "I'm afraid you're going to hear the whole explanation again," he told her. "Of course I do like giving the explanation. But it seems courteous of me to apologize."

"Right idea," she said, "but don't explain your apologies so much. Feeling bad about inconveniencing other people doesn't require explanation."

He grinned like a boy with his first crush, which, of course, was exactly what he was, and said, "Just keep coaching."

She sat down on the couch between me and Hale. Hale woke up, blinked sleepily, and said, "I'm getting warm, if you have a minute to get me out of this coat."

"Sure." Brown Pierre worked all the cuff exchange things you do to make that work, and if Hale got a chance where he could have slugged our captor and started us on breaking out, I didn't see it.

Then Pierre did the same process to me, and I still didn't see a chance to wallop him and make a break. For an amateur, Brown Pierre sure had a gift.

After about ten minutes of maddeningly good smells, Brown Pierre came out with a big pot of tofu-in-tomato-sauce and a load of tortillas, and put much longer chains on us, so we could eat and have some coffee, and he sat there with the gun right to hand and watched us eat. Which, I should say, we managed to do—it had been a while since any of us had eaten, and Pierre wasn't lying about being a good cook.

Then he sat down and told us his whole lunatic story.

"Wait a minute," I said. "This is the part that nobody ever believes in a book or a movie. If there really were any evil villains out there, they'd never tie up the good guys and explain things to them. That would make no sense at all. Because if you got away—I guess you did, considering you're sitting there in a chair in my hotel room, having a beer—"

"Well, knowing what he's up to, so far, has done us no good at all," Travis said. "So it really didn't matter that he explained it to us. And he might have been able to figure out that it wouldn't do us any good, before he did it." He reached over and pulled his third beer from my fridge. I noticed that he had bags under his eyes and a certain haunted look; his skin was a little gray and seemed not quite to wrinkle yet, but to just fit him looser, and the blue of his eyes was more slate, less beryl, than it had ever been before. For the first time ever, my old friend looked tired, even, maybe, old. "It's really just made everything more complicated, bud. And besides, evil bastards do try to explain themselves, to one kind of captive audience or another. All the time. Think about serial killers that send taunting letters to the police. *Mein Kampf*. The Unabomber Manifesto. De Sade's books—"

"Satire."

"Unhhunh. He still liked to beat the fuck out of young boys and girls whenever he got the chance, didn't he?"

Reluctantly, I shrugged, and trying to be a fair-minded academic, even added an example. "Okay, sure, and there's a great little work of feminist criticism—a feminist attack on the whole last generation of Marxism—called *Why Althhusser Killed His Wife*, which makes a good case that he'd been getting ready to, in his writing and ideas, long before he ever did it, which is to say he explained his evil to the whole world before going on to do it to his wife. Yeah, evil likes to explain itself, I'll grant you that. So Brown Pierre sat down and said to you, 'So now, Frash Gawdon, temble at da briyyant scheme of Ming Da Mercaress' . . .'"

"Damn near. Look, Hale and me and Lena all pooled our memories and resources later, to figure out what the sonofabitch was up to. And we went back over all the notes he made for the *Gaudeamus* webtoon, which was another piece of amazing alien tech. Plus we did grab some of his private diary off his computer eventually. So between and among all that, we came up with a lot fuller story than he told us, and I'm not sure what he actually said while we were all chained to that couch, and what we put together later. But I can promise you it will be a fuckload shorter when I tell it than it was when I heard it. Because I'm not going to rant and repeat myself and argue with things you haven't said every time you look disbelieving. It's really pretty simple, and if you pee now, you won't need to again before I get done giving it to you, whereas me and Lena and Hale needed three potty breaks and most of three pots of fresh coffee to get through his whole goddam deal. So be glad this is how you're getting it."

"I'm so grateful."

"You've never learned to do irony well, bud. Now go pee and when you get back, Uncle Travis will tell you the story of The Nut Who Is Secretly Ruling the World."

I took care of business, got a big glass of orange juice from the fridge, and said, "Travis, I've known you all these years, and I'm still never sure when you tell me the truth."

"I know, bud, that's why I rehearse on you."

"Does that mean you don't tell the truth?"

"It means I want to be believed, John." He took another long swallow. "And there can be several reasons for wanting to be believed. One of them, strangely enough, can be that you are telling the exact god's-honest-truth, and you want other people to believe that truth. Now, about this particular case, I'm going to give it to you short, sweet, and as coherent as I can make it, given what the starting material is like.

"But if you're doing your fictiony thing, and you're really trying to picture what it was like the first time I heard this, you have to picture three smart, tough people, in a real bad spot, chained to a couch, listening to a loon as he paces back and forth and argues with everybody since the dawn of time, using a nine-millimeter as his favorite gesturing device. You're getting this without Thomas Aquinas, Coco Chanel, Elton John, or Peter Ramus—all of them came up several times in Brown Pierre's rant, and as far as I can tell they were all working on one side. The other side was Corax of Syracuse, Duns Scotus, Hugh Hefner, and Aldo Leopold. And Walt Disney and Carl Jung stood over all of them, quoting from the *I Ching*. With Brown Pierre, looking like Moses and dressed like the homeless, waving his arms, gesturing with a loaded pistol, and shouting at all of them, for maybe four and a half hours.

"So that's how *I* first got it. Picture that before you ask too many questions. I couldn't possibly make this shit up, John, I don't even have *your* imagination, and I don't think you could make it up either. Now listen."

Brown Pierre's strange name had come about because his father, James Pierre, had been a conscientious objector in World War Two, and had therefore carried a stretcher across most of France and Germany, running back and forth fetching the wounded. This had given him time enough to think about how unpleasant his life was and how much things might be better. By 1944 he had arrived at a conclusion and made up his mind. The older Pierre had decided to live a life that would never require him to move, stand up, or do a lick of work again, and a life he could spend entirely on talk and books, which had been his solaces through all his time with the stretcher.

He'd inherited some money—the Pierre family was old and had had many industrial investments at one time—and with it he had bought a small café in Lyons, married a nice local girl who jumped at the chance to marry a rich American, and set himself up to spend the rest of his days sitting in the corner of his café reading Marx and Mill, Ernest Thomson Seton and Heidegger, Sabatini and James Joyce, Dorothy Day and Ralph Waldo Emerson, sipping at the good cheap wine, while the people he hired ran his café and his customers dropped by to argue.

James Pierre was firm about maintaining the single-syllable pronunciation of Pierre, which had been in the family for many generations, and about the importance of remembering and quoting and comparing everything you read, and about doing what you set out to do. He had promised himself that he would name any children after the last few men who had died while he was carrying them, going in reverse order so that his firstborn would be named after the very last man to have died on a stretcher carried by James Pierre.

As it happened, it was more than a decade until Madame Pierre presented James Pierre with any issue, and so memory was dim and hard to retrieve, old comrades long lost touch with, and government records hopeless, by the time it came time to name his firstborn. He knew the very last had been named Brown, and to save his soul, after nine months of wracking his brains and pulling at his memory, James could not remember what the first name had been; either he had forgotten or more likely he just hadn't been trying very hard to remember.

On the day when Mr. Brown died on his stretcher, James Pierre had still had a long day ahead of him, as far as he knew. He had expected to be running for many more wounded, since fighting was fierce, brutal, and continual, but had broken an ankle in a chuck hole and not recovered until after VE Day, and thus the last man he carried had simply not stuck in his memory, except for his very ordinary last name; when Madame Pierre became pregnant, twelve years after the war, it was a miracle that he remembered even that much of the name (and local folk rather often suggested that in fact the name of a nearby grocer might have been more appropriate). But a promise, especially to the dead, was a promise, and James Pierre believed in consistency.

Brown Pierre had been a painfully bright student, good at arguing with his father—a good thing, because it was the only way he ever got any paternal approval. Between attending lycée and being grilled by the immense, obese voracious reader/eater in the corner, Brown Pierre had formed a deep devotion to intellectual consistency—the only thing that ever got him a little peace and time off the hook—and his devotion grew to be still more fierce than his father's.

Like many tenderhearted people, Brown Pierre had come to like animals and the country better than people and towns. By the time he arrived in the United States to take advantage of the other side of his dual citizenship, at the age of eighteen, he was what one might expect: a devoted vegan, a radical, a Deep Ecologist—and absolutely brilliant at anything having to do with words, numbers, or ideas.

In the summer of 1992, he had just been released from prison after serving his full time for having liberated an entire fish hatchery into the San Angelo River, and was seriously thinking about seeing how long he could survive in a loincloth in the Canadian arctic, thereby having as little impact as possible on the environment, and putting himself to an interesting challenge. That was the moment when some ideas in geometry and physics, with which he had long been playing, popped into the front of his mind, and to his surprise, he thought of a very simple device, for which he would need only the sorts of parts that one could easily shoplift from hobby shops or cannibalize from the nonfunctioning radio alarm clock beside his bed.

In a few hours, in the drab little SRO hotel room that his parole officer had steered him into, working with screwdrivers, needle-nose pliers, and masking tape as his basic tools, Brown Pierre had built a Gaudeamus machine. And within three hours of that, a representative of an alien species, something that looked very much like a hairy fireplug with an elephant's trunk emerging from its top, had arrived to ask him how much of what goods, services, or information he'd be willing to take in trade for his planet.

Now, Brown Pierre had had all greed shamed and humiliated out of him at an early age; he was, in his way, though he hated people, perfectly altruistic and absolutely incorruptible. He wanted to do only what was good, as he understood the good. At the same time, since he had formed the opinion that intelligent life, left to it-self, would always destroy its home environment, plus any other biosphere it could reach, and slaughter other animals—that that was in the nature of intelligence and that intelligence was there-fore a kind of cancer in the life of the universe—Brown Pierre had no reason to like or trust the alien. Most probably the hairy fireplug that stood before him came from a planet where hundreds of other species of squat, hairy things had been hunted to extinction, exper-imented on, tortured, cooked, and skinned; the alien could not pos-sibly be here for Brown Pierre's benefit, and therefore the things to do were to avoid being cheated by the alien, and to cheat it.

He therefore said that he would have a proposal exactly twenty-four hours later. He stayed up most of the night perfecting his ex-act request. The alien, luckily for Pierre, was actually a Nrwyk, a species dedicated to conservation and preservation, and was imme-diately delighted with Brown Pierre's proposals, so much so that the two of them negotiated for a much longer period, since neither could quite believe how much the other agreed with him or hyr. (This is following the standard protocol, Travis tells me, for denot-ing the genders of Nrwyk as she/he/hy/shi, his/her/hys/shis, and her/him/hyr/shir.) By the time that Travis, Hale, and Logan were hearing this story, Brown Pierre had actually become friends of a sort with the Nrwyk, at least as much friends as Brown Pierre was capable of being with anything.

Brown Pierre and the representative of Nrwyk had arranged a simple three-part contract:

Brown Pierre was to receive one matter copier, with perpetual maintenance, capable of producing exact to the atom copies of any object that would fit within its thirty-centimeter spherical hopper. This of course meant that he could immediately produce perfect counterfeit money (as long as he was careful to dispose of the identical serial numbers at different places), as well as do such things as duplicate jewelry for pawning. He admitted that it was more than a month before he realized he would seldom need to buy frozen vegetables again.

His second request was more complex; he wanted a singularity machine—a device that would simply answer any question he asked, if the answer were knowable at all. Sure enough, the aliens were advanced past the singularity, and again the machine came with a perpetual warranty. He could now know anything he could think to ask, if it were knowable at all.

In return for this, the Nrwyk would receive the Earth at the end of Brown Pierre's lifetime, with a special conservation easement: not one inch of it was to be built upon or used for any new purpose by any intelligent species. Every bit of land, sea, or sky that had fallen into human disuse must be left wild forever.

And so, for reasons that Ted Kasczynski might have understood, and with infinite wealth and knowledge at his command, Brown Pierre had set out to depopulate and deindustrialize the Earth, as far as he could, and to live as long as possible while doing so. He intended to fail to some extent, because the continuing existence of the humans would serve as a possible last-ditch protection for both the contract with the Nrwyk and for the Earth itself.

Had he tried to raise an army or even a small band of radicals to do the job for him, he would not have stood a chance, he explained. The experience of a lifetime had taught him that he was the only person whom he could trust. Followers would have betrayed him. The use of force would have invited retaliation. But as it stood, he thought he stood an excellent chance.

While he thought intelligent life was a mistake and human beings a particularly big mistake, he recognized that we were animals, and he did not want to hurt us. He also thought that there was no putting the toothpaste back in the tube; human beings had moved species around and disrupted ecologies everywhere, and if the whole human race all just vanished tomorrow, things would still be an appalling mess, and the environment as a whole, along with many innocent creatures, would suffer horribly as the adjustments worked themselves out.

What was needed was not the extinction of the old human race, but the creation of a new human race that would voluntarily dwindle to almost nothing while restoring the natural ecology. And he recognized, as well, that people could not be threatened into any such thing.

After long thought, he settled on his plan, and asked the singularity machine for the necessary knowledge. One of the first fruits was the Gaudeamus pill, which would achieve two things—getting everyone laid frequently and well, and gradually abolishing secrecy. He had been doing his best to pump it into large corporate and governmental projects ever since.

Now, the longer he went on, the more I realized we were learning everything we needed to know in the course of that endless lecture. So we kind of figured we'd stay there, especially since old Brown Pierre was waving that gun around.

At last that car horn, on the SUV, started honking. Brown Pierre had just been explaining about why the ancient Skeptics and Cynics were misnamed and that this had contributed to centuries of misunderstanding the human predicament. Or maybe that when you watch Snow White you can understand how Disney Corporation ended up owning so many ski areas. I'm not quite sure which of those points was getting made. Lena says it was another one of those things about feet and he was staring at her open-toed slippers, and she would have noticed that more than any of us would have noticed anything else, so maybe she's right.

Anyway, so there Brown Pierre was, in the middle of laying out some grand important point, when—beep! beep! *beeep*! Over and over and over.

"Damn, I'm sorry, Brown—may I call you Brown?—that's the car alarm," Hale said. "The off switch is under the glove compartment, passenger side. And we left it unlocked."

Brown Pierre glanced at Lena's bare toes and obviously decided he wasn't going to get her to go out there. Before he went, he looked over the cuffs and locks on Hale, and then on me. The car kept right on beeping. Finally Pierre went out to turn it off. He opened the passenger side door, and something huge and gray-brown shot out. Brown Pierre hit the thick snow on his back, hard enough to slam his head some, sending snow arcing ten feet in all directions. His gun went off into the air as Beeper clamped down on his wrist and shook it like a rat.

Beeper delicately sat down on Brown Pierre's now-gunless gun arm, put a forepaw on Pierre's chest, and stared suggestively at his throat. We couldn't quite make out words but it sounded like Brown Pierre was talking to Beeper; Beeper seemed to be enjoying hearing it—many dogs like being talked to—but I didn't think he was going to be persuaded.

"Do you suppose that poor dog is being lectured about the political semiotics of women's footware?" Lena asked. She went into the workroom for a moment, came back with bolt cutters, and uncuffed us. "And just for the record, I took a fist full of Gaudeamus with him, every single day, which meant I actually knew what was going on in that mind. Talk about 'it was a nasty job but someone had to do it'—next time someone else can. I honestly think I was the closest thing to real love the poor bastard ever encountered."

Hale shrugged. "Well, if someone has to listen to Brown Pierre, better Beeper than us. He doesn't understand a word of it and doesn't expect to. Now, Beeper will hold him—"

There was a shimmer in the air. All Thumbs climbed down out of it, a gadget that looked like a spaghetti colander and was actually an automatic weapon clutched in one hand. He was followed by all the Irwin brothers, even Elvis. We should have realized that once Brown Pierre took Lena out of that pocket universe in his garage (which he was merely using as a superstorage shed and lab) her transponders would get hold of All Thumbs. Later Hale and I agreed that the reason we didn't think of it was either because we knew we'd rescue ourselves, or because we were busy focusing on our cuffs and Pierre's gun. For that matter, All Thumbs had delayed too—he didn't want to jump through with any of his merry men until he knew Pierre wouldn't get a shot off first.

"How did Beeper know to set off the car alarm?" I asked Hale.

"There is no car alarm. He likes to just sit there, hitting the horn in rhythm, when he gets bored. That's why most people can't stand to work with him."

"And he can do that kind of perfect rhythm?"

"It doesn't have to be perfect—just better than the person hearing it."

"Is it all right to admit I'm impressed?" I asked Hale.

"On Beeper's behalf, I'll do my best to accept it politely."

"If there's a point to that, other than to tell me a silly adventure story, I'm not seeing it."

"Well, it's late, you're tired, your guy choked at the acting competition, and you haven't had enough beer to stimulate your imagination, is all. You'd see it if you were feeling better. See, what happened was, King Kong. It was beauty killed the beast. Lena gave

Brown Pierre his first real human experience, and the poor guy melted. When we went out there we found that he was giggling and telling Beeper what a good boy he was. All of a sudden he didn't want to silence the world, or to be all alone.

"And the guy is smart, and having fun now that he's getting the hang of working with people. That sex-telepathy pill was a damn funny case; he invented it, or told the singularity machine to invent it, with the idea that if he put enough of that stuff into the blood-streams of enough tech people, they would feel too good to stay up all night working on the new gadget. His idea was they might start to think maybe they can just knock off early and take the wife up a nice trail in the park, especially since they would even know that the wife would like that. Soon, every time they took more Gaudea-mus, more secrets are more likely to leak, so the value of secret knowledge and of being way ahead goes way down. Pretty soon in-novation would wither for lack of interest."

"Sounds complicated and slow."

"That's how Brown Pierre likes things." He rested his boots on my bed and added, "You have to remember that he's crazy as a bedbug. So what he did was, he invented the pill that would cure him. He'd missed out on encountering people as people, spent all his time with them as audience and enemy. So he came up with exactly what he needed to take, but he'd only taken it for test pur-poses . . . and then along came Lena. Good-bye heart for Brown Pierre, eh?

"But just now he couldn't be happier. He's letting loose a mix of recreational drugs and some long-term viruses that modify things about people—increase lifespan, decrease fertility, increase emo-tional sensitivity and general serotonin level, decrease aggression . . . pills and diseases to spread love and happiness through the blood-stream of the world. He thinks he can have us all fit to handle a

Gaudeamus machine, by the time that we all have one—February 4, 2011."

"He's working like a talented arsonist," I said, sitting up. "Gotta pee. You figured you could tell the story on one bladder, but you didn't reckon on that bladder being middle-aged."

I splashed cold water on my face and looked at the clock before going back out; I'd been listening to this silly story for an hour and a half. It was really late and I really wanted my sleep.

And just possibly this indicated that I was getting old.

My eyes itched. I took my contacts out, splashed water on my face again, dried it. Maybe I could get him to wrap this up quickly or something?

When I went back out into my room, he was gone. He'd left one Fat Tire in my fridge, with a note on hotel stationery, rubberbanded around the neck:

For a guy who tells stories, bud, you really don't like to listen to them. Catch me outside the "Self-Promotion and Performance Art" workshop on Friday, at noon, if you got time. Meanwhile, drink this, turn the lights out, lie down, and don't set your alarm. You look like you need some sleep, old man.

CHAPTER TWENTY-TWO

I think it was probably Travis's calling me an old man that got me to go to that workshop, which turned out to be taught by Jenapha Lee, who was old buddies with one of the professional theatre liaisons for the conference. There are people who have an onstage personality that is utterly different from the offstage, and she was the best example of that I've ever seen. She sparkled, she charmed, she smiled, she encouraged, and the kids and faculty were eating out of her hand.

Her basic subject was how to make people think they wanted a performance artist, given how poisoned the well was by hostile and stupid media types. "Yeah," she said, "well-noted genius art critic Garry Trudeau drew a naked lady with a pumpkin on her head a few years ago, and ever since, tell any five random people you're a performance artist, and one of them will show you he's, like, so totally *hip* by mentioning a pumpkin on the head. The first thing you gotta do, number one, is not take that crap for a second." She leaned forward, energized. "Every movement and every artistic idea that gets anywhere stops apologizing and start asserting. You watch that

Penelope Spheeris movie, that girl who says everybody should have blue hair? Right idea. Not 'Oh I have blue hair to express myself.' Not 'Oh if you understand it right you'll see there's a good reason for me to dye my hair blue.' Not even 'I feel free to have blue hair.' What you gotta say is, 'Where's your fucking blue hair and why the fuck should I listen to a dumb fuck whose hair isn't even blue?' So you get somebody that says pumpkin on the head, don't say 'Oh, it's not really like that.' Don't try to explain what a naked lady with a pumpkin on her head might be a comment on. Just go right in and make 'em feel like they shat on a Picasso."

"Um, um . . ." a young woman bouncing up and down with excitement, in the front row, said.

"Um what, babe? We only got an hour and I gotta make you brilliant by the end of it."

I filed that away as a usable lecture joke for when questions got long-winded; I was liking Jenapha Lee more every second, especially since three of my students were in the room and their eyes were lighting up too.

"Um," the girl said, "how do you make them feel like they *shat* on Picasso." I don't think she meant to emphasize that word so hard. It immediately pegged her as being from some small religious college someplace, making her first real escape into the bigger world, still pumped about getting to swear in public around people who apparently swore all the time.

Jenapha Lee sat back and smiled. "That guy next to you just rolled his eyes and told you not to ask your question and I heard him whisper, 'C'mon, shut up.'" She leaned forward, focusing her attention on a young man with a thick wad of unruly black hair that looked like he'd rolled over on a tribble in his sleep. "Oh, look at me. Oh, I'm very special. I'm a guy, and I'm good-looking, and I know all about thee-YATER. I am so clever. Clever me. And I have a girl. And she is getting out of line. So I am cleverly going to shut her down and teach her that she is my property and I am important and I have nothing to learn—"

"I didn't say that stuff—"

"But I did. And you got torqued out of your shorts by it, didn't you, pumpkin?" She looked directly at the girl. "You see? Look, when you tell someone you play classical music, most of them don't try to tell you that they know all about that stuff and it's weird and isn't very good, because they read an article about it once in *Newsweek* and anyway didn't Wagner blow Mad King Ludwig to get Bayreuth built? If you say you paint, they don't say, 'Oh, yeah, painting, you get paint on your clothes and you get to stand and look at naked people.' Or if they do, everyone in the room knows they're an illiterate boob.

"They take a dump on your particular art because they don't *want* to understand it and they especially don't want to do the hard work of *not* being illiterate boobs. They're trying to make a public declaration that what you do isn't worth seeing so therefore their illiteracy about it makes them all special and wonderful.

"Well, fuck'em. You're giving your life to it and for them it's a chance to show how much they don't have to know, and pull out their favorite one-liner? Their chance to be smug for a sentence is more important than something you may have put months into? Hurt them. Don't argue with them, you already know you don't share any premises; just hurt. Oh, and lose the dork—you can do better."

That got everyone squabbling, and I quietly slipped out the door, strangely glad I had come, and found Travis by a post.

"If I admit there's something cool about Jenapha, do I get forgiven?" I asked him.

"Shit, bud, you always get forgiven. Here's what we kind of thought—maybe you'd like to go to lunch with us, over to some place with decent barbecue? You might have to miss one of the shows this afternoon."

"Officially I'm not even here," I pointed out. "I'm on leave. I'm only here because the college lawyers didn't want all the Western faculty here to be temps and subs, and I didn't want the guys to have to miss this year. But I'm free to roam around on the loose if I like. Sure."

Over lunch I told Jenapha Lee that I thought her workshop had been great, and she shrugged. "When art is nice, only nice people make art," she said. "Or something." She settled back into staring into space.

Now that all the food was in us, and the table cleared, and there was no large public audience, Jenapha Lee had gone back to smoking importantly and staring out the window, away from Travis. That seemed to make him adore her more. I thought very seriously about slapping one of them and couldn't make up my mind which.

"So the only awkward moment that happened," Travis Bismarck said, sitting back and looking relaxed, "was when we asked Brown Pierre how he knew how to do the Hardware Store Killer procedures so exactly, and he told us that he hadn't killed Susan Glasgow. That led us to a little epiphany, and sure enough, All Thumbs was able to establish that she was alive and well and living off planet, in a pTh'tong n'Wi zoo that she probably thought was a hotel; she'd become afraid, I guess, after Kermit had come close to bagging her a couple of times, and accepted their protection. So they made a brain-dead clone, aged it, shot it in the head, did all those weird things to it, and threw it out the window. One way to keep anyone from trying to kill something is to convince them it's already dead." He shrugged. "She'll come back to Earth, sooner or later, since they'll need her to be here officially. I was going to ask you, though, John, last night you said Brown Pierre was like a good arsonist?"

"Yeah, my father was an engineer for an insurance company, involved with arson investigations quite a bit. The arsonists they almost never catch are the professionals who walk into the place to be torched, think of what fire would be the most natural one to happen here, and do the minimum number of changes to make it happen. The guy who knows which employee keeps a toaster oven in their office, near a wastebasket full of shredded paper, and heats up that toaster oven while shredding a bunch of documents, then throws it all into the trash can. The guy who knows that the cleaning people use the break room and clean things with a flammable solvent and puts a metal can of that solvent into the microwave in the break room. And then they close the door and they leave and it's like they've never been there.

"The ones they always catch are the genius-dork bomb builders who have to try to come up with the biggest brightest ba-boom! in history. Because most workplaces don't contain great big bombs. Unions and OSHA and fire marshals frown on that, you know? That's what's so clever about Brown Pierre in your story. If the human race ends up as a bunch of sensitive New Agers being kind to the animals and treasuring their scenery and hiking trails, with no ambitions to accomplish anything else, well, that's not an unnatural path. Not many people have your taste for danger, or Jenapha Lee's taste for controversy, or even my drive to be able to say 'I told you so.' Out on any hiking trail on any nice day you'll meet people that'd rather have life just pass them by—or would rather live in the moment and enjoy what they have, take your pick of descriptions. If that keeps becoming the more rewarding course of things . . . well, no doubt you can figure it out from there. And it won't look like Brown Pierre is responsible, because it won't look like anyone is responsible—it will just look like what naturally happens. 'Well, they had a rule that the last person out would always put the coffeemaker into the cupboard, so it was bound to happen that sooner or later someone would put the coffeemaker away still hot, and all those napkins would fall onto the plate, and catch fire in a cupboard full of paper and styrofoam.' 'Well, human beings like being comfortable. At the close of the twenty-first century it was clear that what human beings wanted was a clean, safe, painless version of what they had had during the Old Stone Age, with access to the entertainment of thirty centuries thrown in, and the childish dreams of conquering the universe done went blooey.'"

"Is that proper academese?"

I shrugged. "It's certainly the way they'd explain it in retrospect. And after a while the words would get shorter and simpler, I think, mainly because no one would be interested in even talking about it anymore. A few long generations and when the last two-hundred-year-old who could remember anything different died, they'd probably abolish every branch of learning that wasn't amusing. And Earth would have maybe a hundred million happy, healthy granolae named Russ and Katy, who had lots of good ganja, ponytails, and trust funds, and just thought life was, you know, fucking awesome. Dude. The funny thing is, Travis, so far this is the part of your story I'm most inclined to buy. Because when I look around the Colorado mountains, I kind of think we're there already. Brown is not taking the system any way it doesn't already know how to go.'"

"In the Eagles song, it's 'you don't,'" Jenapha Lee put in. "Much better meter."

"So what's your next mission to save the planet?" I asked Travis.

"Oh, oh," Jenapha Lee said, "the professor is so embarrassed at my non sequitur straight out of popular culture."

"Oh, oh," I said, "you're so threatened by my erudition and long-term friendship with Travis."

And, bless her, she laughed. So did I, and Travis looked at us like we were both crazy, and as often happens, that got us laughing again, harder. The waitress came by with the bill, and we paid up, and of course we laughed more in front of her, too.

"Well," Travis said, "if you'll forgive me, there's one more part to the story. So we thought we had it all, and then one bright afternoon, Brown Pierre, who was on a national security parole and required to stay at the facility, very suddenly ran away."

But you know, he was psychically linked to Lena, and she knew where he was if she got within fifty miles of him, so Jenapha and me and Lena, we bounced all over the place, and three times we picked up Brown Pierre's trace in five days, and each time he got away before we got in closer. He was running but not hard, not letting us catch him but not disappearing.

Meanwhile Hale phoned to say that the gadget that Brown Pierre had been building at Xegon was a Gaudeamus detector, some simple gadget he'd built, basically a direction and range finder on a Gaudeamus pulse. Brown wasn't moving at random, he was trying to get to each new transmitter within a day or so of when the aliens did.

So we kept our team, trying to follow Brown Pierre, and we put the Irwins on another team, trying to get ahead of him by scrambling to get to the next Gaudeamus inventor before Brown Pierre could.

For a while they kept getting there late, and all the Irwins found was that Brown Pierre would say or do anything to get a copy of whatever contract these guys had signed. That was it. Brown Pierre just wanted to know what every other contract said.

Hale called in to tell us that a conventional surveillance team had spotted Brown Pierre in a van, and it sounded like, just maybe, he had a Beowulf built into the back of that van—along with a thirty-horse engine to make power for it. That was in Darby, Montana, and it so happened me and the women were in Hamilton, and the Irwins were in Salmon, Idaho, so we had the sonofabitch in a nice clean rundown, like a runner between third and home with another runner already standing on third and a great big old catcher in his way.

We were half expecting there to be World War Three when we got to Darby, and it was nothing of the kind. There he was, van parked in a little diner parking lot, sitting outside on the bench, sipping a coffee to go and waiting to get picked up. Me and Jenapha Lee got out of our car, and she had her hand on the gun in her purse, and she never needed it; a minute later the Irwin brothers were there to back us up, but it was clear that Brown Pierre was turning himself in.

We called Hale, and he gave us directions. Then we drove down 93 to get onto a logging road outside Sula, not very far away, where an SR-17 would pick us and all our cars up.

It had been bright early morning when we busted him, freeze-ass cold the way the Bitterroot Valley is that time of year, since it's so high and so far north, but so gorgeous it makes your heart ache. Jenapha Lee drove, like always, and I sat in the back seat and kept an eye on Brown Pierre. But I had to admit I never saw anybody less interested in escaping.

He was looking out at all that deep crisp snow, and the dark green forests on the mountains to our west, and suddenly he said, "I really do believe that people won't be so stupid that they lose all of this. I really do believe that."

"You going to tell us about it?"

"Oh, yeah, everything. I'll even tell it in front of All Thumbs, if you like, though I admit I'm a little afraid of how he'll react."

So we flew near two thousand miles, the length of the Rockies, in a bit under an hour, without putting a ripple in anybody's coffee, and we convened in the Xegon conference room, and all the usual prelims got said and everyone who didn't know what was actually going on, especially me, made a bunch of wild guesses.

Then, at the meeting, Brown Pierre just stood up and handed it to us. "What I have found," he said, "is a pattern in the contracts that all these inventors are signing. It's a pattern in things that are *not*-mentioned and written-*around* and *not*-discussed (except for clauses that seem to be about 'in the event of things which will go unmentioned but have ample precedent in galactic law.') And once I realized that was what I needed to look for, in the nineteen contracts I did know of, with nineteen different alien species, I found such language in all of them.

"Now, I'm not a lawyer, but right then I wished I was. Because it seems to me when you get similar but not identical language but it's always in there—that's telling you that there's something important they won't mention. And I thought—jury nullification. It must be something like jury nullification."

About half the room nodded. You know what it is, John? I can see you do. Yeah, jury nullification of laws—basically a jury deciding that a law is a bad law and overturning it, as unconstitutional or not in accord with common law or justice—is part of common law, has been for centuries. But it's usually illegal to tell a jury in the United States that it traditionally had that power, and it's illegal for a juror to share that possibility with the other jurors, and they'll keep you off a jury if they know you know about it, and so forth, because lawyers and legislators purely hate the whole idea of jury nullification.

That's what had made our boy Brown Pierre run out on us. His mind, with that freak turn for consistency, kept looking and looking for an answer to one question: "Exactly what is it we're not allowed to know about galactic law?"

And he realized that it couldn't be that we weren't allowed to know the worst they could do to us—hell, every alien and his egg-mates and brothers and clones was telling us that they were considering genociding us and stripping the Earth down to bouillon. It couldn't be that we weren't allowed to know their malign intent, and it couldn't be that we weren't allowed to know about the availability of cops and lawyers to defend us—they hadn't done anything to stop our finding out.

And the only reason for keeping the awareness of a particular power out of the knowledge of one player in the game is—you're afraid they'll use that power. And it must be a pretty good one to lock it away that tight, the same way that if jury nullification got loose the legal system would fall into tatters (and the strength of the people against the government would explode).

So, Brown Pierre realized, there must be a course of action open to us, which would upset the whole apple cart, and which we weren't allowed to know about. Something strikingly effective.

He looked straight at All Thumbs. "Are you authorized to kill me to prevent this knowledge becoming general?"

"I will choose not to. My word of honor."

Brown Pierre took a deep breath, and said, "As far as I can tell, it's implicit in all these contracts that if we invoke the right of armed self-defense, even once, it voids all the outstanding contracts."

There was a very long pause. Then there was the sound of two three-fingered hands clapping, slowly, over and over. All Thumbs was applauding.

Remember *The Rakehells of Heaven,* John? The rules for colonizing other planets in there? The very last rule was the one that said that a planet was to be regarded as too advanced and civilized, fully equal to human, and therefore off-limits to conquest, if it had a demonstrated ability to repel a state-of-the-art invasion. In other words, if you can defend yourself, we don't have the right to take your stuff and kill you.

That's what it was, but even simpler. The galactic government is a weak federation—it has to be, with, jeehoozus, 89,0000 species. Nobody wants it to have the power to raise taxes or conscript troops or anything of the kind. Which means no one wants it to enforce anything against anyone who shoots back.

If we just started shooting, it turned out, at any species, no matter how ineffectively, all contracts with all species were torn up. The Earth had been sold many times, but we could take it all back.

Brown Pierre giggled, suddenly, and sang, very off-key, "All we are saying, is give war a chance."

So sometime soon, John. Don't quite know when. But we're doing some things to lure the pTh'tong n'Wi into bringing Susan Glasgow back for a visit—we faked up a genealogy for her that might give her a claim to being a hereditary empress. They'll probably tell her it's a shopping trip. And when they come to take possession of the property . . . they're getting surprised.

We were standing in one of those small-county-sized parking lots that you find all over the eastern edge of Kansas, in the deep amber sunlight under the fierce blue of the late-afternoon sky, looking down toward the river through the black latticework of the tree branches. We shook hands, Travis and me, and he said, "Watch for me when something weird happens."

"Always have, always will."

I got lost on the way back to my hotel and nearly missed the evening performance as well, a very interesting student-written musical about Vietnam, which, I realized, must have ended two or three years before the student had been born. Parts of it crossed over the line into bad taste, in my opinion, and parts of it were dull and flailing, but enough was really good so that I felt very comfortable being its advocate and defender at every cocktail party I staggered through that night. By the end of the evening I was feeling, a little smugly—well a lot smugly—that Jenapha might be proud of me.

CHAPTER TWENTY-THREE

On January 28, 1998, at about noon, large, bright, apparently burning objects fell over Hanna, Wyoming, and Breckinridge, Colorado. Lay a ruler on the map between those two points and you will see it extend south to touch Albuquerque—which is to say, Kirtland AFB.

The Wyoming fireball passed close enough to a passenger jet so that the pilot reported feeling some turbulence. The Breckinridge fireball was so bright and trailed so much smoke that numerous residents reported it as a plane crash somewhere in their own immediate neighborhoods. No trace of either fireball was found on the ground.

Newspaper reporters in small towns across Colorado and northern New Mexico discovered, across the next week, that many people recalled seeing odd flashes and lights in the sky on that day; but then, in that part of the country, people see strange things in the sky almost every day.

I was staying that night in the Oxford Hotel, which is a block from the downtown Tattered Cover in Denver. The Ox is an old railroad hotel with way too many stories and interesting features to allow it to get into this book at this point; we're almost done, after all. But from a lounge copied from the saloon of a 1930s ocean liner, to a superb seafood restaurant, to several good ghost and celebrity stories, it's got everything you want in a downtown hotel, and I wasn't paying for it, and I could charge stuff to my room. The host bookstore was wonderful too—the Tattered Cover is two bookstores, one downtown and a larger one by the Cherry Creek Shopping Center, that collectively are one of the very largest bookstores in the United States, and they want people to read more than most missionaries want people to convert. It is often a very nice place for writers, though they do seem to think we were all grown in the same vat that supplies *Fresh Air* and the *New York Times* book review section.

This particular time, however, was a complete bomb. A severe snowstorm up in Oregon kept the celebrity, who everyone wanted to see, from arriving, but the weather was nice in Denver, and hundreds of people didn't get the word until they got to the signing. Then, of course, they discovered that the only person available to sign their books was The Author Commonly Known As Who?

That very gratifying crowd, which might have bought a couple hundred books, melted like snow in a furnace. I sucked it up, got on the phone, met a couple of buddies who live downtown for sushi at the place in Writer Square where I usually do, and by nine P.M. I was at utterly loose ends, so, foolishly, I turned on the television.

As soon as I saw the news about the fireball, I started to laugh, and said aloud, "Travis will be dropping by Gunnison." I even got out my road atlas and ruler and confirmed that the two big simultaneous fireballs were along a line that, near enough, ran through Kirtland AFB. "Don't drop by Gunnison tonight, Trav," I said, still shaking my head with the certainty that he would be turning up again with more preposterous stories. "Because I'm here."

"I know, Kara told me," a voice said from outside my door.

I opened it and there he was. "Come in and sit down," I said, "and let me get something up from McCormicks downstairs."

"Will the expense account allow whiskey, a piece of fish, and a mountain of potatoes?" he asked. "Don't want you getting stuck with it."

"Don't fret about that. The worst that happens is I buy you a meal. And who knows. I might get a book out of this someday. At which point it all becomes research—just like taking six Detroit cops to Hooters was research."

"Cool."

I had them send up a bottle of Wild Turkey, two nice swordfish steaks, a big pot of coffee, and a triple of their potatoes.

And he sat down and ate and told me one more whopper.

They had learned last week that a pTh'tong n'Wi ship carrying Susan Glasgow was going to make an upper atmosphere pass to take a look at Great Sand Dunes, where Susan would record a statement, with that in the background, that she authorized them to take the sand. The ship would be passing bang over Kirtland AFB, about fifty miles up, dipping into the atmosphere and then popping out. Its cloaking was less than perfect; the pTh'tong n'Wi have a low opinion of barbarian technology, and had little reason to think anyone in our government knew anything about them.

And since we only had to shoot at one species to void all the contracts, those seemed like the fuckers to shoot at, especially since their ship also carried a human traitor.

"It was trivial, John. We just gaudeamused a ton of liquid propane, and four tons of liquid oxygen, and an empty cardboard box slightly larger in volume than either of those, in that order, blipblipblip, into the same space in the middle of the pTh'tong n'Wi ship, which meant the oxygen compressed the propane into a one-molecule-thick layer, and the cardboard box compressed the oxygen *and* the propane into a one-molecule-thick layer, and it was all white-hot on arrival. They never pulled back out of their upper atmosphere pass; the ship broke up and bits of it rained down all over, a few hundred miles downrange.

"And All Thumbs got the ruling from the Galactic Court, two seconds later. That's the advantage of time travel, you know. All contracts for possession of the planet are void. It's ours. We're the owners, again.

"Think, maybe, we'll take better care of it, this time?"

I poured him a big glass of whiskey, and watched while he gulped it down. No doubt there are more mature, healthy ways to respond, but I couldn't think of any, just then.

The Gaudeamus Effect will be made public on the last day of 2010, if it hasn't leaked out completely before. Brown Pierre's drugs and viruses are supposedly spreading everywhere, quietly, gradually, gentling our harsh hearts. Supposedly the super-technologies like antigravity and zero-point power, and all the old Cold War secrets, will leak out soon; it's interesting that everyone who follows intelligence history and secret weapons stories *did* notice a burst of leaks that began in February 2000 and shows no sign of abating, even with the change of administrations.

I am told that there is nothing intrinsically difficult about making Gaudeamus machines, large or small. In a few years, anyone will be able to blow you up, from anywhere; anyone will be able to leave a rose on your bed. Anyone will be able to have all the energy they want, make anything they want, hurt anyone they want; we will be gods. Do you suppose we can be smart enough, and gentle enough, soon enough?

And I still have no idea whether Travis Bismarck was telling me the truth. If he was, I'll know on February 4, 2011, I guess. But I wish there were some sign I could look for before then, something to tell me that Brown Pierre is working his voodoo on us, that the new technologies are leaking out to make the world cleaner, safer, easier to live in.

Travis said they were going to try to avoid highly dramatic events.

The first sign, perhaps, across the next few years, will be when things unexpectedly start to break for the better, instead of the usual mix of good breaks and bad breaks. Normally every decade has some bursts of hope, and almost all of them then fizzle, like Martin Luther King, glasnost, Cory Aquino, cold fusion, moon missions, Star Wars movies, techno, the Nuclear Freeze—all those within my lifetime. Usually things like that fizzle; even if they turn out pretty well, they're never what they should have been. If all of a sudden, stuff starts to go better than you hoped it might, that might be a sign.

Would it be cheating, the equivalent of lowering the bar or taping the bathroom scale, if we all quietly, covertly, in our own ways and with our own gifts, tried to *make* things go a little better than might be hoped for?

Next time I take Travis on a long drive, I think I'll ask.

ACKNOWLEDGMENTS

As usual, this book incurred some debts on its way to its (very late) birth. I'd like to thank (in roughly alphabetical order):

Travis Bismarck, with whom I spent a lot of time.

Robert Brown, C. E. Myers, and William Sanders, for an enlightening conversation about guns and assholes.

Kara Dalkey, for letting herself appear under her own name here, and for much idea-jamming in the development stages, and because never once did she throw Travis out in the snow, despite everything. Frankly, being Kara, probably she just couldn't.

Tim Edwards, for his very generous sharing of his time and collected materials.

Ashley Grayson, my agent, for, during the entire time I was working on this, beginning every question about this book with "when" and never with "if you ever . . ."

The fabulous staff at Great Sand Dunes National Park, for never once saying "Now, that's a dumb question."

Judy Messoline, of the UFO Ranch (it's on Colorado 17, just

north of Hooper), for one of the most enjoyable interviews I've ever had, and for many interesting insights.

Patrick Nielsen Hayden, my editor, for a generous and extremely patient spirit.

Jes Tate, my research assistant, for superb wide-ranging library work, for being much better at interviewing and photography than I am, for the fun of her company on the research trip to the San Luis Valley, and most especially for not going home with Travis, no matter how much she'd been drinking.